Reviews for

Dangerous Remedy

'Kat Dunn's captivating debut... is part steampunk adventure, part historical thriller... an enthralling, fast-paced adventure with a cast of likeable characters...'

The Guardian

'An intelligent, lush and rollicking opener to what promises to be your new YA obsession. Vivid, dark, and complex...'

Kiran Millwood Hargrave,
author of *A Secret of Birds and Bone*

'Wonderfully atmospheric fill of strange science, mysterious powers and fearless heroines.'
The Bookseller

'Between these pages you'll find heart-pounding romance, wit, trickery, danger and a uniquely brilliant kind of magic – all set against the expertly conjured backdrop of revolutionary France. You'll love it.'

Kesia Lupo, author of *We Are Bound by Stars*

'Dark, deadly and delicious. A thrilling adventure set in a lavish but ruthless world, with a spirited cast of characters you will root for instantly.'

Bex Hogan, author of *Viper*

MONSTROUS DESIGN

Kat Dunn grew up in London and has lived in Japan, Australia and France. She has written about mental health for Mind and *The Guardian*, and worked as a translator for Japanese television. Her debut novel, *Dangerous Remedy*, was published by Zephyr in 2020. She lives in London.

Also by Kat Dunn

Dangerous Remedy

KAT DUNN

MONSTROUS DESIGN

ZEPHYR

An imprint of Head of Zeus

First published in the UK in 2021 by Zephyr, an imprint of Head of Zeus Ltd
This Zephyr paperback edition first published in the UK in 2022 by Head of Zeus Ltd,
part of Bloomsbury Publishing Plc

A catalogue record for this book is available from
the British Library.

ISBN (PB): 9781789543704
ISBN (E): 9781789543674

Typeset by Ed Pickford
Cover design by Laura Brett

Printed and bound in Great Britain by
CPI Group (UK) Ltd, Croydon CR0 4YY

Head of Zeus Ltd
First Floor East
5–8 Hardwick Street
London ECIR 4RG

WWW.HEADOFZEUS.COM

For Mum.

I miss you.

To betray someone, first you must
begin with trust.

The story so far...

Weeks have passed since the Conciergerie job that changed everything. The Battalion of the Dead had broken into the prison to rescue Olympe Marie de l'Aubespine for her father – only to discover the entire mission was based on lies.

Olympe was no aristocrat's daughter, and to start with they hadn't even been sure she was human. Her uncanny ability to manipulate electricity seemed like magic. But Ada knew the truth lay somewhere closer to science – a branch of science the world hadn't yet discovered.

The Royalist Duc de l'Aubespine, who had originally hired them, demanded the battalion hand Olympe over. She was his pet project: an attempt to harness electricity and create a secret weapon that would restore the Bourbon dynasty to the toppled throne of France. As if that hadn't been enough, the Revolutionaries who had locked Olympe up were just as eager to get her back. The desperate fight to deliver Olympe to safety had been the deadliest job the battalion had ever faced, hunted by the duc's henchman Dorval through burning theatres and macabre laboratories – and they had almost managed it. The Revolutionaries thought Olympe was dead, but the Royalists were still after her. And then, at the eleventh hour, Camille's English ex-fiancé, James, had turned traitor and kidnapped Olympe.

Camille and Al left for England in pursuit of Olympe and James, while Ada and Guil stayed behind – the duc remained a threat, and they needed to know what he was planning.

PART ONE

Bone China

1

A Slum Near Rue St Denis

7 Thermidor, Year II

25 July 1794

'So, are you ready to die?'

Ada's face was cast in shadow as she spoke. The cramped medieval streets were unlit, and the buildings gathered too close for any moonlight to reach them. A meaty scent of offal and human waste wafted out of the gutters; in the distance the faint sound of bells tolled midnight. Summer had turned, bringing a sticky heat with it even at night.

Paris was rotting.

Beside her crouched Guil, eyes wide and wary as he watched the narrow opening of the alley they hid in. It was clear: they were unobserved.

Ada raised her eyebrows in question. 'I can do it now or we can keep waiting, but you've got to die in the next half hour or I won't make it home in time.'

'Perhaps we should locate ourselves somewhere a little more noticeable first.' Guil wrinkled his nose. 'If

I die here I'm not sure anyone will be able to tell me apart from the refuse.'

Ada rolled her eyes. 'Fine, I'll take your artistic sensibilities into account choosing the next spot.'

She gathered up the battered canvas bag that held her supplies and followed him to the street. Here at least were a few signs of life: lights in mullioned windows, voices coming from the leaning upper levels of the timber-framed houses.

'There.' Guil pointed to an alcove closer to the main road where dray carts and drunks were trundling past. 'That's our stage.'

'You're sure the resurrection men will come?'

He shrugged. 'Léon may not like me as much as he likes Al, but I trust he still gives me good intelligence. The dead go missing from the slums in the hour after midnight, though no guarantee they will pass through tonight. If they do, we will only have a few moments' warning.'

'You'd better hope they turn up. All these late nights had me falling asleep in my soup yesterday.'

Guil folded himself into the alcove, looking hurt. 'You seem very eager to kill me. I wonder if I should be taking this personally.'

'What, and lose the suitor my father is so delighted I've finally found? Heavens, what a scandal that would cause.'

'I think he would be delighted if you were being courted by a pot plant.'

Ada snorted and tucked herself in beside him. 'As long as the plant had never belonged to Camille.'

She had met Camille when she still used her family name, du Bugue, but when she had formed the battalion she had taken the name Laroche after her mother. Camille du Bugue was the girl she'd fallen in love with, but Camille Laroche was the one with whom she had built a life.

As far as her father was concerned, Ada had abandoned Camille and finally decided to go 'home'. He was only too happy to believe that the business with Olympe and the Revolutionaries had scared her enough to leave the Bataillon des Morts; Guil turning up as her so-called suitor had made him all the happier. His daughter home and a handsome young army officer interested in her hand was the realisation of near all his dreams. Ada was disgusted by how simple his hopes for her future were.

Camille and Al had long since left for England. Ada and Guil had spent the whole time investigating, but they'd learned nothing of the duc's plans. Each plot they formed, each thread they followed, came up blank. The grisly abbey laboratory had been abandoned, the duc's former hôtel had been seized by the Revolutionary army to billet soldiers, and the servants who had worked for him were impossible to track down. He seemed to have no allies, no home, nothing.

He was a ghost.

For a while, Ada had let the thought grow in her mind: maybe he really *had* gone. The blow of being defeated by a gang of outsiders had been too crushing and he'd bowed out. It was a nice thought, but from what little she'd experienced of the duc, she knew it couldn't be true. He was out there, somewhere, doing god knows what to god knows who. Only she and Guil could stop him.

Now they were down to their last hope. Their last foolhardy plan. A very, very stupid, dangerous plan – but that was the Bataillon des Morts. The Battalion of the Dead. They wouldn't give up until they'd tried everything.

Even death.

They had been settled into the alcove for only a few minutes when a scrawny girl appeared. Her lank hair hung loose around her gaunt face and her clothes were held together by dirt and wishful thinking. She looked them over, then gave Guil a curt nod.

'There's two of them tonight,' she said. 'Took Marcel Leclerc already.'

'Are you sure?' asked Guil.

'Yes. I saw them do it. I'm not a liar.'

'I know you're not.' He dug in his pocket and tossed her a coin. 'Get out of here, mousling. Stay safe.'

The girl snatched it out of the air and bolted. Ada thrummed with adrenaline. It was now or never.

Guil pushed her bag of supplies over. His eyes were dark, unreadable. 'I'm ready to die.'

2

A Country House in England

J ames stood in the anteroom of his father's study, trying his best not to pace. A footman had assured him Lord Harford was inside seeing to some other business and would see him shortly. So James waited, sweat drying under his linens, his boots still dusty from the hard ride from London.

The urge to pace was strong. He felt, as always when meeting his father, as if a jar of live bees had been emptied inside him, every moment angry and at risk of being stung. But pacing only made him look weak; it was his anxiety painted on the outside. He would not let his father see it. He stilled himself, clasping his hands behind his back as he'd seen his father do in his Westminster office, listening to complaining constituents or lobbyists in smart waistcoats. A statesman's pose.

The anteroom bridged the gap between the airy, light rooms his mother kept decorated to contemporary tastes and the sombre, tomb-like gloom of his father's study. Tobacco-stained wood panelling covered every wall, Ottoman rugs muffled footsteps, and shelf after shelf was filled with editions of Hansard, biographies of politicians, Greek and Latin texts, and copious snuff boxes, horse bronzes, ivory bookends, and even a Roundhead helmet from the Civil War.

His father had always seen to political business from behind his vast desk, or administered disinterested beatings when, as a boy, James had smashed crockery or hidden mice in his sister's bed. James remembered waiting in the anteroom on countless nervous occasions. In the thick rug a track of bare threads marked where he'd paced each time, a lifetime of worry etched in one spot.

James would not pace. He was a man now. What he had to say was worth hearing, and this time, he would make his father listen.

The corner held a shelf, bare except for a single treasured display piece: a duelling pistol resting on a stand, inlaid pearl handle iridescent beside the dark wood. Its barrel was freshly polished and a small leather pouch of shot and powder sat to one side to complete the display. James stopped before it. He knew this pistol well – the weight of it, the smoothness of its handle against his palm.

A muscle in his jaw flickered.

Its twin had belonged to his father's best friend – Camille's father. Since he'd taken it from her that frantic day in the foundations of the Madeleine church, he'd not been able to bring himself to touch it.

Instead, he'd stuffed it beneath a floorboard in his digs in London, along with any thought of Camille. But he couldn't help thinking of her now. How her pale face had turned up to him, looking so young in her shock and confusion. Then anger had taken over, and the Camille he had known was consumed by someone who had every reason to hate him.

No – he wouldn't feel guilty. He'd done what he had to do, and that was as complicated as this needed to be.

He crossed to the window, looking at the formal gardens and the ha-ha beyond, then crossed back to the door, his legs springy with tension. He turned to loop back to the window – oh, hell, he was pacing – and the study door was flung open in his path.

It took him a moment to realise it was not his father standing in the open doorway. A broad-shouldered man just reaching middle age strode through, all but slamming the door behind him. He had a shock of brown hair that tumbled into his eyes in a windswept fashion, his handsome features made even more appealing by the addition of a dashing scar running from temple to jaw. James was used to seeing him in a rubber apron with his shirtsleeves rolled up and blood splattered to his elbows. Seeing his surgery tutor in a suit and cravat was disconcerting.

Seeing him right *now* was the last thing James wanted.

He recovered himself. *Bright eyes, light smile, give nothing away.*

'Mr Wickham. I did not realise you had business with my father.'

The man's face was twisted, lips drawn back in a snarl. Then he noticed James and, not missing a beat, his expression smoothed into a winning smile, eyes twinkling.

'James, good Lord! How very nice to see you.' He took James's hand and shook it, palms rough with calluses in stark contrast to his crisply pressed shirt and frock coat. 'How nice to see you safe, I should say.'

'Quite safe – though only now returned. I would have come to you first, but I have been away from my family for too long – and my mother's health...'

He was overdoing it. Wickham would surely see through him at once. He'd never been any good at lying to his tutor, not about late assignments or missed lectures, nothing. When Wickham had taken James and his friend, Edward, under his wing as protégés, James had thought he'd finally found the recognition he'd always yearned for from his father. He would never have believed then that one day he'd *want* to lie to Wickham.

To betray him.

With a hand on his arm, the surgeon steered him to a quiet corner. 'Your letters were frustratingly vague. We must talk fully – in London. Aubespine's notes are fascinating; it seems he *did* create an electrical being after all, but in quite the novel manner. A baby! Such a shame you were not able to find the girl. It would have put our research forward by decades.'

James sorted through a series of suitable expressions in his head and settled on earnest interest. The notes he had sent Wickham were Ada's notes, along with the

Duc de l'Aubespine's papers she had stolen detailing Olympe's creation. He'd been working with Wickham and Edward on similar electrical research to the duc, and when Wickham had heard word of the duc's apparent success, they'd agreed James, with his French connections, would travel to Paris to search for her. But when he'd found Olympe and seen what she could do, he'd decided on a new plan, one that didn't involve his tutor or his friend at all.

Wickham was watching him closely. 'Are you *completely* sure there's nothing else?'

James swallowed around the lump in his throat. That was what he had learned about betrayal in France: it hurt. When someone mattered to you, when you had thought your future lay with them, it would always hurt. Wickham and Edward had offered him something once, just as Camille had.

But futures changed.

Everything was a choice, wasn't it?

He had different plans now, and if what he had to do hurt, so be it.

'Nothing,' he said. 'I would have searched further but the city wasn't safe…'

'I can only imagine. We hear of fresh horrors every day, and you must believe I am grateful that you would take such risks to further my – *our* – work.' Wickham's interest in the Revolution drifted rapidly. 'How much of the papers did you have a chance to study? Edward and I have been working through them – applying electrical stimulation in utero is a fascinating approach, but hardly scalable. A novelty. Nevertheless, I think

Aubespine's theories have given us solutions to some of our problems. I am most eager to test them as soon as is feasible.'

As soon as is feasible. What a polite way to say as soon as he had a fresh corpse. It was the grim reality of the surgical student's life: corpses brought from gallows to dissection slab the same day. Wickham had never seemed affected by that aspect of his profession, viewing the human body as simply another resource at his disposal. James, on the other hand, struggled not to be affected; he knew it made him a bad surgeon, but perhaps it made him a good man.

There was something else on his mind that James was unable to ignore. 'What business did you have with my father? Is he still interested in funding your research?'

Wickham's smile faltered. 'Unfortunately not.'

James paled. 'Truly? I was under the impression he thought it significant to the war effort.'

If his father had lost interest, then betraying his mentor had suddenly drained of meaning. His plan wasn't complicated: deliver Olympe to his father instead of Wickham. He'd thought he was content as Wickham's favourite, but when he had seen the possibilities Olympe's power presented, that treacherous thought had crept in. Perhaps he had finally found the thing that would make his father sit up and take notice of him. It might hurt to betray Wickham's and Edward's trust – God, and Camille's trust, for that matter – but it would be worth it. It had to be worth it.

Only, Wickham had just told him it wouldn't be.

His father wasn't interested any more.

'It seems we were both mistaken.' Wickham tugged his frock coat straight, brushing off invisible specks of dust, then continued before James had a chance to speak. 'I saw too much death in my time as a naval surgeon. I offered him the commander's dream, troops who can rise from even the most grievous injuries. If we can harness electrical power, use it to restart that vital spark when it has been snuffed out – why, then England's enemies would tremble in their boots.'

For a panicked moment, James thought about staying loyal to Wickham after all. His mentor wasn't so bad an option, was he? Then he thought about the duc in Paris and the dark paths his work had led him down. The same ruthless streak of ambition he saw in Wickham too. He could choose his tutor but Wickham would never choose him. In the end, their work would always come first.

No. James had chosen his father. He was all in, and now the only thing left was to show his hand.

'What commander would not want such power?' he said. 'He will come around.'

Wickham clapped him on the shoulder, a little too hard, and settled his hat on his head. 'That's the spirit. With you and Edward working with me, I think we can still give the Frenchies a run for their money, eh? He's downstairs, by the way. Think your sister has cornered him so I dare say he'll be glad to see you. We were both worried about you.'

James's heart sank. Edward.

15

'It'll be good to see him too,' he said, and he meant it. It had been too long since their last night together in the coffee house by the hospital, sharing lecture notes and planning their brilliant future. Betraying Wickham was difficult; betraying Edward was a gut-punch. He owed his friend far more than making him collateral damage.

Wickham left and the noise of papers being shuffled in the study drew his attention.

Futures changed.

It was time to make a new one with his father.

James shook himself out of his funk and knocked firmly on the open door.

'Enter.' The low baritone made the skin on the back of his neck prickle.

Lord Harford was bent over a spread of papers covered in cramped, sloping script. His dispatch box lay open on one side of the desk, the other stacked with unopened correspondence. With a flourish, he signed a document, then looked up, acknowledging James.

His lips thinned.

'Oh. I see you've finally decided to grace us with your presence.'

'I'm sorry to interrupt you, when I know you must be busy.'

'And yet you still do.' James felt his cheeks heat and began to apologise, but his father waved him silent. 'Never mind that. Clearly you have decided what you want to say is important enough to bother me when I am tasked with the security of the nation.'

James collected himself. 'Did you receive the letters I sent?'

Lord Harford snorted. 'I received *something* resembling letters, but they seemed more like the novels your younger sister wastes her time on.' He put down his pen. 'What *did* catch my attention is that you took the astronomically foolish decision to travel to France – a country with which apparently I must remind you we are at *war* – in pursuit of some fantastical creature you believe to be imbued with the powers of electricity?'

Well, when he put it like that, it didn't sound good.

'Respectfully, sir, it's not a fantasy but the result of rigorous scientific research – the same research that Mr Wickham has been pursuing in England—'

'As you say in your letters. Don't worry, I didn't tell your mother. A shock like that with her health in the state it is… I would have thought you would have more consideration of your own family. Frankly, James, I am disappointed.'

There it was.

'First, you insist on embarrassing us by pursuing this ghoulish profession and neglecting your role as heir to the estate, and now you have been taken in by Wickham's lunatic nonsense. Do not mistake me, he is a clever, charismatic man, has been since I first met him, but he has a tendency to believe his own myth-making, to concoct grandiose ideas of saving the world. Resurrecting dead soldiers, I believe it is this time.' Lord Harford sighed. 'I had hoped you clever enough not to be taken in.'

'You believed it too, didn't you?' said James. 'You were going to fund his research.'

'A good politician entertains all the options available to him. If Wickham had presented me a genuine, rational proposal I would have been more than ready to back it. But he didn't. He came here today to berate me about my foolish decision, just as you do. Electricity may well provide opportunities one day, but Wickham's "research" is the delusion of a man rapidly losing grip on reality.'

James bristled. Why did his father have to be so stubborn? So convinced anything he didn't know wasn't worth knowing? James had Olympe. He had *proof* the science was real. He only needed to force his father to see the truth.

'The science is evolving every day,' he said. 'There are things we know now that would have seemed like fantasy merely a few years ago. I know it may be hard to understand as an unscientific man, but the foundations all point to this very possibility—' James saw his misstep as he made it. His father's face soured and he leaned back in his chair, hands steepled.

'I am an unscientific man?'

'I beg your pardon, I meant only that your specialism lies elsewhere—'

'Do you know the going rate for gunpowder? How much food it takes to feed an army? How to supply them as they move?'

'No, sir.'

'Do not assume that because I do not interest myself in the same grisly work as you that I am simple; I readily grasp reality, which I fear you do not. Do you know how many rumours and lies come out of France every day? If I believed them all I would be the biggest fool in Westminster.'

James clenched his teeth. He was too old for his father to cane, but it didn't stop the anxiety that flooded through him when his father got angry. Now, it was easier to turn that fear into anger, and they had become embroiled in more than one explosive fight over the years.

'I don't mean to make you a fool. Indeed, quite the opposite.'

Lord Harford held up a hand. 'Stop. I have heard this all from Wickham; I have no need to hear it again. You cannot help the war effort with fairy tales and delusions; I have told him no and I am telling you the same.' He picked up his pen and returned to his letter-writing. 'Say hello to your mother before you leave.'

It was as if James had ceased to exist the moment Lord Harford was no longer interested in him. He had always done this, since James was a child. Their relationship was dictated entirely by his father's terms, and James knew that to push now would only cause his father to dig in further.

Quietly, James let himself out of the study, steps sinking silently into the thick rugs. So much for things being different this time.

Shame was too simple a word for what he felt. He was ashamed of disappointing his father, and ashamed of his own stupidity for misjudging things *again*. Of course his father wouldn't believe Olympe's powers; they had sounded like fiction even to James at first. If he hadn't seen everything that Olympe could do, he would have doubted it too.

Nearly nineteen years of learning how to navigate his father's expectations and he was no nearer to understanding him.

But James had pulled off something his father would never have thought him capable of: he had got hold of the most valuable scientific discovery of the era, delivering it into England's hands while depriving *France* of its newest weapon. He was helping the war, helping England – helping his *father*. If only he wasn't too stubborn to believe it.

James cracked his knuckles, flexing his fingers.

Fine. He would drop the matter – for now. He wouldn't let himself wallow. The task ahead was clear: he must give his father a demonstration of the science no one could not deny.

Then they would see who was a disappointment.

3

A Slum Near Rue St Denis

Guil vomited violently into the gutter. Thin, acrid liquid, little more than bile and the salt water Ada had prepared for him to swallow. She kneeled in front of him in a threadbare skirt and chemise stained with sweat and urine and the splashes of his vomit.

As he retched again, she unlaced his shoes and hid them in her bag before rubbing dirt into his toes and the ragged hems of his trousers. If this was going to work, they both needed to look like they belonged in the slums.

Guil slumped against the whitewashed wall, breathing heavily through his nose.

'That was disgusting,' he rasped.

'Shush. Corpses don't talk.'

But the salt water had done its job. He looked shaky and weak, and he stank of the sewer. From along the street, Ada heard the creak of cartwheels, the mutter of low voices. The resurrection men would pass at any moment.

From the bag she pulled her next trick: a small twist of paper holding cantharides powder made from crushed insects, mostly in the preparation of aphrodisiac sweets nicknamed 'pastilles de Richelieu' after the Maréchal-Duc de Richelieu, a notorious womaniser of the Ancien Régime. Tonight, they would serve a very different purpose.

'This is going to hurt,' she said. 'I'm sorry.'

He nodded and gritted his teeth.

Carefully she shook the powder over his neck and armpits; in seconds his skin began to bubble up in putrid blisters. Guil screwed his eyes shut tight, letting out only a short grunt of pain.

The noise of the cart was drawing closer. There was no time to let Guil recover. Now, she drew a bottle of ink from the bag, took his fingers and dipped them, one by one, into it so the tips looked gangrenous and rotten. Finally she took out another twist of paper, this one filled with ashes which she mixed with the last of the salt water to make a paste that she rubbed into his face and arms so his brown skin began to look grey and sickly.

The creaking wheels had been joined by horseshoes against cobbles, and the soft tones of subdued voices; she rammed everything back in the bag and hid it under the smashed remains of a beer barrel.

'Done.' She rested a hand on his knee as much to comfort herself as him. 'We're on.'

He made no response, but slumped further against the wall, head hanging at an unnatural angle.

Perfect.

Ada took a breath, steadying herself.

Then let out a wail.

'No! Oh God above, no.' She shook Guil by his shoulders then threw herself into his lap, sobbing. 'Emile, please wake up.'

She heard the cart stop. The voices hush.

'Please don't leave me,' she cried into his shirt. 'Please don't die.'

A little on the nose, but she couldn't let this opportunity slip. For a moment, nothing happened. Maybe they'd got it wrong, these weren't the body snatchers passing – or maybe it was but they didn't want to take a risk on a corpse so fresh.

Then behind her, footsteps on the cobbles.

Ada pressed her face closer into Guil's shirt. She could feel the imperceptible rise and fall of his lungs, and prayed the night was dark enough to hide it.

'Miss? Citoyenne?'

She only sobbed harder, twisting her fingers in Guil's shirt.

'Is everything all right? Can we fetch a doctor?'

Blinking away tears, she looked up at the man who had approached her. He was short, with expensive boots and a little dirt crusted under his fingernails.

'It's too late. My brother is dead and gone with the angels, citoyen.'

The man took his hat off in a show of respect. 'My deepest condolences.'

'If we'd had money for a doctor a week ago maybe – but how could we afford a doctor, if we can't even afford bread?' She let her eyes well with tears again as she looked at Guil. 'We can't even afford a burial. My poor brother will end up in the paupers' pit and without him working I fear our whole family will soon follow.'

She held herself still, the picture of mourning and despair. Another set of footsteps arrived and a new voice joined the hushed conversation.

'Come on, Didier, our passengers aren't getting any fresher.'

'I think we've found another.'

'No. No more risks.'

'Look, he's perfectly fresh.'

'Didier—'

'My dear.' Didier came to crouch beside her. 'I can't begin to imagine your pain; a good burial is the last thing we can offer our loved ones. A paupers' pit is an insult.'

'It is, citoyen. I would do anything to save my brother from that indignity.'

Guil's hand had slipped from his lap and landed in some sort of excrement in the gutter.

Didier left a careful silence. Ada wondered if she'd overdone it with the blisters on Guil's neck. Would they take a body if it seemed too diseased?

'There may be something I can—' he started. 'No. I'm sorry. Forget I spoke.'

'What was it?'

'No – you might think I was taking advantage of you.'

'I'm sure I wouldn't.'

He tapped his knees where he crouched beside her. 'My friend and I, we … help people in your circumstances. Those who cannot secure a decent burial through no fault of their own.'

'I am not sure I understand…'

'It's a little unconventional, I'll admit, but there is a place we know that will take the dead and give them the proper rest they deserve. Like the religious orders used to take in the destitute sick before they were closed – except this is a temple of science.'

Ada drew back in horror. 'You can't mean the medical schools? Dissection?'

'No! Not at all. There are no students at this place, no gawping spectators. Only a man of good, respectful conscience with a scientific interest in the human body and how we might prevent tragic deaths like your poor brother's.'

'It is not godly, sir.'

'What is more ungodly is the poor unfortunates thrown into unconsecrated ground like refuse. That, citoyenne, is the true evil. Will you not save your brother from that?' Ada stroked the side of Guil's face.

'Perhaps you're right…'

'What was wrong with him?' the other man interrupted. He had a rattish face with long blond hair tied back in a cue. 'What's that on his neck?'

Ada sniffed, hiccupping around the end of a sob. 'I – I don't know. There wasn't time for a doctor. We thought maybe the plague—'

'Plague!' He took a sharp step back. 'Are you sure?'

Ada bit her lip. There was only a fine line she could walk between success and disaster. 'Maybe – maybe not…'

'Let's go.'

He pulled at Didier's elbow, but he shook him off.

'Don't be a coward. Get his feet.'

'But the *plague*, Didier. Will he even want this one?'

'Of course he'll want the body. You think he can afford to be picky?'

Ada sniffed again, smoothing Guil's short curls from his forehead. 'And you promise he'll be buried?'

'Yes, not a sou's fee. In fact, here's one just for you. Get something filling to eat.'

She gave Guil's face a final, mournful stroke – then snatched the money from the man's hand and backed away with another wail.

'Take him. Do it now. Please, I cannot bear to think of him lying in the gutter any longer.'

The men exchanged a glance, the light of greed in their eyes. They hoisted Guil's limp body between them, hands hooked under his knees and armpits, and loaded him onto the cart. He tumbled into a gap between corpses hiding his face from view. Her heart raced, the coin hot in her sweaty hands. Didier mounted the cart and took the reins, while the rattish man hoisted himself up at the back. He tipped his hat to Ada as they pulled away.

Kneeling in the dirt, she watched as Guil joined the ranks of the dead.

4

Henley House

All the windows had been flung open to let in morning light and the tiled entrance hall was cool and smelled of the freshly cut flowers scattered across end tables. The morning room was empty, needlepoint abandoned on the low sofas, and a maid bent to gather up half-drunk china cups of tea.

'Molly – have you seen my sister?'

The maid startled so badly she dropped the sugar tongs. 'Oh, Mr Harford! I didn't know you were home.'

'Ah – no, I slipped in on the sly, I'm afraid. Just needed a word with the old man.'

'Shall I have your bedroom made up for you?'

'I won't be staying – but I should check in on the rest of the family or I'll never hear the end of it.'

'Miss Harford and Miss Davenport have set up their watercolours on the front lawn with that young gentleman friend of yours who stopped by. I believe Lady Harford has joined them.'

'My mother is up?'

'Yes, sir. Doing quite well today, I think.'

'Thank you, Molly.'

He was out of the room and through the front doors of Henley House before Molly could reply. It was a glorious day, the sky a cornflower blue and the lush green of the trees and grass shimmering in the gentle breeze. A wide, rolling lawn spread all the way down to the distant estate wall. The gardens behind the house were a carefully designed maze of formal beds, fountains and walkways, but at the front, the landscaper had left the natural beauty of the Chilterns on display. A gravel driveway led from the gatehouse to the carriage circle, paths snaking off to woodland in one direction and a lake in the other. A copse of trees shielded the house from public view, and above them, soft, rolling hills reached north towards Fawley and Stonor. It was his sister's favourite view.

To the left of the driveway several folding chairs had been set up under the roof of an ornamental pavilion, with a cluster of hothouse fruit on a silver tray, blankets and cushions spread out, and two large easels facing the lake.

His mother sat in her Bath chair, wheels braced by rocks and a travelling rug mounded over her. Her ashy-blonde hair was pinned up, nearly as pale as her skin, papery thin from illness. James's sister Hennie and another girl were surrounded by an explosion of paints, chalks, brushes, oils, palettes, knives and pencils. Hennie kneeled before her canvas, linen dress speckled with droplets, brushing great clouds of green. Her friend – a Miss Philomena Davenport, who had been a regular fixture at the house since they had met at school – had got as far as painting the sky before retreating to a chair and fanning herself.

And with them, lounging on the blanket in plain olive-green breeches and coat, inky-black hair ruffled by the breeze, was Edward.

Edward noticed James before the others, though he said nothing, only watching him with a carefully studied nonchalance. It wasn't unusual for Edward to join the Harfords in a social capacity, but James couldn't help wondering if Wickham had left him here to keep an eye on him. Perhaps he was being paranoid.

He thought of his tutor's calculating gaze assessing him.

Perhaps not.

If lying to Wickham had been hard, lying to Edward would be excruciating. For months, the two of them had been side by side at the dissecting table, staying up all night studying, sharing a single oil lamp and one pot of coffee, writing up Wickham's notes, preserving his specimens, dissolving bodies in vats of acid to extract bones, and a hundred other fascinating, hideous things done in the name of science.

Edward had always been the one to wrinkle his nose at the smell of rot and turpentine, to give James a side-eye when Wickham was at his most extreme. Though he was loath to admit it, James had always been the blind follower, happy to do as he was told. Edward might question Wickham's fanaticism, or try to pull James away from another night hunched over a corpse, but he stayed all the same; he had nowhere else to go. James did. And now he had chosen to trade their friendship for the chance of his father's approval.

Philomena squinted at her canvas. 'Really, Hennie, I don't know why you keep insisting I do this painting lark with you. You know I've got the artistic talent of a toad. I'm not even that fond of *looking* at art – unless it's a nice picture of a horse. Your father has a great portrait of Eclipse, fabulous racer. Such a shame he never was any good at stud.'

'Phil, I beg you, stop being such an utter Philistine, or I shall have to believe you're only lying about being christened Philomena when the truth is your parents sniffed out your boorish ways at birth and named you for it.'

Phil threw a grape at Hennie. It bounced off her forehead and plopped into the jar of murky water used for washing their paintbrushes. Hennie turned on her friend with a look of petulant outrage and reached for the nearest projectile.

'Henrietta Harford, put down that pencil at once.' Their mother emerged from the depths of her chair, fixing her alert gaze on her only daughter. 'You have been brought up as a lady, and ladies do not resort to violence.'

James ducked under the shade of the pavilion. 'To be fair, Phil resorted to violence first.'

All four turned to James at once, his mother's pale face, his sister's ruddy cheeks and blonde waves a mirror of his own, Phil's square face framed by dark hair curled into ringlets at her temple. Edward was the palest of the lot, all smudge-dark eyes under a strong brow and cheekbones sharp enough to draw blood.

'James!' Hennie flung herself from her easel and into his arms. 'There you are! You neglect us, it's a terrible thing.'

He gave her a squeeze then unpeeled himself from her.

'I do not neglect you.'

'Father neglects us too. I believe you are attempting to copy him.'

'I'm doing no such thing.'

'You've been gone a month and no one knew where you were,' Phil piped up.

'I am extremely busy with my studies, and I'm afraid that can't be helped.' He *had* vanished on them when he'd gone to Paris, but they didn't need to know the truth about that.

Edward caught his eye and arched a brow. For a tense moment, he thought Edward might give him away, but then he spoke. 'Our tutors are all taskmasters. Hardly get a chance to come up for air all term.'

James flashed him a grateful look but it wasn't returned. At least with Camille, the betrayal had been over in a moment. This was torture.

Hennie threw herself into a chair with a flounce. 'Oh, yes, such a terribly important man with vital man business. Don't let your blood relatives who love you get in the way of being busy.'

'Hennie—'

'James.' His mother reached out a hand. 'Come. Sit with us a while. Your sister is not entirely without

31

justification. It has been a long time since we've seen you.'

He hesitated. The sun was almost directly overhead; if he meant to get back to London before nightfall he would have to leave soon and ride hard. He'd already been away one night, breaking his journey at a coaching inn in Windsor before riding on that morning. He didn't like to stay away longer.

Wickham would be expecting him.

And Olympe.

He had secured her as best he could and left food and water, but it was a constant worry at the back of his mind that meant he couldn't fully concentrate on anything. He had brought her this far, he couldn't lose her now.

But his mother's hand reached for him. Delicate, with slim fingers beginning to curl in on themselves like a claw as her illness progressed.

He took it, pulled a chair up beside her and sat.

'Was that so hard?' Hennie grumbled to herself, turning back to her painting. The grape had splashed dirty water across the trees, and now the green of their leaves was dripping down their trunks. 'Edward comes to visit us willingly but we practically have to tie you down to see you.'

She turned a little pink as she spoke and James had the horrible thought that Hennie might be developing a crush. Edward only smirked and helped himself to a grape.

'She says mean things, but really they're just worried about you.' Phil had picked up her paintbrush again too and was idly daubing clouds onto the sky. 'You are looking quite peaky.'

'I'm fine.' James squeezed his mother's hand gently. 'I promise.'

His mother smiled faintly, the slightest upward tug of her lips. To James, that was the worst thing about her illness. The shaking palsy froze not only her limbs but also her expressions, turning her brilliant, shining face, with its crow's feet and lip that quirked when hiding a laugh, into a placid mask. As though his mother had been spirited away and one of Hennie's porcelain dolls had been left in her place.

'I'll stay tonight,' he conceded. 'But I'll have to go early tomorrow.'

Olympe would be safe for that long.

'Won't make much of a change,' said Hennie. 'I never see you at breakfast anyway — good lord!'

Hennie and Phil had both frozen mid-brushstroke and were staring at a post-chaise driving towards them at some lick.

Edward sat up, shading his eyes. 'Are you expecting visitors?'

James watched the carriage approach in confusion. It couldn't be Wickham – he'd left already and would have been travelling on horseback.

'Clearly not!' said Hennie. Abandoning her painting, she left the pavilion to get a better look.

Now the carriage was almost upon them, James could see it was splattered with mud and dust as though it had taken a long journey to get there – but there was no luggage strapped to the top. He squinted at the windows. It was impossible to make out who was inside. The carriage looped round the circle and drew level with them, then the driver hopped down to let out a dishevelled blond man in a travelling coat, who in turn gave his hand to help the woman behind him.

James went cold.

The woman emerged and pushed back her hood. He knew that face.

Oh, how he knew that face.

Camille Laroche had arrived in England.

5

The Grounds of Henley House

Camille shook as Al helped her out of the carriage. It had been weeks since she'd last laid eyes on James; too many long weeks crawling her way from Paris, first to the Harfords' London house, and when they found that shut up and empty, on to Henley. Weeks of hiding, avoiding the authorities or anyone who might give away their whereabouts, running whatever dirty jobs she could for money, sleeping in fields and eating scraps, driven by the memory of James turning her own gun on her before kidnapping her friend.

She would make him pay.

Henley House – once her other home – was laid out before her like a painting, and perfectly arranged in the foreground were the characters of her childhood: Lady Harford, Henrietta, James – though the picture had changed; Hennie was older, a few inches taller; an unfamiliar girl sat nearby and with them, a dark-haired man with intense eyes.

But it was Lady Harford who stopped Camille's breath in her throat. The last time Camille had seen her, she was walking with a stick and struggled to use a pen – but otherwise unchanged from the cheery socialite she'd always been. Now…

If only Ada was here. She was always better at this part.

Camille took a hold of herself and looked away. There wasn't time to have feelings about this. She had a plan to execute.

The curtain had risen, it was time to take the stage.

She took a hesitant step, blinking in the sun as she allowed the party to take her in. Then she rolled her eyes back and slumped sideways into Al's arms. He was ready, catching her and exclaiming in shock, 'Mon dieu! 'Elp! 'Elp! The pauvre child is overcome!'

'Camille!' Hennie came racing over first, her hot hands unfastening the cloak around Camille's throat. 'Oh, Maman, pass your smelling salts.'

Camille kept her eyes shut until the ammonia reek of the salts reached her, then fluttered them open to see Al, Hennie and the other girl leaning over her, and James wheeling Lady Harford towards them.

'Gosh!' Hennie peered directly into her face. 'It's really you! You didn't get your head chopped off!'

'Henrietta!' chided Lady Harford.

'What? That's what we all thought had happened. The newspapers are full of people getting their heads lopped off by that frightful Robespierre. I think it's awfully smart of you to have made it all the way to England.'

Lady Harford smacked her fan against Hennie's shoulder.

'Oh, my darling Camille. Can it really be you?'

Lady Harford's eyes were glistening with tears.

'Help her up, get her into the shade.'

From her Bath chair, she ordered their relocation to the pavilion, Al and the dark-eyed man carrying Camille between them to be daintily rested on a wicker couch and propped up with enough pillows to wedge her in place. Al stayed by her side, playing his role of dutiful guardian and babbling in an affected mixture of French and English. The two strangers were introduced as Phil, a friend of Hennie's, and Edward, a friend of James's, and the party settled down, passing her water, grapes and smelling salts in turn.

Only James kept his distance. Camille assessed the tightness of his jaw, his fist clenching and unclenching at his side. When she caught his eye, a look of fear flashed across his face. *Excellent.*

'Forgive me for bursting in upon you in this manner,' she said, after taking a sip. 'I realise our appearance must be quite alarming.'

'You must think nothing of the sort. You are here, and that's what matters.' Lady Harford squeezed her hand. 'When I heard what had happened to your dear parents, I was devastated. I would have done anything to get you out of there – I would have sailed to France myself, if it weren't for my health. What can you have been through, my poor, poor girl?' With difficulty, she reached to touch Camille's face with one hand. Tears were flowing down her cheeks and Camille found herself blinking away tears of her own.

It was stupid, but in all the gruelling days and sleepless nights it had taken them to work their way to the French coast, onto a ship that was willing to take them to England, she hadn't once thought about what it would be like to see Lady Harford again. Oh, she had thought long and hard about seeing James, letting her anger and hurt fester into something unpleasant. But his mother? The woman who had been a fixture of her family until the Revolution cut them off. The woman who was one of the few people still living who remembered her parents. Who meant that her past hadn't died with them.

No, she hadn't factored this into her plan at all.

Lady Harford passed her an embroidered lace handkerchief and they both dabbed at their tears. 'You and your friend are most welcome.'

'Ah! I must introduce my companion.' Camille turned to Al. 'This is Aloysius de Landrieu, he is also wanted by the Revolutionaries. We made it out by the skin of our teeth, and I wouldn't have got here without him.'

'Then he is our friend too. Do you have people here?' Lady Harford asked Al.

He gave a pained look. 'I fear I am the only member of my family who escaped that ... that monstrous *hell*.'

He looked away, as though emotion had overwhelmed him. Camille winced; Al had taken one too many acting lessons from Léon. It had taken him a week to pick an outfit for the occasion, before realising the outfit he had fled in, with its fine silk fraying and travel-worn wrinkles, was the perfect disguise.

'Then you must stay with us.'

'Thank you. That's very kind.'

'Er, terribly sorry.' Hennie's friend cut in, cheeks pink with embarrassment. 'My French isn't up to much, could someone tell me what exactly is going on?'

'Oh, Phil, you are boring.' Hennie sighed, switching to English. 'This is Camille du Bugue, a very old family friend from Paris who we thought really *ought* to be dead. But it turns out she's not! Which is quite splendid. Also, she's James's fiancée.'

'Leave the juiciest bit to last, why don't you!' Phil looked at Camille with renewed interest, sizing her up.

Camille looked at James again, but his attention was elsewhere. He was casting a nervous eye over his friend Edward, who had set himself as helper, bringing Lady Harford drinks, plumping cushions and adjusting parasols for shade. He seemed at ease with the Harfords, so presumably he was a close friend of James's. Camille didn't know him – so he was close, but also recent. Handsome, in an intense, brooding way, long, slim fingers and narrow frame. Curious. She had thought James was nervous because of her arrival – but perhaps she wasn't the only problem he was facing.

Several maids came carrying a teapot, cups, a cold jugged hare, and half a loaf of bread to add to the fruit already in the pavilion.

'I know we French make – 'ow you say – *fun* of your English food, but now I salute it!' said Al. 'Roast beef is the dish of liberté.'

Camille kicked Al's ankles under the cover of her voluminous skirts – at some point even the thickest person would twig they were being laughed at – but he smiled sadly at her. 'Lady 'Arford here has set the example, n'est pas, ma chère Camille? We must adopt England as our new 'ome. If such a beautiful French-woman can become an English lady, then so must we.'

Lady Harford squeezed her hand again. 'You will find it not that strange, after a while.'

Hennie leaned over to pour Camille a cup of tea. 'Does that mean you're staying for good?'

Camille closed her eyes, letting the image of the traumatised émigrée rest in their minds for a moment. 'I have matters to attend to – I will stay until I see them done.'

Edward cornered James as the women went to find Camille fresh clothes and Al disappeared in another direction with Lord Harford's valet. They shut them-selves in the morning room.

'You're back,' said Edward.

'I am.'

'Don't look glum. You made it out of revolutionary France, you can dine out on the story for years.'

'You know I can't tell anyone about it.'

Edward leaned back on the settle. Everything about him projected an air of casualness, but there was a shadowy cast to his face, the shape of his eye sockets and cheekbones too prominent.

The week before James had left for France, he and Edward had dissected a human head. They had peeled back tissue, thin layers of skin, to expose the glistening muscles and arteries, each sliced out with precision, eyelids and tongue and lips, and cartilage of the nose, and soft jelly of the eyes, until the hollows and curves of the skull showed through. When James had thrown up, Edward had hidden the evidence from Wickham.

'Anything else you can't tell?' asked Edward.

'What do you mean?'

'You know what I mean.'

'I put everything in my letters,' said James. 'I didn't find the girl. I've already told Wickham I'm sorry I couldn't do more.'

Edward considered him for a moment. 'You went to see your fiancée, didn't you? Is that what took you so long?'

James blushed, but said nothing. Camille was a problem he didn't want to think about. He had known she wouldn't let his betrayal slide, but once he proved Olympe's powers to his father Camille could play whatever silly games she liked. He would have already won.

'I'm not sure I see why you would,' said Edward. 'Quite plain, really.'

The urge to snap at him, to defend Camille, rose, but James caught himself. She wasn't his to defend any more. Camille would never forgive him; Edward wouldn't either, when he discovered the truth, and it was inevitable he would. But if that happened *now*, everything would be lost; he'd tell Wickham, they'd take Olympe and every awful thing James had done would be for nothing.

He joined Edward in the act of nonchalance, sitting at a card table and pulling out a tin of snuff. 'I ran into her, yes. Didn't expect her to follow me back to England like a love-sick puppy.'

'Don't be cruel, James, it doesn't suit you.'

It didn't, did it? That's what everyone thought of him: *nice*. Not clever, not strong, not sharp. He didn't want to be *nice*. He wanted to be *someone*.

'Look, she's here now but it will be easy enough to keep her busy with Hennie, it needn't get in the way of the work. Wickham says he wants to try again, with these new ideas in place.'

'Are you sure you're still interested?'

'Of course I am—'

Edward carried on as if he hadn't spoken. 'Only, you're a terrible liar, James. Those letters – vague to the point of obfuscation. You're hiding something. Perhaps it's just this fiancée, but I can't shake the thought it might be something else.' He leaned forward, an intensity burning in his eyes. 'I don't have any family, James, I don't have a fiancée or a country house or anything other than my own wits. Wickham, the work, you – that is all I have.'

The room was too quiet. James's thoughts too loud. 'I know, Ed. I know,' he said.

They were both all in, but they'd chosen different places to lay their bets.

Edward's voice softened. 'We were like brothers, once.'

'We still are.'

'Are we? I'll ask you again. Is there something you aren't telling me?'

Sweat prickled under James's arms and his stomach cramped with nerves. 'There is nothing. You are mistaken.'

Those intense eyes fixed him in place like a pin through a butterfly. Then Edward stood abruptly. 'You can't play both sides at the same time. Whatever it is you are doing, decide quickly.' He stalked out of the room, pausing on the threshold to look back. 'Before we decide for you.'

6

Henley House

Soft candlelight flickered in the dining room, illuminating the party that had expanded considerably since Camille's arrival. It hadn't taken long for word to get out that two genuine French refugees from the Terror had arrived in Henley-upon-Thames, and before they knew it half the local gentry had invited themselves to dinner and Lady Harford was in a flap about how to stretch a leg of mutton among thirteen people.

As carriage after carriage arrived, disgorging more nosy neighbours, Camille's heart sank. A healthy audience for her performance as a pitiful orphan fleeing bloodshed was one thing, an entire company of onlookers was quite another. She could feel the focus slipping from her. In a haze of coal and pipe smoke, her lungs felt too tight, as though she could never fully catch her breath. She needed Ada. Ada had brought out the best in her; attempting this alone could bring out the worst.

The plan was only half in place. Camille had been welcomed into their home – now she needed to back

James into a corner and force him to reveal Olympe's location. It was going to be bloody difficult to do that stuck at the far end of a table stuffed with drunken landed gentry. Every time Camille caught a glimpse of his golden head amid the shimmering candle flames, dishes of roast beef, mutton, mackerel with herbs, beetroot and spinach that had been conjured up to sate Lady Harford's panic, she felt the vast distance that split them.

As she watched James, she realised someone was watching her too; Lord Harford trained an assessing gaze at her across the table. She offered a small smile but he didn't return it. They had spoken once, briefly, in the drawing room waiting to go down to dinner, where he'd echoed his wife's welcome in tones that rang hollow. Perhaps he was thinking about his affair with her mother – Camille certainly was. Did he know it had led to her death?

She pushed an over-cooked carrot across her plate. As much as she wanted to confront him about it, she couldn't lose sight of why she was here. She was leader of the Bataillon des Morts, and she had a job to do.

The local vicar and his wife, a Mr and Mrs Banbury, had been the first to arrive uninvited, to offer spiritual succour to the poor afflicted young people. Soon after followed Lord Beauchamp, a baronet from a few villages over, his wife in a towering wig, and her spinster sister in no wig at all. Finally the party had been completed by a Mr Penge, a lawyer with chambers in Henley itself, who had been due to visit Lord Harford on other business anyway, and considered it prudent to stay in order to get a first-hand account of the state of the world across the Channel and expropriate a large quantity of claret from Lord Harford's cellar. James's friend Edward had departed before Camille had emerged from being fitted in a spare outfit of Hennie's. That had only piqued her curiosity further.

Al blossomed under the attention, laying on an accent thick enough to cut with a knife. The party fell into rapt silence as he embroidered the narrative of their passage from Paris to England, inventing Revolutionary forces set at dramatically satisfying points along the way ready to thwart their desperate escape.

'What a breathless tale.' Lord Harford spoke softly. 'It could almost come out of *The Morning Post*.'

He was still watching Camille closely.

Ah. Perhaps he was thinking about something else.

'Indeed, sir, we live in extraordinary times.'

'You must be entirely relieved to have reached a bastion of civility once more,' said Mr Banbury over his wine. 'England stands ready to protect those in need, sir, and it always will.'

Al nodded somberly. 'Alors, oui, I am – 'ow you say – so terribly grateful for la gentillesse – the kindness – your great country has shown me, when my own country rejects me completement. C'est tragique, la belle France reduced to a brawling mob.'

Camille gave him another surreptitious kick under the table.

Al looked at her sadly. 'Vraiment, I think that ma pauvre Camille has suffered so much more than I, she has quite lost her sense of humour.'

'Oh, Camille never had a sense of humour, did she, James?' said Hennie, chewing a piece of mutton. 'If she ever cracks a joke, that's when we'll know she's really lost it.'

'Henrietta,' admonished Lady Harford. 'A lady does not speak with a full mouth. Do not make me reconsider your readiness to join the adults at the dining table.'

'Sorry, Mother.'

Camille could barely stomach the rich food. It was surreal to see so much luxury spread across the table – fistfuls of candles, fragile china, mounding heaps of food. And the people, ruddy-cheeked, in lace and silk, old-fashioned wigs and glittering jewels. The Revolution would have chewed them all up and spat them out without breaking a sweat.

Dinner drew to a close, and the women left for the drawing room while the men stayed at the table for port and cigars. Camille fidgeted through two rounds of tea and mind-numbing small talk, cursing the stupid English tradition, until finally the men rejoined them. Thankfully, the vicar and his wife had taken themselves off home, so the room grew a little quieter.

Before Camille could buttonhole Al to report back, Hennie drew her and James to sit with Lady Harford.

'I have been thinking about it all day and Phil has too so we absolutely must know: Camille, will you and James still marry?'

James choked on the glass of port he'd brought with him. All coherent thought fell out of Camille's head like the trapdoor opening under the gallows: a short, sharp drop and she was entirely gone, dangling at the end of the idea.

Marriage.

Then she struck a second thought, toes finding purchase on the ground so she could breathe.

Wedding.

She needed James distracted, off-kilter. Prone to mistakes.

This could work nicely.

Hennie was still talking. 'I think I would look very well in lavender and it would be a lovely flower to decorate the church with—' She caught up with herself and blushed. 'Though I suppose you'll need some time to recover.'

Lady Harford had tears in her eyes again. 'Oh, but you must, Camille. Once we have you as legally part of the family you will be safe. No one can ever force you back into that dangerous, awful place Paris has become.'

Camille looked down, as if overwhelmed by emotion. 'Since Maman and Papa were … since they died, I have been so perfectly alone. I could not dare let myself hope to ever be among family again. Now that I am, my feelings towards James remain the same, but I understand if things have changed in my absence…'

They all turned to look at James expectantly. He stared back, expression fixed. For a moment, Camille wondered if he would have the guts to reject her in front of everyone. The silence stretched out too long, then he spoke, voice little above a whisper.

'No. Nothing has changed.'

'Oh, James, that's not very romantic. Maman, make him be nicer to Camille.'

'Look, Hen, maybe we can talk about this later—' he said.

'Of course, we must discuss details when Camille has slept,' said Lady Harford. 'I will see you safe. It is the very least I owe the memory of your dear parents.'

Camille leaned back in her chair, forcing a weak smile to her lips. Inside, she felt cold. All she could think of was Ada. This might fit the plan, but it came at a price and now she wasn't sure she wanted to pay it.

Oh god, what had she done?

7

A Slum Near
Rue St Denis

Ada tracked the snatchers' cart from the Right Bank, past Les Halles market and over the river as they wound further and further south. It moved slowly, drawn by a tired-looking dray that picked its way wearily though the night-time streets. She kept as close as she dared, slipping noiselessly from doorway to alley to keep out of sight. They stopped once to add another body to the pile – a middle-aged woman who had been hit by a mail coach and left for dead. Ada watched the men heft the body on top of Guil, bile rising in her throat.

God, she hoped this gamble was worth it.

Across Paris she could see the rot spreading. Inflation and disease boiled out of control. Assignat notes were worth more for the paper they were printed on and the poor of Paris died in droves – Robespierre might have fixed the price of bread, but even the lowest price was too high when you had nothing.

Instability had rippled from the competing centres of government, the National Convention, the Paris Commune and the Committee of Public Safety, after the Festival of the Supreme Being; Robespierre had hardly been seen since his failed attempt to cement his authority and rumours abounded. The Law of 22 Prairial that had sent Al to the guillotine had made a capital offence of so many things that the gutters flowed with blood, and even the mob grew tired of executions. The war with Austria was over, soldiers with nowhere to go flooded into the city, and people had begun to question whether terror should still be the order of the day – or if it ever should have been. What was the point in their new republic if more people died at home than in war?

Ada heard the news day after day as she sat at her father's breakfast table, sneaking the papers after he was done with them. She wanted the Terror over as much as the next person, but she was afraid of what would follow; a kinder revolution seemed no closer. Robespierre had retreated further into dictatorship, losing what scant support he had remaining, and anyone else with half a plan had already lost their heads to Madame La Guillotine. Once his grip on power failed, what stood between the people and the return of everything they had fought against? Monarchy, subjugation, starvation, all waited in the wings.

In that void, it would only be a matter of time before the duc struck.

Ada's biggest fear was that by splitting the battalion, they had doomed themselves. Their strength was together. Divided, she felt lost. Camille should have been the one to stay in Paris. She was the one who could execute a plan amid chaos.

Still, Ada had to try. So she'd gone back to the last reliable way they'd found to locate the duc: dead bodies.

They had discovered his abbey hideout before because Léon had told them about deliveries of cadavers. With the rise in executions the medical schools had no end of headless corpses, so the body snatchers had been put out of work. Only the duc would need intact bodies now; the last place left where the snatchers could still get good money. Léon hadn't exactly been delighted to see the battalion again, but he had agreed to help.

It was a bloody awful plan, but it was the only plan they had.

The weight of Camille's expectations rested at the back of Ada's mind. Camille had trusted her with this. She couldn't let her down.

As the first pale grey hints of dawn stretched across the sky from the east, the cart lumbered past the Luxembourg, the deconsecrated monasteries of the Carmelites and Capuchins and the monumental Val-de-Grâce just barely preserved. Then through the city gates and into the Faubourg St Jacques where, beyond the mounded earth embankments of the new city walls, Paris rapidly faded into farmland. At the Observatory they turned sharply right.

Ada flattened herself against a wall as the carriage rumbled to a halt outside an unassuming house with a shabby frontage and a dirty yard wrapping around the side.

The street was silent. It was just her and the snatchers.

And whoever was inside that building.

The plaster might have been flaking, but the shutters had been newly restored, and candles burned in the windows. There was money here. The blond man rapped his knuckles on a side gate, and a servant opened it wide enough to allow the cart through. The gate was locked behind them.

Ada swore.

She was no use to Guil stuck outside.

Keeping flush to the buildings, she followed the high wall that bordered the yard until she found what she was looking for: a gnarled tree that stretched a branch over it. Half the gardens out here had been planted as orchards long in the past, and now fruit trees made their home wherever they saw fit.

Tucking her skirts into her belt, she clambered onto the branch that overhung the duc's yard, then dropped onto the packed dirt, skinning her knee in the process. The yard was half-earth, half-straggling remains of a grove of apple trees. Stables stood at the far end, several horses closed in for the night, and a small carriage tucked under the roof.

The body snatchers had pulled up to the servants' entrance and waited impatiently.

Ada hunkered down behind the tree trunk and held her breath.

The wait dragged on, and for a tense moment, she thought they might give up and leave, before the sound of a key in the lock broke the silence.

The door eased open.

A tall, smartly dressed man with closely cropped grey hair and piercing blue eyes stepped outside.

They had found the duc.

8

The Drawing Room, Henley House

Lady Harford waved her husband over to inform him of the wedding news, which he took coolly, another assessing eye cast over her. Camille wondered if he could smell the revolutionary on her somehow. Offering their congratulations, the Beauchamps and the lawyer Penge took their leave, and the family – plus Camille and Al – were alone. Hennie pulled James in to make up a four for a game of whist, so Camille requested Al join her to take a turn about the room.

'What did he say?' Camille hooked her arm through his and steered him towards the outskirts of the room. It was large enough to contain various arrangements of sofas, card tables and writing desks. The walls were hung with a silvery lilac paper that perfectly matched the upholstery and pale, glossy wood.

'What did who say?' said Al.

'James, you fool, who else?'

He shrugged. 'Not much. Sank several glasses of port and stared into the middle distance like a brooding hero in some novel. I can understand what you saw in him, if you like that sort of thing.'

Camille ignored the comment. 'He's rattled. Good.'

'Your dramatic entrance was, in fact, dramatic. But why are we talking about that when, unless I am very much mistaken, you have you arranged for yourself to be married at the earliest convenience? Do you think Ada will mind having three people in your relationship?'

She pinched his arm. 'Stop it. You know it's a good idea. If they think I'm nothing but a helpless girl fixated on some romantic notion of marriage, then they're not going to notice anything else.'

He narrowed his eyes. 'Hmmm. Almost convincing, but a little shaky on the dismount. Looked to me as if you were backed into a corner.'

'I can handle it.'

'Don't get in a huff, you know I'm on board. Wagon hitched firmly to your star. Anyway, it's quite fun watching you put on a pretty dress and pretend to be a girl.'

Camille glanced at the silk confection she had borrowed from Hennie. 'I *am* a girl. That doesn't mean I have to like dresses.' It was the sort of thing that would look beautiful on Ada and made Camille feel like a potato – only, Ada would have made her feel beautiful in it. The dress squished her breasts over the scooping neckline and Hennie's maid had curled strands of her hair with a hot poker. Camille thought she looked like an idiot. A potato with delusions of grandeur.

Thinking of Ada brought no comfort; all she could picture was Ada's face when she found out what Camille had done.

'No, I suppose you are rather wearing it like a sack.' They had made it almost two-thirds of the way around the room and were nearing the card players. 'What do you make of James's mysterious friend? Quite dishy. Do you think he's spoken for?'

'Edward? I don't know what to make of him, but James doesn't seem all that comfortable around him, for a friend.'

Al arched an eyebrow. 'You've got a look.'

'Have I?'

'Yes. A scheming look. Go on, tell me.'

'Well … we need to find James's weak spot and we might have stumbled across it already. Keep an eye on him, follow him – I don't think Lady Harford is going to let me out of her sight.'

'Yes, milady. As milady commands.'

'Never mind that,' she said. 'How about you tone down that appalling accent before people start thinking you're making fun of them? I know you speak perfect English.'

'Ah, non, ma chérie, c'est impossible. The English folk, they think we are the sad little victims of an unspeakable horror that could never possibly visit their lands. The more I play into it, the more they'll believe anything I say. You're not the only one who knows how to act a part.'

'I suppose you have a point.'

'Don't I always?'

Her expression changed. 'Don't push your luck.'

He patted her hand as they parted. 'I think the hardest bit of this plan is going to be tolerating each other for so long.'

Camille had a feeling he was right.

Lady Harford beckoned her over. 'My darling girl, keep me company a little. I have missed you.'

Camille joined her, sitting on an overstuffed stool beside her Bath chair. Lady Harford was flagging as the evening stretched on, and now she sat so quietly she had almost disappeared from the room. It still shocked Camille to see how far her illness had progressed – somehow, she had imagined everything in England standing still while she'd been separated from them. But it hadn't. The world had changed, and she had become a stranger to it.

'Oh, blast.' Hennie threw down her cards. 'Whist is an awful game. I detest it.'

'You don't know how to concentrate, that's your problem,' said Phil.

Hennie twisted in her chair to speak to Camille. 'Will you be married by special licence? I think that would be far more romantic. *Nobody* gets the banns read any more. Do they, Maman?'

Lady Harford inclined her head. 'A special licence would be preferable. William, you must arrange it as soon as possible.'

Lord Harford looked up from his paper. 'Oh, must I?'

'Don't argue. I know you will return to town tomorrow. Your son is just like you, he insists on leaving too.'

Lord Harford shot James a look and James seemed to deflate even further. Camille watched the exchange with interest.

'Oh, Maman, why don't we all go?' Hennie beamed. 'We can get Camille some gowns of her own, and even start a wedding trousseau! She doesn't want to have come all the way from Paris just to moulder away in this old place.'

'What a wonderful idea. William, we might as well open the London house.'

'I am perfectly happy staying at my club. I don't think the travel is the best thing for your health...'

'Nonsense, a man needs a home, and my health is my own to worry about. London it is.'

Lord Harford huffed and disappeared behind his paper.

Hennie clapped her hands. 'We'll find you some lovely things, Camille. Silk suits you – I heard Robespierre banned silk. Whatever for, I ask you! What have the poor weavers done to him? I thought the Revolution was supposed to be about helping people like them. How can they be better off if no one is buying their wares?'

'Well, it's rather complicated,' said James, speaking for the first time. 'You see, the Revolutionaries think they're doing the right thing, that they have some grand master plan to save the world. But really they're stumbling about like children with no supervision.'

He delivered the lines looking straight at Camille.

She bristled. 'How true. An inflated sense of righteousness is a terrible thing.'

If he wanted to play, she was ready.

'Enough talk of unpleasant things.' Lady Harford interrupted them. 'I am quite exhausted. Hennie, ring for Molly.'

'Of course, Maman.'

A servant came to wheel Lady Harford to her bedroom, and with their hostess retired, the party was over. Lord Harford disappeared to his study, and Hennie and Phil followed Al, asking him a litany of questions about Paris.

Camille caught James's eye as he reached the door. He hesitated on the threshold, then stepped back inside and shut it.

With his back to her, she crossed the room in a few quick strides, pulling out the knife that was strapped under her skirts. As he turned, she shoved him against the wall, blade to his throat.

'Where is she?'

James stared at her, eyes wide, flickering down to the knife just out of his view. When he swallowed, his Adam's apple bobbed against the blade's edge. 'I'm telling you nothing.'

'Did you somehow miss the part where I have a knife to your throat?'

'Go on, then.'

'What?'

'Cut my throat. Isn't that what you're threatening?'

Camille faltered for a second, and a triumphant look flashed across his face.

She rallied. 'I don't have to cut your throat to make you suffer.'

'No, you're planning to marry me to do that.'

With a growl, she pushed the knife closer. 'Don't think that was my idea.'

'What exactly *is* your idea, Cam? You lost in Paris and all you're going to do now is embarrass yourself. There's still time to leave – unless you actually want to marry me?'

'I'd rather drown in my own vomit.'

'Charming. Put the knife down, will you? Why the theatrics?'

'Maybe I felt you should be on the receiving end of something unpleasant for a change,' she said. 'What with threatening to shoot me in the head a few weeks ago.'

'Mmm. Unconvincing. Try it again but with less of a shaky hand.'

Camille's eyes darted to her fingers wrapped around the handle. He was right; they were trembling, blade wavering against the faint stubble at his throat. She was exhausted, lungs never quite recovered, shaken by the prospect of the wedding, and god *damn* this stupid boy for making her feel like an amateur. Like she could still entertain *any* feelings for him.

A bubble of frustration rose up.

She pressed the knife into flesh, denting his creamy-white skin until a vivid red bead of blood welled over the steel.

James drew in a sharp gasp.

She smiled. 'I don't know. A shaky hand seems to get the job done.'

'You're forgetting I know you, Cam.' His breath was warm against her cheek. 'I know what you're capable of. And I know when you're bluffing.'

They were so close she could feel his heartbeat hammering in his chest, smell the mix of linen and stables and eau de toilette. The last time she had been this close to him, they had kissed. 'You don't know me at all.'

'I do. I know you like grand gestures and wild plans, and I know you can never pull them off. You're all bluster, you always were.' His lips curled in a smirk, and he leaned forward, letting the blade cut him more. 'You're in my world now. Do you really think you can outsmart me here?'

Before she could reply, there was the sound of footsteps at the door and Camille leaped back, hiding the bloody knife behind her as Molly came into the room.

She took one look at their rumpled appearance and breathlessness and went pink.

'Excuse me, Miss du Bugue, but Lady Harford says that your room is ready if you want to retire. And there's a bed made up for you too, Master Harford.'

James straightened his collar to hide the cut at his throat. A tiny starburst of blood on his cravat was all there was to show of it.

'Goodnight, my love,' he said, ducking his head to kiss Camille on the cheek. 'Sleep well.'

He sauntered from the room as though nothing had happened. Molly caught Camille's eye and winked. 'I hear the morning room doesn't get much use in the evenings,' she said. 'In case that's of any interest, miss.'

'It's not,' snapped Camille, then caught herself. 'Sorry. It's been a long day.'

'Of course, miss.' The maid bobbed a curtsey and hurried out.

Camille sank into the nearest chair, heart racing, and dropped the knife onto the table before her. She'd been gripping it so hard her fingers felt numb.

One day down – how many more to go?

She was starting to think saving Olympe's life would be the death of her.

9

The Faubourg
Saint Jacques

Ada stared at the duc in shock. Weeks of searching with nothing to show for it, then, in one short evening – there he was. Maybe Camille had been onto something with her wild plans. The biggest, stupidest risks could reap the greatest rewards.

The duc stepped out of the pool of light spilling from the doorway and into the shadows with the snatchers. Ada felt a thrill of excitement and panic at the same time. It was really him. He was expensively dressed, but his waistcoat was unbuttoned, and his rolled-up shirtsleeves exposed muscled forearms. Without the old-fashioned wig, he looked younger than she remembered; his short grey hair made him look hardened, less pampered.

A threat.

'Ah. Gentlemen. I was expecting you earlier.'

The rattish man hung back, arms crossed. 'It's a long journey.'

Didier elbowed him into silence. 'A little late, but worth it, I assure you.'

'What have you brought me today?' The duc neared the cart. The woman they had added last had slipped sideways, and now Guil's long limbs sprawled across the top of the mound of corpses, exposed to the duc's hawkish eye. Ada could only imagine how horrible it must be.

Oh god, what if the duc recognised Guil? No – Guil was just another dead peasant. The duc would see what he wanted to.

'Only the finest resources, monsieur. You know we wouldn't let you down.'

'I will be the judge of that.'

He lifted a lantern to inspect the body on the top of the pile – Guil.

A frown crossed his face.

Ada's heart stopped as the duc reached out. Lifted one of Guil's eyelids and held the light near his eye. Then he put two fingers against Guil's neck.

With a sneer of disgust, he stepped back.

'You fools, this one is still alive.'

The snatchers exchanged a look. The rattish man looked ready to blow. 'I *told* you this was a bad idea.'

Didier ignored him. 'His sister said he was dead.'

'And you didn't bother to check?'

'He was practically gone when we took him – we know you prefer them fresh. Give him a few hours, he won't pull through.'

The duc gave him a withering look. 'This man is perfectly healthy and the two of you are idiots.'

Ada pulled the knife from her boot and braced herself. This was it. The moment it could all go wrong.

'Look, if a dead body is what you want, we can fix that easily enough. No one will miss him.'

'I have no interest in murder being brought to my doorstep,' said the duc coolly. 'You attempted to trick me and have been exposed by your own stupidity. I have made it perfectly clear that this arrangement only survives with your discretion. I've half a mind to turn you over to the Commune police.'

The rat puffed up. 'Do that and we turn you in as a traitor to the Republic. We know who you really are—'

'Shut *up*, Maurice. Ignore him, no one needs to tell anyone anything. We can still do a deal on the others?' Didier lifted the arm of the middle-aged woman they had collected last. 'This one is definitely dead.'

The duc snorted and returned to the house. 'Get off my property before I throw you off.'

With that, he slammed the door shut and Ada sagged in relief.

But the danger wasn't over.

The body snatchers had descended into argument, Didier shoving Maurice in the shoulder. 'We can't just abandon the cart here, you fool.'

'Why not? What can we do with a live one? I say cut our losses and get the hell away before his sister changes her mind about that story you spun her.'

Didier weighed the rock thoughtfully. 'Maybe this night doesn't have to be a total loss. We could try and sell them to the new medical school over near Les Invalides...'

Oh god, this was going south fast. Ada held the knife in a shaking hand, mind racing. She needed to do something – anything – to distract them long enough for Guil to run. They had come this far. Anything was worth a try.

She picked up a rock of her own and lobbed it at the men. 'Hey! You! I did change my mind. Give me back my brother!'

As they turned towards the direction of the rock, Guil didn't waste a moment to leap out of the cart and start running. Maurice spotted him – but too late. Guil was halfway to the gate. Ada dived from behind the tree, flinging another rock, this one catching the rat on the shin.

'Hey – wait! Damn.' He swung back round to Ada, eyes narrowing. 'You set us up.'

Didier squinted at her. 'So she did. You lying little bitch.'

'Guil! Run!' Ada yelled – but Guil had already hopped the gate and disappeared into the night.

The men hesitated, uncertain who to follow, and Ada took the opportunity to scramble over the wall out of the duc's yard. Lungs burning, she ran headlong back towards the city. She ran and ran until she was through the city gates and able to fling herself down an alleyway to watch for any sign of pursuit. Her mouth was filled with the bitter taste of her raw throat. A minute passed, and then a minute more and still no one came. Either the snatchers were smarter than she gave them credit for and were waiting for her to come out – or they'd given up.

Ada could only hope that Guil had made it too. They'd agreed to each make it out however they could; it had seemed a sensible plan at the time, but now, alone in the dark of the city, she wished they had stuck together.

For a moment she felt a flash of unease, a premonition. They had already split the battalion in two for Olympe.

To see this through, how much further would they have to fall apart?

The Streets of London

8 Thermidor
26 July

The hackney carriage bounced over the cobbles and potholes, jostling James against the other passengers as it rumbled east along High Holborn. It was scarce a mile and a half from Bedford Square and its wastelands of half-dug foundations to his university digs – but he wasn't headed there.

The carriage crawled through traffic; brewers' drays stopped dead in the street to deliver barrels of ale to pubs, drovers herded cattle towards Smithfield, sedan chairs and their runners bobbed and weaved through the traffic. From the first moment James's family had crossed into London in their large, well-sprung post-chaise that morning, dark clouds had loomed low on the horizon. The sunshine of the week before had vanished, and the sticky heat had built and built as they drove further into the city. A storm threatened, a tension in the air ready to break.

And in their London house, the tension had grown worse. As servants folded away dust-sheets, made beds and stowed travelling clothes, James and Camille had continued their awkward dance. Wherever he turned, she or Al seemed to be there, watching him, whispering between themselves. And worse, his mother looking at them both fondly, a light he hadn't seen in months returned to her eyes.

James's hand went to his throat, and the scab that had formed where Camille's knife had cut him. She would be planning something. As sure as night followed day, so trouble followed Camille Laroche.

The carriage lurched to a halt and a flurry of shouts came from the driver and the delivery cart he'd nearly collided with. James and the other passengers settled themselves, wedging into the cracked leather seats. He pulled the window open a fraction, letting in the smell of the city: coal, horse manure, sewage, street food, livestock, perfume.

God damn Camille. He was angry at her for showing up and disrupting his plans – but what did he expect? If there was one thing he knew about Camille, it was that she took delight in being difficult.

He couldn't work out what she wanted. Olympe – of course – but why? Was it just her hurt pride? Were she and Olympe truly friends? Camille had made it clear she wanted the girl out of the Royalists' and Revolutionaries' hands – so why did she care that he'd taken her to England? In Paris, Camille had sat on the fence between both sides. She was naive if she thought she could do that for ever; allying with Olympe would force her to pick a side sooner rather than later. Edward was wrong about him on that count too. James had chosen a side.

The only problem was that they were no longer on the same one. James had chosen his family. His father.

The cab slowed and the driver thumped on the ceiling, bellowing their location. They were far enough from Bedford Square now, so James hopped down and began walking back west. His university digs were east, near St Paul's Cathedral and St Bart's Hospital, where he and Edward had trained in surgery under Wickham, and the last place he would want to hide Olympe if he meant to keep her secret from them. The slums of St Giles had proved the answer.

Known as the Rookery, the slum covered the triangle between Great Russell Street and Broad Street, bounded by Charlotte Street and High Street. It was barely ten minutes' walk from the polished stone and flashing windows of the Bedford Estate, but he didn't dare go directly unless some emergency forced his hand.

Within paces, James had left behind the carriage-crammed thoroughfare of Broad Street and disappeared into the dark hollows of the slum. Once-respectable townhouses had been divided and divided until three families lived in each room. Crumbling tenements were squeezed into the gaps, built without foundations and walls only half a brick thick, and everywhere, the rubble of collapsed buildings, a spectre of future ruin. Spider-webbing between was a warren of alleys, courtyards and cul-de-sacs, windows stuffed with rags or papered over, gutters choked with cabbage stalks and refuse, walls bulging, whitewash peeling with mould. James had come here to hide from his past – instead, it only reminded him of Paris, and running with the battalion.

He had taken a room above a public house called The Rat's Castle on Buckbridge Street, the closest the Rookery got to a main road. The building was a wreck of the area's former fortunes, a redbrick house with ornamental carving decorating its frontage, though the ground floor had been long since ripped out to make space for the pub.

It was a raucous pub, with a steady stream of clients passing at all hours and in all states of disrepair – perfect for slipping in and out without attracting attention. Edging past a party of drinkers clutching tin cups of spirits, James mounted the stairs two at a time to his room at the very top. He had taken care never to meet his neighbours; he could be rubbing shoulders with murderers for all he knew – and given the Rookery's reputation, he probably was. Despite its position under the eaves, his room was unusually fine – small but ornately panelled, with a vast fireplace and two windows, their glass panes intact. Olympe couldn't complain he kept her in complete squalor.

That itch in the back of his mind was stronger than ever: he'd left her alone for too long. She had enough food and water, he was sure, but god help her if she escaped and became lost in this nightmare of a city.

At the top of the stairs he paused, waiting for the

footsteps thundering down below to stop, then fished the key from his pocket and let himself in.

To find Olympe holding a pistol aimed directly at his head.

PART TWO

Entente Cordiale

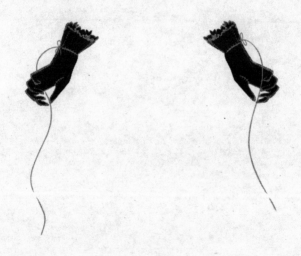

1

A Room in the St Giles Rookery

'Let me go, or I shoot.'

Olympe's silk-gloved hand was wrapped tightly around the handle of the pistol.

James stepped inside and locked the door. The hairs on his neck prickled as he turned away from her, even for a moment.

'Stay back.'

The gun wavered in her hands, tracking a bead between his forehead and throat as she squared up, a head shorter and dressed in nothing but silk: silk dress, silk stockings, a silk scarf around her throat. A rope around one foot bound her to the bedstead, her silk gloves, each tied at the wrist, giving no purchase to undo the knots. Her hair was loose and wild, curling away from her temples to hang in an unbrushed tangle down her back. The smudged grey-blue storm cloud of her skin roiled with tension and, in the darkness, the pinpricks of star-like light in her eyes were as bright as a burning match.

Behind her was the floorboard she'd levered up to locate the hidden pistol.

'I'm not bluffing.' The gun was too big for her; she held it in an awkward, two-handed grip.

James raised his hands. 'I can stay back, or I can untie you. Which one would you like me to do?'

'Don't patronise me!' Her finger twitched on the trigger.

'I'm not patronising you. Believe me, I take you very seriously. But if you shoot me, I can't help you. Agreed?'

A look of uncertainty flashed across her face. 'Yes, but it will hurt you and that will be just as satisfying.'

Olympe had learned a few things from Camille, it seemed.

'I'll untie you, and then we can talk, okay?'

'Untie me and unlock the door. Then you can talk as much as you like, I won't be around to hear it.'

'All right.' James manoeuvered around the trembling point of the gun towards the rope at her ankle. As he crouched, he felt the cold barrel brush his ear.

'There,' he said. 'Done.'

The rope came loose.

Olympe looked down, and James lurched, grabbing for her wrists.

With her powers locked away behind layers of silk, she was just a teenage girl; in a simple contest of strength, he knew he could win.

Olympe panicked and her finger squeezed the trigger.

The gun went off with a bang at his temple. Powder

flared, filling the air with the acrid smell of smoke; the sound punched so hard against his ear he felt drunk.

But – there was no bullet. She hadn't loaded it.

James almost laughed. Of course she hadn't; she wouldn't know how.

The recoil was still fierce on a big old pistol like that. It hit Olympe hard enough that she fumbled, pearl handle slipping against her silk gloves. Ignoring the ringing in his ears, James snatched at the pistol – even if she couldn't shoot him, it could do damage as a bludgeon. They struggled for a moment, Olympe slipping in her silk stockings, and they went tumbling to the floor. James knocked the pistol out of her hands, sending it spinning; Olympe dived after it, but James grabbed her ankle and hauled her back. She kicked at his face. He ducked out of the way, putting himself between her and the gun.

'Stop! Stop it! It's over, Olympe. It's over!'

'I won't let you tie me up again.' She scrambled upright, hair in her face and panting. 'You're like Docteur Comtois, you lock me away like an animal. Like I'm nothing.'

'I'm not like them. For god's sake, look around you. Is this a dungeon?'

'You can put me in silks and call it mercy, but you still treat me like a dog,' she spat. 'You betrayed your friends. You're a monster.'

'Shut *up*.'

It stung. Why was Camille a hero when she went after what she wanted? Why was he a monster when he did the same thing? He remembered the pleading look on Edward's face at Henley House, begging him not to throw away their friendship. Edward, Olympe, Camille – they were collateral damage, yes, but it didn't make him a monster. He was a good man. He had to believe it.

His heart rate slowed after the burst of action, and a headache from the gunshot was starting to build. Olympe hadn't fought him like this since France. At first, she'd struggled to escape at every opportunity, but the further they got from anywhere she knew, the quieter she grew. For the last few weeks, she'd barely spoken.

Olympe gave a final longing look at the gun, then slumped, skin clouding blue-grey with frustration, and rubbed her eyes with her hand.

'Are you crying?'

Olympe sniffed angrily. 'No. I hate you.'

'I know.'

'When Camille finds me, she's going to kill you. I want to watch.'

James leaned against the bed frame, unutterably weary. Weary from the journey to Henley and back in two days, weary from constantly looking over his shoulder, weary from fitful sleep during their agonisingly slow journey from France, always hiding, sneaking, walking by moonlight until his feet bled, hoping Olympe wouldn't smother him as soon as he shut his eyes.

'No one is going to kill anyone,' he said tersely. 'There is no revolution in England.'

Olympe folded her arms. 'Maybe there should be. Just a little one, to make arrogant men like you taste humility.'

'I told you at the start. If you cooperate, this will be over so much faster.'

'I'll cooperate when I'm a corpse and you can stuff me and mount me on the wall like the medical curiosity you think I am.'

'Please. Give me a chance—'

'Why? Why should I trust you? Everyone who's kidnapped me, locked me up, experimented on me, thought of themselves. Only Camille and my mother were ever *for* me, ever thought me human.'

'I promise I don't want to hurt you. I am not like Comtois – or the duc.'

She narrowed her eyes. 'And yet here I am, your prisoner. I am not a commodity to be traded and exploited. You're as bad as the rest of them, whatever you tell yourself.'

James tipped his head to look at the ceiling. The white-washed plaster ceiling was spotted with damp and a spider was patiently building an empire in one corner.

Maybe Olympe was right. After all, he didn't know what his father would do with her. But surely she would be better treated here than in France. He had to hand her over to prove the science was real – before Wickham got there first. This discovery would be for nothing if he didn't act fast.

Like the spreading damp, a stain of guilt marred his thoughts. The truth was: he hadn't thought about what would happen to Olympe in the end. It hadn't factored into his decision and perhaps it should have. The more time he spent with Olympe the more questions he had.

How was she storing electricity – or was she generating it? Did every human have this latent ability, or was she special? Why did the shock hurt? Why did it kill?

He had too many questions and the uneasy feeling he wasn't smart enough to answer them.

Ada was smart.

She had figured out so much with no formal scientific education. Of course Camille would pick someone like her. Smarter than him, sharper, better. Here he was, dim and ordinary and offering her nothing—

James stilled mid-thought.

There was a creak on the stairs, then the softest of sounds at the door.

The handle turned. Rattled against the lock.

James grabbed Olympe before she could utter a cry, clamping a hand over her mouth, rolling them both under the bed.

The sound at the door stopped; for a moment he thought whoever it was might have gone. Then a piece of paper was slid under the door. Slowly, the key he had left in the keyhole was pushed out, and dropped onto the paper waiting below, before it was pulled back to the other side.

With a jolt James remembered the gun still on the floor.

Reaching with his foot he could just about toe it into the hole and push the floorboard into place.

The lock clicked.

He whipped his foot out of sight as the door opened.

And someone stepped inside.

A Dressmaker's, London

'How many heads did you see chopped off?' Hennie leaned across the carriage, eyes wide in horrified delight.

'Henrietta, shush.' Lady Harford flicked open her lace fan and wafted herself gently.

'Was there a lot of blood? Was it *awful*?'

Camille looked between Hennie and Phil's attentive faces, at a loss. She had thought she was good with words, sharp with a plan at any time. And she was – in Paris. In the middle of a revolution. When stabbing someone and running away was always an option. Here in London, in sprig muslin skirts and genteel society, Camille was finding herself more than a little helpless.

And hurt. It was almost a curiosity, the capacity she still had to feel hurt by naive, insensitive children who thought the Revolution a game.

'Yes. It was quite awful to see my parents murdered in front of me. I did not particularly enjoy that.'

Hennie's face fell. It was cruel, but Camille felt a

moment of satisfaction. She had suffered in ways Hennie could never – hopefully would never – understand. It had marked her, and for the rest of her life she would be working around this raw wound, like the gap of a pulled tooth.

'Oh. Oh, yes, of course. I'm terribly sorry. We both are, aren't we, Phil?'

Phil was still staring at Camille, like she was at an exhibition of medical curiosities on display for penny-a-view at a saints' day fair. 'Oh, er, yes. Awfully.'

It was the four of them driving into town: Camille, Hennie, Phil and Lady Harford. James had barely arrived at the London house before vanishing. Camille just had time to instruct Al to follow him before she was caught up in an expedition to the dressmaker to outfit her with a new wardrobe.

She had watched jealously as Al sauntered unimpeded into the city. In Paris she would have left with him without another thought; in London, playing the role of pitiable refugee and James's fiancée, her freedom was severely reduced. More than that, everything that made her confident – her contacts, her array of weapons, her knowledge of the sprawling mess of alleys and rooftops of her city – was gone. All she had left was herself.

Not that her body felt like much of an asset. Her lungs were bothering her still. She'd blamed it on the fire, then the stress of their exploits with Docteur Comtois and the duc, and finally the journey from France to London. She had lost so much weight that she'd been able to fit into Hennie's cast-offs.

'Still, a tragic orphan is far more likely to be the heroine of a novel and that is at least something of a comfort,' said Hennie.

'Oh, girls, not these silly novels again. So ghastly and improper,' said Lady Harford.

'*Gothic*, not ghastly, Maman. You haven't even read one.'

'And I never shall. That strange Udolpho book you were in such a passion about – in my day we wasted money on dresses not bound heaps of paper! Trop bizarre.'

Hennie turned from her mother with a *humph*. 'It is *literature* and I'm sorry you are too stuck in your ways to appreciate it. I will lend you my copy of *The Mysteries of Udolpho*, Camille.'

Camille blinked. 'Thank you.'

'Ah! We're here.'

The carriage had finished its stop-start trundle, arriving finally in Pall Mall at the tasteful frontage of a linen-drapers. Above the large windows hung a sign: Harding, Howell & Co. The four women stepped over the horse manure and overflowing gutters into the haven of the shop.

Lady Harford was immediately recognised, and they were whisked through a series of airy rooms separated by glazed partitions, past displays of furs, fans, suede gloves, lace trimmings, bonnets, jewellery and perfume, until they reached their destination. Lit by a grand domed skylight above, this room was given over entirely to fat bolts of every fabric imaginable: sprigged muslins, slippery silks and weighty brocades, shiny black bombazine, velvet, calico, linen and printed cotton, stashed in alcoves that reached from the floor to the ceiling, two storeys high.

Camille was ushered into a chair and a book of fashion plates was pressed into her hands. Hennie leaned over her shoulder, flipping between different illustrations of diaphanous young women wearing an array of gauzy, fluttering, high-waisted dresses in the new style. Camille let the hum of chatter from the other shoppers wash over her, the sound of scissors slicing silk, the distant hoof beats from the street outside. She hadn't quite adjusted to hearing English all the time. She understood it perfectly well, and that was the problem. Out in public, with countless voices all speaking at once, it was an onslaught, her mind straining to catch it.

'Oh, what about *this* one for Camille's trousseau?' Hennie snatched the pattern book to show her mother and Phil. 'I heard if you dampen your chemise beneath the dress it looks *quite* indecent and all the most dashing ladies wear it that way at the balls. Of course, I don't know for sure, as Maman won't let me near a ball.' She shot a sullen look at her mother.

'Balls are dreadful things, my dear. I won't inflict them on myself any sooner than needed.'

The shop assistant came and took an extensive order for dresses, chemises, underthings, pelisses, short spencer jackets, a riding habit and finally a ball gown, reeled off with casual disregard for the bill that must be racking up.

'I'm sure I do not need *quite* so many things,' said Camille, after Hennie added in a third nightdress.

'Nonsense.' Lady Harford was firm. 'This is your wedding trousseau. Do not begin to think of the cost, we shall pay it, of course; it is only what your dear, dear parents would have wanted.'

Camille looked about her at the sheer excess, the gilt furnishings, the glittering jewels and silks. She thought of the children she had seen begging on their carriage ride over, the soldiers missing limbs and rattling tins at indifferent passers-by.

No. She wasn't sure this was what her parents would have wanted at all.

Though, given what she had found out about her family – her mother's affair with Lord Harford, her father's revenge that had sent her mother to the guillotine – maybe she didn't know that much about her parents. Watching Lady Harford flick through fashion plates, Camille wondered if she knew of the affair. Or – a darker thought – perhaps her illness had been Lord Harford's excuse to stray. Camille wasn't sure she wanted to know the answer.

The patterns decided, it was time for the huge bolts of cloth to be brought for inspection under the domed skylight, and candles that were brought for the express purpose of testing how a colour would look when firelight was all that was on offer.

Camille let the other women take the lead. She felt exhausted, hectic spots of colour burning in her cheeks, her pulse fluttering in her throat. She hadn't realised how outnumbered she was going to feel, faced with so many people to manage, or how stressful it would be to play the long con. This wasn't a job with a clear get-in and get-out; it stretched on indefinitely, demanding more than her quick wits or skill with a knife.

Seeing James's family made her miss her battalion, Guil and Olympe and Ada, especially Ada. The rosewater smell of her skin, the brush of her fingertips and the crumple of her nose when she was about to tell them how short-sighted they were being – and, oh god, how she missed her parents too and a million other things she could never go back to.

Even so, it was still a job. She had to make it work. James was rattled; now they had to work out where he was hiding Olympe. Camille knew from experience it was no easy task keeping someone hidden, and James was an amateur. If Al could follow him, they could learn where his base was – and plan how to strike. This wasn't her world; the rules she played by in Paris wouldn't work here, but moving quietly and playing the role expected of her could be just as effective as any other weapon. Ada had taught her that.

She thought of Ada as she'd last seen her, expression heavy with worry, stray curls falling into her eyes. A hand at Camille's waist, then warm lips pressed firmly against hers. Not a goodbye – a 'see you again'.

She would see Ada again, she swore it to herself. Until then, she would use everything Ada taught her.

With renewed energy, she threw herself into the fabric selection, holding cloth against her throat for Hennie to judge. Into the conversation, she peppered a series of quiet questions about James. Had he been busy lately? How was his medical study? What did they think of the Revolution here? Between Hennie, Phil and Lady Harford, she began to piece together a picture.

'I'm afraid it is my sisterly duty to inform you that you are marrying a man who exists only notionally,' said Hennie. 'We've hardly seen him since he started that surgery nonsense with Mr Wickham. I don't think Father ever forgave him for going to medical school and disgracing the family name by actually *working* for a living.' She affected Lord Harford's tone. '*Shocking behaviour for a firstborn son who should be stewarding the estate safely into the next generation.* James always thinks he needs to do something flashy and impressive to get Father's attention, when all Father wants is for James to be dull and normal.

'Father said he was okay with the medical school, because we know he was expecting James to get bored and drop it, but he didn't and they end up fighting and ruining family outings. Which is boring because now it means I will have to marry ever so well to make up for it, and that rather puts paid to my plan to marry a tragic émigré French count with nothing but a dashing scar to his name.' She looked at a bolt of cotton printed prettily with wildflowers. 'By the by, your pal Aloysius…'

Camille cleared her throat. 'Spoken for, I believe.'

'I supposed as much. His eyelashes are very pretty. Ah, well, plenty of other émigrés out there, isn't that so, Maman?'

Lady Harford snapped open her fan and flapped it ineffectually. 'I do not know what your fascination with France is. How often have I told you about the time I visited the palace at Versailles and they did their business on the floor behind curtains? The whole place stank. No, no, England is much better. You must marry a proper Anglo-Saxon. Though I suppose Norman stock would be acceptable.'

The conversation drifted and Camille let it.

Pieces of the puzzle were starting to fit together. Her assumption had been that James was working for his father – if anyone wanted to get their hands on Olympe it would be the War Ministry, surely – and she knew what stock he put in his father's approval. It wasn't a stretch to make the connection. She hadn't known about James's surgical tutor, though. Perhaps James had other allies. It made things trickier, there was no denying it, though Camille would not be discouraged easily.

James had said he knew her, but she knew him too.

And she knew exactly how to unravel him if she must.

3

The Printing House of
L'Ami d'Égalité

Ada yawned as she stepped from her father's carriage outside the offices of *L'Ami d'Égalité*. She'd barely snatched a few hours' sleep before blearily washing her face and stumbling into the first clean clothes she could find. A plain day dress in cream cotton. A shawl crossed over her chest in the older style and tucked under a belt. Not her finest hour. But right now, being upright felt like a victory. Her muddied and torn street clothes were stuffed under her mattress, ready for when she next needed to sneak out.

'You see, if literacy has not spread to the masses, then there is no need to direct printing efforts towards them.' Her father had been holding forth on his latest business strategy as they drove from his townhouse in the Marais to the Section de la Butte-des-Moulins, where his offices were rammed into the tangled backstreets near the Jacobin Club. 'The cause will be far better served by aiming our work towards the educated man, and through him the message can be spread.'

And what cause would that be? Ada let the unkind thought linger. Her father was so insistent he still stood for some sort of revolutionary purpose, but from where Ada stood she saw only his self-delusion and daydreaming.

It was another sweltering day, the stink rising from the overflowing gutters. Inside the printing house, the heat built with the thud of machines, the men stripped down to bare chests as they worked the huge levers and screws to churn out her father's projects. Ada scanned everyone, but there was no sign of who she was looking for.

Guil.

Their rendezvous was still a little way off, but she hadn't realised how much she'd been hoping to see him here already. Ada knotted her fingers together in worry. She had been sure Guil had got away last night. What if he hadn't?

Her father disappeared into his office. Ada lingered a moment longer, holding on to her fantasy that Guil would come sloping past the bow-fronted window, a little distorted by the mullioned panes of glass, then at the doorway resolving into her friend – solid, real and safe.

But he didn't, so Ada pinned her broad-brimmed straw hat in place and took herself off to the little shop on the Rue des Moineaux, where she picked up a stack of binding samples wrapped in brown paper and string for her father.

As she returned, she passed the shop selling naval supplies where she would always pause, pressing her face against the glass to take in the cluster of sextants, barometers and other navigation equipment on display. On impulse, she went in. She might have accepted the need to give up most of her scientific pursuits to please her father, but no one could stop her doing a little window-shopping.

It was cramped inside. Loops of rope hung from the ceiling, along with oil lamps, umbrellas and sheets of waxed canvas. Shelves and glass-fronted cabinets were stuffed with all manner of devices, only half of which she could put a name to.

She stopped in front of a set of taxidermy knives for skinning pelts. The sharp flash of the blade reminded her of the scalpels lined up in the duc's abbey laboratory. As she reached a gloved finger to trace their sharp line, someone came up beside her. She turned to apologise, move out of their way. Her heart stopped in her chest.

It was the duc.

'Hello, Adalaide.'

For a moment, she was transported back to the Festival of the Supreme Being, when she'd felt the same icy shock on discovering her father had been working with the duc in order to force her home.

The duc picked up the knife she had been looking at. Turned it, so the sunlight caught its blade.

'Do you know what this is for?'

Her voice stuck in her throat. The shopkeeper seemed impossibly far away. The duc stood between her and the door.

Ada swallowed. Lifted her chin. 'An eight-inch curved knife, used for taxidermy. When naturalists make their scientific voyages, they can't bring back every specimen alive; it isn't practical. So the men will kill the creature, use a knife like this to skin it and dismember it. Then they bring it to Europe in its component parts.' Keeping her composure, she added, 'It kills, sir. That is what it is for.'

He smiled.

'Correct. A clever girl, indeed.'

He placed the knife back in its case.

She fought to hold her nerve. Not for the first time it crossed her mind that Camille should have been the one to stay in Paris. Camille knew how to play this game. Ada didn't.

She would have to learn fast.

Lightly, she turned to another display, touching a set of glass beakers.

'You seek supplies. May I venture a guess that you undertake an experiment at the moment?'

'An astute guess.' He didn't elaborate. 'I hear rumour that you have come round to our point of view. I understand you returned home to your father?'

Ada chose her words carefully. 'I'm not a fool. I know the Terror is no good thing, *Monsieur* le Duc.' She made a point of using the old aristocratic title. A crumb dropped in his path: her loyalties to the Revolution slipping.

'I am glad to hear it. After seeing what your Camille did to poor Monsieur Dorval, I feared you had grown a taste for it.'

Dorval had died in the foundations of the Madeleine Church, bludgeoned with a rock as Camille escaped. Ada made a careful show of nodding, seeming pained at the memory. 'Certainly not. I will readily admit things went too far. It's part of the reason you find me here now, and not with Camille. But I know it is not so easy to make amends for the blood on my hands.'

It hurt her to say, because what of the blood on *his* hands? On Dorval's hands? She knew the role she had to play, but it didn't mean she would like it.

'I think we both know that Dorval's death was not your fault, my dear,' he said. 'It is for the best that Camille Laroche is out of your life.'

'I thank God every day.'

'Away to England, so I hear?'

'I wouldn't know.'

'Hmm. Your father told me you were clever.' He shifted, placing himself more clearly between Ada and the exit. 'Which is why I am disappointed that you are still lying to me.'

Her mouth went dry. 'Am I?'

'Oh, yes. Perhaps I believe you do not know Camille's whereabouts. But I wonder how you care to explain your presence throwing rocks in the grounds of my house last night. Such a commotion. I went to my window immediately, only to see you climbing over my garden wall, and young Guillaume vaulting my gate. I would kindly suggest that spying is beneath you.'

'I – I'm not—'

'The question is: who would you be gathering information for? Not Camille. At the behest of your father, perhaps? A man as stupid as that is a dangerous force; he knows not what problems he stirs up.'

She had been frightened, but as he spoke the feeling was replaced by a simmering resentment. Why did she have to be someone else's tool?

'No – I would posit a third theory. Perhaps you are here entirely for yourself?'

Ada stilled.

'Ah, how interesting.'

'And if I am spying on you? Then what?'

'Perhaps *spying* was not the right word. Observing you now, I have something of the impression of a child with their face pressed up against the window of a sweet shop, hungry for something always kept just out of reach.'

A moment passed. The shop was so quiet she could hear her own breathing. She knew she should be afraid.

But she wasn't.

She had the feeling of walking from a dark cellar into a wash of stark daylight. Of being seen.

The duc continued. 'Your father is an idiot. He makes assumptions, acts as though only he truly understands the world. It makes him blind to what is right in front of him. When he approached me about removing you from that dangerous mess, I was all too ready to accept. Your father had the gall to paint you as a naive young girl caught up in something she didn't understand; I knew at once he had made a grave error of judgment. You understand very well.'

He reached into his frock coat and pulled out a piece of paper. It took Ada a moment to recognise the looping handwriting that sloped up the page. It was her own.

He held the paper out so she could see what she had written. It was the notes she had made at the duc's old hideout in the abandoned abbey. She had found his records explaining how Olympe had been created by experiments with electricity in utero. She must have left them behind when they fled Dorval.

And the duc had found them.

He went on. 'I must say, I was quite taken aback to discover that a member of your little gang harboured such an intellect.'

'It's nothing. I was just copying.'

His eyes went steely. 'Do not pander to the fools who want you to undersell your own potential. I have known clever women before, and I know you are capable of far more than people assume. What surprises me is that you allow others to hold you back.'

'I...'

'Say thank you when someone compliments you.'

She was pinned under his gaze, unblinking and fixed.

'Thank you.'

He tucked the paper away. 'The people around you are not interested in you reaching your potential. If I had such a talent to nurture, I would not make the mistake of snuffing it out.'

He let the moment hang between them. Ada thought of his workroom in the abbey, the bodies obscenely spread, organs plucked out like meat on a kitchen worktop, and of the intoxicating thrill of her first experiments with Olympe. She had been hungry, then, to know more, to try more, to take things further. At a certain angle, she could see how the two of them stood at either end of the same trajectory.

Given free rein, who knew where she might end up?

'I ... understand your offer.'

'And?' He arched an eyebrow in question.

'Let me think about it.'

4

A Room in the St Giles Rookery

The door opened, and someone came into the room.

James tightened his hand over Olympe's mouth. The stranger wore Hessian boots splattered with mud, their tassels swinging as he walked. Then came the sound of drawers opening and closing, boards creaking.

The room was being searched.

James glanced at the loose floorboard concealing the pistol and the bundles of notes he'd made on Olympe. The rest of the room was little more than a shell – a bed, some broken furniture, a jug of water and a small stash of food. If the stranger was hunting for something, a plank of wood wasn't going to stop him finding it.

And sure enough, a minute later the boots stopped and the figure crouched, slipping a knife into the crack between floorboards to lever it open. A lock of blond hair tumbled forward and James tensed.

It was *Al.*

He pulled out the gun and the papers, flicking through them. James went cold and hot at the same time, panic and anger flooding him – how had he been such an easy mark to follow?

Olympe had clocked Al too; she scrabbled like a cat, a low hum of static building before being smothered by the silk; it was all he could do to keep her still.

Al's reading was interrupted by the door bursting open and a clamour of drunken voices flooding in. He snapped upright, stuffing the papers inside his jacket.

'Who the hell are you?' He had dropped the overdone French accent, now speaking English in the posh, clipped tones of James's schoolfellows.

'Oh!' squeaked a female voice. 'Sorry, would you mind pissing off? We've only got the room for an hour.'

'What's this? I'm not paying to share you,' said a man.

Al stalked round the bed commandingly. 'This room is not for rent. Get out.'

'My mistake!' The woman giggled, which turned into a hiccup. 'Come on, Joe – we've got the wrong door.'

'Bloody rich boys thinking they own everything,' the man muttered. Their voices receded, and with a hand on the stolen papers in his coat, Al left too.

James waited until it was quiet, then wriggled out from under the bed, snatching up the rope to secure Olympe again before she could run.

'See. I told you they'd come for me,' she crowed.

'Don't get your hopes up. Camille is all sound and

fury. She says the right things, but she couldn't fight her way out of a paper bag.'

'You're worried. You know you're running out of time.'

He ran his hand through his hair, tugging on it. He hated to admit it, but she was right: time was no longer a luxury he had to waste. Al was only ten minutes from Bedford Square, where he could report to Camille and give her the key to the room. They could be back here to get Olympe before the day was done.

'Look, stay put. I promise you, this will be over soon. I don't want to hurt you.'

'Says the man keeping a teenage girl locked up in his bedroom.'

'*Please*. Trust me.'

She cast her inky gaze over him, but said nothing.

James felt hot and sweaty and panicky, his collar too tight and thoughts too messy. Fine. If he was running out of time, he would make things move faster.

He folded the pistol, powder and shot in a handkerchief and buried it at the bottom of the bag. Through the rippled panes of ancient glass, he watched Al weave along the street heading north. With a curse, he hurried out, taking the stairs two at a time. Al had the key so he couldn't lock the door. Olympe was tied up; it would have to do.

The space between the Rookery and Bedford Square was swallowed in a blink as he near sprinted the distance, wriggling through slender alleys and courtyards. The storm had finally broken, lashing rain into his eyes and sliding down the back of his collar.

'James!'

He turned in shock at Edward's voice. There he was – on the corner of Charlotte Street, with Wickham behind him.

No, no, no. This couldn't be happening. He couldn't handle this.

'We've been looking for you.' The memory came back to him – Edward leaning close in the morning room of Henley House.

We were like brothers, once.

Whatever it is you are doing, decide quickly. Before we decide for you.

It was a snap decision. James could deal with Edward and Wickham, or with Al, and in that moment, all he could think of was Olympe snatched before he had a chance to talk to his father.

Edward and Wickham would have to wait.

James darted into traffic, swerving between a dray cart stacked with barrels and the thundering line of carriages turning in from Tottenham Court Road.

Edward followed. 'James, wait!'

A yell went up as James skidded to the other side of the road, horses whinnied, then came a sickening crunch, and he looked back.

For a second he couldn't understand what he was seeing; the shape of horse and carriage and body mixed up unnaturally. The newly laid cobbles were glossy with water and tinged with red. Edward had slipped or the carriage had struggled to stop on the rain-slicked streets. Either way, he had ended up under the wheels.

Pulled up short by the accident, the door of the

carriage two behind was flung open and Hennie's head poked out.

'What happened? Oh, goodness—' She saw Edward and let out a shriek. Camille appeared, an arm looped around her waist to pull her back.

Wickham was crouching by Edward, barking orders. James knew he should go over; he was a medic, he should be helping. But he was frozen, every thought in his mind, every breath in his body dissolved.

His best friend was dead.

And it was his fault.

Lord Harford's Study

S haken and soaked through by the rain, Camille
and the other women arrived back in Bedford
Square on foot.

Edward had been carried off by Wickham and
James to the hospital, and the footmen were clearing
the broken debris from the crash. That sound wouldn't
leave Camille's head – the crunch and the sudden
silence after. It almost surprised her that she could still
be shocked by violence after everything she had seen
in the Terror; for some reason this had shaken her all
the more for its mundanity. To die at the guillotine was
to be part of history – to die in a carriage crash was a
forgettable accident.

Camille was on her way to change out of her blood-
and rain-spattered dress when Lord Harford's study
door opened and he appeared, blocking her path.

'Camille. A word.'

She followed him into his office. She'd expected
this meeting.

'I will speak frankly with you,' he said, hands

clasped behind his back, 'because our long connection bids me not to prevaricate or play games. By coming here, am I to believe you renounce your loyalties to France and the Revolution?'

Camille swallowed. It wasn't hard to let tears prick her eyes. 'The *Revolution*,' she spat, 'murdered both my parents. I owe it nothing.'

'I am glad to hear it,' said Lord Harford. 'However, you will forgive me if I am not quite so readily trusting as the rest of my family. A foreigner in the home of the war minister could be seen as quite the security risk.'

She'd spent long stretches of the journey from Paris to Henley House trying to reframe her understanding of the people she'd called family. Her father wasn't a faultless, stoic man – he was petty, violent and possessive. Her mother wasn't a pure, revolutionary flame – she was a human being who wanted love badly enough to make the mistake of an affair with Lord Harford.

And Lord Harford. Her 'Uncle' Will. What should she think of him now? She was filled with an anger she hadn't expected; anger that her mother had died, and he had lived. A quirk of chance had meant her mother was in the firing line and Lord Harford had escaped. He sat behind his desk, master of house and family. He had torn *her* family apart, and now had the gall to demand she justify her presence in *his*.

Camille cast her eyes down, let the grief and confusion she had buried come to the surface. He might wield the power here, but she could still act. 'I confess I had not thought of how this must seem to you.'

His expression did not soften. 'I have not made it as far as I have without a modicum of caution. The picture you present is indeed a pitiful one, but I also know where you come from, Camille du Bugue. You might mistake me as a friend to your parents' erstwhile cause, given our past, but know that I stand with England now. Whatever sympathies I had before have been destroyed by the wanton bloodshed across the channel; violence will never be the right way to bring about change. No, my naivety was exposed, and I have learned to adopt a more measured stance. I can only hope that what you have seen has stripped the wool from your eyes too.'

'Indeed it has.'

'Very well. I will take you at your word, I will allow you and your friend in my house and your engagement to my son to continue.'

'Thank you—'

'But I will be watching you,' he said. 'I hope you can see the generosity given to you here. Do not repay us with betrayal.'

'Never,' she replied, letting a little fire into her voice.

He dismissed her.

She paused artfully, hand on the doorknob, biting her bottom lip. 'There is something you should know. Georges Molyneux is dead.'

They had been close friends once, her parents, Lord Harford and Molyneux. Now only Lord Harford was left alive. Camille thought of her battalion; perhaps that would be them someday, dead one by one until someone was left to mourn alone.

Lord Harford blanched imperceptibly. 'The guillotine?'

'No. Murdered far more conventionally.' She smoothed her skirts. 'I thought you would want to know – though I suppose you must be better informed on these matters than I. As you say, you are the war minister.'

His hand moved unthinkingly to the briefcase on his desk, and the papers stacked neatly next to it. They were covered in dense writing, several wax seals split apart; she thought she saw something written in French.

'Thank you for informing me. I shan't keep you longer.'

With a perfunctory curtsey, she left.

In her room, she changed clothes, pausing only when a coughing fit struck, folding her double and forcing her down onto the edge of her bed. She felt too hot and too cold, dizziness made her head spin. When she took her handkerchief from her mouth, it was spotted with blood. She threw it onto the fire then loosened her stays before going back downstairs.

Lord Harford didn't trust her. So be it. At least she knew where she stood. And he wasn't wrong; someone with differing loyalties, in the home of the war minister, could come across very useful information *indeed*.

In the hallway, the front door was open and a footman was carrying in a red case on a silver platter. The rest of the Harfords and Phil sat in the morning room in varying states of shock from Edward's accident, waiting for news. Lady Harford looked too small in her Bath chair, the blow of death so close too much for her to bear. Phil was doing her best to stay cheerful, making conversation, while Hennie clutched a bottle of smelling salts and wept into a handkerchief.

Camille stopped in the hall, out of their line of sight. She didn't have time to get drawn into their grief.

She caught the attention of a passing maid. 'Those briefcases that get delivered to the house...'

'Lord Harford's dispatch boxes?'

'Is that what they are?'

The footman came back down carrying a different case on his tray – the one Camille recognised had been in Lord Harford's study a minute ago.

'Yes, miss, his papers from the government travel very securely. No one is allowed to touch them, not even the family.'

Camille watched the exchange between the footman and the man attending the carriage outside.

As War Minister, Lord Harford would have access to the latest, most sensitive intelligence. Her mission might be to rescue Olympe – but Ada's was with the duc. They knew so little about his allies, his plans. Who better to have this information than the politician dedicated to understanding everything happening in France right now? Lord Harford had information and the battalion needed it.

Perhaps Lord Harford was both a problem, and an opportunity.

6

St Bart's Hospital

The storm lashed the courtyard as James and Wickham arrived at St Bart's. People scattered in a bristle of umbrellas opening and coats being thrown overhead. The driver had raced down Holborn, past Smithfield Market and on to St Bart's Hospital with all the speed Wickham could urge him to.

Together, they carried Edward's limp body to Wickham's operating theatre. The gash on his head had bled profusely, sticky blood covering James's hands and running inside his cuffs. His mind jolted along like the staccato rhythm of the horses' hooves: it was going to be fine – they had made it in time – they were both surgeons – of anyone in the city suffering such an accident, Edward had the best chance of survival.

A memory had played in a loop: they had met when James had slipped on a patch of vomit in the operating theatre and Edward had caught him, a firm hand under his elbow, arm clamping around his waist. The exchange of words, Edward's hesitant smile, his black hair falling into his eyes.

Inside the hospital, younger students followed doctors and surgeons on their rounds, and visitors threaded the hallways, clutching parcels of food, newspapers and gifts. The operating theatre was like a real theatre, a horseshoe of wood, at the base an oval of space strewn with sawdust to soak up the blood, where the surgeon would undertake dissections or surgical procedures. Ringed around like tiers on a cake were balconies placed so that students could stand with their notebooks and watch their teachers below. Old blood spattered the boards up to the second level – James recognised a stain from a particularly memorable amputation that had hit a huge artery in the poor dockworker's leg, sending jets of hot, salty blood over the first few rows.

As newer students, James and Edward had been confined to the top tier, their necks aching, straining to see through rows of wigs and hair. Hour after hour spent watching Wickham finely slicing through layers of tissue to expose the glossy kidneys, the spongy lungs, the filigree of blood vessels charting the human body like a map.

Now it was Edward splayed out on the dissection table, a tray of bloodied instruments ready by his side. Wickham, like many surgeons, took pride in leaving them dirty, the layers of dried blood demonstrating his years of experience wielding saw and scalpel. He had taken a needle and thread and was sewing up the cut on Edward's forehead. It looked bad, shining white bone flashing between flaps of skin and red gristle. Edward lay like a doll dropped on the nursery floor.

James thought he might be sick.

Finally the cut was stitched closed, an ugly tear in Edward's beautiful, ashen face. His chest didn't move.

'What do we do now?' James faltered. 'Tell me what to do.'

Wickham stepped away, blood smeared up to his elbows. 'James…' His voice was soft. 'We're too late.'

'No. We brought him here in time, you said it was going to be okay.' His voice was rising, slipping out of control.

James grasped Edward's limp hand, heavy with fading warmth. His features had gone slack, eyes half-open and glassy. One pupil was blown wide, as big as a farthing, the other a dark speck.

It was too big a thought to swallow: Edward was dead.

James had lied to him, made their friendship collateral damage. He had discarded the only person who really *saw* him. And for what?

'He only has us, he said that to me.' James stroked the line of Edward's thumb, his wrist. 'We're his family.'

Wickham rested a hand on his shoulder. 'We did everything we could. It was an accident.'

It happened all the time in London. James had seen enough victims of the crowded streets on Wickham's operating table. If only he hadn't run, Edward wouldn't have followed him. He had done this.

'Come on.' Wickham pulled James into his private rooms.

The door was open, and from where he was deposited in an over-stuffed armchair James could see

Edward, dark hair matted with blood, his arm hanging over the side of the table. A flash of lightning lit the room at the same time as thunder boomed, shaking the windowpanes.

'Here.' Wickham pushed a tumbler of something amber into his hands. It burned his throat, but James knocked it back greedily.

Wickham's private quarters were as chaotic as always – a whirlwind of shelves of medical specimens, stuffed creatures from all corners of Britain's growing empire, skeletal animals, fossils, lumps of quartz, a baize board peppered with butterflies and moths, stacks of books and papers, jars of preserved tumours, resined kidneys, varnished bones, all crammed into a room little bigger than the one James had rented in the Rookery. The boards here were dark with bloodstains, and at the back was a person-sized vat for boiling bodies down to extract their bones. Around all of it hung a smell: the mix of flesh and rot, acid and preserving alcohol.

They sat in silence, letting the storm swallow them.

Edward's blood was on his hands now, flaking around the nail beds and darkening the lines on his palms.

'Useless,' said James. Wickham moved to pour James another measure but he covered the glass. 'I'm useless. What's the point of studying medicine if I can't help people when I need to?'

'We can't help everyone. It's a hard lesson all surgeons must learn. I'm sorry you're learning it like this.'

James laughed. 'I knew there was nothing to be done for an illness like my mother's – but *this*. My god. Edward was alive a minute ago and now he's *dead*, because this' – he gestured to the contents of Wickham's room, to the both of them – 'is useless. No better than some medieval quack and his bag of leeches. We study and we learn and come up with new techniques and people still die in *accidents*.'

The alcohol had gone to his head fast, or maybe the shock had.

Wickham was quiet, looking into the distance. No – at the cloth covering the glass cylinder they used to generate electricity in their experiments. It felt like a long time since James had last been here. But he'd already chosen to throw away his place before Edward died; now there was no getting it back, whatever he did.

'Did you read the research notes you sent me?' asked Wickham, frowning.

'Why does it matter?'

Wickham rose and pulled the dustsheet back to touch a hand to the cylinder, the collection of wires hooked up to it. 'They were most useful. I think I have fixed the issue with insulating the generator. I just need to test the new set-up...'

'Is now really the time to—'

James broke off. Wickham was looking at him expectantly.

Everything came together suddenly, like a bucket of water being dumped over his head. A test – Wickham had mentioned it before, at Henley House. A test needed a body.

'No,' James said.

'Why not?'

James shook his head. 'Because – it's *Edward*.'

'Don't be sentimental,' scoffed Wickham, as he began to gather the equipment. 'It's what he would have wanted.'

'To be an experiment?'

'To change the world. You claimed our work was useless if we couldn't save people – don't you want to help find something that might? Think, James. When have we had a better opportunity? If things were the other way around, I know Edward would be out there himself setting up.'

James went cold. He could see it now – his own corpse on display, wires snaking to a great glass tube, Edward's fingers working the handle.

James looked again at Edward's corpse, blood-drained and cooling quickly.

The accident had been his fault. If Wickham's ideas had any chance of working, didn't James owe Edward that?

With trembling hands, James took a rubber apron and tied it on.

'Tell me what to do.'

6 Bedford Square

Tucked into a chair by the tall sash windows, Camille yawned and turned the page in her book. She didn't know how Ada read for such long stretches of time. She'd been trying off and on for the past hour, but her attention kept wandering. She wanted to get up, move around, *do* something, but by the end of her shopping trip with Lady Harford and Hennie and Phil, she'd felt as flat as a pressed flower and as fragile. Each breath was shallow, as if she'd laced her stays too tight. It frightened her.

Everyone was still shaken by the accident, so it had been easy enough to retire to the library. At random, Camille had plucked a few books she thought Ada would want to read off the shelves. It was a comfort, if nothing else, to feel the ghost of Ada here with her, turning the page and remarking on a particular word or line. She skimmed through a slim volume; it was in French, translated from Chinese. She wasn't sure she understood it, but something caught her eye:

*Pretend to be weak, that your enemy may
grow arrogant.*

She ran her finger underneath the line, turning the words over in her head. There was something there.

The door swung open and Al came in. His hair was damp with rain, his white stockings splashed with mud. He'd adopted a more sombre dress in London, favouring the tan buckskin breeches that buttoned below the knee and a sharply tailored black tailcoat Camille had seen on half the fashionable young gentlemen in town. Though the clothes were borrowed from James, Al somehow made them look like they'd always been his.

She shut her book and waited expectantly.

'There you are.' Al flopped down in a chair facing her, throwing his legs over the arm and pulling out a squashed packet of cherries. 'I didn't know you could read,' he said, nodding at her book stack.

'Al, don't test me.'

'I assure you that is one thing I would never do. Can't abide a test. Why make life any more challenging than it already is?' He popped a cherry into his mouth, chewed, then took the stone out and threw it into the fireplace.

'I am stricken with mirth at your wit,' said Camille.

He beamed. 'Finally, you're warming to me.'

'Get to the point. Were you able to follow James?'

'Oh, *that*. Yes. Nearly lost him when he left the cab, but he's not exactly hard to spot. Thinks he's being clandestine when really he's so suspicious he might as well have "up to no good" tattooed on his forehead. Didn't even notice me following.'

'Are you sure?'

'Quite sure. He doubled back on himself and ended up in a slum not far from here. I poked around his rooms and found your pistol he stole back in Paris and his research – not to mention food, water and even a few silks. He keeps her there all right.'

'So we know his hiding place.'

'Give me five minutes and a cup of proper coffee and I could feel up to a little light heroism. What do you think, stake the place out?'

'No. We wait.' She explained her plan to search Lord Harford's documents for intelligence on the duc. 'Keep following James. See if he moves Olympe.'

Al frowned. 'Are you sure you'll find something worth the risk of waiting?'

'This is bigger than just James and Olympe,' she said. 'We get back to France – then what? We'll still have the duc to reckon with and I'm more afraid of him than I am of anyone in this poxy country.' She turned the book over in her lap, running her finger along the edge of the pages. 'Ada's risking her life in Paris trying to get close to him. If we can find something on him, we owe it to her to get it. Lord Harford is the war minister. If there's anything worth knowing about Royalist movements in Paris, he'll know it.'

Al cocked his head. 'Careful now, you're making something dangerously like sense. I'm impressed. I'd have thought you'd be distracted by other things.'

'What other things?'

Al threw a cherry in her direction. 'Oh dear, have you forgotten about your upcoming nuptials so quickly?'

Camille caught the cherry and angrily yanked the stem out. 'Ah. That.'

'Yes. That. Tell me if I'm overreacting, but I'm not sure Ada's going to be thrilled about this development.' Al's voice briefly lost its joking edge. 'She deserves better.'

Camille pressed her thumb into a bruised divot in the cherry. It was soft, rot setting in. 'I know she does. Just – let me figure this out. The wedding gives us a place here. It keeps James from running. The rest – I'm trying.'

Al looked around at the mess of books lying open on the table.

'Yes, I can see. There has been quite an attempt. A very good try.'

'Are you ever going to be useful or are you just sent here to be my own personal living hell?'

'Don't murder me with your sexy thigh knife, but you are the one who insists on keeping me around.'

At that she looked up, eyes flashing. 'You'd get into trouble otherwise. I risked a lot to keep your head where it is, I'm not going to let you throw yourself into harm's way again.'

Al stilled, a tension entering his body. 'About that. I've … been thinking.'

'There's a turn up for the books,' she said, but the joke felt sour on her lips. Something was wrong.

'I'm not going back to Paris.'

'What?'

'I'll help you to find Olympe but after this job is done, I'm out.'

Camille stared at him, floored. 'I don't understand. You mean – leave the battalion?'

'Yes.' He shrugged. 'I don't know what else to say. The worst has already happened to me, Camille. I watched my whole family die; I nearly died myself. I'd rather stay here and be no one than go through that again.'

She felt almost breathless with shock. Oh god, it was happening: that image of her battalion dropping away one by one was coming true. Olympe stolen from her, James's betrayal, now Al leaving. She would be alone, surrounded by ghosts.

'You can't just leave. We need you.'

'Do you?' His voice was cold.

'Yes. Of course we do.'

'Hmm.' He was silent, watching the runnels of rain coursing down the windowpanes. Camille cast around for something to say, something persuasive or comforting or whatever it was Al needed, but she found nothing. This wasn't her skill. God, she barely understood her own feelings, never mind other people's.

Al bounced up on his seat, tension vanishing in an instant as though he had taken off a coat. It seemed he was done talking. 'Cheer up. I'm still here for now. With all your racket I haven't had time to tell you the most important thing.' He pulled out a key, then tossed it to her. 'For James's room. Sadly I am light-fingered and couldn't stop myself pocketing it. Such a shame. No redeeming me.'

Camille's face lit up. A spark of hope flared as she held the key. 'You got it! You're such a little shit, Al. Don't ever hold out on me like that again.'

Now she had two leads: access to James's rooms, and Lord Harford's government intelligence. Finally they were no longer on the back foot.

Al stood, stretching until his bones cracked. For a brief moment, that shadow crossed his face again. 'I'm serious, Cam. I've made up my mind. This job will be my last.' He didn't wait for her reply, the library door swinging firmly shut behind him.

She turned the key over in her hand, feeling its teeth against her fingers. If they couldn't stop the duc, it might be the last job for them all.

8

St Bart's Hospital

A shock of black hair and chalk-white skin so thin James could see the flurry of veins and arteries spread like the roots of a plant. That was Edward, sprawled on the cutting table, stripped naked and covered in wires looking like so many leeches.

Together James and Wickham had moved with slow, precise motions, reaching across Edward's corpse to attach them along his chest, to his head, the soles of his feet and the palms of his hands. At the foot of the slab and connected to the wires was a large glass tube, set with a hand crank.

There was one last chance to do right by his friend. Whatever came next, he had to face it head on. For Edward's sake.

Another crack of thunder broke outside.

James locked the operating-theatre doors, and they set to work.

While James cranked the handle, Wickham monitored the flow of electricity. The current would pass along the wires and into the body; the theory was that if they could send a large enough charge, they could restart the vital spark of life. James had seen it done with frogs' legs and small animals, the jerking, twitching movements of their limbs as, for a moment, life surged through them – but the current was never strong enough. Wickham had been convinced they were losing too much electrical charge at the point of generation but had been unable to crack a workable solution. It seemed that the research notes James had stolen gave the answer.

A sudden flurry of rain smacked the windows, like someone battling to get in. The storm lamps guttered. A hum and crackle filled the air. James's hair rose in a halo around his head and his tongue fizzed.

Muscles twitched. Edward's legs convulsed. His eye opened, the white turned yellow.

Then he fell still.

James felt faint, sick. His hand was clammy on the crank and some ancient instinct told him to run. This was *wrong*. Life wasn't a toy to be played with.

He remembered Edward calling out to him. Dashing into the road, the clatter of horseshoes and the crunch of impact. *We were like brothers, once.*

There was no turning back now.

Wickham muttered to himself, adjusted the wires and gestured for James to start the crank again.

Edward's body spasmed, contorting in a grotesque echo of the patients who squirmed and cried in pain as Wickham performed surgery on them.

Lightning flashed in a starburst that illuminated the laboratory, Wickham, the corpse, the blue sparks of the charge as it strengthened.

The body jerked again, writhing and writhing

and then – like a chorus of dancers moving as one – the movements coalesced. Arms and legs drawing together like a swimmer thrashing at sea, face twisting into a grimace.

Edward's eyes snapped open.

When he fell still this time, James knew it was different. The current crackled in the air, though he had stopped turning the crank. Edward's hand reached to touch his face. Tracing the blood-smeared jaw and cheekbone. The curl of dark hair.

'Edward?' asked Wickham gently.

James was lifted by a wave of elation. A flash of memory: candle flame, Edward spattered with blood and hair stuck with sweat fresh from his first successful surgery, grinning with exhilaration.

Edward had died, but they had used electricity to bring him back. James had done it, something all but impossible. He'd saved his friend.

He'd undone his mistake.

'What – what happened?' Edward's voice was raspy and low. One pupil was still blown, and he blinked slowly, eyelids moving out of sync.

'There was an accident,' explained Wickham. 'But you're all right now.' His face was alight with excitement. 'Can you move? How do you feel?'

'I feel – cold.'

They helped Edward sit, wrapped a blanket around him.

'This is brilliant,' said Wickham. 'Here we have living proof my theory is viable. The War Ministry will have to listen now.'

James couldn't stop staring at the stitched cut on Edward's forehead, where shortly before he had seen bone, the shallow indent like a thumb pressed into clay.

At his friend, who had been a corpse, and now was not.

Wickham had his proof; it was a straight race between them now to see who would get to his father first.

'You came back,' Edward croaked, and hooked his stiff fingers around James's. 'I knew you would.'

James twisted his hand away. The feeling was too strange.

He only realised now that Wickham couldn't have known how Edward would come back. How death might have changed him. It was his Edward sitting in front of him, but it could have easily not been. The wrongness hit him all at once, a wave smashing him off his feet. They had treated Edward's life like another experiment. Olympe was right; he was no better than the duc. He kept telling himself the things he did, the lines he crossed, the people he hurt, were worth it.

He wondered if there was an end to the path he'd started on.

'I – I have to leave.' He fumbled with the apron strings, grabbed his topcoat.

'Where are you going?' A note of threat in Wickham's voice. 'This news *cannot* be shared.'

'I won't – I'm sorry.' He couldn't look at either of them. 'I – need some air.'

'James!'

Once out of the theatre, he ran and didn't stop until

he was halfway up High Holborn where he huddled under a shop awning along with several other people sheltering from the storm.

He waited, wondering whether Wickham would follow.

Lightning flashed, but the thunder had moved further away.

When no one came after him, he breathed deeper. Shut his eyes.

He saw Edward on the slab again. Saw him jerk and twitch. His eye open. He had met death and returned.

James shivered despite the muggy summer warmth.

He had to bring Olympe to his father before Wickham could tell him about Edward.

Through the last of the rain he cut back to the Rookery and up to his room. At the top of the stairs, he frowned.

His door was slightly ajar.

Oh god, he really *was* too late. He flung himself inside.

But Olympe was already gone.

9

The Printing House of
L'Ami d'Égalité

'My dear, my dear – you'll never guess who I found waiting in my office.'

Ada's father stepped aside to present Guil coming down the stairs. He looked as exhausted as Ada felt, but his suit was crisply pressed, his cravat exquisitely folded; he'd learned Ada's lessons of dressing for bloodless battle well. Still in shock from her encounter with the duc, it took her a minute to truly register that Guil was here, alive, safe. She felt a rush of love and relief, and it was no pretence when she embraced him, kissing both cheeks.

'You gave me such a – *surprise*!' she said.

'I know. I'm sorry.'

She squeezed his arm. 'Well, you're here now.'

Her father clapped his hands. 'So, what is it you young people have planned for the day? A play? The pleasure gardens?'

'With your permission, citoyen, I had been considering a visit to the Observatory.'

Ada bit her tongue. She had forgotten they were due to meet Léon today at the Observatory. It was too close to the duc's new headquarters for comfort, but there was no changing it now.

Guil continued. 'Ada mentioned she used to have a telescope, so I wondered if she might be interested in viewing theirs. I hear it's something of a popular curiosity.'

'What a brilliant idea. You must go at once.'

Ada found herself packing picnic baskets and organising a carriage to take them, yawning all the while as their late-night activities caught up with her. Finally, they were alone together on the drive across the city, tracing the path they had cut the night before with the resurrection men. In daylight the city was no less sinister, with corpses left in gutters, effluence flowing in the street past fine buildings shuttered and barred.

The journey was torturously slow. Ada had travelled faster on foot as part of the battalion, but she was a lady now, and a lady had to mind her delicate slippers and fine skirts.

She knew she should tell Guil about her run-in with the duc, that he had seen them last night. But the longer she left it, the harder it was to get the words out. Every time she tried, she choked at the duc's offer, swallowed by shame because she couldn't deny she was considering it.

So she fell silent, letting the shape of a plan resolve itself. Once she knew what she wanted to do, she would tell Guil, she *would*. Once she knew how to make him understand.

They arrived at the Observatory a little before lunchtime. Ada unfolded herself from the carriage, sticky with sweat, in front of an imposing two-storey building that stood alone, surrounded by a sweeping grassy terrace overgrown with weeds. Ada had seen engravings from its happier past, when countless astronomers, nobility and their servants from around the country had gathered there to set up telescopes and other equipment for measuring the stars.

In the mundane light of day, it looked nothing special. A few of the tall windows had been boarded over, the limestone walls grimy with coal smoke and blooming patches of moss crawling up from the ground. At the door, the housekeeper was accepting visitors in return for cold hard cash.

The Revolutionary regime had neglected the Observatory, the housekeeper explained, due to the old director, Comte Cassini, being a Royalist. There was a temporary director in place, but with no real money to speak of, the grandeur was barely more than a memory.

'You can have a look at the big telescope if you like,' she said, 'but don't break anything.'

The housekeeper took them through a room full of smaller telescopes and lenses gathering dust to the first floor, where a long, high-ceilinged gallery stretched the width of the building. Sunlight flooded through the windows, and above one was drilled a hole the size of a fist. It sent a coin of light onto the floor and along a marble path measured in brass markers and decorated with astronomical symbols.

Ada dragged Guil over to it, caught up in sudden delight.

'Oh my goodness, look! It's the Paris meridian line! I came here once before with Camille, but this room was closed.'

'I … see. Very interesting.' Guil's attention had drifted to the view outside, and the duc's house beyond. 'Léon left word that he had some urgent intelligence to share, but clearly not urgent enough for him to arrive on time.'

'Oh, don't worry. You don't have to pretend you're interested.'

In that moment, Ada missed Camille something fierce. She didn't much understand what Ada would go on about, but she would listen attentively all the same, curling an arm around her waist, turned to her like a flower follows the sun.

Guil softened. 'No, tell me.'

'The meridian – it's a way to measure the height of the sun. It's how we can work out what shape the earth is.'

'A stage, my dear, that's the earth's shape.' Léon arrived in the gallery like a leading man entering on cue. 'And we are but players on it.'

Ada's lips quirked. 'I see now where Al gets his Shakespeare quotes from.'

Léon was dressed as though it was the last thing he had thought about, in clean but worn breeches and jacket, a paisley scarf flung carelessly around his neck in place of a cravat. His exquisitely embroidered waistcoat looked as if it had been lifted from the

Théâtre Patriotique costume box, and his shoes needed a polish – like all of them, he was surviving, but at a cost.

'How is Al?' Léon spoke off-hand, but he wasn't a good enough actor to hide the way his eyes stayed sharply trained on her.

'We've had no word,' said Ada. 'But he will be safe in England, I promise you.'

'I would say I can't believe he fled the country and let me think he was dead, but unfortunately it is quite in character.'

Ada had thought Al and Léon only a casual thing, though it had become clear it was something more – from the tension in Léon's jaw when they spoke of England, or the faux nonchalance when Al's name came up. She thought of Al and his fraught childhood, barren of love, and how he guarded it now so closely and secretly.

And she thought of Camille the last time she had seen her, eyes glittering and a crackle in her lungs.

They both would be safer there, she had to believe it.

'You said you had something for us?' asked Guil.

They crossed to the far end of the gallery, away from other visitors clustering around the meridian line. Out of the tall windows and across the grounds the view spread over the city; between the fluttering canopy of treetops, Ada picked out roofs and spires – perhaps of the Palais du Luxembourg by the battalion's former home above the café Au Petit Suisse – but more likely just the gutted shell of the Val-de-Grâce.

'How did my last tip go?' asked Léon. 'One always likes to know about one's successes. It *was* a success?'

Ada and Guil exchanged glances, and Guil nodded. 'He has been found.'

'Congratulations. In which case, this might be even more interesting to you. Someone I reckon is this self-same duc has been sniffing around the soldiers littering the city.'

Ada frowned. 'Why?'

'Muscle for hire, I had assumed. Since you disposed of his right-hand man, he would be in need of a replacement.'

'No shortage of people looking for work,' she said. 'I'm sure he's been able to equip himself with a personal guard.'

'Ah, well, that's where you are wrong.'

Her curiosity was piqued. 'No takers?'

'Plenty. But that's not what he was after.' Leon pulled a piece of paper from his pocket. 'I found myself introduced to one of the soldiers he'd approached. Ex-soldier now, I suppose, like you.' The last part directed at Guil, who bristled. Guil had deserted, unlike the men who had been disbanded. 'Far too happy to talk, not so fond of paying his bar tab. Once I cleared that problem up, I learned quite a bit. The Royalists are stirring; there's something about to go down. Something brewing. People criticising Robespierre as though consequences were a thing that happened to other people. And your duc is looking for bribable soldiers who can access the prisons.'

Ada's breath caught in her throat. 'Prison? But he already got Olympe out...'

Léon shrugged. 'I bring you the news, you figure out what it means.'

Guil's lips were a tight line. 'We need to speak to this man.'

'I thought you might.' He slipped the paper into Guil's hand. 'His name, and where you can find him. Take something to make it worth his while.' Léon's eyes slid back to Ada. 'It didn't come cheap, buying out his debt.'

She dug into her pocket and pulled out a roll of assignat notes.

Leon's nose wrinkled. 'Don't insult me.'

Grudgingly, she swapped the notes for a purse of pre-Revolutionary coins. 'Stay in touch. If you hear anything else—'

'You'll be the first to know.' He caught her wrist. 'And if you hear about Al...'

She softened. 'We'll tell you anything we hear. Camille won't let him get hurt.'

With a nod, Léon left, and Guil took Ada's arm again to promenade along the gallery.

Another chance for her to tell him about the duc's offer.

Another moment of cowardice.

'So when do we meet this solider?' she said.

Guil unfolded the paper as they walked, scanned it, then handed it to her silently. All the life had drained from his face. Quickly, she read the name and location.

'I don't understand. What's wrong?'

Guil was silent a moment more, before he said, 'I know him. We were in the same light infantry demi-brigade. We scouted together in Spain, when we served under General Dumas in the Army of the Western Pyrenees.' He stopped by the north window, looking at the city, his expression unreadable.

'He was the man I betrayed.'

10

Buckbridge Street

James hurtled downstairs. The passage outside the tenement was as busy as it always was, drinkers spilling out of the pub, out-of-work men thronging on corners, girls carrying children in doorways, games of knucklebone, sewage thrown from windows, cats fighting over split bones.

Where was Olympe? Had Al and Camille come for her? Had she run away?

Oh god, oh god, oh god, he should never have left her.

His heart was racing so fast he felt faint, struggling to suck in full breaths. In minutes he was onto the fractionally calmer Broad Street, where men strolled by shaking off their umbrellas now the storm had passed, and women clopped along the cobbles on their metal pattens like horses.

He scanned the crowd, but of course Olympe was nowhere to be seen.

Picking a direction, he started walking, hunting the faces of everyone he passed for some sign of her.

He was an idiot. An *idiot*. His father was right. What was wrong with him that he hadn't seen this coming? He'd let himself get distracted and he'd been outmanoeuvered.

At the end of the street he stopped, glancing in both directions. This was hopeless. Looking for one person in London was worse than looking for a needle in a haystack. Needles stayed still. Olympe would be on the move and expecting him.

The street was full of cabs and carts, men on horseback, private carriages wedged into the traffic, peddlers pushing handcarts, milkmaids with pails of fresh milk hanging from the yokes across their shoulders, cress sellers and cat's meat men knocking on kitchen doors. The cacophony overwhelmed him, the sound of iron on cobbles, yells of traders, animals bleating – it was too much.

He forced himself to slow down and think.

There were two possibilities: either Al and Camille had taken her, or she'd left on her own.

If Camille had taken her, then chasing after them would do nothing. He knew where they were staying. He could confront them – lord, but Camille would probably want to crow about it anyway.

And if Olympe had got out on her own? Then she was in a hell of a lot of trouble. She didn't know the city, she was wearing nothing but a collection of borrowed silks, she had no money – hell, she didn't even understand English. The longer she was on her own, the more she was at risk. The Rookery was a dangerous place for a girl – the rest of the city no better. There were too many horror stories in the papers that his mother would pore over and pointedly put in Hennie's face to explain why she absolutely wasn't to go gallivanting around without a chaperone. If there was even a chance Olympe was out there, he had to search for her.

That was something to go on, then. He was hunting for a girl on her own. A girl who was probably lost, and scared, and trying to hide from people. It would be hard for her to avoid attracting attention.

He began to make a methodical sweep of the streets, alleys and courtyards radiating from the tenement, avoiding the busiest, people-filled thoroughfares and sticking to the quieter back alleys.

Then, on Great Queen Street off Drury Lane, a street lined with chemists, haberdasheries and bookbinders, he almost walked past a heap of rain-soaked rags bundled into the opening of a mews. He doubled back, picking out the storm-grey face that blended into the dirty silks. She'd pulled the scarf tight around her face and buried her head in her hands. People walked past unseeing; Londoners were used to ignoring vagrants and beggars. By making herself look pitiful, Olympe had unwittingly stumbled on the best disguise of all. Just another fallen woman, soon to end up in the murky waters of the Thames. He heard a few muttered comments from passers-by. *Those French refugees coming over here, and they don't even speak the language. Don't know how to behave on the street. Look at her face. Bringing diseases.*

James tuned them out and sat next to Olympe on

the wet pavement. At any moment he expected her to dart away.

But she didn't.

She only cried harder into her hands.

Awkwardly he patted her knee.

'Hello.'

Looking up at him through a blur of tears, a warring mix of relief and despair crossed her face.

'Did I get far?'

'Far enough to frighten the life out of me.'

She looked down at her feet, the silk stockings ripped and dirty. 'Was I going in the right direction?'

'To find Camille?'

She nodded.

James decided to be kind. 'Almost.'

'So not at all. I couldn't even get ten minutes away before I was lost. I don't know where I am, I can't find my friends, I can't even *speak* to anyone. I hate stupid English. It's very rude that no one here speaks French.' She slumped into her folded arms. 'I'm a child running off in a fit with no plan.'

'I don't know. I think it was brave.'

'It was stupid.'

Above, the clouds lowered, threatening another storm. Olympe's skin had settled into a dull grey, like the paving stones beneath them.

Olympe wiped her eyes and rearranged the scarf to better hide her face. Then she turned to James.

'I give up.'

His eyebrows shot up. 'Really?'

'Really. Take me back. I'm done.'

Broad Street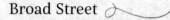

James lifted the steaming pot of coffee and poured two cups. He nudged one towards Olympe, but she didn't take it.

They were folded into the corner of a noisy coffee house on the main road, just beyond the Rookery proper. Olympe was soaked through from the rain, looking so wretched that he let go of the urge to cloister her again and took her to dry off first. The coffee house was crowded enough that no one looked too closely at her, and with her back to the room she could sit unnoticed – at least for a short while.

'Drink something. You must be cold.' He couldn't quite believe his luck that she'd stopped fighting.

Mechanically, Olympe took her cup, drank, replaced it on the scuffed wooden table. James sipped his slowly. She pulled the scarf closer around herself, fingers clenched tightly and he realised she wasn't downcast. She was *angry*.

'Do you think Camille would be disappointed in me?'

'If Camille expects you to magically locate her in a city of several hundred thousand people when you don't speak English and have no idea where she is, then she's an idiot.'

Olympe's eyes snapped up. 'Camille is not an idiot!'

A smile tugged at the corner of James's mouth.

'No, she's not. My point is, she absolutely wouldn't be disappointed in you.' He hid his face in his cup for a moment. 'If she's disappointed in anyone, it's me.'

'With good reason.'

He shrugged. 'I suppose. Only, I assume she must have gone off me beforehand otherwise she wouldn't have been looking for someone else.'

'You mean Ada?'

He didn't reply. He hadn't meant to let that slip, but he'd had no one to talk to about it, and somehow it came out anyway. It was a hurt that lingered. In his darkest moments, he wondered if that pain had made it easier to hurt Camille back, to betray her. An eye for an eye.

'Are you jealous?'

'Of course I'm jealous.' James spoke quietly. 'We were engaged.'

Are engaged, and his mother planning the wedding. Oh god, what was he going to do about that?

'Have you spoken to her about it?' asked Olympe.

'I don't need to. It's obvious where things stand.'

It had been clear from the moment he arrived at Camille's rooms over the Au Petit Suisse café. The look of shock and guilt when he'd walked in. Even before she'd admitted she'd fallen in love with Ada, he'd known. The way they looked at each other, moved easily in each other's personal space, an unspoken dance of familiarity with each other's bodies. It was the way he used to be with Camille. Now the space between them was brittle, frozen.

If he loved Camille, he should be happy that she

was happy, he had told himself. But, oh, it had still hurt. A long, chaotic time had passed since they'd last been in contact, let alone seen each other. But Camille had *left* him. Without telling him. More than their engagement, it was their friendship he mourned. The Camille he'd known told him *everything*, wrote him letters about every decision she was agonising over. Shared her life with him as if it was the most natural thing in the world.

Now she shared that with Ada, and James was no one to her.

No – that wasn't quite right, not now. Now he was her enemy.

Perhaps that was better than being nothing at all.

'I think Camille and Ada are very good for each other, but that doesn't mean you can't also be hurt,' said Olympe. 'I would understand.'

He shot her a sideways look. 'Are you trying to get on my good side so I take you to Camille?'

'Yes. Is it working?'

'No.'

'But you *are* jealous. Why do you need to hide it? Are you ashamed of having feelings?'

'They're private.'

'Hmm.' She poured herself another cup of coffee, a smirk playing on her lips.

James glared. 'Picking at this will not get you anywhere.'

'Maybe you should try moving on too,' she said sweetly. 'Brooding isn't going to make you any happier.'

'I don't have time for that.'

He couldn't deny he still had feelings for Camille. But was loving her just a habit? Maybe one he could break. Or at least – that's what he'd hoped before she'd showed up two days ago and everything had hit him at once. He loved her and he was furious with her; he felt guilty and scared at the same time.

Olympe smirked. 'Oh, yes, I forgot, you're terribly important.'

'Look, I didn't have to buy you coffee and be nice to you.'

'It's true, I think you're going soft.'

He eyed her more seriously. 'So do I have to tie you up again? Are you going to make another run for it?'

A flash of mottled navy blue and purple clouds bloomed up her throat and across the side of her face. 'No. I've decided: I don't like being useless, and I don't like being locked up. So, here's the deal: I will help you do whatever it is you need me for, and then you let me go.'

He opened his mouth to speak but she held up a finger.

'I'm not done. Al knows where you were hiding me now; that game is up so don't pretend you're in any position to negotiate. You want something from me and I'm not unreasonable, I will help you. But no more tying me up. I decide what happens to me. Also, I want to go outside – show me some of the city. And you must teach me English, I don't want to be helpless like that ever again.'

He held his hands up. 'Whoa, whoa, whoa – I need to start writing all this down.'

'Don't worry, I won't let you forget.' She smiled. 'But this is the big one: take me back to Camille. You're out of time, we both know it. Camille will make your life not worth living until you hand me over. So let's skip all that.'

'What if you and Camille disappear before helping me?'

'Then you made a mistake trusting me.' She shrugged. 'There's never a guarantee in life. You consider your options and make the best call you can. At some point it all comes down to taking a risk. I'm taking a risk trusting you to come good on your side of this deal. You have to trust me I'll do mine.'

He leaned back in his chair, feeling light despite her threats. 'You certainly did learn a lot from Camille.'

Olympe's eyes sparkled. 'Do you think she would be proud of me now?'

'Most definitely.' He stuck out his hand. 'It's a deal.'

Olympe peeled a glove off and he took her cold, swirling-grey hand in his own.

James thought of Edward's limp fingers dangling from the operating table, the way they had twitched with each jolt of electricity.

He would be a fool to think this truce with Olympe meant his problems were over.

But he had no idea then how much they were just beginning.

11

6 Bedford Square

Sharp shards of moonlight cut slices out of the corridor, thick shadow and pallid light chequer-boarding the parquet and stretching up the walls. Camille stumbled barefoot, one hand at her throat, the other tracing the window ledges.

She needed air. She couldn't breathe.

She tugged at a window, then the next. None would give. She'd woken, gasping for breath and so hot she felt like she was on fire. The windows in her room were locked and she couldn't find the key.

With no candle and wearing only her cotton nightdress, she wandered from window to window, alternately sweating with fever and shivering with chills. The familiar hallways and furniture of the Harfords' London townhouse were made strange by night. Somewhere outside, a fox screamed.

For the first time, she allowed the thought to enter her mind.

Maybe she wasn't completely well.

Why were all the goddamn windows locked?

Camille rushed faster and faster from window to

window. What was wrong with her, why couldn't she breathe?

She yanked at a sash, cursing, fingers scrabbling at the latch. Lurched to the next – tripped.

A hand closed under her arm, catching her. Her heart stopped.

A voice spoke. 'Don't die here. It'll look very suspicious.'

Al steadied her against the window ledge, arching a brow. Camille sank against him. He smelled of brandy and tobacco and familiar Al-ness. 'Oh, thank god. It's just you.' She shut her eyes as she tried to suck in a few even breaths. 'You scared me.'

'Er, no, you scared me, Miss Streaking-Around-in-a-Nightdress.' He leaned against the wall next to her and pulled a snuffbox from his pocket. He was still dressed, though a little dishevelled, shirt untucked and cravat loose. The smudges under his eyes had grown darker since they had arrived at the Harfords' and she wondered if he was getting any sleep. 'I thought you were the ghost of some Civil War casualty come to haunt me for being French.'

She rolled her eyes. 'First, this building is only forty years old, how is a Civil War victim here? Secondly, I don't think the Civil War had anything to do with the French. And thirdly, what are you doing up?'

'Sleep is for the weak.'

'Sleep is necessary.'

He shrugged. 'My whole family is dead. Sleep doesn't seem particularly important. Nothing seems important anymore.'

'Al,' she started softly, but he interrupted her.

'And anyway, they're English, it's always the French's fault. Even when they're killing each other, somehow it's because our cheese is too good and we have better weather so they get angry and cut their own feet off. Silly country.'

'I don't think we have a leg to stand on right now.'

'Touché,' he snorted. 'More to the point, what are *you* doing? Don't tell me, your bed's too cold without Ada in it. No wait – sleep is too boring for you. You're pining after a good crisis?'

Camille didn't reply immediately. Her chest still felt tight, and the memory of jerking out of sleep, heart racing, cold with dread, was too close. She sank to the floor, pulling her knees up to wrap her arms around her legs. 'The opposite. Sleep is … too much. I dream.'

Al sat beside her. 'Go on, then. Tell me.'

'Really? You want to listen to me talking about my feelings?'

'Oh, only so I can hold this over you later.'

'How generous.'

'Think nothing of it.'

She sighed, thinking of the dream that had come again that night. It had followed her from France, a cloud of blood and fire and pain. 'I'm not sure I know *how* to talk about it.'

'Well, start with what you're thinking right now.'

Camille looked at her toes peeking out from under her nightdress. At the speckled half-moons of her fingernails.

'All right. Do you feel guilty?'

'About what?'

'About the things we've done.'

'What, you mean rescuing people? Not really, I thought that might be my ticket into the good place, if Him upstairs is as against my type as my family tells me he is.' He took a pinch of snuff. 'Told me,' he corrected himself.

'No. I mean when we do what we do, and people get hurt.'

'You've never had an issue with that before.'

The fever that had gripped her when she'd woken was gone. She felt cold in just a nightdress and acutely vulnerable, soft skin protected only by a thin layer of cotton.

'I ... didn't tell you everything that happened before Ada and Guil rescued me from the Madeleine.'

'Oh?'

She moistened her lips. 'Dorval died because I killed him.'

'So you feel bad for hurting someone. My god, that's natural, Cam.'

'No.' She couldn't look at him. 'I feel bad because *I know I'd do it again.* He was trying to kill me. I tell myself I'm better than Comtois and the duc because I don't kill and they do, because they hurt people and cross the line. But here I am, on the other side of the line alongside them, and I know I'll cross that line again if I have to. So who am I now? What other lines might I cross? Where does this all stop? If I give up, abandon Olympe, then worse things will happen. I have to keep going, keep doing what needs to be done to stop something more awful from happening. Don't I? I lie awake at night and think: *is that what they tell themselves too? That it's a necessary evil?* How can one person make that decision? How can I sleep when I have blood on my hands and I am running headlong into more?' Camille stopped. Somewhere in the middle of all that, she had started crying and she couldn't stop.

Al stared at her, eyes wide.

'Oh, Cam. Oh, you ridiculous human.' He wrapped his arms around her and pulled her close. Petted her hair. Rocked her. 'I didn't know you had feelings like this. I assumed everything was easy for you because you make such snap decisions, as if you're born to lead. And here I am having to eat my words because you're a mess like the rest of us.'

She sniffled. 'Yes. I am. Don't tell Ada.'

'My dear, I think she already knows. I'm sure that's what she likes about you most,' he said.

Hiding her face in his shoulder, Camille let herself say the thing she had wanted to earlier in the library. 'I'm sorry. I failed you. I couldn't save you from what happened to me, but please don't leave. I can't bear the idea of losing you too.' When he said nothing, she added, 'I'm your family as well, you know. We're all each other has left.'

He didn't move away, but she could feel the subtle shift, the loosening of his arms.

'I don't know about that, Cam. Seems like you've got a whole extra family here waiting for you.'

And just like that, another stone of guilt joined the pile in the pit of her stomach.

'I don't belong here any more,' she said.

'Are you telling me that, or yourself?' he asked.

They let silence fall and she peeled herself away from Al's warm body, wiping her face with the sleeves of her nightgown.

Al spoke at last. 'You don't have to do this, you know. If you're afraid what it might make you. No one dropped down and knighted you saviour of the broken, the beaten and the damned.'

She thought, for a second, about what it would be like if she did stop fighting, if she married James, like she'd always meant to, and quietly put down her responsibilities, retired from difficult decisions. The Harford family name and money would protect her from any consequences.

Then she saw Olympe's face in the Conciergerie prison when she'd taken off her iron mask, upturned and hopeful. She thought of the horror of the duc's experiments. The knowledge of what would happen to the people of her city if the Revolution fell.

And she knew she could never give up.

'I know,' she said. 'But I'd rather be a monster than a coward.'

She would save her friends. Her city. And she would save anyone else from having to cross those lines for her.

Idly, Al stroked a stray lock of her hair, and regarded her sadly.

'Oh, my dear. Conscience makes cowards of us all.'

12

The Faubourg
Saint Jacques

Ada held her skirts out of the dirt as she strode down the Rue Faubourg Saint Jacques. The evening was hot and a trickle of sweat made its way down her neck. She'd picked the wrong outfit again; it was too tight in the bodice, an old-fashioned thing in striped silk, pinched in at her natural waist. She was cursing herself as she panted for breath on the long walk from the Marais.

Her mood was as sour as the smell from her old dress. After Léon had left them, things had not gone well. From the Observatory, she and Guil had piled back into the carriage and crawled north towards her father's house through Paris's gridlocked traffic. Guil had been silent. Ada hadn't known what to say. It was an awful thing for Guil to find out, but she knew there was no point pretending they could pass up this chance to find out what ally the duc was trying to bring on board.

'Will you be able to do it?' she asked, as they passed the Jardin du Luxembourg.

He came back to himself. 'Of course. Do you doubt me?'

'No. Never.' Now was the time to tell him about the duc and her nascent plan. 'I've been thinking … perhaps we can use another route to get to the duc. What if we try to get inside the house, now we know where he's set up?'

Guil looked at her sharply. 'That's too risky.'

'Risky worked for us last night.'

'It very nearly didn't—'

'Hear me out.' She took a breath. 'I think we're being too cautious. The longer we take, the more chance the duc has to slip out of our grasp entirely, to hurt more people – to move against the government, even. We know he wants the Revolution overthrown at any cost. From what Léon has heard, it sounds as though things are already in motion. If we hold ourselves to higher standards, he'll win while we're still deciding on the *safe* thing to do.'

Guil considered her words. 'Léon's lead is a more sound route. The more we learn about the duc from a distance, the better equipped we will be when the time comes. If we stretch ourselves too far too soon, all we will achieve is attracting trouble.'

'And if we sit on the sidelines, we'll achieve nothing,' she snapped. 'We might as well not bother. Camille trusted me to stop the duc. To *help* people. What's the point if I sit here worrying about my own hide?'

Guil's tone became frosty. 'Only you? Did she not also entrust that responsibility to me?'

Ada felt immediately guilty. Guil was right. Perhaps it was the claustrophobia she felt being with her father that drove her to action. It felt too much as if she was going backwards; day by day she was losing all the things she had grown to like about herself.

Drawing a slow breath, she pinched the bridge of her nose, brought her emotions back under control. 'I'm sorry. You're right. We're doing this together.'

'I am sorry too. You are correct, we cannot linger.' He drummed his fingers on the lapel of his coat. 'What is your plan to gain access to his house?'

Ada swallowed, winding her sweaty fingers together to keep them still, and haltingly recounted everything that had happened: the duc finding her, telling her they had been seen. His suspicion. His implied offer.

Guil's expression grew unnervingly still. Ada had forgotten how much she hated this about him; when Camille was angry it was written across her face in ten-foot letters. Guil was far too careful to reveal anything he didn't want to. Perhaps it was why she had not noticed his feelings for Camille for so long.

'He didn't offer anything directly,' she said. 'It was more like an overture to a larger conversation. But I think he means it; if I want a place with him, I can have it.'

Guil shut his eyes, swaying with the carriage. 'You kept this from me until now, so I can only presume you are planning to accept.'

Her cheeks burned. 'I needed some time to think it through.'

'And informing me that our most dangerous adversary not only witnessed us spying on him, but had the tenacity to approach you in the open – that was unimportant to mention?'

'No. I – I couldn't find the right time.' Her stays were prodding her in the armpit and she was too hot and her scalp itched and she *hated* feeling so stupid and childish.

He opened his eyes and looked at her with a piercing gaze. 'You want to work for the duc.'

'*With* him.' She folded her arms. 'Tell me it's not the best way to find out exactly what he's up to.'

'It is absolutely not the best way to find out what he's up to.'

'Guil, this is a gift horse. I'm not going to look it in the mouth.'

'Your definition of *gift* is strange. I would suggest this is more likely an extremely dangerous trap.'

'You don't think I can pull this off.'

'Ada—'

'If it were Cam suggesting this, you'd be all over it.'

His jaw clenched. 'That is not true. You were not privy to my conversations with Camille, but I assure you that more often than not I was advising her against some risky or morally indefensible course of action. Must I remind you that it was your father who agreed to work with the duc before? I seem to remember you thinking *that* was unacceptable.'

'This is different.'

'Because now it is you who is doing it?'

'Yes! I mean – the reason is different. Surely you of all people know sometimes you have to do distasteful, risky things for the right reason.'

Guil's voice went menacingly quiet. 'What exactly is that supposed to mean?'

'Well, you know.' She tried to backpedal. 'You left the army because you had to, in the only way you knew how.'

But the conversation was broken. She'd known as soon as she'd said it that she'd crossed a line. Guil was a thunderous presence, too-long limbs folded into the opposite carriage seat. She tried to catch his eye but he wouldn't look at her.

And she hadn't had word from him since. She felt guilty for an afternoon, before her guilt turned to anger. They wanted the same thing, why did he cast her as the villain for it? She had passed a distracted day turning the problem over in her mind, and came to a conclusion: if Camille was here she wouldn't hesitate. She would make a choice and act.

Ada was done with being cautious. She didn't want to simper and tag along after her father, repressing every passion and talent that made her *her*. What was the worth of her, then?

No. She wanted to make things happen.

Outside the glossy front door of the townhouse, she paused to catch her breath. Neaten her hair. Smooth her skirts.

In her head, she rehearsed what she was going to say.

When she couldn't put it off any longer, she reached for the knocker and rapped twice.

A maid answered, and Ada waited on the step as her message was delivered.

The duc appeared.

Ada didn't give him a chance to speak. 'You're right: I've been wasted, and I'm sick of it. Take me on, make me your apprentice. Put your money where your mouth is. I'm willing if you are.'

The duc smiled and opened the door wider.

'Welcome, Adalaide. I am so very excited to begin.'

13

A Flophouse in
the Rookery

9 Thermidor
27 July

James woke with a start when the string was cut and he went tumbling out of the pew. Olympe caught his arm before his head made contact with the row in front.

'Morning. Sleep well?'

Around them, people were stirring, stretching. The flophouse had been full the night before and they'd only managed to get a space after James pressed an extra coin into the landlord's hand. It was little more than a single room, crammed with pews salvaged from a church. All the 'guests' jammed in close together, and then a rope was slung across their fronts and tied tight so they could sleep sitting upright.

James only knew these sorts of places existed from the charity work the hospital sent them on. It was the cheapest possible place to get a night's shelter – and the hardest place for anyone to sneak up on them unawares.

Who he was hiding from at this point, James wasn't sure. It felt like everyone.

He thought of Edward easing himself from the operating table, beautiful face crusted with blood and body burned where the electric nodes had been affixed. He shouldn't have run. Perhaps Wickham would chalk it up to shock, but Edward already seemed to think he was hiding something and disappearing wouldn't have helped. *Choose a side*, Edward had said. Had running made it all too clear he hadn't chosen them?

One problem at a time: he needed to convince his father about Olympe before Camille made her move. If Edward and Wickham found out he'd betrayed them after that – well, it would be too late. He'd lose Edward's friendship, Wickham's mentorship, but he would have gained his father. For the first time in his nineteen years, his father would be proud.

He and Olympe had come up with a plan last night, over oysters. They would go to Lord Harford and demonstrate Olympe's powers. His father was hostile, so they'd need something impressive to persuade him. Something he hadn't seen in any scientific demonstration before. Something he couldn't accuse them of faking.

After, James wouldn't stop Olympe going to Camille. He couldn't say the same for his father.

They went back to the room in the Rookery to practise what Olympe had in mind. It was the only place they'd get any privacy. James hurried the whole short way, one eye over his shoulder. He couldn't shake the feeling they were being followed.

Upstairs, Olympe sat under the skylight, gloves off and grey hands held out before her. A blue-white spark shimmered along her finger, gathering at the tip before jumping to her next finger, and the next, like a coin rolling between her knuckles. She frowned, stormy aspect drawn to a churning knot around her eyes. The pinpricks of light in their inky darkness were iridescent, like the night sky in the deep wilderness.

The spark of electric charge danced faster and faster across her outstretched fingers, the intricate ball of static growing bigger and bigger until, between one finger and the next, it spilled out of control. In half a breath it had engulfed her hand, blazing bright. A dangerous hum had built in the air, shadows gathering in darkened corners, and James felt his skin prickle as his hair rose in a halo around his head.

'Olympe—'

'I know, I'm trying!' Her look of concentration took on a tinge of panic as the glove of energy stretched over her wrist and licked at her cuffs. For a moment the tide seemed to reverse – and then the whole thing flared in a blast of power that singed James's eyebrows.

Olympe gave a huff of frustration and slumped against the bed frame.

'See, *that* bit's easy. Why can't I keep just doing that?'

James patted the cinders from his face. 'That bit we can fake. Any idiot with the right equipment can make a flash – what we need is control. To show my father what this really *means*. Imagine – if you can pass the charge between your fingers, could you pass it between your hands? Could you project it from your body? Pass a charge into something else? So many new possibilities open up.'

She frowned. 'Possibilities for what? You know I won't hurt people.'

James paused, chose his next words carefully.

'I don't want you to hurt anyone.' It wasn't a lie, but when his father finally understood Olympe's powers, he was all too sure that's what *he* would want. 'If you could pass a current into something else, for example, there could be countless technological applications. Or medical – we've hardly begun to understand what electricity could be used for because we struggle to generate it in any large quantity or store it.'

Olympe wrinkled her nose. 'I'm not a resource for you to plunder. I know that's the sort of thing you people do. Empire and conquest.'

He realised then that she knew. She knew he would hand her to the war minister, who might lock her up like the Revolutionaries or experiment on her like the Royalists; she also knew she had no chance on her own. She was taking a calculated risk, using him to get closer to Camille. Their alliance was untested, but it was the only option either of them had.

Olympe climbed onto the bed and leaned back on her elbows to stare at the skylight. In the hours since she'd agreed to work with him, she'd gone from crouching in the corner hissing if he made any sudden moves, to demanding he buy a better quality of meal. He outwardly took umbrage, grumbling that a slap-up dinner wasn't a priority. But he bowed to her orders.

The more she trusted him, the more she relaxed, the easier this would be. And if it soothed his guilt, then that was a pleasant side effect.

'Do you really think this is science?' asked Olympe. A solitary spark shimmered on her knuckles.

'What do you mean?'

'Once, a priest came to the house where I lived with my mother and tried to set me on fire.'

James dropped his snuffbox, scattering tobacco over the rug. 'Jesus, Olympe!'

'Don't worry, Mother put it out quickly.'

'But why?'

'He said I was the Devil. That I had no soul.'

'I … don't understand.'

Although, beneath his shock and disgust, he did.

'Isn't that what Al thought? I overheard them all talking about me. I wasn't surprised; the duc told me he wasn't sure I had a soul like regular Christian Frenchmen, because I wasn't made by God.'

'You were born from your mother, weren't you?'

'I assume so.'

James shrugged. 'Then I don't know what he's talking about.'

'But is it really science? Ada said it was. Also that it was mine to control. I have been wondering and thinking all these dull days locked up on my own – even if this is something that scientific experimentation awoke in me, the rest is still me, surely? Something I can choose to use for good or bad. I can make myself an angel or the Devil. It's what Maman called me. Mon ange.'

As she spoke, she sent a fine filigree of sparks dancing like snowfall across her cloudy skin, like a net of stars cast around her. Like she was only caught on earth for a brief time, before she bucked and broke the net to return to wherever it was she rightly belonged.

A moment of silence hung between them as James stared at her. Her face was dark, the blooms across her skin falling still. Cloud-cover spread overhead, blocking out the sun. The prickle of stars in her eyes seemed to seep across her temples, her forehead, her cheekbones. She was a human girl, but in that moment she was something more. Something powerful and ancient.

A slither of fear crawled along his skin.

Then the clouds passed. The sun broke through.

James shook it off.

'Come on. The sooner we figure this out, the sooner it's over.'

Olympe grumbled, but slid back onto the floor to sit opposite him. The sparks netted over her swooped to gather in a glowing orb at the tip of her index finger. She tried to skip it between her fingers again. Hit, hit, miss – and this time the spark snuffed entirely.

Olympe swore. 'One thing I do not understand. If this thing comes naturally, why isn't it easier for me to control?'

James laughed. 'I have no idea why anyone could ever think you're not human.'

'Oh?'

'Olympe, that is the most human thing I've heard. I know who you are. You are clearly one of us.'

And he meant it. Before now, he hadn't let himself think of her as anything other than a means to an end. Betraying Edward and Wickham, Camille, the lies and the violence, all of it could be justified. He thought of the confusion and hurt in Edward's eyes when he'd fled the operating theatre the day before. Perhaps he had been wrong about all of it.

After a few more attempts, she called a halt and refused to do any more unless James brought her a baked potato from the carts she'd seen outside. He trotted downstairs, jingling the coins in his pockets – then froze on the landing.

It was dark in the stairwell. In this halfway place, with the pub too far below and everything stairs and doorways, James felt a step outside the world. He was alone and it was oh-so-dark.

Although not so dark he couldn't see the figure in the doorway.

On the landing, a door was open. The doors were never open.

But now one was, and the darkness within took human shape.

Then the smell reached him. The smell of old blood.

Dread plunged through James like a knife.

He had been found.

PART THREE

Empire of Death

1

The Duc's Headquarters

Ada faced off with the stack of documents that tottered above her head. With delicate precision, she lifted the top folder off. For a tense moment, the stack swayed and she imagined herself crushed to death under the duc's badly-kept records. Then it steadied and she breathed out.

Returning to the desk, she looked again at the light under the door into the duc's private rooms. Occasionally, he paced back and forth, cutting shadows. She had spent a whole day stuffed in this dank backroom of his house in Faubourg Saint Jacques, going through years' worth of receipts, household accounts, correspondence and research notes, organising them into something resembling logic.

When she'd presented herself on the duc's doorstep that morning, she'd expected to find a replica of the abbey laboratory – but the duc's rooms were far more mundane. No sign of dissected bodies, not even a bloodied scalpel in sight – though Ada knew he had continued to take deliveries of cadavers.

Instead, it seemed the duc had turned his attention entirely to electricity. The room played host to shelves of Leiden jars, sulphur globes, coils of copper wire, jars of acid and turpentine, folded sheets of rubberised cloth, swags of silk and countless other oddities Ada hadn't had the chance to investigate.

She'd stood in his rooms, taking it all in as he quizzed her.

'What exactly is it that you think I do here?' he had asked, leaning against the edge of his desk.

'Why, continue your research, of course. Now Olympe is lost to you, surely you wish to recreate her talents?'

The duc watched her for a beat, cold blue eyes studying her carefully. 'No. It would be foolish to try to replicate a miracle. Olympe is unique. I have turned my attentions to electricity itself, and the practical applications it could be put to.'

'How fascinating.'

'I would say I'm sorry to see you left behind by Camille, but that would be a lie. Now I have the luxury of keeping your talents to myself. Though you have my commiserations – I didn't think she would leave you for the Englishman either.'

Ada's cheeks went hot. 'She didn't leave me. I left her.'

'Oh! Is that so?' He sat behind his desk, pulling out a set of keys. 'But she *did l*eave you here, did she not, and go to England herself? For him.'

'That's not— I chose to stay.'

'And she chose to leave.'

'She had to—' Ada caught herself at the last minute. 'We had different priorities.'

The duc held her gaze. Ada felt like an animal pinned on the dissecting table, waiting to be sliced open. Then he stood abruptly, pulling a key off the ring. 'You were right not to trust her; that girl can only see her own ambition. Here, you'll need this for the document cabinets.' She caught the key he tossed to her and slipped it into the pocket tied at her waist.

The urge to defend Camille was strong, but she swallowed it.

'Does this mean I'm hired?'

A smile spread across the duc's face. 'Consider it a trial.'

It had turned out what the duc lacked most was a secretary. He'd shown her to the room crammed to the rafters with piles and boxes and folders of paper – whatever he'd managed to salvage when he'd been forced to run after the king's execution and he'd fallen from favour. They'd been rotting in this dingy house since, gathering dust and mould spots. Now, the duc wanted his affairs in order – for what, Ada hadn't yet worked out.

She'd shut herself away, sifting through the detritus, filing and indexing a lifetime's scientific work, searching for any useful information, any hint at what he might have planned. The highlight was when the duc stepped out of his private rooms and handed her his recent notes to write up. These gave a tantalising glimpse of *something* brewing. The duc was currently investigating the conductive properties of different materials, comparing the dullness of wood or silk to the quickness of metal or water when an electric current was applied.

The clock chimed five, and Ada stretched, tidied away her quill and ink and gathered up the notes. Before she knocked at the duc's door, she took a moment to fix her hair, pinning back the stray curl that fell in her eyes, and brushing the dust off her skirts. She'd finally found the right outfit, something that toed a careful line – smart and modern, but not the flimsy white cotton that had come into fashion and would never stand up to a day's hard work. Nothing too rough or low class either, which ruled out half the hard-wearing things she kept for jobs with the battalion.

She'd settled on an expensively made, high-waisted dress in a plain beige, but covered it with a muslin pelisse in dove grey to hide the dirt she accumulated throughout the day. She needed to remind the duc of her station as her father's daughter, her wits and intelligence, as well as her practicality.

Ada tucked the fresh notes inside a leather wallet then, clutching them to her chest, knocked.

'Come.'

When she entered his study, the duc was at the desk, brooding over a letter in front of him.

'I've written up everything until the second set of Leiden jars,' said Ada, laying the wallet on his desk. 'I've made a note where I wasn't sure of the quantities listed. You say one thing at the start but logically, it couldn't be more than— here, I've shown my working.'

'I'm impressed,' he said, turning a page. 'These are thorough and methodical, and yet so vivid.' He shut the wallet and passed it back to her. 'You are an invaluable resource.'

'Thank you.' He went back to his letter, and Ada hesitated. The letter was half-obscured by his elbow, but she could just about make out the words *England* and *success*. She had grown more confident in her decision, but she was also growing impatient. 'Could I assist you in your next experiment? I'd like to learn more practical skills.'

The duc arched an eyebrow. 'Ah, bored, are we?'

'No, sir. But I like a challenge.'

'A trait that I value.' He tapped his index finger on the letter. 'As it happens, I must increase the pace of my own work, and an assistant would go some way to achieving that. But I would caution you against running before you can walk.'

Nerves fluttered in Ada's stomach. Her instinct was caution, but it held her back. Made her wait for Camille to reach a decision or tell her what to do. Caution was a weight dragging her down, always to be in second place, always to be overlooked.

Caution made her weak.

'Weren't you the one who said I shouldn't be wasted?' she said. 'If you think my notes are good, imagine what help I could be if you let me bring my ideas to your work too.'

Amusement curled his lip. 'Is that so?'

She held her chin high. 'Yes.'

For a moment, the duc drummed his fingers on his

desk. Then he spoke. 'I would not want arrogance or presumption to get in the way of recognising talent. Very well.'

Ada was thrilled. 'I am happy to be of service.'

'Tomorrow, then.'

Another question was on her lips. She knew he studied electricity, but what *for*? The whole purpose of her being there was to find out what he was doing and how they could stop it.

But she didn't ask. She let herself be content for now with her first victory.

Caution might be unhelpful.

Cunning wasn't. With each step closer to the duc, she needed to be sharper. Play her cards closer to her chest, earn his trust in careful measures. If she pushed too fast he'd get suspicious and drop her.

So she nodded. Smiled. Agreed plans for the morning.

Her father's coach was waiting. She'd fed him a line about tutoring the daughters of a fictional respectable family in English and composition, and he'd hardly noticed, absorbed as he was in his own little empire.

In her mind she let a dozen different visions of the next day play out. What she might discover about the duc – and what she might learn from the experiments themselves. Society might not grant her the right to attend university, but that wouldn't stop her learning whenever and wherever she could.

She tied her bonnet and climbed into the carriage.

Guil sat in the far corner, hand wrapped so tightly

around the leather strap hanging from the ceiling that his knucklebones showed through his skin.

'Hello, Ada,' he said. 'You've been keeping secrets.'

2

The Rookery

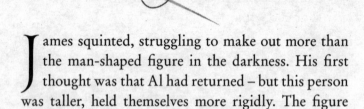

James squinted, struggling to make out more than
the man-shaped figure in the darkness. His first
thought was that Al had returned – but this person
was taller, held themselves more rigidly. The figure
shifted, and James's eyes flew wide open.

'Why are you hiding in a place like this?' asked
Edward.

Shock immobilised James.

His mind filled with memories of Edward tangled
beneath the carriage, his ashen body laid out on
Wickham's operating table. It struck him again: they
had really *done* it. Wickham's theories had worked
and Edward, who had slipped over the threshold to the
Underworld, had been returned. Coin out from under
his tongue, Charon and his ferry receding on a distant
shore. It was a miracle.

He might have betrayed his friend, but thank god
he'd been able to save him.

'Edward. You found me.'

A miracle, and a complication.

The shadows shifted and Edward stepped into the

paltry light, enough for James to see his face, pallid and hollow at his eyes and cheeks. Across his forehead the deep gash that had been sewn closed, skin puckered and mottled. James had thought of the wound as a thumb pressed into clay but now it looked like bruised fruit, rot spreading slowly, as though life had only been reluctantly coaxed back into his body, and with every passing hour it seeped away, decay reclaiming him.

Hairs raised on the back of James' neck.

'Why did you run?'

It was his friend, yes, alive and standing before him, but like an image distorted in water, or a badly made mirror. Something a little warped, something uncanny, like a flame guttering in the wind, stuttering between life and death.

'I – I'm sorry,' stuttered James. 'I shouldn't have. I was – overwhelmed.' Shock was fading, and now he was all too aware that Olympe was only a floor above them. He'd known this moment would come, but he'd hoped to put it off a while longer. He wasn't ready to lose Edward's friendship so soon after thinking he'd lost him for good. 'I'm so glad you're alive.'

Edward looked at his hands. Turned them over. It might have been the light, but his fingertips looked grey, rims of black around his nail beds. 'I'm told the blow was severe, but I feel no pain. I don't feel anything.' His once-eloquent friend worked through each word like a challenge. He had come back, but there were gaps, ruptures – of course there were – no one could go through that and be unchanged. 'If this is all the life I could salvage, I owe it to Wickham.'

Edward looked at James, a dark light in his eyes. 'Do you understand? I owe him everything now.'

James began to speak, though he was unsure what he could possibly say – only to be interrupted by Olympe running down the stairs.

'James! I have changed my mind; I don't want a baked potato, I'd rather a pie, and some gingerbread – and I saw a woman selling cherries from a great basket on her head, get some of those and— Oh!'

Reaching the landing she caught sight of Edward and stumbled, letting off a shimmer of sparks in shock.

Edward's eyes widened. 'You found her.' His voice was raspy and low. 'You *lied*. I asked you outright and you *lied*.'

James held a hand up in appeal or defence, he didn't know which. 'Edward—'

'You mean to take our work for your own. Traitor.'

Instinctively, James closed his other hand around Olympe's wrist. The triumphant vision of presenting her and her powers to his father as his own discovery was rapidly vanishing.

Could he bargain with Edward? No. What had been his words? He owed Wickham *everything* now. The choice he'd made was clear.

It all happened in a jumbled second.

James yanked Olympe towards the stairs and yelled, '*Run.*' Edward lurched after them, catching Olympe's waist, and the three of them crashed together. The space was too small – the steps suddenly underfoot – and then they were toppling down in a chaos of arms and knees and splintering bannisters.

Olympe, in her panic, set off another burst of sparks, giving James a bad jolt as he landed with the wind knocked out of him. Edward staggered up just as Olympe sprang into a crouch, face a thunderstorm in full force, a crackling blue net of electricity strung over her hands.

Edward held his ground, staring at Olympe's hands in hungry fascination. 'So it's true. This is far beyond what Wickham achieved with me.'

Olympe frowned, the net fracturing and reforming. 'What do you mean, *achieved with you*?'

Edward didn't answer, only reached closer till their hands met. Sparks cascaded over his arm. James waited for him to pull back in pain – but nothing happened.

I feel nothing now.

The swirl of movement across Olympe's face increased. 'Why doesn't that hurt you?'

Edward looked in fascination at where their hands joined. 'I don't know.'

'Are you human?'

His brows furrowed. 'I had thought so.'

James wrapped his hand around a curtain they had torn down, and in an awkward movement flung it over Edward. It was stupid and would only buy them a moment or two as he disentangled himself, but it could be enough – it *had* to be enough – to buy them time.

James and Olympe pelted out into the noise and chaos of the Rookery.

James was gathering enemies faster than he could deal with them.

3

6 Bedford Square

Lord Harford strode through the front door, tailcoat flapping, a blast of rain and storm wind following him in. A muggy summer storm had finally broken with a crack of thunder so loud Hennie had dropped her dish of tea.

Now, sheet rain lashed the windows and the household was stuck inside. A fretful mood had fallen over them since Edward's accident. Phil discordantly plodded through the same prelude on the pianoforte and Hennie refused to do anything but stare out of windows and dab at her eyes with a handkerchief, while Lady Harford had thrown herself into wedding preparations.

Lord Harford had left before breakfast on parliamentary business; now he had returned, handing his top hat and umbrella to a waiting servant. Behind him, a footman followed with his dispatch box.

Camille had positioned herself in the morning room with a piece of embroidery on her lap and a view through to the front door. She caught Al's eye and nodded imperceptibly. He stood up from where he had been sprawled on a sofa with the newspaper and stretched languorously.

'Excuse me.'

Hennie sighed. 'Do you think we should prepare some clothes for mourning?'

Phil paused her playing. 'Don't think about it, Hen...'

Through the door, Camille watched Al intercept Lord Harford. She gave it a moment, then put down her sewing.

'I'm afraid I must retire for a while. All this talk of death...'

She let the spectre of the Revolution fill the silence, the horrors she had been witness to.

'Oh, of course, how awful of us not to think—'

Camille rose and cut her off. 'Not at all. I only need a little rest.' Heart racing, she forced herself to remain sombre as she left the room. She bobbed a curtsey to Lord Harford as she passed him and Al in the hallway. 'Good morning, my lord.'

'Good morning, Camille.' She felt his eyes follow her as she climbed the stairs. When she reached the top, she tucked herself out of sight and listened as Al picked up their conversation.

'... Lady Harford did seem insistent on discussing the matter again. It seems she has agreed a neat price for fresh tongue...'

Lord Harford huffed in irritation. 'I have told her more than once that we cannot host all the home counties, however fine the tongue.'

Al shrugged. 'I am only the messenger. I believe she is in her dressing room.'

Lord Harford glanced towards his wife's rooms on the ground floor. 'Oh, very well.' He waved the footman carrying his dispatch box up.

His study was at the top of the staircase, and his dispatch boxes were delivered immediately to it whenever he returned home. Camille had monitored his comings and goings, the box always trailing him like a prize held ever out of reach. As War Minister, he was privy to the most up to date intelligence on the situation in France – which had to include a player like the duc.

The footman reached the top of the stairs and turned towards the study. From her hiding place, Camille watched him in her hand mirror. When he came close enough she pulled a bottle of smelling salts from her pocket and uncorked it; the smell overpowered her for a moment and she felt her eyes water.

Barrelling around the corner, she collided directly with the footman as he unlocked Lord Harford's study. The bottle shattered, coating his uniform with the foul-smelling liquid, and the dispatch box burst open on the floor in a flurry of papers.

'Oh my goodness, I'm so sorry!' Camille tried to dab away the salts and only managed to rub them in further.

The footman's face twisted in disgust as the smell hit him. 'I apologise, Miss du Bugue. I wasn't looking where I was going.'

Camille almost felt bad; she didn't want to see him

fired or disciplined. It wasn't his fault he stood in between her and what she wanted.

'Oh dear, I hope it doesn't stain.' He was starting to look green as the awful smell engulfed them both. She used her handkerchief to cover her mouth. 'It is quite a *unique* scent, isn't it?'

He took her hint. 'I will change immediately. After I deliver his lordship's papers—'

He looked at the mess of documents scattered around their feet.

'Don't be silly. I'll pick these up – they're to be delivered to Lord Harford's study, correct?'

'Yes, my lady, but—'

'This is my fault; I will fix it. Off you go.' She shooed him away and started to gather the papers. Reluctantly, he left, looking not far off throwing up.

On her knees, Camille ignored the lingering smell and rifled through the documents, scanning them for anything of interest. Most were dull: reports from underlings, accounts, projections of department expenditure, requests for new military uniforms, disciplinary hearings – then something caught her eye.

Robespierre's name. The words: *Trial. Accusations. Collapse.*

At that moment, two voices echoed in the hall below. Without thinking, she stuffed the papers down the front of her dress.

'Camille! What on earth are you doing up there?'

Lady Harford had come into view at the bottom of the stairs, pushed in her Bath chair by Lord Harford.

'Oh – I – er—'

Lord Harford had caught sight of the dispatch box and was up the stairs two at a time.

'What are you doing with that?' he snapped. He pulled the papers away from her. 'Where's Watson?'

'Is that your footman? I'm so sorry, I spilled my smelling salts on him and he had to change – I was trying to tidy these away and put them in your study for you.'

'You are not to go into my study under any circumstances.' He rammed the papers into the case and slammed it shut.

'I'm sorry. I was trying to help.' She let fear come into her voice, a tremor into her hands. She was a traumatised girl, trying to be a good house guest. She wasn't a threat.

Before he could speak, Lady Harford called from the bottom of the stairs. 'My dear Camille, come and sit with me. I have some wedding preparations I want to discuss. We're having the tongue, William, I won't have penny-pinching over our only son's wedding.'

Lord Harford softened, turning to his wife. 'Very well, then. Tongue it is.'

'Now, say thank you to Camille for trying to help.'

He tucked the case under his arm and muttered a gruff thanks before shutting himself in his study and locking the door.

Camille sagged, half in relief, half in frustration. She'd found something promising – but at the cost of arousing Lord Harford's suspicions quite thoroughly.

She was running out of time.

And there was still so much left to do.

4

A Gin Palace Near
the Rookery

The gin palace was an abundance of gilt and glass and velvet, towering mirrors behind the bar, rambling shelves of bottles lining them, and not an inch of floor space free. James set two glasses and a bottle on the sticky table in front of Olympe, who was hunched inside a veiled bonnet they had snatched off the display outside a pawnshop.

He knew the palace from drinking with other medical students – they had ventured into the edges of the Rookery now and again when they were feeling cocky – but this time he had avoided the gentlemen's entrance and taken Olympe in through the working man's door. Frosted glass partitions split the room by class of patron, extending even over the bar, so that the wealthy didn't have to catch sight of the unwashed masses when ordering their seventh drink.

After running a zigzag path through the slum, Olympe had signalled to the pub and they had entered.

They would be hard to spot in such a chaotic crowd, and almost impossible to sneak up on, so they had hunkered down among the raucous noise, the smell of anchovies and oysters and straw strewn across the piss-stained floor, the whirl of perfume mixing with sweat and tallow grease. He'd worried Olympe would look out of place but she fitted in well; she wasn't the only eccentrically dressed person in her shabby silk outfit.

James poured a measure of gin and knocked it back. He didn't know if it would steady his nerves or make them a hundred times worse, but it was worth a try. Olympe ignored her cup. She focused on her bare hand, held in front of her, a faint blue cloud of sparks washing over her palms like a rising tide.

'My powers didn't work on him. Did you see?'

'I did.'

'What's wrong with me?'

He reached across the table and held her hands tightly. A crackle stung his skin. 'Nothing is wrong with you,' he said firmly.

'You know him?'

James took a breath. 'I do.' Still holding her hands, he told her about the research he and Edward had been helping Wickham with. How the three of them had agreed James would go to Paris, looking for the rumoured electrical creature the duc had created – but when he found Olympe, he had thought to steal the scientific discovery for himself. He left out the part about so desperately, pathetically, wanting his father's approval.

Then he told her about the accident, and Wickham's

insistence on trying his new theory – how it had worked, snatching Edward back through the veil between their world and the next. Somewhere along the way, he started crying. The shock of seeing his friend nearly die had shaken him to his bones. This was no game they played. This was life and death.

Olympe listened in silence, the storm clouds of her skin roiling dangerously.

'So perhaps he is like me now: human, but not in the same way as rest of you. I would be curious to speak to him again. Don't worry,' she added at James's horrified look, 'I believe you that your tutor is dangerous, but you said Edward was a friend. He must be frightened by what has happened to him. Perhaps we can make him an ally.'

James shook his head. 'You don't know him. He won't forgive me quickly.'

Olympe poured another measure of gin into James's glass and pushed it into his hands.

'Well, then. It's time to take me to Camille.'

'But—'

'James. You've made a lot of enemies, and you have no one on your side. You can run, but then what? Wickham will still find out what you did. You need help. You need Camille.'

He clenched his jaw, battling with himself. Then he knocked back the second gin and nodded. 'Fine. We go to Camille. But if we get the chance to show your abilities to my father…' The gin cut a burning line down his throat.

'Camille first. Father second.'

James sank his head into his hands. 'I'm such an

idiot. I had everything lined up, I swear I did, and now it's collapsing, like the bloody Spanish Armada, swept out to sea the moment before victory.'

She patted his hand. 'At least you acknowledge you're an idiot.'

Decision made, they ordered a plate of bread, whelks and samphire in place of the lunch James had set out to get when Edward had found them.

'Do you still mean to go back to Paris?' asked James. 'Even though the duc and Comtois are there?'

Olympe narrowed her eyes as she fished a whelk from its shell with a pin. 'Is this you trying to persuade me to stay?'

'No. Only, I wonder why I do the things I do, when they turn out to be so stupid or dangerous. I wondered if other people have better reasons for their choices.'

She chewed thoughtfully. 'We never know how our choices will turn out before we make them; we will always grieve the path untaken. But to *not* choose, to take no path at all? Then we would end up grieving everything.'

Food finished, they edged out of the gin palace, watching corners and alley mouths for any sign of pursuit, and set off for Bedford Square and Camille. James led them down the mews that connected the backs of the grand houses, where horses were stabled and coal deliveries arrived.

At number 6, they hopped the fence and sneaked

into the stables. Only two horses were there at the moment, whickering in their stalls.

James hovered in the entrance. 'I'm sorry I can't get you into the house – there are too many servants; there's no way you'd go unnoticed.'

Olympe raised her hand to a horse's nose, letting it snuffle and lick. 'That's okay. I'll be all right here.'

'Hallo – there you are!' He slammed the door and spun around. Hennie was wrapped in a decorative shawl and a smart satin evening dress.

'Don't sneak up on people,' he snapped. 'It's rude.'

'Well? How's Edward?'

He startled, then quickly smoothed his hair from his face. Of course, the last time Hennie had seen him he'd been taking Edward to the operating theatre. It flashed through his mind again – cold skin, crackle of electricity, blood under his nails.

'Edward is – he's recovering.'

Her face lit up. 'You did it? Oh, I knew you would!' His sister flung her arms around him in a tight hug. 'Can we go and visit him? Was it awful? When I heard that crunching noise—'

'Give it a rest, Hen.'

'Oh, fine. You never tell me anything.' She folded her arms, pouted. 'I hope you haven't forgotten we're to go to the Vauxhall Pleasure Gardens tonight.'

'Right. Yes. Pleasure Gardens.'

'We're off in an hour. Don't be late, or Maman will never forgive you.'

Hennie went back inside and James returned to the stables, heart racing.

Olympe wasn't where he'd left her. But there was only one way in and out. She had to be here.

He passed the stalls, steps muffled by the straw scattered across the packed earth floor. The smell of horse and manure was strong, and familiar; he'd spent enough early mornings helping muck out when he was younger. His father had insisted a gentleman should know how every part of his estate was run, from the stables to the groundskeepers to the accounts to the tenants. James had liked spending time with the horses more than learning how to fill out a ledger, and his father had never let him forget it.

He found Olympe in an empty stall at the far end of the stables, crouched over something black and feathery. A dead bird. Leaning over it like a child inspecting an insect, she prodded it with one finger, sending a pulse of electricity into its body. A flash of blue sparks and the smell of burned feathers – and nothing more.

'Olympe?' His voice was just above a whisper. 'What are you doing?'

She sent another burst of power into it, the blue static lighting her face and the dark hollows of her eyes.

'An experiment.'

'An experiment to find out … what exactly?'

Turning to him, he could see the spark of curiosity on her face.

'To find out if I can do it too. If I can bring something back to life like Edward.'

'I'm … not sure that's how it works.'

'Why not?'

'I … never mind. Something's come up – I'm supposed to go out with my family tonight, and they're starting to get suspicious of me avoiding them all the time so I can't say no. Camille is going too, so I can try and talk to her about … the situation.'

'Go, James. I'm not helpless.'

She flapped him away and hunched over the bird again. A jolt of electricity pumped through it. The power seemed to rise from her skin in a fog, before clustering at her fingertip and pulsing out.

'No,' he said softly. 'No, you're really not.'

He slid away, the image of the dead bird fixed in his mind.

It was hard to tell in the shadows, but it looked as though its wing had twitched.

5

A Carriage on the Rue St-Jacques

'You've been keeping secrets,' said Guil. 'And I want to know *why*.' Hostility radiated from him, and he kept his hands tightly curled around the leather strap.

'No, I haven't. I told you this was my plan.'

'Ada, don't,' he said, pained. 'I have been *frightened* for you. I came to make amends this morning but your father said you'd gone out already, "tutoring". I had to quiz the damn coach driver to find out where you were and when he told me the Faubourg Saint Jacques—' He cut himself off.

In profile against the window, he looked like the portrait of a general. Strong furrowed brow, square jaw, the firm line of his full lips. She sank back into the carriage seat, pinching the bridge of her nose. 'I'm sorry. You're right.'

'Am I not a part of this job any more?'

'You are.'

'And yet you make decisions without me.'

'I know, but I—'

'Thought you knew better?'

Ada hated the way he looked at her, the tone in his voice as though she was a disobedient child. 'It was my risk to take.'

'It is *not* just your risk. What if something happened to you?'

'If something happened to me it would hardly be *your* fault.'

'How did you feel after I was hurt in the theatre?' he said quietly. 'That it was nothing to do with you?'

'All right. Fine. I felt guilty.'

'You are avoiding me because you know you are in the wrong.'

'No, actually, I don't think I'm in the wrong. I'm sorry I didn't tell you my decision, but this is my life, Guil. You don't get a say in how I run it.'

'You know if Camille was here she wouldn't support this. Do you really think you can do this on your own?'

The giddy high she'd felt leaving the duc's study had vanished. For a moment, she'd felt competent. Useful. Respected.

Guil had reminded her that wasn't true.

'Camille isn't here, is she? She dropped all of us to go chasing after James. I am not her lapdog. I can do this, Guil. Trust me.'

Ada wanted to kick the door open and rage her way through the streets. She knew she was guilty on all counts, and yet it hit home so much harder than she'd expected. What she felt was more than guilt – it was shame. Because maybe, in her heart of hearts, she *enjoyed* what she was doing. The life the duc was offering her was far closer to what she wanted than their struggling existence as the Bataillon des Morts, always at risk, always hiding, eating stale bread and freezing under the eaves come winter. There'd been Camille as reward, and the freedom of escaping her father's house, of course.

But was it her future?

No.

The future she wanted wasn't something her father could offer. Or Camille. She wanted to learn, to discover, to be in the room where it happened when the world was split open, its secrets splayed out like she was God and every mystery was a puzzle to be solved.

Maybe this *was* more than just a plan to her.

And that knowledge made her squirm.

They fell into silence, staring out of opposite windows as the carriage crawled through the crowded streets around the river's edge, then across the Pont Notre-Dame towards the Right Bank. At a lull in traffic, Ada leaned out of the window to change their direction – instead of the Marais and home, the Palais d'Égalité. They were due to see the solider Léon had informed them about; she'd planned to meet Guil there, explain to him what she'd done. It wasn't supposed to go like this.

'So tell me how this plan works,' said Guil as she pulled up the window. 'Shutting yourself up with a violent and dangerous man.'

'He's not like that.'

'Oh? Sympathy for the Devil, is it now?'

'Stop it,' snapped Ada.

Guil said nothing. His expression had shifted from stony anger to something more complicated. Ada let the silence spool out.

Finally, Guil spoke. 'I ... I saw things go wrong in the army. Time and time again, tactics, strategies, risks that didn't pay off. I have seen the dire consequences when we throw ourselves into something unprepared. I cannot let that happen again, especially not to someone I care about.'

And the fight went out of her. Guil held himself so carefully, rose above the mess of the rest of the battalion, like a lone competent adult in a band of squabbling children; it was easy for Ada to forget he'd had had a life of his own before she knew him, had seen and done things that still haunted him.

She reached for Guil's hand, and he let her take it. 'Nothing bad is going to happen to me.'

'You should not be so sure. If you continue to shut me out, then that is all that will happen. No one can succeed alone.'

Outside, the view had shifted from the river to the Rue Saint-Honoré. The Palais d'Égalité wasn't far.

Guil was right. Fighting each other would get them nowhere. 'From the notes I've been writing up, it seems the duc has been testing which materials are the best conductors of electricity. Now he's trying to understand the principles of transferring electricity through flesh. You remember the demonstration at the theatre, where people stand in a circle holding hands and a current is passed through them? Like that.'

'That does not sound good. Why on earth would he want to know that?'

Ada looked out of the window, at people hurrying about their day: street sellers, shopkeepers, beggars in doorways and the well-to-do, lifting their skirts to avoid them. All trying to keep some semblance of normality through the chaos of revolution.

'I don't know,' she said, pressing her forehead to the glass. 'And that's what worries me.'

6 Bedford Square

Leaving Lady Harford's dressing room, Camille edged along the wall to keep out of sight of Hennie and Phil in the drawing room – and knocked into an end table, nearly sending flying the china dish where guests left their calling cards. She dived and caught it before it slid off the edge, but a cascade of cards fluttered to the floor.

'Camille?' Hennie's voice rang out. 'Is that you? Is there more news of Edward?'

Camille held her breath. The shadow of a figure approached the doorway.

'Come back, Hen, and turn the page! I'm almost at the end of this bar.' The piano slowed.

'Oh, all right.'

The shadow turned and left.

As silently as she could, Camille replaced the dish and picked up the cards. She'd forgotten how communal life was in a place like this. Not the easy camaraderie of her battalion, where she could come and go as she pleased, but the enforced group movements between mealtimes and leisure. In this world, Camille's place was with the other young women, embroidering handkerchiefs for her bridal trousseau, or in some other way making herself pleasant and useful. She was only alone when she slept.

She didn't know how she used to stand it.

Cards replaced, she padded noiselessly in her silk slippers to a little-used drawing room. She would have to dress for the pleasure gardens shortly, but first, she had an appointment to keep.

Al was waiting, hands in his pockets as he paced nervously in front of the empty fireplace. 'Did you get it?'

She pulled the documents out of her dress. 'I got something, but I think Lord Harford suspects me. We need to be more careful.'

'I suppose there's no dodging the wedding now,' said Al. 'If you try to pull out, it'll only make him think he's right.'

Camille's heart sank. She'd been thinking the same thing.

'We'll just have to make that work to our advantage,' she said. 'If James gets sucked into wedding preparations, he'll have less time to keep an eye on Olympe or us.'

'In the meantime, we'd better hope you've managed to steal something useful.' Al held out his hand. 'Go on, then, give us a read.'

'Hang on, I've not even looked properly yet.'

She dropped into an armchair and read.

As she realised what she'd stolen, a chill swallowed her whole. Wordlessly, she held it out to Al.

It was a report on the state of things in Paris, from an English spy. The information was only two days old – someone must have ridden more than one horse to the point of collapse to get to Lord Harford.

He would definitely realise this was missing.

But what scared her more was what it said. Unrest. Robespierre's grip on power sliding. A resurgent right wing in the National Convention angling to take control. Royalist factions gathering strength; potential routes to funnel funds to them, to free useful agents from prison. Rumours of a coup.

The duc and his Royalist allies must have another plan in action.

The fragility of the Revolution was laid out in stark words Camille could no longer ignore. Paris was a political powder keg, and she'd left Ada and Guil on their own to navigate it. No, worse – she'd sent them into the heart of it.

She'd already lost one family to the guillotine. Was she at risk of losing another?

The feeling of having made a terrible mistake overwhelmed her, and Camille reached for Al's arm to steady herself. Her chest hitched, panic filling her as she couldn't catch a proper breath.

Al had gone paler than usual.

'Good thing we left Paris. If the duc gets his minor-royal-of-choice into power, he'll have the entire secret police in charge of hanging us by the ankles and skinning us alive.'

'Shut up – please just shut up.' Camile stood, heart beating too hard. 'We need to do something.'

'All right, what?'

'I don't know! We shouldn't have left Ada and Guil. Robespierre is about to fall, and the duc will have his pawns in power. God only knows what will happen to Paris next.'

Al folded the letter and handed it back to her. 'You never know, everyone might think it's about time for a rest. They might leave off executing each other for a bit.'

'You think now is a good time for jokes?'

'Fine, do you want me to rub it in your face that I was right? Paris is too dangerous for us. We should get Guil and Ada over here and cut our losses.'

'Cut our losses?' she said incredulously. 'Can't you see they need us?'

He sneered. 'Don't be so big-headed. France doesn't need us. We fought for months and look where it got us. I'm out, and you should be too. Let someone else pick up the slack this time.'

'And what if no else does?'

'So be it.'

'You'd really walk away and let the duc win?'

Al shrugged. 'No skin off my nose if I'm over here. Why should I care?'

Camille stared at him. The feeling of hysteria was only building. Her throat was closing up, her thoughts spiralling. 'I don't believe you really think that. I know you care.' She couldn't just sit here, she had to *do* something. 'Come on.' She pulled Al off the arm of the chair. 'Have you still got that key to James's room? Both of us need to get dressed as though we're going to the pleasure gardens, but the first chance we get, we sneak off. Get Olympe and *run*.'

'Camille—'

She pushed him into the hall and towards the stairs. She felt like a blazing star, burning too fast. 'No, I don't want to hear it. You said you'd finish this job with me, so do as I say and finish it.'

'*Camille*!'

'What?'

'I just saw James and Lord Harford go into his study, looking quite thunderous. Something is up.'

She stopped, looking at the sweeping staircase to the door above. 'Oh.'

'Yes, *oh*. Well, go on, then.' He nudged her towards the stairs. 'Be a good little revolutionary and have an eavesdrop.'

The tightness in her lungs faded into the background of her mind as she mounted the stairs. *Her quarry was cornered. Soon, she could pounce.*

7

6 Bedford Square

James felt like a stranger stepping inside the house. Around him, the bustle of normal life whirled, carriages and cloaks being readied for the evening out at the pleasure gardens. It was all so perfectly familiar, but it was as though he was watching through a glass pane – normal, safe, mundane life happening with his family on one side, while he was stranded on the other in a world of death and danger.

Lord Harford's London study was a smaller replica of his grand study in Henley, but without the anteroom in which to keep anxious visitors. Stepping inside, James was only a few paces from his father's desk. The ceiling might be higher here, the wallpaper cleaner, the shelves stacked with newer volumes, but the feeling was the same. Lord Harford had already settled in his chair, pulling papers towards him.

'Spit it out.' Lord Harford didn't look up.

James clasped his hands behind his back. 'It's about the electrical research I spoke of previously.'

'Oh, for goodness' sake—'

'No – please, hear me out. I have a demonstration with me to *prove* electricity is much more than a gimmick.'

His father folded his hands and waited. 'Very well. Go ahead, show me.'

James's cheeks heated. 'I don't have it on me exactly, but if you come with me outside...'

'Ah. It never is quite the truth with you, is it?'

'It will take but ten minutes—'

'Do you see what is on my desk?' Lord Harford interrupted.

'Sir?'

'It is a simple question. Answer it.'

James looked at the desk, the expensive quills and ink, paperweights, blotting paper, the sheafs of documents, and the dispatch box that sat on one side.

'Your dispatch box, sir.'

'It is the governance of a nation. The matters of state that trouble the greatest minds of a generation.'

He paused. Looked at James expectantly.

'Yes, sir?'

Lord Harford sighed, face pinched like the cat had dragged in a half-dead bird and was expecting him to accept it with pleasure.

'And you bring me ... paranoid theories. I had high hopes for you, my son, but you fall for a hoax and spout stories of mad scientists and inhuman girls wielding electrical powers to anyone who will listen. You waste my time and humiliate yourself.'

'But Wickham—'

'Wickham is an idiot. This is why I didn't want you

at the medical school. To be perfectly frank, you have always been a flighty boy with little sense of duty and propriety. You should know your place is here as the heir to the estate, learning the duties and obligations that will fall to you when I am gone. Instead you choose to play strange, immoral games with human life. It was a mistake to allow it, and you have made me regret it.' Lord Harford leaned forward, steepling his hands. 'What's more, you fail to see the threat directly in front of your face. Camille's arrival here was … convenient.'

James frowned. 'I don't follow.'

'Of course you don't. If the girl had wanted to escape Paris, why on earth did she not tell you so when you found her? Why did she wait several weeks and turn up with that wastrel?'

Clenching his fists behind his back, James swallowed. Before, this is exactly what he would have wanted. His father suspicious of Camille, wanting her out of here as much as he had. Now she was his only hope.

His father wasn't going to listen, that much was clear. He was a fool for having held out hope. Edward must have told Wickham about Olympe by now and they would be plotting *something*.

'I don't know, sir. Perhaps seeing me reminded her that there was another family still waiting for her.'

Lord Harford snorted. 'That girl doesn't have a sentimental bone in her body. She's keeping something from us, and I intend to find out what.'

'I am sure she is keeping many things from us.

The true horror of the Terror is not something easily shared.'

'Don't play coy. You know what I mean. Her parents were fervent Revolutionaries and lost their lives for it. You think the apple falls that far from the tree? Revolution is in her blood. She is French, we are English; she does not have the same loyalties.'

'That's not…' James struggled to find the right words. 'We don't doubt Maman's loyalties and she's French. Doesn't that make me half-French?'

'Don't play semantics with me.'

'Please, for once, believe me. She is not here for *you*.' Camille might be telling his father lies, but he knew all too well her real target.

Lord Harford arranged his papers, dipped his quill in the inkpot, and began to write. 'You've been a fool before, James. Don't be one again.'

James stood rooted to the spot. It couldn't just end like that. There had to be something he could say.

'Now, do what is expected of you – escort your fiancée to the pleasure gardens and at least try to act respectably for one night. I don't want to hear about this again.'

The nib scratched across paper, a small, obstinate sound that filled the space between them.

Because there was never any space for James there. There was only space for the person his father wanted him to be.

8

6 Bedford Square

The door to Lord Harford's study opened suddenly and Camille skittered sideways. James came out looking furious and she made a half-hearted attempt to appear interested in a porcelain shepherdess on the side table.

'Camille. Enjoy your eavesdropping? Catch any good gossip?'

She adjusted the shepherdess so she had her back to the red-cheeked farmer leering next to her. 'I don't know what you're talking about. You're really not as interesting as you think you are.'

He opened his mouth to snap something else – then stopped. Downstairs, laughing voices rose from the drawing room, full of anticipation for the evening ahead.

'Actually, I'm glad you're here,' he said. 'I need to talk to you.'

She arched an eyebrow. 'Do you now?'

She had heard only muffled, unintelligible snatches of their conversation, but enough to know James and his father had been fighting. She would have thought she was the last person he wanted to see.

Dark smudges circled his eyes, and his cheekbones stood out in too-sharp relief. She wondered when he'd last slept through the night.

Crooking his elbow, he offered his arm and, hesitantly, she let him lead her downstairs.

'Look, if I were to … what I mean to say is, would you—'

'Any time today, James.'

'I need your help.'

'I beg your pardon?'

What on earth could James need her help for?

Curiouser and curiouser.

'It's gone wrong,' he said. 'Wickham is—'

He was interrupted by Lady's Harford, looking regal in red satin with a feather in her hair. 'Oh, look at the two of you! It's such a pleasure to see you together again. Like old times.' She turned a glistening eye over both of them. 'But what is this? You are hardly dressed, my dear girl, and James, you look a fright! Both of you, to your rooms at once.'

Camille knew when to stop fighting, and allowed herself to be chivvied along, transferred into evening wear, her hair dressed and rouge dabbed on her lips and cheeks.

I need your help.

What had happened? What had changed James from the stubborn, crowing enemy she'd faced so recently? Her anger at him warred with her curiosity and the stubborn sliver of her brain that still worried about him. It wasn't the *worst* feeling to have James begging for her help.

And then there was the ever-present dread that had followed her since her mother had first been arrested, the shifting-sand feeling that any success was fragile, and without constant vigilance could be lost.

She and Al could get Olympe and go at the first opportunity – but James had said something had gone wrong. She needed to find out what.

Once she was deemed fit for public consumption, she was released. The first of the dresses Lady Harford had ordered for her had arrived, and it was barely more than a cloud of gauze and silk. Standing in front of the mirror with the light behind her, she could plainly see her figure through the fabric. She'd worn trousers enough times that she didn't care about anyone seeing the shape of her legs – but like this, a teasing glimpse, it felt more salacious.

Embarrassment quickly turned to annoyance, and she stomped down the last of the stairs. She was Camille goddamn Laroche and she would not be embarrassed by her own goddamn legs.

Downstairs it was quiet. In the drawing room, she found Al alone – except for the footman he was tangled up with.

'Get out!' he yelped.

Camille shut the door firmly and crossed her arms. 'Time to leave,' she said to the footman. The footman shrugged back into his frock coat and made himself scarce. Al collapsed into a sofa, shirt still untucked and tailcoat abandoned on the floor.

'For god's sake, Al, try to be a bit more discreet. For example, anywhere other than a well-lit public room with lots of people around.'

'You're such a spoilsport.'

'Get dressed before someone comes in.'

'Yes, Mother.' He made himself more presentable.

She fiddled with the petals on a flower arrangement. 'Is this a serious thing? You and…'

Al interrupted her. 'Is it serious with the footman whose name you don't know? Shockingly it is not.'

'I was only trying to be a friend. Do you like this man? Is he nice?'

Al buried his face in his hands, cringing. 'Cam, oh my god, shut up. This is embarrassing.'

'I thought you and Léon were … exclusive.'

'Don't talk about Léon.'

'Why not? Does he know you're in London?' When Al didn't reply she raised her eyebrows. 'Ah. I see.'

'He'll have seen my execution notice in the papers. He's better off thinking me dead.'

'Really? You think it's better that he *mourn* you? Christ, Al, and you call me callous—'

'What's done is done, okay? You really think I could face him now? Sorry! Whoops, that whole getting my head chopped off thing was a bit of a mix-up, actually I'm fine and dandy and on holiday abroad.'

'Is that the real reason you don't want to go back to Paris?'

'No. Maybe. Yes.' Al couldn't meet her eye. 'And the other stuff I said too. It can be both.'

With a sigh, she tucked her flimsy skirt under her

and dropped onto the sofa next to him. 'I know what it's like to lose your parents in the way you did, but it doesn't mean your life is over too. You could be happy, you know.'

'Spare me the heartfelt speech,' he sneered. 'You're deluded if you think you and Ada have a future together. She deserves better than you, and when she realises that, you're done for, Cam.'

Camille stared at her own knees. 'If Ada wants to leave me, that's up to her.'

She meant it. She wasn't good enough for Ada; she'd always known it. She'd lied about James, begrudged her a relationship with her father, and used her like another weapon in the arsenal of her battalion. It was only a matter of time before Ada saw it too.

'You really are pathetic. I tell you the so-called love of your life is going to leave you sooner rather than later, and you're just going to roll over and accept it?'

Camille shrugged. 'What else should I do? Lock her up?'

'I don't know – *fight*? Be a better person so you actually deserve her? Don't marry your ex just to make him miserable? It's basic stuff.'

There were thoughts she never let herself think, not now, not in the middle of a job, not with so much on the line. When her parents had been killed, the grief had made her weak; she'd been unable to save them because the pain and fear had overwhelmed her, and she'd ended up dragging her friends into danger, making mistake after mistake.

Loving Ada was so huge it frightened her. The

power it had to destroy her. She wouldn't think about it. It wasn't safe.

Before she could reply, Al changed the subject. 'Anyway, you didn't tell me about your eavesdropping.'

'All I could hear from the study was an argument – but you'll never guess what James said when I spoke to him afterwards.'

'He's tired of being filthy rich and is retiring to the country to raise goats and starve like the peasantry?'

She ignored him. 'He said he needs my *help*.'

'Excuse me?'

'I didn't get a chance to ask him what the hell he meant before I was remanded for 'delicate young lady' duty and stuffed into this stupid frock. We're *so* close to getting Olympe. I swear if James drags us into more trouble…'

A servant arrived to announce the carriages were ready, and the Harfords assembled for their outing.

Al patted her arm. 'Ah, defeat snatched from the jaws of victory. Just like old times. Anyway, it's not really a Bataillon des Morts plan if it doesn't go wrong, is it?'

9

Palais d'Égalité

The last time Ada had walked the colonnades of the Palais d'Égalité, it had been in search of Al, missing from the battalion once again, and she had found him somewhere darker, drunker, poisoned by the impending execution of his family.

This time, it was Guil who moved like a man condemned. The Café Corrazza at numbers 9 to 12 was a smart affair, with a black lacquered frontage with gold lettering and a black-and-white tiled floor. A popular meeting spot for the Jacobin Revolutionaries. Ada kept a nervous eye out for Docteur Comtois, the Revolutionary scientist who had kept Olympe locked in the Conciergerie and who had given the Bataillon des Morts hell trying to get her back.

Thankfully, it was a quiet evening – only a few tables of men playing chequers, reading the newspapers or leaning together over bottles of pastis and jugs of cold water. But there was an undercurrent of unease – glances exchanged, conversations falling quiet as they passed.

Ada remembered what Léon had said. *Something brewing.*

They found their appointment tucked into a shadowed table towards the back, where a servant was lowering the chandeliers to light them. The man was short and stocky and must have once been handsome before a deep weariness had consumed him. He was dressed as a civilian, plain black breeches and tailcoat and a shirt turning yellow from the laundry.

Guil hung back, so Ada strode forward with a confidence she was struggling to find.

'Citoyen Jean-Baptiste Baudot?'

The man looked up, then glanced at Guil. 'Ah. I was warned it would be you.'

Ada pushed Guil into a seat and took the other chair. 'Thank you for meeting with us.'

'I'm not doing you a favour. What's it worth to you?'

Jean looked fixedly at Guil, who sat as blank and motionless as a theatre prop.

'If you will tell us what you know, a great deal.'

They ordered coffee for the table and Ada brought out half the money as a show of good faith.

'I'd help you for free if you really are working against the Royalists,' said Jean, hand hesitating over the money. 'But I suppose we are all sell-outs now.'

'Jean—' Guil spoke finally, but Jean cut him off.

'Do you know, I never once wondered what happened to you? I thought about how everything that had come before was a lie. I thought about what a worm I must have been friends with, that he was capable of abandoning us in the field.'

'I never wanted to leave you,' said Guil. 'But I could not fight for such men—'

'I never *once* thought about where you ended up. So, don't think I'm interested in hearing about you now.'

Guil clammed up, turned away. Ada wanted to reach out to him but she didn't think it would be welcome.

'Tell us what you know and we'll leave you be,' she said.

Jean sipped his coffee, considering her. 'What is it like to work with a man you know you can never trust?'

'Your information, or the rest of the money and I walk away.'

'I don't know how you do it. Always keeping one eye open.'

'I'm not going to play this game.' She stood, putting the coin purse away. 'Guil is a good man and has proven that to me – not that I owe you any defence of his character.'

It had begun to rain outside, and she fixed her hat in place.

'Wait.' Jean held up a hand. 'Wait. Sit. I can keep my peace.'

'Can you?'

He drained his coffee cup and refilled it. 'Maybe not, but I meant what I said. I would be happy to help anyone stop the Royalists.'

Stiffly, Ada sat and folded her arms. Guil hadn't moved the whole time; she thought he was lost in introspection but when she looked closer she saw his tension, the shaking of his limbs. He was barely keeping himself under control.

'We've been told someone is looking for soldiers

susceptible to a bribe, particularly ones who work in the prisons – and that he approached you. Why?'

'Why else? He's looking to break someone out.'

'Who?'

'Sounded like an old ally – someone important, someone the Revolutionaries *really* don't want getting out. Security was too tight around the cell so I wasn't interested in the work – not that I'd ever turn traitor and work for someone like *him*.'

Ada felt a pang of shame. 'What did he say?'

'Nothing much. Whatever's going down, he wants a real accomplice for it. Not hired muscle; someone he can trust. So that means gathering his oldest allies.' Jean shrugged. 'I think he found a way to get them out in the end.'

Ada swore loudly and creatively in her head. To Jean, all she said was, 'I see.'

But Jean had been thinking about something.

'You know what? I changed my mind. I do want to talk about it.' He stabbed in Guil's direction with the end of his pipe.

He leaned forward. 'Very well. What is it you would speak about?'

'There you go, pompous as ever. Do you remember what we called you?'

'The Scholar.'

'No, I mean, behind your back. *The Gutter Prince*. So mannered, so *noble*. When you're just another nobody like the rest of us.'

Guil said nothing, taking the blows with that same solemn expression.

'You'd have to think yourself *better* to be able to walk away from your friends. The men who fought with you, who saved your life. You thought it was nothing, didn't you? Not as important as your *principles*.'

'You are correct. I chose my principles over my loyalty to you.'

Jean's mouth twisted in a snarl. 'You have the nerve to admit it? Then let me be the one to tell you what happened to those men you didn't think important enough to stick around for. You ran when we were redeployed to the Vendée. They told us to target the women, but I suppose you knew that. And the generals, they expected us to act without complaint. To be machines for them. To burn and kill and destroy and when we wouldn't they shot us too. *Thank you*, for leaving us to that. If you weren't there, I suppose you got to pretend it wasn't happening.'

Guil was shaking, knuckles showing white. 'The opposite. Every piece of news convinced me I made the right decision. I would do it again tomorrow. I am sorry to have hurt you. I am. But I did the right thing.'

'You're a *traitor*.'

'Enough,' interrupted Ada.

Jean pocketed the money and pushed his chair back with a discordant screech against the tiles. 'Save your fancy words. I'm not the one who needs to hear them. You owe your apologies to the dead.'

'I don't like the idea of the duc getting any more allies,' said Ada.

Guil was walking her back to the Marais along Rue Saint Honoré and up Rue Avoye. He was always quiet compared to the rest of the battalion but this complete silence was worrying her.

'You were right, this was an important lead to follow.' She elbowed him gently. 'I said you're right, would you like to crow a little?'

He stirred, straightened his shoulders. 'No. I cannot find it in myself to take pleasure in any of this.'

'Well, then, how about agreeing the rest of our plan? It sounds like whoever this ally is, they're at the Lazare prison. So that should be step one. Back in familiar territory.'

'I have the soldier's uniform still,' said Guil. 'I can reconnoitre the area.' Ada wondered what it would cost him this time to wear that uniform. 'You will go back to the duc?'

She nodded. 'If I vanish now it will only look suspicious. And there's value in learning what his experiments mean.' Rue Barbette and her home were a few more streets away. Ada chewed her lip. 'You can tell me what happened, if you want to. If you need to. You know I would never judge.'

They walked the next block in silence before Guil shook his head. 'I do not think I am ready to speak of it. I never … I did not expect to see Jean-Baptiste or any of my comrades again. I thought that part of my life was dead.' At the corner of the Rue Barbette, Guil stopped and unlaced their arms. 'Jean was right. I have too many deaths on my conscience. I—' He stopped himself sharply.

Ada's worry only grew. 'Guil, you know I trust you with my life. Camille trusts you too. Whatever happened, it doesn't define you.'

She reached for his arm but he stepped back into the shadows so his face was hidden. For a moment, she had a sense of him slipping out of time entirely, back to his days as a soldier, scouting battlefields and sharpshooting from concealed vantage points. She saw the ghost of another man, one who had lived with death so closely it had become part of him.

Perhaps none of the battalion really knew each other; they showed each other one face and kept all their others shut away. Even Ada and Camille picked the sides of themselves they were willing to share, kept secrets that had begun to unravel them.

Perhaps none of them really knew her either.

And no one knew what she was truly capable of.

10

Bedford Square

arriages pulled up outside the townhouse, all gilt and gold with fine chestnut mares pulling them. Camille and James were at the back of the group, Al had manoeuvered to take a blushing Hennie's arm, while Phil pushed Lady Harford's Bath chair. They would travel to the river in two groups and take the boat to Vauxhall for an evening at the pleasure gardens. A supper box was booked, and there were to be fireworks. Above the square the sky was tinged dark blue as evening slowly settled on the city.

James thought of Olympe alone in the stables and wondered again if he should try to stay. But Hennie had already climbed into the first carriage and was hanging out of the window, yelling at them to hurry up. He was being watched; it was no use.

Camille paused at the top of the steps, turning away as she started coughing. Her face was too pale still, with a vivid flush to her cheeks and sunken eyes. He could feel how thin she had become when he held her arm in his. A thought struck him: the cough, the weight loss, the fever in her cheeks and the glitter of her eyes. He knew what this looked like. He had been so wrapped up in himself, he'd missed something vital.

'Are you sure you're up to this?' he asked gently. Did she know something was wrong?

'I'm fine.' She straightened, wiping her mouth on a handkerchief – then seemed to notice the red speckles on it.

Quietly, he took it from her and folded it away in his pocket.

There was no truce between them, but it didn't mean he'd stopped caring about her entirely.

Hennie, Lady Harford and Phil pulled away and the second carriage drew up; Al climbed in first, and between him and James they lifted a fragile Camille into her seat.

Before James could join them, the traffic cleared for a moment, and he saw through to the newly planted garden in the centre of the square.

There, as plain as day, stood Wickham, watching him.

James dropped back from the footplate.

Time was up. He'd been found out.

'What's wrong?' said Camille.

'I – nothing.'

Camille cocked her head. 'Is this about that help you needed?'

A passing cab obscured his view and his eyes flicked to Camille. 'Yes. I'll tell you soon – there's something I need to do first.'

Camille didn't reply, gleaming eyes watching him

from the dark interior of the carriage. James shut the door and rapped the side to signal to the driver to leave. It pulled away at a trot to the end of the square, then swung into Great Russell Street.

He'd known it was a matter of time before Wickham came for him.

The only option left was to face the consequences head on.

His tutor's usually dapper dress was dishevelled, his collar askew and frock coat stained at the cuffs, but his eyes were sharp. James knew Wickham to be obsessive, ruthless – he'd proved that when not even Edward's death could sway him from his single-minded dedication to his work. James had also known Wickham wouldn't take his betrayal well. Now, he wondered if he'd underestimated how dangerous an enemy he would be.

In a heartbeat, James ran through the calculations in his head: was Edward here too? Was Olympe safe? Why had Wickham come to his home? Was it a threat? This must be how Camille felt all the time: so many moving parts to track at once, the knowledge that failure meant disaster, death. But Camille wouldn't cower. Camille would make her choice and act.

With a deep breath, he plunged in.

'I wanted to speak to you,' he called across the road. 'I shouldn't have run yesterday. I was overwhelmed and, I will admit, a little frightened by what we did.'

'What could be so frightening about saving the life of your friend? Unless, perhaps, you are not the friend we once thought. Perhaps it would have made things easier for you if I had failed.'

James fought to hold his nerve. 'I would never wish Edward dead.'

'But you would wish us out of your way, hmm?' Outside the operating theatre, Wickham never quite looked right; tucked into a suit, walking the city streets, something of the dark still hung about him. A smell of blood and turpentine, calloused hands that seemed to reach for a blade.

'Sir, I—'

'Oh, don't start lying,' Wickham snapped. 'Edward told me everything. What trusting fools you must think us both.'

'I didn't go to Paris with the intention of betraying you.'

'Lie! Do you want to try again?' All James could see was Wickham's silvery scar, threading from ear to eye. The unblinking way he watched him. 'Drop the act, James. You were working for your father all along, you infiltrated my trust to *steal* from me. Your father wants this discovery for himself, to make his name in the War Ministry. *That's* why he won't fund my research. He doesn't want the competition.'

James felt sick. 'Wait – that's not—'

'I will *not* be bested. This is *my* discovery. *My* life's work. I will not be humiliated by you or your father.' He had grown fiery. 'I like you, James. That's the bitter irony of this, I really thought I could make something of you as a surgeon. Edward likes you too. Did you laugh at us as you wrote those letters, telling us Paris was a bust? Did you pity us for being so gullible?'

'It wasn't like that.' But the words sounded hollow

to his own ears. Wickham wasn't wrong; James had betrayed them and been calculated about it. He'd weighed up his loyalty to his mentor and his friend against his need for his father's approval, and his own craven nature had won. 'Whatever you think I've done, nothing will change my father's mind about you. He won't support your work.'

A spiteful smile split Wickham's face. 'You misunderstand me. I don't want his support. I want him *gone*. I will show him that I am not to be trivialised. I am not to be dismissed. I have power and knowledge, and his life is at *my* mercy, not the other way around.'

Everything came into sharp focus with a rush, the threat in Wickham's words writ large. A week ago, James might have dismissed it as posturing, but not now. Now, he had seen what Wickham was capable of.

'Stop this. My father isn't competing with you. He hasn't seen the girl. He thinks electricity is a fad. You're not competing with *anyone*, so you can leave him alone.'

'Is that so?'

'I swear on my life.'

Wickham hesitated on the opposite curb. 'Oh, well, then. All right. I yield.'

James blinked. 'Really?'

Wickham laughed. 'No, James. You're so good at telling lies I thought you might at least be able to spot one. Not nice to be taken for a fool, is it?'

'I wasn't—'

'I don't care. You've chosen your side, and now you must live with the result. You will not get in my way again. Any of you.' Wickham looked at the house, then back at James and smiled. 'There are so many of you. You cannot keep your eye on them all at once.'

James flew forward, driven by guilt and anger.

Hennie, his mother, his father, Camille – all in Wickham's sights because of James's choices.

'Don't you dare threaten my family—'

A scream, the crash of hooves. James flung himself back just in time to dodge the speeding carriage that had come hurtling round the corner. The driver was yelling at him, horses bucking and rearing in their harnesses. In a single breathless, terrifying second, he saw himself take Edward's place on the operating table. Wickham's next experiment.

He landed on the pavement hard, light and shaky from shock. Someone climbed down from the cab to check on him, but he looked past them with mounting dread.

Wickham was gone.

11

The Vauxhall
Pleasure Gardens

The boat bumped up against the Vauxhall stairs, nestling among countless other ferries that brought people from across the city to this small, glamorous spot on the south bank of the Thames. Camille took Al's hand as they stepped onto the wharf, craning up at the grand stuccoed entrance to the pleasure gardens. They passed between ornately clipped hedges, and then spilled out into the riotous gardens.

On both sides were long curved stretches of chinoiserie pavilions and draped cloth, set for suppers, drinking, tea, illicit liaisons and public spectacle. At the centre was a huge circular building many storeys high, ringed by balconies like tiers of a cake; an orchestra played on the central level, and on the others drunken revellers hung over the edges. Around it a dance floor took up a huge space, countless couples swirling together, and along the fringes were acrobats, jugglers, sword-eaters and strongmen. Beyond, the gardens disappeared into a dense forest, punctuated by follies and ruins, pavilions and benches, and lit by torches as the summer nights grew shorter.

Camille clung to Al's arm. The chaos of excess was overwhelming. A bloody riot or a violent crowd she knew how to handle; this was too alien. All she felt was scorn at these naive, self-assured people, so confident that the world was safe, their lives happy, and all there was to life was celebration.

As their party swept past a display of tightrope walkers and tumblers, the hair prickled at the back of her neck with the sensation of being watched. She shook it off. She was worried about too many things: Ada and Guil in Paris, Lord Harford's suspicion, the 'trouble' James had come to her about. Her mind was full, that was all. No use jumping at shadows.

'What shall we do first?' Hennie was practically bouncing, darting back and forth between them. 'There's the Turkish tent or the rotunda and fireworks soon, and – oh, look! Look! Balloon rides!' She spun back to her mother. 'We must go, I insist upon it.'

Camille tensed at the thought of a hot-air balloon. She had only seen one once, back at the start of the job to rescue Olympe when she had sent Ada up in it to cause a distraction. It had ended badly, with Ada crashing into the very prison they'd been trying to break into.

Lady Harford watched her beaming daughter with delight. 'Of course. We wouldn't want you young people missing out.'

It was only a short wait at the balloon ascent site, and soon they were being ushered into the basket, Molly helping Lady Harford the few steps from Bath chair to bench inside.

Camille felt queasy. 'I – would rather not.'

Al patted her hand. 'All right, old thing. I'll stay on terra firma with you.'

Hennie and Phill hopped into the basket. 'Spoilsports.'

The balloon began to rise; Camille's face upturned to follow it. Was there anything she could have done differently, back at the start of all this? If she'd known the truth about Olympe, would she have turned down the job? Could she have found another way to thwart the duc?

She had sat on the fence between the Royalists and the Revolutionaries, thinking she could play both sides against each other, that she didn't care what happened to the Revolution. Was that really true?

The balloon crested the trees and she lost sight of it.

She gripped Al's arm and steered him away. 'Let's talk.'

'About James?' Al plucked a glass of champagne from a passing servant. The crowd swelled and rolled around them, laughter and shrieks punctuating the cacophony of music competing from every direction.

'Yes. We're so close to getting everything we came for and getting *out* of here I don't want whatever mess he's made getting in our way.' She took a deep breath, despite the catch of her lungs. 'But first, I owe you an apology for earlier. I was cruel.'

He gave her an odd smile. 'Apologies, dresses, crying. English Camille is strange.'

In her flimsy gown and slippers, hair curled and pinned, it wasn't just the pleasure gardens that felt alien. Her own body wasn't hers any more. Al was right. English Camille *was* strange, and she wasn't sure how well she liked her.

'Maybe English Camille is trying to be a better friend.'

'Surely a sign of the apocalypse.'

'Ada said something to me once: that I'm hard on you because I recognise too much of myself in you. I think she's right. You say and do all the things I want to but don't let myself because I'm worried if I do everything will fall apart, and then I wind up angry and jealous because you do it and nothing *does* fall apart, so maybe I'm keeping such a tight rein on myself for nothing.'

'Funny way to be my friend – to apologise, then tell me how much you don't like me.'

'You're right,' she said. 'Let me try again. How are you? That's what friends ask, right?'

'Oh, you know.' He waved a hand. 'Bored, hungry, cripplingly depressed. The usual.'

'Won't you be more bored if you leave the battalion?'

'Oh, certainly. I will have a long, boring life ahead of me. I'm thrilled.'

Reaching the depths of the gardens, they came across a hedge maze, well-tended and over six foot tall. A woman in an owl mask stood at the entrance taking pennies.

'Risk getting lost with your sweetheart, sir?' she called to Al. 'It's mighty quiet inside and no one knows what may go on.'

Al looked mildly ill at the prospect of Camille being his *sweetheart*, but she wasn't paying attention.

She'd felt it again. That sense of being watched.

Halting by the entrance, she scanned the crowd. Had James caught up with them?

Only – no – a shadow darting across the corner of her vision. She spun, tracking its moments – but it was nothing. Just a trailing swag of fabric flapping from a branch.

'Well? Shall we?'

She startled. 'What?'

'Get lost for a bit?' Al gestured to the maze.

Camille looked for the balloon against the night sky, trying to judge whether it had begun its descent. As the last of the red-stained clouds faded and dusk fell, a prickle of stars began to wink to life.

'Weren't you just saying you were jealous of me for being an impulsive, feckless dandy? This is exactly the sort of ill thought-through, self-indulgent thing I would do, so I think it would be good for you.'

'I'm not sure those were the words I used, but...'

Al was already pressing a coin into the woman's hand and she removed the ribbon barring the way. The maze was dense and dark, and entirely unknown.

To hell with it.

Camille stepped inside, and at once the noise of the gardens ebbed.

It was cooler in here, the smell of loamy earth

trading places with perfume and sweat, the gentle rustle of wind in the laurel hedges covering fiddles and organ music. They took the first two turns at random, following the sharp corners and dead ends until Camille had no idea where they had started.

'What would it take for you to stay with us?' she asked, as they paused at a fork in the path. Occasionally, they could hear voices through the leaves, giggles and the panting breath of other attendees wandering the labyrinth.

'This isn't about you offering me better terms,' he replied. 'The battalion made sense for me for a while, and now I'm not so sure it does.'

'We need you.'

'That's sweet.' He patted her hand. 'But, no, you don't.'

'I'm not a charity, Al, I don't keep people around out of the goodness of my heart. If I say we need you, we need you.'

He laughed. 'I think you'll find you *are* a charity, my dear. Helping those in need? Never seeing a proper bloody pay cheque for it? Charity, through and through.'

The maze was getting darker, the passages narrower; she was certain they must be nearing the centre. 'We're your family.'

'My family is dead, Camille. It doesn't matter how many people we save, they'll still be dead, and your parents will be too. It's about time you got that through your thick skull,' he snapped, and for a moment she saw behind his mask of indolence and red wine. Saw the death of hope, the loss that hollowed him. The unravelling.

She saw herself.

Before she could speak, they ran headlong into one of the parties of revellers they had heard through the hedge-walls. Seven sheets to the wind and reeling like boats bobbing in a storm, they brought a moment of chaos, apologies, heels stepping on toes, skirts caught on branches, laughter and noise and chatter, and once Camille had disentangled herself Al was nowhere to be seen.

Bloody typical. Things get difficult and off he runs. She pulled her shawl tighter around her shoulders and considered the path ahead and behind her. Which way had he gone? Was there any point following him? It was a maze, for god's sake; what chance did she have of tracking him down? They could both find the exit and regroup.

Camille strode on, making choices as best she could. There had to be an end. The party carried on here too, wilder and darker, beauty turned to horror. The sharp yapping of two lap dogs fighting. A man pissing noisily into a bottle, grunting and hunched against a hedge wall. A couple locked together in the shadows, like a many-limbed beast, a medical curiosity from the duc's labs, the human form conjoined and distorted.

Heat rose to her cheeks. And worse, a flash of longing: she missed Ada. They had never been apart so long.

What if Ada didn't miss her?

A dark smudge broke the solid line of green hedge

before her, and Camille found the exit. Or, rather, *an* exit. It was not the one they'd come in through. It was blocked by two planks, which she pushed out of the way to step into a dark, forest-like cluster of trees. Rose-strewn trellises blocked either side, so she couldn't follow the edge of the maze back around to the front. There were only the trees, the distant sound of the river lapping its banks, and the moon above.

Surely there would be another path back to the party? It would be better use of time to find that than risk the maze again. Camille walked into the trees.

Her lungs were beginning to bother her, her breathing a little too shallow, that ghost of a fever hovering around her thoughts making them curl and twist and flit away from her grasp. The stars were so bright. A net of silver spread above her; she remembered the way Ada would take her hand and point to each constellation, explain the paths they took across the sky.

All things had an end. Maybe even stars could die.

Her thoughts stopped abruptly.

She heard something.

The crunch of footsteps behind her.

She stopped, and the footsteps stopped too, a moment out of sync. Her heart began to race. The lights of the party were all but gone, even the maze had vanished from view.

Camille gasped. Beneath her feet the ground was cold, her useless slippers so thin she felt every ridge and bump. She strode faster, hating the hitch in her chest, so fast her feet slipped on the gravel, her skirts tangling around her legs, and she tumbled into a clearing.

Once more, the footsteps stopped a moment after hers.

On the grass of the glade, she moved silently, scanning the trees. Her nerves alive with adrenaline as she listened, listened.

But there was nothing. Only the distant sound of voices, and a cold breeze.

At last, she relaxed, and rubbed her hands over her face.

Stupid stupid stupid. Jumping at shadows. What happened to Camille of the Bataillon des Morts, who broke into prisons, jumped off buildings and stormed the guillotine scaffold?

Pathetic.

A scream went up from somewhere distant, the crowd enthralled by a fire-breather or a tumbler perhaps. Camille turned.

And found herself face to face with a dead man.

12

Ada's House, the Marais

The spread in front of Ada was obscene.

It was just dinner for two, her and her father, but the servants brought dish after dish – pats of glossy butter, a large round pie, steaming tureens of soup, and a whole side of salmon swimming in sauce. There was one sop to revolutionary solidarity in the loaf of tough, gritty pain d'égalité served alongside. They sat at either end of the table, dishes and bottles and jugs a barrier between them. It was late; with only a few clusters of candles on the table, the rest of the room was thrown into shadow. Ada picked at her food in a silence, punctuated by the clatter of cutlery on plates, the ring of glassware.

What was Camille doing right now? Had she found James? Ada let herself entertain the fantasy for a moment that Camille had already succeeded in rescuing Olympe and her *real* family were on their way back to her, that they would stand side by side and face the duc together. Instead of Ada alone, stumbling into the unknown.

'How was it today?' her father asked between spooning sauce over his fish. 'What little adventures did you get up to? How were your pupils?'

The lie Ada had told came back to her and she only stumbled for a moment. 'Quite well. They took to the piano nicely and will make good players with some study.'

'I thought you were tutoring English composition?'

'Oh. Right. They asked for a little music too.'

Ada thought about what she'd been doing instead, the research notes she had written up, the study she had made of the duc's work.

'Have you given any thought to what you will do after? I haven't seen that charming young man of yours around recently. I found myself wondering what his intentions were...'

She put down her fork. He really didn't understand her. Even this fictional tutoring was only a distraction from her real job of marriage.

'I thought I might enquire at the university about sitting in on lectures. I understand they are considering admitting female students on an individual basis, though they are not yet intending to grant any degrees.'

Unbidden, the memory of the duc came to her mind, the words he'd used: *talent, invaluable.*

Her father laughed, awkwardly. Poured himself more wine. 'Come, come. Perhaps a lecture or two might make interesting entertainment now, but what of your poor beau? When you marry, you will be far too busy running your own household.'

The thought of Guil sent another flash of guilt

through her. Here she was, comfortable at home, pursuing her passions in the name of doing the battalion's work. And where was he? Courting danger on his own and wearing a uniform that only brought back shame. She shouldn't be enjoying this mission, especially not her time with the duc.

And yet, at times, she was.

She took up her cutlery again, bowing her head as she cut her food into bite-sized morsels. 'I would hope that whoever I chose to spend the rest of my life with would understand my passions and want me to live in a way that made me happy.'

'Yes. Well. Within the bounds of what is appropriate.'

'And who decides what's appropriate?'

Before he could reply, the door opened and the footmen brought in the next service, a large stew put in pride of place in the centre of the table.

Ada let the conversation take a more civil turn. Her father might be frustrating and unable to see beyond the end of his nose, but she knew he did care for her, in his own way.

It was only a shame that he didn't understand her.

She found herself longing suddenly to be back at the duc's house, away from this false propriety and family obligation. She wanted the pen in her hand, the words in front of her full of possibility and challenge, instead of this suffocating tomb.

Her father had started some story about the printing rooms that day and Ada tuned him out, making the right noises whenever he paused. Despite herself, she *was* hungry, so she reached to serve herself a portion of stew. Her fingers closed around the ladle and she yelped. A searing heat met her palm; she pulled back, upending the spoon from the pot and sending a splatter of stew across the tablecloth.

Her father was at her side in a flash, servants dashing for a cold compress, a poultice, another mopping the spill, another at her side offering water. Her father crouched next to her and unpeeled her fingers one by one, until he could see the angry red weal across her skin. He drew in a sharp breath.

'Does it hurt?'

'Yes,' she hissed between clenched teeth. 'Of course it hurts.'

A maid arrived with a jar of honey and a clean cloth, and set about washing, covering and bandaging the burn.

The pain was raw, a shock that rooted her to the chair.

But it had brought a new thought with it.

As her hand was wrapped, she looked at the offending ladle, now being covered in a napkin as the table was cleared. The ladle itself hadn't been cooked – it was the stew that had sat over a flame until it bubbled, then the ladle had been placed inside and carried up. The heat from the stew had carried along the metal and burned her.

It was already known that electricity could move along copper wire in the same way. She thought of Olympe, kneeling on the floor when Dorval had attacked them in the duc's laboratory, how she ran her electric charge into the water so that it flowed across

233

the whole floor. The conductive material didn't just receive the charge; it moved it. It could be generated in one place and felt in quite another. Destruction could be carried out from a distance.

She watched the blistered skin of her palm disappear beneath a layer of honey and cotton bandage.

The duc was trying to harness and transfer an electric charge for a reason, one that would help his cause. She knew too well that his cause was violence. The beginnings of an idea formed in her mind, still shapeless, indistinct. She felt frustratingly on the edge of understanding something much, much larger.

Dinner was over, and she was packed off to bed with a glass of watered-down laudanum and an instruction to rest.

Alone, Ada pushed the laudanum aside. She didn't want to sleep. She wanted to *work*.

From under her bed, she pulled out the books and pamphlets and treaties the duc had lent her. She burned through candle after candle reading until her eyes ached.

In the small hours, as she stretched and yawned, the quiet of the night was split by a yell. Ada started, sending a book sliding off her lap and thunking to the floor. Another yell came, then another, then so many it was like a wall of noise rolling along the street outside.

She wrapped herself in a shawl and went to the window. When she'd returned to her father's she refused to stay in the same room as before, the one he'd locked her in not once but twice. Her new rooms faced the street, a gesture of his goodwill. She pushed back the shutters, and looked down onto a riotous crowd, lighting the darkness with torches, candles, anything to hand. Young and old, men and women, shouting, laughing, dashing forward with excitement.

Ada hung over the window ledge and called out.

'What is it? What has happened?'

A girl paused in the flow of people, and looked up at Ada, eyes alight with glee.

'Robespierre has been arrested!' yelled the girl. 'The Terror is over!'

13

The Vauxhall
Pleasure Gardens

J ames jumped off the boat, tossing a coin to the ferryman, before he and Olympe raced up the river steps towards the pleasure gardens. They couldn't have been far behind Camille and the others, but it felt like a lifetime. Wickham's smug smile replayed in his head, the pure fury he'd seen in his eyes. The way he'd looked up at the edifice of James's family home and vowed to bring it tumbling down.

He'd shaken off his near miss with the cab and gone pelting to stables. Olympe had been there, confused but fine – which had only brought more dread. If Wickham hadn't found Olympe, then maybe he was going after another target.

There are so many of you, you cannot keep your eye on them all at once.

And where was Edward while Wickham confronted James?

His family. Too many moving parts. Too many to protect all at once.

The pleasure gardens would make that job even harder. If Wickham's threats were serious – and James was sure they were – he had a clear run to whichever of James's family he wanted.

Inside the gardens the crowd was thick and raucous, the ground churned to mud. Olympe wrenched out of his grasp.

'Al! It's Al!'

And it was – sloping past was Al, smartly dressed, hands in pockets. He stopped dead, eyes wide. 'Good god, that was even easier than I thought.'

Olympe flung herself towards him. 'Thank goodness you're here.'

He looked down at the bundle of girl in his arms. 'That's what everyone always says.' He quirked an eyebrow at James. 'Er, is this you surrendering? Because if so, can we tell Camille I heroically disarmed you and persuaded you to see the error of your ways? I know you already asked her for help, but maybe you can let me have a bit of the glory.'

James was in no mood for it. 'Where's my family? And Camille?'

Al shrugged. 'Your family are messing around with balloon rides, last I saw. Lost Camille in a hedge maze, which sounds ridiculous but is unfortunately the truth. She'll be around here somewhere…'

The future yawned in front of James. The decision he made now would determine more than his own fate.

It was time he accepted which battles he'd already lost. He stepped back, leaving Olympe with Al.

'Take Olympe with you and look for Camille.

I've got to find my family. There are people after us. Olympe can explain.'

Al's brows drew together. 'James, what have you done?'

He grabbed Al's arm, squeezing too tightly. 'Listen to me. This fight between us, it's over, okay? Whatever I did, it's not as important as keeping everyone safe.'

Al studied him, mouth drawn into a sneer. '*Whatever* you did was pretty awful and no, it's not over. But the battalion doesn't leave people in the lurch. Unlike some others.'

James clenched his jaw. 'Find Camille, then get out of here. And for god's sake – watch your back.'

The three of them split up, Al and Olympe disappearing into the crowd while James peeled off, following the rough directions to the launch site Al had given him. He arrived as the balloon touched back down. Hennie was hanging over the side of the basket and waved enthusiastically when she caught sight of him.

'You took your time! And you missed all the fun.' The attendants opened the basket and Hennie and Phil stepped out.

'What's wrong? You look like you've seen a ghost,' said Hennie.

His family were safe, thank god.

That only left Camille. Alone, lost, and unsuspecting.

His eyes caught on the maze Al had mentioned and saw a path to one side leading to another part of the gardens behind it.

It was a start.

14

The Vauxhall Pleasure Gardens

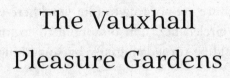

Camille stood face to face with Edward.

Edward, the boy she had seen dragged under the carriage wheels. Edward, the boy who should be dead.

She was rooted to the spot in strange fascination. Sensitive mouth, gently curling dark hair, deep, soulful eyes. And a puckered scar along his temple and forehead, a putrid bruise spreading from it like mould.

How strange to see death standing in front of her. Death, or one of his outriders.

'You're alive,' she whispered.

'In a sense.' His voice was brittle. 'James and Wickham brought me back using electricity, but you know all about that, don't you?'

Camille frowned. 'Wickham – is that James's tutor?'

'Don't play stupid. The game is up. We know James has your electric girl. We know you came here from France to help him betray us.'

'Sorry – *what*? You think I am working *with* James to betray *you*?' She gaped.

'How else do you explain it? We have worked side by side in blood and sweat for the same goal, the same glory for months – and then suddenly he acts as though we are nothing to him. And here *you* are.' Edward circled her. 'I'm disappointed to know his head could be turned so easily by something pretty in skirts.'

Her eyes narrowed. 'You have me so well assessed I'm surprised you didn't realise sooner that James had turned on you,' she said. 'Or perhaps you were never as important to him as you thought. Either way, you say he has the girl and you have … what, exactly?'

'We will have it *all*.' Edward pounced, hands closing around her throat.

They felt like a vice, cold and solid and stronger than anything she had felt before. Immediately her breath was cut off and she panicked, scrabbling at the fingers around her windpipe. Pain screamed through her jaw and neck, stars flashed in her eyes, black growing around the edges. Her chest strained.

She was alone, and she was going to die here.

Ada might never know what had happened to her.

Something slammed into Edward's side, sending him staggering backwards. Not something – some*one*. Camille barely had time to register her shock before he bucked, shaking off the small figure dressed in silk, who was thrown into Camille. Together they toppled to the grass. The figure's veil fell back, revealing a stormy grey face and dark eyes.

'Olympe!' she cried. 'Oh my god, what are you doing here?'

Olympe threw her arms around Camille in a quick hug. 'Less talking, more fighting.'

Edward was already on his feet, hands raised, ready to pounce again. His beauty had gone, and now all Camille saw was his ragged fingernails, bunching muscles, the edge of rot, as though he had come back *wrong*. She yanked up her skirts, grabbing for the knife strapped to her thigh – but Edward had stopped a second before his attack. He was focused entirely on Olympe, a look of recognition dawning on his face. His jaw worked, lips pulling open like the tearing of flesh.

'You again.'

'Yes, me again.' They circled each other, a thread of current playing between Olympe's hands. 'I've come to defend my friends.'

'Your friends scheme and plot and betray. They are not worth defending.'

'What would you have me do? Go willingly with you? I have been the toy of scientists before and found it was not to my taste.'

'If you mean to defend your friends then giving yourself up would be the safest way to save them hurt,' he said. 'We will have you, one way or another.'

Camille hung back, throat and lungs raw like a burn. Edward seemed reluctant to attack. He looked shaken, hands flexing as though in memory of squeezing her throat, as though it had frightened him as much as it had frightened her.

'And yet you hesitate,' said Olympe. 'Perhaps your task is not so easy when it means hurting another person.'

'I don't want to hurt anyone.'

'You just have. On his orders, yes? Wickham certainly has no such moral qualms. James told me about how they brought you back – you are an experiment to him now, that is your value.'

'We are partners.' Edward started forward, indifferent to the blaze of sparks Olympe sent his way – but he did not grab for her.

'Does he still think you're as human as him? Or does he look at you differently? Maybe not directly, but from the corner of your eye you catch him watching you, like a specimen to be studied. Perhaps he asks too many questions, wants to know why you don't feel the cold or why your wounds don't heal. He is re-categorising you, and once he does it will be all too easy for him to ask you to do so much worse. Hurt us today, see what he expects of you tomorrow.'

'Shut up.'

'You and I are not so different. We both know that being human is more complicated than it seems.'

His hand went to the gash on his forehead, to the rubbery, gangrenous flesh.

'I'm not a monster,' he said.

A stillness hung in the air, the stillness of the surface of water, subtle and shivering with tension.

Olympe held out her hand, a swirl of bruise-purple and grey, in a sign of peace. 'Then let us go. Don't become one.'

From the tree line, Al burst out, brandishing a walking stick.

'Olympe! Get back!'

Olympe tried to stop Al – but it was too late. He cracked Edward around the head with the stick, clumsy with nervous energy.

Edward didn't go down.

A low growl filled the clearing, and, with a dreadful slowness, he turned and set his sights on Al.

Al lashed out with the walking stick again, narrowly missing Olympe, who threw herself between them.

'No! Stop! Don't hurt him!'

Edward grabbed the stick before it made contact and thrust it back to strike Al in the chest. He doubled over, gasping. Olympe tried to reach for Edward, but he smacked her aside, flesh meeting in an audible crack.

Camille used the chaos to slide her knife from its holster and pounced, slamming the blade into Edward's side. He howled – but still didn't drop, only reached for the blade and yanked it out.

She scrambled towards Al, hands shaking.

'Good job!' he shrieked. 'Now he's got a weapon!'

The growl became a roar – not of pain, but frustration. Edward weighed the knife in his hand, appraising them in turn. Camille, with her fists raised, Al ready with the walking stick. And Olympe, reluctantly stepping to their side, hands crackling blue.

Olympe edged forward, sparks jumping back and forth between her outstretched hands.

'You don't have to do this. You're more than Wickham's pawn.'

'I'm not a pawn,' Edward spat. 'I owe Wickham my *life*. Your friends may betray quickly, but I am not so fickle.'

'He saved you. That doesn't mean he controls you.' Olympe let the electric field die down, extended her bare palm. 'You make your own choices. My friends taught me that.'

A branch cracked behind them, footsteps in the trees.

Wickham stepped into the clearing, James held in front of him with a knife pressed to his bare forearm.

'Children, children. No more dramatic speeches, I beg you. I have my knife to your friend's radial artery. None of you have studied anatomy, so I shall explain: it runs across the top of the radius bone, and when severed can cause unconsciousness in thirty seconds. Death in two minutes. Not even enough time to go for help.'

James looked ashen. Even Edward had gone still, eyes trained on the blade against his friend's skin.

'He's right,' said James. 'Camille, stand down.'

'But—'

'I'm sorry. I should have come to you sooner.' He looked her in the eye and Camille knew he meant it. She saw an apology there, and something else that frightened her – acceptance.

'This is over,' said Wickham. 'The girl comes with us.'

'Stop it. *Stop* it – I don't want anyone getting hurt because of me.' Olympe started towards them, at the same time that Camille grabbed for her yelling, '*Olympe, no!*'

Wickham loosened his grip on James, licking his lips in anticipation – reached for Olympe—

She made it halfway across the clearing, when a flash of light ripped through the trees, and a bang so loud they all fell to the ground. The metallic smell of gunpowder drifted on the breeze. Camille covered her ears with her hands, blinking in confusion. Another bang, a flash, and gold glowing in the night sky. Fireworks – they must be near the launch site.

Through the light and smoke, in glimpses she saw James on the floor, red smeared down his arm. Olympe in Edward's arms, shocking him to no effect as he carried her off. Wickham hauled James up, threw him over his shoulder and followed.

Camille got to her feet, only for another detonation to rip through the clearing, a wall of noise that threw her down.

There was a moment where she lay, pressed into the grass, cool under her skin and the ringing in her hears like a lament. And then it was over, the darkness closing in.

PART FOUR

Cry Havoc

1

A Supper Box in the Pleasure Gardens, after Midnight

Unnoticed amongst the drunken debauchery of the Vauxhall gardens, two figures emerged from the woods, stumbling and clinging to each other as they staggered across the piazza towards the oasis of a vacant supper box.

Camille and Al weren't the only people looking the worse for wear by this time of night, and their lurching progress drew no attention despite the dirt and leaves clinging to them. Camille's ears were still ringing so loudly the music and laugher was only a distant suggestion of noise. She'd come to with Al's arm around her waist, hauling her away from the firework launch site. Olympe and James were long gone.

The display was still going on, a cacophony of noise and light erupting too close above them. Gunpowder burning her nostrils and chest tight with smoke, she let Al help her into a chair. They needed to go after

Wickham now, before the trail went cold – but she couldn't *breathe*.

'Camille – Cam!' Al was shaking her shoulder as she sank down, head between her knees to fight the drowning feeling. She felt too light, as if she was floating out of her body, dissolving into thought and starlight.

A sharp slap brought her back. Her cheek stung and she and Al stared at each other in disbelief, Al holding his hand out like a strange tool he had never had need of before. 'Did that work? You're not going to keel over on me, are you?'

'You slapped me.'

'You were having hysterics.'

'I was not having—' She stopped, her hand moving to her throat.

Al looked worse than she felt; the little colour he had was completely drained from his face, so that he seemed painted in lime wash and shadows. 'Where's a bottle of whisky when you need one?'

'I don't need a drink.'

'I wasn't thinking of you.'

A waiter arrived and Al sent him away for sherry and oysters, which appeared in short turn. A mishmash of ornate Venetian style and chinoiserie, Ionic columns, Gothic arches and flared scrolls, the garish boxes were little more than rooms, open to the party on one side, with rustic tables and chairs arranged to best view the action. Al poured them both a big measure and downed his in one. Camille sipped hers, feeling the burning line of her throat in contrast to the hitching numbness of her chest.

Al refilled his glass and clutched it between two white-knuckled hands. 'So. What the bloody hell was all that?'

'I ... don't quite know myself.' Camille recounted her meeting with Edward, his resurrection and his suspicion that she and James were working together to usurp their research.

'They resurrected him?' Al looked queasy.

'By all rights he should have been dead. You didn't see him under the carriage.'

'Thanks, I don't need more imagery. He already looked ... gone off.'

'No one has ever survived death like that before, who's to say what's normal?'

'No offence to Ada,' said Al, 'but so far scientists seem an absolute bag of dicks.'

Camille held the glass to her mouth but didn't drink. 'I don't know if it's a miracle or a nightmare.'

'So the duc has an English rival in this Wickham. They must be working on the same sort of research, or why else would they have taken Olympe?'

The words 'eliminate the competition' crossed her mind but she didn't voice them. 'They took James too. This must be the trouble he wanted help with.'

She thought of the flash of red she'd seen on James's arm. He'd been hurt, Wickham had threatened to kill him. Maybe he already had – no, no, she couldn't let herself think like that. Until proven otherwise, James was alive.

She was still so angry with him, but the thought of him dead was like a cold stone weighing her down.

One by one, she was losing everyone she had left. Maybe she really would end up like Lord Harford, alone, surveying the wreckage of her past.

The fireworks had finished and the crowd was dispersing from the viewing area, pouring into the supper boxes and dance floor, wrapped in silk and feathers and lace, chattering and laughing, oblivious to the drama that had taken place so close by.

Al rolled his shoulders. 'All right, stop moping. The way I see it, nothing has really changed. The job is still the same: find Olympe. Only now we're up against someone a bit scarier than your pathetic ex-fiancé. Two people – this Wickham, along with that chap killed by the carriage, but who seems to have shaken it off all right. I suppose there's James too – but it didn't exactly look like he was on their side. It's two against two, at worst. I don't mind those odds.'

He was right, they'd faced worse – though Edward seemed unaffected by Olympe's powers and Camille didn't know what to make of that.

'You're right. The plan is still the plan.' She rested her head on her arms and shut her eyes against all the awful things that would not stop coming. She felt so impossibly bone weary. 'Al. Tell me it's going to be okay.'

'It's going to be okay.'

'Liar,' she mumbled.

He gave her a soulful look. 'I have never uttered a lie in my life, I will not start now.'

Before Camille could say anything else, Hennie appeared from out of the crowd, bouncing towards them.

'Maman, I found them! The beastly things have started eating without us.'

Phil followed Hennie, pushing Lady Harford's Bath chair. Lady Harford clasped a hand to her chest. 'Camille! You frightened us, disappearing like that. I worried you could have been hurt!' Hennie stopped, looking at the mud and leaves clinging to the hem of her dress and frowned. 'What happened to you?'

But before they could answer, the waiter arrived again and seats were rearranged to accommodate the Bath chair, along with more food and drink.

'Where is James?' asked Lady Harford. 'He promised me he would not miss this evening, and yet I have seen him for only five minutes!'

Camille and Al exchanged a look. 'We saw him – he gave his apologies. He had to go.' It sounded unconvincing but she was too tired to think of anything better.

Lady Harford seemed to accept it easily enough, tutting about children neglecting their parents, and soon they were distracted by their meal and Hennie and Phil's breathless stories of the balloon ascent and the contortionist and the quadrille that had gone so fast Hennie had nearly been sick.

As they left the gardens, Camille paused.

Looking back at faux stucco buildings, the dancers, the lanterns, the life and the excess, she felt the spasm of a cough building. The tightness in her chest. The fever lighting her skin.

Dark things lurked behind the lights and laughter. They left, trailing the stench of rot.

2

Ada's House, the Marais

10 Thermidor
28 July

Ada woke early, sweaty and tangled in her sheets. Her hand throbbed like a heartbeat, an exquisite point of pain that wiped her mind blank.

Her maid arrived to dress her, bringing a tray of breakfast. As she sipped at her coffee, her burn was cleaned and redressed. She observed the puckered, shiny skin rising in a bubble in the shape of the ladle where it had nestled in her palm.

The night before came back to her slowly. The shouting crowd. The exultation.

Robespierre has been arrested! The Terror is over!

Quiet dread crept in.

If Robespierre was gone, who next? What would become of the Revolution?

Paris was raw and split open, like a wound not yet scabbed over. Every tussle, every blow would break its fragile skin open again, and the city would bleed.

Her father peered around her door as her maid carried out a bowl of soiled water.

'How's the patient today?'

'Well, thank you.'

'Are you sure you should be up?'

Ada smiled placidly, held her neatly bandaged hand for him to inspect. 'Why, I've had worse from tending fires.'

He took her hand, face drawn tight in concern. Then seemed satisfied. Pressed his hand against her cheek. 'My angel. Such a good girl.'

It was as if their conversation the night before had never happened. Her father was so good at fooling himself.

'Your gentleman caller is downstairs,' he said. 'I wouldn't keep him waiting, you string that poor boy along too much as it is.'

'In a moment, Papa.'

He pressed a kiss to her forehead, then left her to finish her toilette.

Her outfit was already chosen. The reliable grey pelisse over a refined yet sensible dress. On her dressing table lay her tricolore cockade. She had pinned it to her breast every day since – for as long as she could remember. Should she wear it today? Ada thought of the crowd the night before, the glittering hunger in their eyes. *The Terror is over.*

Perhaps – yes. But carefully.

Ada pinned it to her chest, where it could be tucked under her pelisse if required.

Alight with nerves, she went to leave her room

and without thinking, she closed her hand around the door handle. She fell back, nauseous with slicing pain. When it receded, she took the glass of laudanum from the night before and drained it.

She could not afford to show weakness today.

In the parlour, Guil was in lively conversation with her father. He was a better actor than she gave him credit for; seeing him now, there were only the smallest tells betraying the state he was in after seeing Jean-Baptiste. He spoke lightly, but Ada could see his hands knotted behind his back, the tap of his foot on the floor.

She cleared her throat to announce her arrival.

'Ah, good morning, citoyenne.' Guil kissed her hand.

'Good morning.'

She was grateful to see him. He hadn't abandoned her, however much she had pushed him away. However much he was hurting.

Her father grew sombre. 'What news we wake up to this morning. A different world to the one we left last night. Robespierre is no more.'

'Indeed.' Ada hooked her hand through Guil's arm and led him towards the door. She couldn't stand hearing her father give forth on the Revolution. Not now. 'We must be going, I don't want to be late.'

On the street outside, the carriage was waiting. Guil opened the door and held out his hand to help her up.

'Are you ready?'

Ada nursed her burned hand, running a thumb over the bandage. Then she pulled out a pair of thin cotton gloves from her pocket and put them on.

Show no weakness.

'As I'll ever be.'

The carriage crossed the city and outside the windows, Ada watched crowds pull down notices from the Paris Commune, from the Committee of Public Safety. A rotting head was paraded on a spike. In a square, a well-heeled mob turned on a band of sans-culottes. All around, rumours swirled. Had Robespierre tried to shoot himself before he could be arrested? What would the result of the trial be – surely they must convict – but what if they didn't? Who would take over? Who was left?

Paris whirled around the power vacuum now at its centre. The duc was a spider that had waited at the edges of its web, and the city thrashed and tangled itself in his threads. He was already gathering his allies – how much longer did they have to stop him?

'What news from Saint Lazare?' she asked.

Guil shook his head. 'It was chaos by the time I worked my way in. Allegiances were shifting too quickly; no one knows who to trust, so no one would talk to me. The prison was home to any number of Royalist sympathisers, and I witnessed more than one walking free. Whoever the duc was targeting, he will have them by now.'

They passed the Luxembourg and the Au Petit Suisse again, and Ada felt another pang of loss. She wondered what Camille was doing right now. If she would be proud of what Ada had managed, or disappointed.

'I'm sorry,' she said quietly. 'I shouldn't have acted without you, you were right to be angry.'

Guil looked up, eyebrow raised. 'A change of heart?'

She pinched the bridge of her nose. 'Please, don't rub it in. Father was right; we have woken up to a changed world. I don't want to navigate it on my own.'

'You will not have to. We may argue, but I am not going anywhere.' Guil squeezed her hand again. 'Have courage. We cannot falter now.' He hopped out of the carriage a little way before they arrived at the duc's and paused for a moment. 'Remember, you must play the players, not the game.'

The Rue Faubourg Saint Jacques was quiet compared to the city, peppered with carts and foot travellers drifting along the road. The misrule of the city had not reached this far, and the duc's house looked terribly normal. Shutters were open, windows cracked to air rooms. A maid was scrubbing the doorstep. Ada lifted her skirts and stepped down to the cobbles.

It was time.

The duc was waiting for her in his study, facing the window that looked over the orchard behind the house, and westward across open fields. Ada swept in and presented herself.

'Good morning, Monsieur le Duc. Is everything ready for our work today?'

When he turned to her, the look on his face was something she'd never seen before.

Excitement.

'Our work today? Yes. Oh, yes. We have much work to do. Come.'

Together, they descended to the cellar. It was a

full height room, stacked with boxes, wine bottles, empty crates, broken furniture and other supplies. A well-trod path led between the boxes and stopped at a dead end.

Or what looked like one. The duc felt along the edge of the wood panelling, and with a click the wall swung open. Behind, a ragged hole cut into the earth.

'After you.'

The skin at the back of Ada's neck prickled. If Guil could see her now, he'd call every risk she'd ever taken child's play.

She stepped into the tunnel and felt a rush of hot, damp air against her face. The duc lit a storm lamp and followed, sending shadows lurching in front.

'Did you know there are mines stretching all across Paris?' he said. 'Mostly here on the left bank. For centuries, men dug for gypsum and Lutetian limestone, that noble stone that gives Paris its beautiful face. Immense caverns stretch under the Val-de-Grâce, the Observatory, all the streets around here. Twenty years ago, when I was a young man and just beginning to put the pieces of my work together to create Olympe, the Rue d'Enfer collapsed into the mines not far from here. It was then that I discovered these tunnels. This abandoned world.'

Their path sloped down, square cut into the rock face. The walls were covered in a thousand chisel and blade marks, each inch carved by hand, and the floor was clean of rubble. Her descent was all too easy.

'I bought this house, seeing then its value. To have access to one's own private Paris, to come and go unseen, to work in private, the freedom these things grant – essential for the scientific mind to do its best work. Of course, since then Monsieur Lenoir has emptied the cemeteries into the tunnels like a woman throwing a slop bucket from a window. But he barely touched a fraction of the space. And so my reign in the underworld continues.'

They reached a crossroads, the tunnel forking in three directions. One led up, the air cooler. Another had caved in entirely a little way along. The third led down again, a set of broad stone steps cut roughly into the rock. From below came a red glow, and the soft sound of movement. The duc lifted the storm lamp, casting light on the first few steps.

'I am trusting you, Ada Rousset, showing you this realm of mine. You have proved yourself to be quick, to be bold. I hope you are also clever. I hope you understand who can really offer you a future.'

Ada swallowed, her throat dry. 'I understand.'

'Good.' He smiled and led her down the steps. 'Welcome.'

The tunnel bloomed into a large cave, easily twice Ada's height and broad enough to contain a whole laboratory. Storm lamps were strung from cables hooked along the ceiling, and the whole room was warm and humid. Here were the bodies she couldn't find. In jars and stuffed displays, wired skeletons and bristling resin arteries, the laboratory they'd found in the abbey had been replicated. Ada looked around in horror and fascination. How easily she'd been duped by the display above ground.

'I thought you said you weren't trying to recreate Olympe?' she asked, fighting to keep her tone even.

'I am not. But why throw away a strand of research that has been so fruitful? Electricity and the human body are a puzzle I will solve, one way or another.'

'Yes … of course. And is that what you have planned today? The experiment I am to assist you with?'

'Ah, today, today. And what a day it is.' The duc almost seemed to be speaking to himself. He went to the far end of the room and hooked his lamp to a peg in the wall. 'I woke to a world changed this morning. The sun shines on our dear France again. The way forward is clear. The future presents itself to us, fragile and needing protection. Needing bravery. Needing someone to step into the breach and do what must be done.'

Ada folded her hands in front of her, careful to avoid aggravating her burn.

'Indeed. France does need … direction.'

'And with that madman gone, our allies are free again to join our number.'

She stopped breathing. Oh god, this was *it*. The duc caught the edge of a curtain hanging at the back of the cavern that Ada hadn't realised covered another entrance.

'There is someone I think you might be interested to meet.'

He disappeared for a moment, then returned leading someone. Ada held herself still. It was a woman, perhaps in her late thirties, with striking blue eyes and black hair pinned into a messy knot on top of her head.

She wore a dress a good while out of date, but Ada could tell that meant little to her. There were burns and stains along its sleeves, and the hem had begun to fray. But those eyes drew Ada's attention back to her face. There was something familiar in the line of her brows, the tilt of her mouth.

The duc ushered her forward. 'I'd like you to meet my sister.'

Ada reeled. On reflex she curtseyed as the woman crossed the room and offered her hand.

Ada took it, searching her face. Yes – she could see it. The resemblance to the duc was there. This was the person he had been trying to free from prison? Of course – his family would be as important as any other ally.

But there was something more. The expectant way the duc watched her.

Ada placed it just before the woman spoke.

'How do you do? I'm Clémentine,' she said, with a cool smile. 'I believe you have met my daughter, Olympe.'

3

Wickham's Study,
St Bart's Hospital

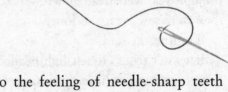

James woke to the feeling of needle-sharp teeth
devouring his arm. He swam towards conscious-
ness, tugged by the searing pain along his forearm,
to surface in a room, storm-dark and lit by lamplight.
Wickham and Edward loomed over him. Something
flashed, and he watched the curved surgical needle
descend, puncture his skin, and rise again, pulling the
two sides of his wound tight. His arm – he had cut his
arm. The thought formed and slipped away. The pain
was too much, like a bell ringing inside his head and he
dry-heaved, before sinking under again.

When he woke again, the bell was gone. The pain
still hummed insistently, but it was confined to his
arm; the rest of him felt mercifully clear.

He sat up and found his feet were bound, and his
good hand tied to the leg of a desk. He recognised
Wickham's rooms at the hospital, the muddled,
overflowing shelves and cabinets as familiar as his

own bedroom. His tutor and Edward were gone, the only proof of his pain-fuelled dream in the neat set of bandages around his arm.

And he wasn't alone. Olympe was at the other end of the desk, trussed up even more thoroughly, a silk stocking stuffed in her mouth. It pulled at his stitches, but he could just about reach with his injured arm to remove it.

'Thank god.' She was tearful, voice hoarse. 'I thought you were dead. There was so much blood and they were sewing for so long.'

'I'm fine,' he said.

It wasn't true. He felt lightheaded and queasy and as he came back to himself his utter failure settled over him like a heavy cloak. Everything he'd done, all the lines he'd crossed to be able to bring Olympe to his father, it had been for nothing. He had dangerously underestimated Wickham. James had known he was a brilliant surgeon who purused his research with an intoxicating fervour; he'd known he *had* to be willing to do things regular people wouldn't in order to break ground in surgical fields. But he'd never thought it would come to *this*.

'Edward persuaded Wickham to fix your arm.'

'What?'

'I think Wickham wanted your corpse, but he gave in.'

James blinked, sized up this new information. He had hurt Edward badly with his betrayal, but his friend had still looked out for him. It was more than he deserved.

Olympe was deflated, close to the girl he had found lost on London's streets only two days ago. 'It's so stupid, I have all this power and I can't do a damn thing to *help* anyone.'

He looked at her bindings, a thin cord around her ankles and wrists. Her hands were gloved, but a seam was coming loose at one finger.

'Yes, you can. Stay still.'

He leaned over again, reaching and reaching with his bad arm, skin twisting and straining at the stitches, to grab hold of the loose thread and pull. With a grunt of pain, he tugged at the seam until it unspooled itself, the two sides unpeeling.

'There. Now you can do something.'

He'd had his own experience of trying to contain Olympe's powers and was thankful to see Wickham had thoroughly miscalculated.

'Do what?'

'Remember what we practised?'

She caught his meaning, a hint of hope in her eyes, and summoned a ball of electricity the size of a farthing. Slowly, it flowed up her finger towards the rope around her wrist. When it made contact, the rope sizzled and an acrid smell filled the air – but it was short-lived. The ball flared and shrank in size and Olympe screwed up her face in concentration, roiling clouds of grey and purple and blue bursting across her cheeks – then she lost control, and the electricity surged, and died as soon as it hit silk.

James looked anxiously towards the door, but no one came.

'Try again. You need to get close enough to burn through the rope.'

She did, two, three times more, but each time no sooner had she got the charge to the rope than it slipped out of control.

Her expression stormed. With a yell of frustration, she let a burst of electricity flare from every exposed part of her body. It caught a nearby jar that shattered, and a diseased heart went skittering onto the floor.

'This is *hopeless*.'

James tensed, suddenly on high alert. The show of power was almost impressive, forceful and controlled like a muscle flexing, but also inhumanly powerful and so vulnerable to her emotions.

'Be quiet,' he said. 'He'll hear you.'

'I don't care! He's got us trapped, what does it matter what he hears?'

'It's not over yet. We have to try and do something. My father—'

'Oh, shut up about your bloody father! This isn't about you, James!' Her hair floated away from her head as a wind whipped around them. 'This is about me, okay? About me getting to live a life that's more than being someone's pet project, some object to be fought over. All these men, so desperate to understand what I am, but what about what I want to know? Do you get that? What it feels like to wonder if you're even human? If you have a soul?'

'You're human, Olympe—'

He'd been so selfish. He'd thought only of himself. Hurt and used people because of course what he wanted mattered more than what other people wanted. The truth broke over him like a wave, the world shifting around until he saw that he stood in a much different place than the one he'd thought himself in.

He had so many amends to make.

'Am I?' said Olympe. 'No one will treat me like it. I am more desperately alone than you could ever imagine. So, *yes*, I am going to get upset. I am going to sulk and scream and you have no right to tell me not to.'

Another wave of sparks billowed across her face, dissipating into nothingness. He looked at her, kneeling on the floor, hair hanging loose around her face, eyes shining with unshed tears, and bowed his head.

She shut her eyes, drew in a few shuddering breaths. 'These bad things seem to follow me. First my mother, then Camille, now you. Sometimes I think I might be something worse. Wherever I go, it's as though I'm some evil charm that tempts men into greed and avarice, ambition and arrogance. I poison everyone around me.'

'That is *not* true.'

'Isn't it? Would Wickham be trying to hurt you if it weren't for me?'

James thought about all the choices he'd made and the justifications he'd given himself. 'What people do is their own choice. You can't blame yourself for it. We all have to war with our worst instincts; if people give in, that's on them.'

A small, hopeful smile crossed her face. 'You really think that?'

'Yes. I've made my own bad decisions, but I can't blame them on anyone other than me. What the duc and Comtois did, what Wickham is doing now, that's never going to be your fault.'

She didn't reply, and the silence in the study seemed loud. Rain spattered against the window, a shock of noise and movement. Night was closing in.

'Okay.'

'Okay?'

'Before, I told you I give up, but I don't. Bad things might keep happening, but I have to believe good things will too. They're worth fighting for.'

James blinked back the sudden tears that threatened.

The door slammed open and Wickham came in, followed by Edward.

'Ah. You're awake. No sudden movements, you don't want those stitches to tear. Edward – set the girl up,' ordered Wickham.

'You don't have to do what he says,' said Olympe, but Edward hid his face as he untied her.

Now James knew Edward had fought for Wickham to stitch his arm he saw something different in his expression – a war in himself, torn between loyalties.

As soon as her arms were loosed from the desk leg, Olympe threw herself at Edward, a cloud of electricity rushing over him; but like before, it ran over him like water, his skin blistering red with jagged lines and he didn't seem to feel it. He threw her slight figure over his shoulder and carried her out to the operating theatre as she hammered her fists on his back.

Wickham paused, hand on the doorknob, to take in James with a small, smug smile. Then shut the door with a click and James was alone.

Bad choices had got him here; only good ones could get him out.

4

The Catacombs

Sometimes Ada thought about who her mother would have been if she hadn't died when Ada was ten, tangled in her bed sheets and slick with fever sweat.

What she would have thought of Paris – if they would have even come to this dreary, angry city. Ada thought about how her face would have matured, when grey would have started to speckle her black curls. If crow's feet would mark her eyes, or laughter lines would arrive first. As the memory of her mother's voice, her smile, the feeling of her arms holding her faded, Ada held on to whatever little things she could.

How her mother would talk to food as she cooked it, or always have a pencil tucked behind her ear. That papaya was her favourite fruit, or that she would put rum in her coffee after fighting with Ada's father. Ada held onto her mother in fragile, crumbling pieces, and someday she knew when she opened that box to look at those memories she would find nothing but dust.

Olympe would have no such problem. Marie-Clémentine de l'Aubespine was sharp, young, standing upright with healthy flesh on her bones. Of all the reactions she thought she'd have on meeting Olympe's mother, anger was not one. It rippled through her like a fire catching. Resentment at how *unfair* it was – how *unjust* – that Olympe's mother was here and hers was rotting in the loamy earth across an ocean. In that moment she wished her dead. She wished all mothers dead, so that everyone could know the pain she felt. It was the impotent rage of a small child. If Ada couldn't have her mother than *no one* should have one.

But now was not the time for that. It was never the time for Ada to think like that. She rolled her anger into a tight pellet and swallowed it whole. Ada was a good girl. Ada didn't get angry or jealous or spiteful. She did the right thing.

She did what was needed.

'How do you do, Madame de l'Aubespine?' She kissed Clémentine's hand.

'No need for such formalities,' said Clémentine, withdrawing her hand. 'My brother tells me you liberated my daughter from that awful prison. I am in your debt.'

'We would have done the same for anyone,' said Ada. 'All we've ever wanted was to help people.'

'Philippe has told me about you. Your mind, your intellect.' Clémentine watched her so closely it was as though she could see through Ada's lies.

Ada blushed. 'I'm nothing special.' She would rather it was anyone else acknowledging her talent, but at least *someone* was.

'Do not minimise yourself,' said Clémentine. 'It is

something I promised myself when I was young, that I would never speak badly about myself – other people would do that enough for me. In my generation, a scientific education was even further out of the hands of women, but Philippe saw my potential and we worked together.'

'You worked together?' Ada asked.

'Has he not explained?' There was amusement in her voice, and Ada had a sudden image of their relationship, the sharp younger sister running rings around her distracted older brother. 'I was his laboratory assistant for many years. As you can see, there is something of a large age gap between us. Our parents passed when I was young, and I grew up as his ward. He pursued his studies, and so I was exposed to science and its methods, far more than any other woman around me. And when Olympe came along, he looked after us both, in a way not many men would have done.'

Ada's stomach turned. None of this made sense. If Olympe's mother had been involved with the duc's research, then surely she would have known about the experiments he'd done on Olympe? Or had it somehow been kept from her? How was that even possible?

She remembered Jean-Baptiste in the Café Corrazza, hands wrapped around his coffee, speaking darkly of the Royalist ally the duc was trying to free.

'How … progressive.'

'Come, it is hardly shocking.' Clémentine circled the room, keeping her gaze trained on Ada as she passed from dissecting table to resined organs to acid vat. 'I am not the only woman to assist the man in their life – through my brother, my discoveries could be shared, known, in a way that would never happen if I was on my own. You must know of Marie-Anne Lavoisier, working with her husband in chemistry, or Caroline Herschel in England discovering half the stars herself, though her brother is the one with the international reputation.'

Ada was lost for words. She felt like she stood in shifting quicksand, sinking deeper into confusion every moment. 'Yes. I suppose this is true.'

Could they have misunderstood everything so greatly? Was the duc only their enemy as a Royalist? No – Ada had read his diaries. She knew what he thought about Olympe: that she wasn't human. So why would Olympe's mother want anything to do with him?

The duc cleared his throat. 'I know this must come as a shock. You will forgive me for not being completely transparent with you and your friends previously. As you know, trust was not something we shared. But now you are with us, Ada, and I have made myself responsible for your education, the realisation of your potential, I knew it would be important for you to meet Clémentine. To see a woman with the same inclinations as you, and understand that my words are not empty. I truly do wish to see you prosper.'

'I see.'

Ada considered the pair of them, trying not to let her lip curl in derision. Two rich, well-connected white aristocrats who thought themselves daring. How inspiring.

But at the same time, she had never met a woman like Clémentine, who spoke off-hand about Lavoisier, who felt no need to apologise for herself.

It was … interesting.

'I am glad to see you freed, Madame,' said Ada. 'I confess I am a little confused. I understand that the Revolutionaries were interested in Olympe and her abilities, but why imprison you too?'

Clémentine turned steely, and for a moment Ada could see the duc in her face entirely. 'Because if they left me free I would not rest until I found her.' Then she clapped her hands together, shifting back to the woman Ada had first met. 'If we are to talk any longer, I insist we sit and do so in a civilised manner. Come into my salon.'

She took Ada through the curtain and into a second, smaller cave room. Here, a camp bed had been pushed against one wall, a desk and chair against another, a wash jug and basin. Piles of books, paper, candles and other supplies littered every available surface.

'A little joke. Much fallen from the salons of my youth, but it will do for now. Philippe, a pot of coffee is in order, and bring in the rest of the chestnut cake.'

Clémentine might only have been out of prison for a matter of hours, but already she had asserted herself. Ada watched in faint amusement as the duc busied himself brewing coffee and bringing plates and cake at his sister's beck and call. It was unsettlingly domestic. In this light, the duc seemed all too human.

'It has been so long since I could live like a civilised person, I find myself overcome with need for simple pleasures, like taking tea and talking,' said Clémentine, sitting on the bed as if it was the finest Louis X chaise longue.

Ada made a noise of assent, hiding her face in her cup for a moment, choosing her next words.

'Perhaps this is indelicate to ask, but if you are Olympe's mother...'

'Ah, you are wondering where my husband is? I will freely admit I did not take one. It is hardly unusual among the aristocratic circles of our youth for men and women to take lovers, to have affairs as suited them. You are an intelligent girl and I'm sure you understand most marriages are more about money and power than love.'

Ada thought of her parents. How her father had danced with her mother on their porch as the sun set. How he'd cried when they buried her. How they buried the man he had been with her.

'So you fell in love.'

Clémentine laughed. 'Hardly. I felt in lust. You understand me, I think? Philippe has told me about your flight from home for the sake of a pretty girl.'

Ada blushed furiously.

Clémentine carried on regardless. 'I enjoyed myself – but suddenly found myself in a way I had not expected to be for many years. Marriage and children would interrupt what I truly wanted to do with my life – to pursue scientific discovery. I was lucky that my brother understood. Many women in my position would be forced to give up their child, but he agreed to provide for us in seclusion in the country. I could continue my work, and our reputation would be secured.'

The question was on the tip of Ada's tongue: had experimenting on Olympe been the price for keeping her? Could anyone do that to their own child? Ada thought about what she would be willing to do to have the life she wanted – what she had already done to escape the suffocating rules set out for her, the sneers and hatred of people who thought she shouldn't be there at all.

Perhaps Olympe's mother was not quite the same as the duc. She hardly seemed beholden to him – if anything, her loyalty was to Olympe, and that could make a big difference to Ada, Guil and their plans. They had thought the duc was gaining an ally – but perhaps they could make her theirs.

She needed to talk Guil.

The duc returned with the coffee and cake. 'I hope you aren't sharing too many of our secrets, my dear.'

Clémentine looked at him sharply. 'Do not imagine you have any control over what I do or say, Philippe. You let those men take my girl, you left me in prison, and you didn't get her back. You speak so grandly, but don't forget I know you.' A moment of tension passed between them and Ada held her breath. The duc broke first, wilting under his sister's steely eye. 'All I want is my girl safe from you petty men,' said Clémentine. Then she turned with a flourish and pulled the chair out from under the desk. 'Ada, you sit here. Philippe, we need more chairs.'

The chairs were supplied and a crate was pulled in to use as a table. They settled around it, freshly poured coffee steaming in front of them.

'Now.' Clémentine leaned in conspiratorially. 'I hear you are planning an experiment today. Tell me everything.'

5

Theatre Royal, Drury Lane

The theatre foyer was packed, so it wasn't hard for Camille and Al to slip away from the Harfords. Arm in arm, they drifted into the churn of London, turning down Russell Street, then past Bow Street with its magistrates' court and the infamous Bow Street Runners, skirting the tumble of fruit and vegetable stalls packed into Covent Garden, all ringed by coffee houses, taverns and brothels.

The Harfords had brought them to a matinee performance of some Restoration comedy or another. It was so hard to find a moment's privacy to talk to Al, they'd had to manufacture one where they could; it would be plausible enough to claim Camille had had an attack of her chest complaint and Al had taken her for some air.

Since their run-in with Wickham and Edward the night before, they had been plotting. Camille had sent Al to gather intelligence, and as they walked, he updated her on what he'd discovered. Wickham was holed up in his usually busy surgical theatre, which was now suddenly and suspiciously shut to visitors and students for undisclosed reasons. Quite how he'd found this out, Al refused to say, only giving her a meaningful look and mentioning something about the Marquis of Salisbury, three bottles of port, the rumoured execution outfit of King Charles the First, and a very, very heated game of Faro.

Slipping down New Street, they crossed Saint Martin's Lane and passed through Cecil Court towards their destination: 28 Leicester Square, home of the late Sir John Hunter and his surgical museum.

They paid the entrance fee and walked through the house, half in dust sheets now the man himself was no longer here to use the study and parlour and day room. While living, Sir John had added and added to his collection until it was too big to contain in one building. He had bought the house that backed onto his and constructed a museum between the two, containing a picture and print gallery, rooms for teaching anatomy pupils, and even a fully working operating theatre. It was said that the corpses for dissection were delivered to him via the back door on Castle Street.

Camille wondered if he and the duc had known each other.

They moved quickly past the gallery and the gravel garden, through the twelve-foot glass doors that opened onto the Conversation Room which housed shelves and cabinets of surgical instruments, pickled tumours and twisted bones, a lamb with two heads bobbing in camphorated spirits of wine, carefully positioned knots of tissue injected with oil of turpentine, then finally, into the operating theatre.

The space was cavern-like, ceiling as high as a church and atmosphere just as hushed. Rings of seating reached to the skylight above and at their centre was an oval slab of slate for the operating table. It had been scrubbed clean as it could be, but it was still stained dark with years of blood.

They couldn't get close to Wickham's theatre without risking being spotted, so this was the second best option for working through the next part of this job.

'The English plays are so dull,' said Al, dropping onto one of the benches and beginning to stuff a pipe with tobacco as Camille circled the space. He looked more pale and pinched than ever. She wondered if either of them slept. 'Léon would have eaten that lead role for breakfast, but look who they had doing it. Some morose sack of bricks with all the artistic feeling of a lampshade.'

'I thought it was all right.'

'You would.'

The theatre was bigger than she had expected, and every inch – the surgical floor, the viewing benches – was exposed. They would never be able to sneak up on Wickham.

'Why are you so grumpy today?' she asked.

'I don't know what you're talking about. I am a ray of sunshine in all situations.'

'I think the theatre made you miss Léon. It's okay, you can say it.'

'You have no idea what I'm feeling.' He tapped his foot. 'You thought Léon was just a fling. You looked at me and made assumptions. It's not. It matters.'

Camille pulled his feet off the bench and sat next to him. 'I miss Ada.'

It was a relief to finally say it. It felt too stupidly obvious a thing to need to put into words, but in reality she knew she'd been hiding from herself, hiding from her feelings. Loving one person so much was terrifying, but it felt better to look it dead on, in all the fear and elation and joy.

Al looked down his nose at her. 'As well you should.'

'I miss Guil too. It didn't realise how much I needed him until he wasn't by my side any more. I miss all the clever things he said, the way he saw through me, always told the truth whether I wanted to hear or not – I miss all of us together.'

'Not tempted to stay and live the easy life with the Harfords paying your way?'

'You know I'm not.'

'More's the pity we can't swap places. I quite like the idea of leeching off some dim, rich family. Such a shame my family didn't let me do that.' Al clamped the pipe between his lips and fumbled for a light. 'Instead I watched their heads plop into a bucket like horse manure and I get to treasure that piece of trauma for ever.'

He lifted the flame to the pipe and a museum curator rushed over, wringing his hands. 'Put that out at once, don't you see the signs?'

Camille looked at the notices the man was pointing

to. *Caution. Highly flammable liquids and objects.* Interesting.

'Which bits in particular are dangerous?' she asked, with as much innocence as she could muster.

'Why, all of it! The preserving fluids you see. Alcohol, turpentine, all of it as good as gunpowder. We must be extremely careful to protect Sir John's collection, so I request again that you put that out, or exit forthwith.'

Grumbling, Al dampened the flare and returned the pipe to his pocket. The curator left.

But Camille's mind had latched on to something. An idea blossomed. 'I know what we can do about Wickham, and I need your help.'

'Please,' said Al coldly. 'Don't pity me. You've never really needed my help, don't pretend you do now just to make me feel better.'

'I'm serious. You put yourself down, but the battalion couldn't do what they do without you – you found out where Wickham was.'

'I'm good for gathering gossip. That doesn't make me like the rest of you.'

A small party filtered into the theatre, squealing at the blood caked into the operating table. Camille dropped her voice.

'I know what you're feeling. I know what you went through because it happened to me too, so don't tell me I'm taking pity on you.' She shut her eyes, letting the past come back to her. 'It's as if you're standing on a cliff edge you were never aware existed, but now the mist has cleared and all you can see is this yawning

282

void, above and below. There is no one older to tell you what to do, no path to follow for life – and worse, there's nothing now between you and death—'

'If you *know*,' he hissed, 'why won't you leave me *be*? I don't want to do this stupid job any more, I want to lie down in the street and never move again. I don't *care* about this job. I don't care about *anything*. Save Olympe, don't save Olympe. Revolution, monarchy, I don't give a *single flying shit about any of it.*'

She held his arms, turned him round to face her, and looked him in the eye. 'I know, Al. I *know*. I'm going to say something and you're not going to like it, but I think you need to hear it.'

He pulled away and folded his arms, waiting.

'You want to lie down and die with them but you *cannot*. You family is dead. All of them.'

'No shit.'

'But you aren't. At some point, this pain will ebb and when it does you'll want your life there waiting for you. So I won't let you throw it away, all right? You don't like me, but you don't have to because we're family. That's how it works. I don't always like you, but I do always love you. And it's because I love you that I'm telling you this. The only meaning I ever found in losing both my parents is this: they are dead, and I am not, and that's that. I have a life to live and they don't.'

'What exactly is your point? Making me cry in public?'

'The point is: what are you going to *do* with your life? Exile yourself to England and mope around until you end up in debtors' prison or dead of drink? Or are you going to stay with the people who care about you, and do something *goddamn worthwhile*? Stop acting like you're dead already, because you're not, and we need you.'

Al blinked furiously, twisting away from her, taut as a bowstring.

'I really hate you, you know that,' he said.

'I know.' She rested her hand on his arm, the closest to affection she could muster.

'You're just the worst. Ada should leave you immediately.'

'I know.'

'And you should get boils. Big boils all over your face so you end up pickled as a medical specimen for everyone to stare at and be horrified by.'

'Absolutely. The biggest boils.'

He turned abruptly, and squeezed her in a tight hug, mumbled, 'Thank you,' into her neck – then let go and smoothed his hair down, looking for all the world like he'd never experienced a negative emotion in his life.

Camille blinked back the tears that stung her own eyes – how often did she really let herself think about the death of her parents? What it had done to her? – and joined Al in the illusion that things were okay.

'So. What is it you need from me? Other than fashion advice. That dress really is ghastly.'

Camille grinned and leaned forward, ushering him into the conspiracy.

'I know how we get in – but how we get out, that's where I need your expertise.'

She explained her plan and a grin spread slowly across his face.

'Oh, I know *exactly* what we need.'

6

The Catacombs

The slab of raw and bloody muscle in front of Ada twitched once, twice – and then nothing. The duc swore and stopped cranking the electrostatic generator.

In the cavernous main room of the duc's underground laboratory, an experiment had been set up. Storm lamps were gathered in a cluster in the centre to illuminate the dissection table, which had been covered in a sheet. Across it had been placed a series of muscles taken from the cadaver Ada had seen when she first arrived.

There was a long, sinewy stretch of arm, shoulder, a hunk of thigh and even the heart, closest to the generator. They had wired them together in a circle, in a mirror of the experiment Ada had seen at the Théâtre Patriotique a month or more ago, where audience members had joined hands onstage and had an electric current passed through them.

The principle here was the same: what were the effects of running a current through flesh? They had begun with a single piece hooked up to the generator, then added more and more – and had seen the effect lessen the more they added. The muscle closest to the generator always pumped frantically, in slick squelching spasms, the muscle wired up after it flexing and rippling. But the further they were from the generation of electricity, the less they responded.

The duc strode the length of the room, rolling a glass paperweight in his hand. 'The electricity is leaking somehow,' he muttered to himself. 'Through the material it lies on, perhaps? But when we insulate the surface, there is no electrical effect. They cannot all be receiving the same charge if the reaction of the deltoid is so much weaker than the heart.' He stood at the far end of the table, observing his macabre display. 'But how to get the same charge to pass through each piece simultaneously?'

Clémentine sat in a corner of the room, taking notes, an arm slung casually over the back of the chair. 'Oh, Philippe. Always biting off more than you can chew.'

The duc gave her a cool look. 'You are free to offer some input if my mistakes are so risible.'

Clémentine kept her amused gaze on him, then picked up her quill again and made a note. 'Don't mind me. I'm only the clerk today. Perhaps your charming assistant has a thought? You did ask her here for a reason.'

They both turned to Ada, who flushed at the attention.

'Well?' asked the duc. 'Do you have something to add?'

Ada shifted her weight, eyes darting between the elements of the circuit, the glistening slabs of raw flesh. She had almost too much to say. 'I burned myself on a soup ladle yesterday.'

'Fascinating,' said the duc dryly. 'Let's move on—'

'Hear her out,' said Clémentine. 'You might be surprised.'

He sighed, then gestured for Ada to continue.

Ada worked a little spit into her dry mouth.

'I was burned because the heat from the stew had travelled. Really, the heat from the fire had passed into the stew, then up the handle and finally into my hand. We've all encountered something similar. Perhaps the problem here is that we are trying to force the current to move in a way it doesn't want to, when what we should do is let it move the way it does naturally, like heating up a ladle. Think of when you touch a metal handle in cold weather, and the electric charge jumps naturally from you to it. Think of lightning leaping to the ground.'

He frowned. 'What are you suggesting?' He was paying full attention now, and even Clémentine had stopped eating her apple.

'What if instead of joining the … the *pieces* together, creating multiple points for electricity to leak, you make only two points – a conductor above that you run a current through, and a conductor below. A floor and a ceiling. Let the electricity complete the circuit itself. Let the spark jump to all of the objects at once.'

Ada finished speaking, realising she had run away with herself. The duc and Clémentine were both staring at her. A look of excitement spread across the duc's face.

'Of course, of course. Complete the circuit all at once.' He crossed the gap between them and grabbed her shoulders. 'Ada Rousset, you are brilliant.'

A warm flush of pleasure flooded Ada. The words might be coming from the duc, not her father, but *oh*, was that not the very thing she had longed for? To be recognised.

And was it really the wrong person, if he was the only one to say it?

L'Odéon

Guil was waiting for Ada at the rendez-vous they'd arranged the day before. While Ada was working with the duc, Guil would wait at the same time each day near the old Odéon Theatre that was halfway between Ada's father's house in the Marais and the duc's on the outskirts of the city, only a few streets away from the battalion's ex-headquarters above the café Au Petit Suisse.

When they broke for lunch, Ada invented an urgent errand and slipped away. An emergency cord of sorts; if things started to go south she had a reliable way to get back-up. A new sign had been raised above the entrance, naming the theatre now Théâtre de l'Égalité, recently reopened and performing 'par et pour le peuple'.

This time, Ada lost no time running through everything that had happened since she arrived at the duc's that morning. The secret laboratory in the catacombs, the twisted experiments and, most importantly, the appearance of the duc's sister – Olympe's mother.

Guil let out a low whistle. 'Perhaps we should have guessed that the "important person" the duc wanted would be connected to Olympe.'

'What should we do? All Olympe ever asked of us was to reunite her with her mother. She trusts her.'

'But the duc's *sister*—'

'I know, it's hard to understand. Maybe she didn't know what was going on?'

'Ada, you are not that stupid.'

She sagged. 'I know, I know. Let a girl hope.' From her reticule, she pulled a lace fan and wafted too-warm air over her face. 'Perhaps if we're her means to be reunited with her daughter, then she will side with us…'

In that moment, their choice felt impossibly daunting. Here they were again, trying to work out how to protect Olympe – and protect the city, France, the Revolution, even – and every path was murky. How easy it was to see the right thing to do from afar or with the distance of time. How much harder when you were pressed up close against it.

'You're the one who has met her,' said Guil. Ada had never heard such a note of uncertainty in his voice. 'Do you think that likely?'

Ada shook her head. 'I am not quite sure what to make of her.'

A moment of silence yawned, both were frozen by the enormity of the decision that lay before them.

'I should go back – before the duc gets suspicious.' Ada chewed her lip. 'We haven't spoken about Robespierre's trial.'

'Indeed. I saw the crowd storm the Hôtel de Ville and drag him out. He looked in a bad way.'

'What do you think is going to happen?'

'I don't know.' Guil pulled a cheap sailor's watch from his pocket. 'The trial should almost be over now. I do not see how he could be acquitted, not after everyone he has sent to the guillotine.'

'But then who takes his place?'

The answer hung in the air: no one.

And anyone who dared try.

'A power vacuum is a dangerous thing,' he said, that mask of stillness back again. She wanted to take his arms, shake him, tell him it was okay to feel whatever it was he was feeling, that she would *listen*. But she knew that couldn't be forced.

He offered her his hand as she climbed the step up to the cab they had hailed and she paused, looking around at the people, the wilted swags of tricolore bunting. 'I wonder how history will look back on this time? Will it all seem so obvious to them when it's laid out in a line? Right now, it feels like mud; anything could happen, and barely any of it good.'

On the way back to the Faubourg Saint Jacques, Guil escorting her a while longer, they passed through familiar ground – and then there it was outside the window. The Au Petit Suisse, looking the same as the day she'd last set foot in it. On an impulse, Ada stopped the cab. Guil tried to speak to her but she waved him off. 'I only need a minute.'

Pulling out the key to their rooms, she ran her thumb over the shape that had meant home for months. She had kept paying the rent quietly from the allowance her father gave her, but she wasn't sure how long she could keep it up. She always had the key in the pocket tied under her skirts. Whatever happened, she would carry this piece of home – of her other family – with her.

Discreetly, she let herself into the cramped courtyard, then wound up the stairs to the battalion's rooms. The last time she'd been here was before they'd gone to the duc's hideout in the abandoned abbey. So much had happened since then, and the Ada who had left this place was not the Ada who came back.

The wet, warm weather had swollen the door in its frame and Ada had to give a shove with her shoulder to push it open. Inside, the air was musty. Motes danced in the light, swirling around a knocked-over chair, a water jug evaporated dry. The detritus of their old life abandoned.

She tried not to look too closely.

In her and Camille's bedroom, she kneeled by the bedside table and opened the drawer. Tucked in the back was a handkerchief knotted tightly and she could feel from the weight that there was something inside. She undid the knots and let the silk unfurl like a blossom. Nestled in the centre was a pair of emerald earrings: her mother's. The last real thing she had of hers.

Clémentine was not an easy person to figure out, but Ada *did* understand what it was to be mother-and-daughter, separated. What she would have endured to get her mother back.

What Clémentine might have done to keep her daughter with her.

Ada re-tied the handkerchief and slipped it in her pocket. As she was about to leave, her eye was caught by something else, a glint in the drawer. She pushed aside a torn stocking, a candle stub, and pulled out a gold locket hanging on a chain.

Oh. Camille's locket. Inside, she knew there were two miniatures of her parents. Ada was surprised she hadn't taken it to England.

Maybe she hadn't wanted the reminder of France, of everything painful in her past. Ada wondered how easy it might be for Camille to forget her.

Out of sight, out of mind.

Maybe she didn't know Camille as well as she thought.

Ada dropped the locket back into the drawer and slammed it shut.

Outside, the sun broke through the clouds, sending a blast of heat. Guil was waiting by the carriage. Ada paused, making a show of fanning herself before getting in.

'I've decided what we should do.'

'And?'

'Robespierre is gone; Royalists are *everywhere*, it's not just the duc. A coup is coming, we both know it. The Revolution has already fallen; they're just waiting for someone to announce the death.' She steadied her nerve. 'No fate. No destiny. Everything is a choice – remember? So we make the only choice we have: we trust Olympe's mother. We tell her we can reunite her with Olympe and ask for her help. What else can we do?'

Guil's expression was unreadable. 'I'll follow your lead.'

She wanted Guil to say something comforting. But he was silent, and the carriage pulled away, leaving him stranded, a solitary figure fading behind her. She thought of him walking north with his old *demibrigade* from Spain towards the Vendée, orders to rain destruction weighing him down. She wondered when his decision to desert had been made, whether it had come quickly or crept up on him slowly over weeks. Either way, his leaving only took a moment.

Ada sat alone, fan gripped tightly in her hand. She could feel the lump of her mother's earrings in her pocket.

She would do what she had to.

Whatever that meant.

7

Wickham's Study,
St Bart's Hospital

Wickham let himself into the study, drying his hands with a cloth. James's head snapped up to track his movements across the room, assessing his enemy.

The events of the past few days hardly seemed to have left a mark. Wickham's rich brown hair was long enough he could tie it back in a cue, a style left over from his time as a surgeon in the Navy. He was dressed in rolled-up shirtsleeves, his waistcoat hanging open, but somehow he still commanded the room; the tense, uncontrolled man James had squared up to the day before was gone. After all, he had won. Olympe was his, and James was at his mercy. Once, James had found his presence inspiring. Now he knew what Wickham was capable of, James saw the cruelty in his authority, the violence in the strength of his hands.

'Here, take a look at this.' Wickham tossed him a preserved resin liver with a strange growth attached to its side. James caught it awkwardly with his good arm. 'Cut that out of a man stationed in St Kitts in '82. Seemed perfectly healthy, until the day he dropped dead. Captain had me autopsy the body in case there was something on board the ship killing the men. Surgery on ship is more often a saw and a bucket of pitch while the guns fire, so I leaped at the chance. Turned out to be a massive haemorrhage in his brain. But I found that while I was rummaging around. Do you know what that growth is?'

James frowned, turning the liver over in his hand. It was a strange echo of their past tutorials – Wickham lecturing on some point, James taking hurried notes or holding a magnifying glass over a specimen. Wickham thought him no threat, he realised. This world was his world, and if he wanted to stop a moment to elaborate, show off his intellect, then it was his prerogative to do so.

'A cancer, perhaps?' said James.

'You'd think, but no. Look a little closer.'

He squinted at the hideous mass of swollen flesh. It looked like nothing, and then at once it came together in his mind like a trick-eye puzzle.

'It's a person. I can see limbs.'

'Bingo.' Wickham clapped his hands. '*That* is the man's twin. Died in the womb and was absorbed into his body. He lived his entire life not knowing he carried inside him the husk of his unborn brother.'

James felt sick. 'How fascinating.'

'Isn't it? The human body is a marvel. We know so little about it, or what it's capable of. We are explorers,

James. As surgeons, we hunt the dark interior to uncover hidden treasures.'

What had Olympe said? *I'm not a resource for you to plunder. I know that's the sort of thing you people do.*

James eyed the liver. 'A conquest.'

'Of course. We strive, we struggle, we win. To the victor the spoils.'

James had seen Wickham in this triumphant mood before, when the three of them had made some breakthrough; he liked it less now that it was Olympe strapped to the dissection table.

'Tell me, so I don't have to sit here wondering about my fate: what's your plan? Kill me so I can't steal your secrets?'

Wickham took a dented metal tray and began to load it with tools and pieces of equipment. 'Perhaps. I have done worse in my life for less. But it is no longer you that I'm concerned about.'

'My father—'

'Your father has stood in my way for too long. He has dismissed and belittled me, and so many others, time and time again. If he encounters an … accident, then I don't think I am the only one who would be pleased.'

James felt the hair at the back of his neck prickle. 'What about Olympe? You've demonstrated your theory is true with Edward, what do you need her for?'

Wickham paused with a trepanning bore in his hand and laughed. 'What do I— You really do lack ambition, James. What *won't* I need her for? Think of the possibilities – if nothing else, now I have a constant source of power I can truly begin to discover the potential of electricity. No one will be able to deny my legacy then.'

'Killing the competition doesn't sound like a *glowing* reputation to foster.'

'Oh, stop being so sanctimonious. Men who make history don't often make friends. If you have the strength to do what it takes, then glory can be yours; a legacy that will outlive you for generations to come. If you don't … well…' He looked at James, tied and prone on the floor, the bandages fresh over his wounded arm. 'I would be doing a service to science and progress to eliminate obstacles in my path.'

James thought for a moment about the Revolution. About Robespierre and the guillotine, about the duc and his work. About his own father, deciding which men to send to die in battle. About Camille, putting her battalion in danger in the hope of saving people.

'The ends justify the means,' he said softly. 'Like using Edward for your test.'

Wickham held his gaze, the light in his eyes replaced with something of that frightening coldness James had seen outside his father's study a handful of days before – before this all went so wrong.

'There, you grasp it now.'

He had grasped it long ago.

A few months before, he would have said the same. Now, he didn't know what he thought.

James fell silent as Wickham gathered the last of the things he needed for whatever he had planned for

Olympe. It was raining incessantly, rattling down the windows and misting the insides of the panes.

Wickham selected a long, thin blade, and held it to the light as thunder rumbled.

'Now, where to begin?'

8

Paradise Lost, a Gambling Den in Covent Garden

Camille placed her chip onto the Faro board and tried not to glance at Al. He was sitting beside her at the green baize table, bet already placed and his snuffbox attracting more of his attention than the other players taking turns to set their chips.

She was sure he was cheating, but she hadn't the first idea how. The board had a suit of cards stencilled onto it and bets were placed by laying chips on the number or face card you thought would be drawn. The banker pulled his two cards from the top of the deck; first the losing card – the Six of Spades this time – which he placed to the right side of the dealer's box, and then the King of Diamonds on the left – the carte anglaise, the winning card.

Al looked up long enough to accept his pay-out from the banker and push his stack of chips onto a new position on the Faro board, before going back to his conversation with one of the men crowding around the gaming table. Camille frowned. She was sure Al's chips had been on the Queen, and yet there they were, on the King to win.

Her own chips lay on the Three – not a winning bet, but not a losing one either. She had the choice now to swap location or try her luck for another draw of the cards. She hesitated, finger resting on the scant three chips she had bought in with. She wished Ada was with her; she would have calculated the odds in her head already and have an entire game plan. Camille never felt so stupid as when Ada wasn't there and she had to use her own intellect.

A mixed pang of longing for the comfort of Ada's presence, and the sting of knowing she wasn't good enough for her distracted Camile from the betting for a moment, until Al made his move. He had amassed a fortune in chips, a small stack in play now positioned on the Ace, but most heaped in front of him like a dragon's hoard. They were halfway through the deck, but they had already gone through three of the Aces – it didn't make sense as a bet, but he seemed entirely unconcerned. There was more than just money riding on the bet; it had been nearly twenty-four hours since she'd seen Olympe and James dragged off by Wickham and Edward, and the longer they took to rescue them, the more time there was for something awful to happen. Given free rein, she didn't know how far Wickham would go.

The dealer called time, and Camille left her chips where they were. At the other end of the oval table, their quarry, a dandyish young man with thick chestnut curls brushed into a quiff, frowned intensely at his chips. He had only two left. At the last moment, he tossed them on the Three, along with Camille's. The dealer pulled the cards – the winner's card was a Ten; the loser, a Three. Camille and the mark's chips were collected by the banker. Al, safe on the Ace, leaned over to pour the man another drink.

'Buck up, Malvern, some of us are simply born winners.'

'And some of us are born losers, I take it?'

Al smiled blandly. 'If the shoe fits…'

The mark was Alastair Malvern, Viscount of somewhere Camille had no interest in learning about, and regular patron of the gambling house Al had been making himself acquainted with since their arrival in London. With no membership of a gentlemen's club, Al had happily ensconced himself in the seedier gambling dens and backroom drinking clubs that littered the city.

Paradise Lost was a club that touted itself as catering to the finer gentleman, who wanted to lose their fortune in a room that had been cleaned at least once in the past decade and where the brandy was almost entirely made up of real brandy. Camille thought it looked like the fever dream of some designer who had never encountered the concept of taste. Tucked above the stately colonnades of Covent Garden, the rooms were decked in gaudy silks, rugs as thick as her fist, smoke-blackened paintings reaching to the ceiling, and mirrors everywhere, so the sweaty, undulating mass of patrons was doubled.

They had waited until the Harfords retired, weary from the pleasure gardens the night before and the matinee that afternoon, then Camille had borrowed a set of Al's breeches and the two of them had climbed out of her bedroom window and made their escape through the mews. Al had spotted Malvern immediately and button-holed him in a game of Faro, where he proceeded to haemorrhage cash as if he was allergic to being wealthy.

'Lend me some iron, will you, Ravenscar?' Malvern asked the man beside him.

'Will I hell. I'm hardly flush in the pocket myself, dear boy, you owe me for enough. I've no interest in throwing good money after bad.' Ravenscar quit the table.

'Tell you what,' said Al, topping up Malvern's glass again, 'my friend and I are having a pleasant time, so I'm happy to make a proposal to let you try to win some of your money back – I do seem to have rather a lot of it in my lap. I hear you've come into some sort of whizz-bangs from abroad. I'm having a party and they're just the sort of thing to make a mark on the social calendar.'

'Oh – I—' Malvern tugged at his collar. 'They're not mine, exactly. My father imported a sample…'

'Don't play coy, I saw you demonstrate one for Old Rumpy in the smoking room and nearly singed his eyebrows off. I know you have a supply on you.'

'Maybe I do.'

'Stole them off the old man, did you? Worried about going back empty-handed? I'd be more worried about going back without a farthing on you.'

Camille thought Al might have pushed it too far; the man looked genuinely anxious at the mention of his father. The memory of blood on James's arm, Olympe's terrified expression as Edward dragged her away, flashed across her mind. They couldn't mess this up.

The Faro dealer had finished paying out from the last round and was calling for last bets before he drew again. Malvern made a snap decision and held his hand across the table to Al.

'Deal.'

Al shook his hand, then tossed him a chip to stand in for his wagered goods. Malvern agonised for a minute while Al placed his own bet, positioning a stack on the Jack, along with a hexagonal copper token that Camille had twigged indicated a reversed bet – if the Jack was pulled as the losing card, the token would flip the result and make it a winning bet; if it was pulled as the winning card, the token would make it a losing one. Malvern, a desperate look in his eyes, copied Al's bet, placing his one chip and his copper token on the Jack.

In the jostle of players reaching to place their bets, Camille hardly paid attention to where she dropped her last chip – either Al was being incredibly clever, or incredibly risky.

Knowing Al, it was probably both.

The dealer pulled the first card – the banker's card, the losing card – and it was the Nine of Clubs. She leaned forward, eyes trained on the dealer's fingers plucking the next card off the deck. Lifted, turned and placed down for all to see: the Jack of Hearts.

Malvern went pale. He had reversed his bet. The

Jack would have won him everything back; instead, he had lost it, and the firecrackers.

'Tough luck, old thing.' Al scooped his chips into his hoard, along with his new pay-out.

'Hang on a minute.' Malvern frowned.

Camille had to bite her tongue to stop herself from smiling. The copper token Al had seemed to place had inexplicably vanished, making his bet a winner. In the confusion of the crowded table she hadn't seen him do it, but the result was the same.

'You're cheating! You should have lost too!' Malvern exclaimed. 'You coppered your bet, I saw it.'

'I don't know what you mean,' said Al, eyes narrowing. 'And I don't like your accusations.'

'Where's your copper, then? I've seen men like you have the damn thing on a wire so you can move it about like a toy – I demand you show it to me.'

Al stood up from the table with more drama than was necessary. 'How dare you, sir! An insult!'

'So you claim, yet you do not show me proof otherwise.'

'I have nothing to prove to a deluded man that far into his cups. But I shall humour you.' With a small audience now paying attention to the brewing fight, Al presented his copper token and threw it down for Malvern to examine. 'Do you see a wire?'

Malvern faltered. 'No – but—'

'Then I wait to hear a retraction of your accusation forthwith, or I shall be forced to demand satisfaction, sir!'

'Now there's no need for that.' Malvern threw the token back at Al. 'I withdraw my words.'

The crowd dispersed, denied the spectacle of a duel, and Malvern led them to a quiet corner, swaying with drink and entirely subdued.

'Take your damn firecrackers.' He pulled a paper packet from his jacket and thrust it into Al's hands. 'Come for some other fool next time.'

He sloped off and Al grinned in triumph. 'Another man ruined at the card table. What a tragic story.'

'Good job.' Camille looked at the small packet, so innocuous. 'They'd better work.'

'They will, just aim them at the right thing.' He looped their arms, tucking their spoils away. 'One more for the road? Oh, don't give me that look. All right, all right, I'm getting my coat.'

They left the club and hired a waiting sedan chair to run them across the city, along the Strand and Fleet Street.

'Out of curiosity,' she said, as the sedan chair lurched in time to the chairmen's gait, 'how *did* you move the copper? I saw you place it.'

In the dark of the box, he smiled and produced the token from his pocket. Only this one had a fine thread dangling from it. 'He was right. I cheated.'

At St Paul's they turned north up Old Bailey and Guiltspur Street, until the lofty pediment of the gate to St Bart's Hospital drew into view.

Camille and Al stood side by side in the deserted night-time street.

Inside, who knew what horrors they might find. Perhaps they were already too late; perhaps Wickham had already strapped Olympe to his dissection table and started experimenting. Camille had never tried to pull off a rescue with only two people. Given the choice, it wouldn't have been Al by her side. But maybe she'd been wrong about him – he'd proved his worth more than once. Al was who he was. At some point, either she trusted him or she didn't. She thought she'd made the right call.

Tonight would put that trust to the test.

9

The Operating Theatre

Wickham had decided against leaving James unsupervised, so he was bound to the lecturer's chair a few feet behind the operating table. Olympe was tied down on it in the same way as he had seen so many patients before. He was glad he was by her feet. He couldn't bear to see her face.

The storm had blown in loud and fierce; flashes of lightning illuminated the theatre like day, throwing lurching shadows up the rows of viewing platforms. Edward looked worse in the poor light; the grey had spread from his fingertips, discolouring his wrists, and James noticed two of his nails torn from their beds. As if his grip on life was slipping.

The wrongness of what he and Wickham had done – turning Edward into *this* – hit James again. They should have let him die with dignity; instead, Wickham had made him into another medical curiosity, like the strange things floating in jars in his study. Wickham had said Edward would have done the same if their positions had been reversed, but James didn't think that was true any more. Edward was a far better friend than he'd ever been. Now he was running out of time to make things right.

Edward had taken the tray of equipment and was setting up the Leiden jars that stored electricity alongside the table, with their trailing wires and rubber insulation mats. Wickham had disappeared into his study for long enough to make James even more nervous.

'Why are you doing this, Edward?' Olympe asked.

'Don't talk to me.'

'No, I think I *am* going to talk to you. You have decided to hold me against my will, so I would like to know why.'

'This work is my life. Why wouldn't I do whatever is needed?'

'Because I don't think you're like him. You feel loyal to him but you *are not him*. I understand what it is to have little family other than the one you make for yourself,' she said. 'Do you not see that Wickham is unhinged? He's *kidnapped* people.'

Absentmindedly, Edward touched his fingers to the unpeeling stitches on his forehead.

'I owe him my life,' he said. It sounded like something he had learned by rote. And that disturbed James most; all Edward's curiosity and questioning snuffed out by a debt that could never be repaid.

'Well, he will have it, because if Wickham carries on like this, he'll either get you killed again or spending the rest of it locked away. Did you know he threatened to hurt James's family?'

Edward looked up sharply, pausing from connecting the wires to the jars. 'No, I didn't know that.'

James wondered if he should intervene, but he lost his nerve. Everything between him and Edward was tangled, fraught with fractured trust and unspoken history. He would make things worse. Remind Edward of *why* he was on one side and James on the other. No, better to let Olympe work on him. She was perhaps the only other person in the world who could begin to understand what Edward had gone through; to know what it was to exist because of a twisted science experiment.

'All we have are our choices, and I don't think this is the one you truly want to make. It is frightening to be alone, yes, but better than turning yourself into a monster in order to stay in the company of others. Braver.'

James had never seen Edward this unsure. He had always been the first to pick up the dissecting knives in their classes, the pupil with the strongest stomach. Always ready to challenge Wickham, questioning what he didn't agree with, pressing their tutor when he evaded or bluffed. He had never known Edward to doubt himself.

'We are not the same,' said Edward, as though confirming it to himself. 'I am more human than you will ever be.'

'Does Wickham agree? We both want someone to be loyal to, a family to tell us we belong. Just because Wickham claims to offer you that does not mean you must accept. His place for you now is at his heels, like a dog.'

Edward hesitated by the leather straps that bound her, warring emotions playing across his face. James held his breath. Willed him to make a *choice*.

The study door snapped open and Wickham emerged.

'Edward! Take a note. I have decided on a course of action: we have observed that pain causes the subject to generate an electric charge, so I would test this hypothesis. And if a charge can be generated, then we must test whether it can be stored. We have a range of tools at our disposal,' he said, running his finger over the tray of surgical knives. 'Let us begin.'

A sheet of lightning flashed, and an almighty bang echoed around the theatre as a tree branch smashed through a window, throwing a shower of glass across the benches. Wickham startled, and dropped the scalpel with a curse.

'Oh, for— Edward, clean that up.'

'Yes, dogsbody,' said Olympe. 'Hop to, master's orders.'

Edward glared, but went to fetch a broom and sweep up the shards. Wickham turned back to his notes, and in the quiet, James heard something at the door. A soft, metallic scratching, like little claws.

Or lock picks.

He kept still – Wickham hadn't noticed anything yet.

'Did you ever study the Greek tragedies at school?' asked James.

'Keep talking and I'll have to gag you.' Wickham replaced the scalpel on the tray and set it aside.

'Only, I think there are a few concepts you might have found useful to learn about. Hamartia – "to miss the mark" in Ancient Greek. The fatal flaw.'

The scratching at the door grew more insistent. Wickham moved to the shelves of bone saws and mallets.

'Peripeteia, there's another one. The reversal of fortunes, the turning point.'

Wickham picked up a mallet, weighed it in his hand, then crossed towards James, who braced himself, teeth clenched for what came next. Whatever it was, he deserved it.

Something clicked in the door, and the scratching sounds stopped.

'Hubris, though, that seems the most relevant, don't you think?' said James. 'What is it they say – pride comes before a fall?'

Wickham went straight past James to yank the door open, and Camille and Al tumbled into the room. Lying on her back, Camille looked up at him, face pale. 'Oh. Sh—'

Wickham brought the mallet down.

10

The Catacombs

The lights were dimmed, the brass polished to a shine and each slick organ put lovingly in place. They were ready to start.

Ada was ready to crank the electrostatic generator. Her experiment had been set up; the plate metal had only taken a little effort to integrate into the workroom. One piece they'd laid on the table, then they had arranged the slabs of muscle in similar positions to before, but this time not connected by individual wires. The curved piece they'd hung overhead from lengths of silk and hooked to the generator so they could pass a current through it. Clémentine had been the one to suggest snuffing out half the lights. In the gloom, the sparks of electricity would shine like blue fire.

At the other end of the work bench, the duc surveyed the scene, hunger plain in his eyes. 'Ready the charge.'

'Readying,' she echoed and began to crank the handle.

She couldn't deny she felt that hunger too. The ache of curiosity. The irresistible urge to step into the unknown.

The glass cylinders in the generator spun faster and faster. Hairs rose along the back of her neck, haloing around her face.

'More!'

She cranked harder, shoulder aching, but she couldn't stop now. The anticipation was too great. The knot she'd been struggling to untangle was about to come loose.

Tension mounted in the lab, the light seeming to draw in on the bench. Even Clémentine leaned forward, notepad and quill forgotten.

For a sickening second, Ada thought it wasn't going to work. That her idea was nothing but a fancy.

And then at once, like a crack of shattering glass, electric currents arced from the curved plate above to the pieces of flesh below. Blue light, a loud pop, and the smell of burning meat. It was over. Ada let go of the crank and the generator wound down. Her heart was pounding, limbs light like feathers.

She realised she was *grinning*.

'Magnificent. *Magnificent*.' The duc hunched over, examining the charred muscle. 'How extraordinary. How – how—'

'Violent,' finished Clémentine. A frown had appeared between her eyebrows.

The duc ignored her. 'The theory is sound. We must now test its limits.'

'I agree,' said Ada. 'We should try and measure the—'

'Later,' the duc interrupted. 'Right now, I have something prepared I've been waiting for this moment to try. Clear the space.'

He went into the tunnels and Ada got to the grisly work of prying the fried flesh off the brass plate. It wasn't just cooked, it was *burned*, little hunks of crispy meat glued down. It smelled like dinner.

Ada's stomach turned. Clémentine passed her a bucket just in time and she retched into it.

'I won't tell him, don't worry,' said Clémentine, with a tight smile.

Ada was swilling her mouth with water when the duc returned. He was carrying something large and square covered in a cloth. Distressed squeaking noises came from inside. The sheet came off, and a cage of rats was revealed. Five in total, clambering over each other inside the small space.

Ada recoiled. 'What do you intend to do with those?'

'Why, test the limits of our theory, of course.'

He opened the cage lid and tipped the rats onto the brass plate where specks of flesh still smoked.

Ada felt faint. The rats snuffled and scrabbled over the metal, all pale pink paws and worm-like tails. 'Are you sure this is … wasn't that enough?'

Clémentine stood up abruptly. 'I can't watch.' She marched out of the room, yanking the curtain back into place.

The duc and Ada were alone. Suddenly the dim lighting was sinister, and she felt too, too aware of the weight of rock pressing down from above, the labyrinth of tunnels that stretched around them, filled with the bones of the dead.

'Are you up to the task, Ada?' asked the duc. 'Or will you give in at the final fence?'

The choice was there. She could walk away. The experiment would still happen. And then everything she'd done so far would be for *what*? The memory of the disaster at the Théâtre Patriotique came fresh to mind. That vision of countless people crushed, turning blue and swollen, and the awful, awful silence. Just because the battalion tried to do good didn't mean they hadn't been the cause of some awful things, whether accident or collateral damage. They already had a body count. She would be a hypocrite to draw the line here. Or were those people worth less than a cage of rats?

She swallowed, balling her hands in her dress. 'I – I can do this.'

'Excellent.' With brusque movements, the duc swapped their places and Ada flushed with relief and shame. 'Here, you keep the rats from jumping off. I will operate the generator this time.'

Slowly, he began to turn the crank. 'Do you know of the rat king?'

'No,' said Ada. Her eyes were trained on the writhing mass of pink and grey bodies on the brass. Like a serving tray of strange sweetmeats.

The duc continued, turning faster as the hum of electricity grew. 'In Germany, a phenomenon was often observed, where a nest of rats became hopelessly tangled together by their tails, forming a ring of bodies around a single fleshy knot. It is considered a bad omen, a harbinger of dark things to come. The secretions from their own skin would stick their tails together as they slept, bundled close together in the coldest of winters. When it woke and found its predicament, the rat king would struggle, drawing the knot ever tighter. Until it was so immobilised that the only kind thing to do' – the glass cylinders spun impossibly fast, an acrid smell filled the air – 'was to kill it.'

With a crack, blue sparks split the air. Bolts of lightning burst from the brass breastplate and in an instant all five rats were rooted to the spot, the current pulsing through them as their insides boiled and their hair burned away. An awful, high-pitched screaming filled the room. Ada clapped her hands over her ears and turned away. Everything smelled like smoke and death.

'It's over.' The duc's voice was shaky.

Ada turned back, filled with a cold, sickening wash of guilt.

The rats were dead. They had died painfully, if not at her hand then by her invention.

The duc was surveying the destruction with avid curiosity. 'A roaring success! You should be proud of yourself; this is a milestone discovery. Electricity can end life, as decisively as it can give it. And look how efficiently.' He swept a hand over the scene of destruction. 'We thought the guillotine was the greatest advance in ending life – but we have gone one step further.'

'Thank you.' She heard herself say the words but she couldn't remember speaking.

He began to dictate notes, and stiffly she took up the quill and paper Clémentine had discarded and started writing. She could cope with this, if only she didn't think. If only she filled her mind with something other than the screams of death.

She'd thought there could be nothing worse than the silence of the Théâtre Patriotique. She'd been wrong. That had been an accident. This, she had done on purpose.

The duc declared it time for refreshments and they packed up. Ada collected the rats in a sack. It was so heavy in her hand she wanted to cry. She followed the duc, winding up out of the catacombs, carrying death into the land of the living.

In the yard they waited while the footmen dug a hole. The bag fitted perfectly into it, like a perverse present, neatly wrapped.

As dirt was shovelled over the five bodies, a servant came running out of the back door, looking flustered. She pushed a letter into the duc's hand.

'They've done it, Monsieur. They took him to the guillotine this afternoon – Robespierre is dead.'

A smirk crept across the duc's face.

Ada shivered.

'And like that,' he said, 'the rat king has been exterminated.'

11

The Operating Theatre

Camille woke with a crick in her neck and a pain in her skull that felt as if she'd been cracked over the head with a mallet.

Which she had.

She was tied to a chair, arms behind her back, in a line with James and Al on the operating stage. Olympe lay before her, held down on the slab with leather straps. The side of Camille's face felt tight where a splatter of blood had dried and her fever was back, everything dizzy and light.

'Good evening,' said Wickham, from where he leaned against the foot-end of the operating table. 'I wanted to thank you for making this so terribly easy for me.'

'Don't mention it,' replied Camille, through gritted teeth.

'I might have worried that our little traitor James still had allies out there working against me, but no. Only children playing games they don't understand.'

Camille glanced over the set-up. The space was as

bleak and open as the surgical theatre they'd visited in Leicester Square, with as few places to hide. Wickham and Edward stood top and tail by Olympe. She was unnervingly calm, the usual scudding clouds of her complexion entirely still; her head was tilted sideways, and those large, black eyes watched her blankly. Camille caught her attention, then winked.

'Edward, check the Leiden jars,' instructed Wickham. 'Attach one. Make a note of it. And be quick.'

Edward followed the instructions. Camille thought he did it with unnecessary slowness – though that could have been down to stiffness in his limbs. Like a badly operated marionette, he jerked and fumbled with the tools. She cocked her head and watched with curiosity. He had declined from only the day before.

'Now, hand me the scalpel.'

'Are you sure you need to—'

Wickham cut Edward off. 'You think you know better than me?'

'No, but do we really need to hurt her? Why don't you just ask her to create a current?'

'Don't turn weak on me,' sneered Wickham. 'Science doesn't care about your feelings. It is about facts, discovery, progress. Leave *emotions* to the women.'

Silently, Edward handed him the scalpel. His expression was unreadable. Wickham turned his back to his audience and considered his incision.

That was his first mistake. Quietly, Camille began to work the small blade she had stashed up her sleeve into her hand. She had seen the operating theatre in

Leicester Square and known there was no way they could sneak in – so instead she'd had Wickham usher them in with open arms.

From the corner of her eye, she saw Al doing the same, slipping the sliver of razor into his hands and working it against the ropes. Getting their feet free unnoticed would be the hard part – the only blessing was that Wickham seemed to be running low on rope between the three of them, and there wasn't so much to cut through.

Wickham raised the scalpel, but before he could lay a hand on Olympe, her finger twitched, slipping through the open seam in the glove and brushing against the bottom of his waistcoat to trail a line of sparks. In a flash, the fabric smoked, and a flame caught. He yelled, leaped back and smacked out the fire, while Olympe cackled.

'Subdue her!' he snapped to Edward.

'What do you want me to—'

'Hit her – whatever you think will teach her to take this seriously! My god, use your brain.'

Edward hesitated.

Olympe looked up at him, her face a challenge. 'You're not his monster.'

'Do as I say or get out of my surgery.' Wickham's voice was icy cold.

Edward closed his eyes for a moment as if gathering himself, then opened them and gave Olympe a sharp, open-handed smack across her cheek that made her gasp. The sound was obscenely loud in the silent room.

He turned away, busying himself with the Leiden jars, checking wires that had already been checked five times before.

Camille wanted to carve the self-satisfied smile from Wickham's face.

The blade was slippery between her sweaty fingers but finally it cut through the last thread and her bindings fell away. The operating theatre was ringed at the back by racks displaying anatomical specimens in jars of ethanol, resin lumps of flesh full of turpentine and oil. Wickham was busy rescuing his singed waistcoat, and with his back turned, Camille slipped a free hand into her pocket to retrieve one of the firecrackers she and Al had portioned up between them, and lobbed it directly into the middle of the display.

It flashed bright white and there was a bang worse than the fireworks display – but it only bounced harmlessly off a glass jar and she swore.

'What the hell was that?' Wickham spun round, frantically checking his precious collection.

Quickly, Camille yanked the ropes from around her ankles, as did Al. They exchanged a glance in the briefest of seconds, then leaped in opposite directions, Al tackling Edward headlong into the display with a crash, sending the jars smashing to the floor with a shout of 'God save my beautiful face!', while Camille made for James to slip him the blade, then on to Olympe, still strapped to the table.

She had unbuckled one strap before Wickham was on her, an arm locked around her throat and a hand twisted painfully into her hair.

'How dare you, how *dare* you?' he hissed into her ear. 'Who the hell do you think you are?'

'We are – the Bataillon – des Morts,' she grunted with the last of her breath. 'Who the hell are *you*?'

As they struggled, Olympe undid the rest of her straps and in an instant she had James untied. He bounded into the fray with Edward, hauling his erstwhile friend away from Al who was biting and scratching like a cat whose tail had been trodden on. Al scrabbled free and reached for his stash of firecrackers.

'Get down!'

Camille just had time to swing them round so Wickham took the brunt of the blast when Al threw a firecracker into the mess of glass and flesh and spirits. Camille sent up a prayer as it arced through the air, and this time it landed perfectly, the flash of gunpowder lighting the preserving fluid like a match to kindling. Sparks danced behind her eyes; she could hardly breathe, the arm around her throat too tight and her lungs already drowning. The edges of her vision crept black.

Wickham dropped her as his body jerked. Olympe touched a bare hand to his crown and sent another pulse of electricity through him. His jaw clenched, limbs spasmed and she thought he might bite through his own tongue – then Olympe fell back, face wild with horror.

'I can't – I can't—'

Camille struggled up, looped an arm around her waist. 'It's okay, you don't have to. You did good.'

'I can't kill him, Cam, I can't become a monster – a weapon.'

'You're not. Come on, we've got to go.'

The fire had caught, burning through the oiled floorboards and blocking their escape. Camille and Olympe fled up the stairs between the rings of viewing benches to where Al crouched, lobbing firecrackers to cover their retreat. Wickham hadn't stayed down for long – he was crawling around the floor, lurching like a sailor newly on land, two palm-shaped burn marks on either side of his face. Smoke was filling the air, rising to cloud the upper levels they had climbed to.

Where the hell was James? Camille doubled over and coughed. And coughed and coughed and coughed, until she thought she must tear apart her own throat. Her hands were bloodied where she held them to her mouth, and her head spun and throbbed. The fire was burning too hot – not again, this couldn't happen again. She wouldn't lose anyone else like this. She peered down at the haze of flame and smoke, looking for a body – a figure – anything.

Anything to cling on to hope.

12

The Operating Theatre
on Fire

James circled Edward, smoke making his eyes sting. They knew each other too well; when James moved, Edward moved with him, when Edward feinted, James sidestepped a second before.

Only now did he feel the true extent of the injury to his arm, the blood loss; the wound ached and his head was dizzy. The preserving chemicals burning in the fire filled his mouth with a bitter taste. He wondered if it still affected Edward, or if meeting death once had armoured him from feeling its effects again. Then again, judging by the mottled pallor of his skin, perhaps death had not left him so far behind. Edward raised his hand, and James saw something glitter. He had found a scalpel from the dissection table, spattered with blood but still wickedly sharp.

'You don't have to do this,' said James, echoing Olympe. 'This isn't you, Ed.'

'What do you care, James? You made your choice and you didn't choose *me*.'

James blanched from the hit. 'No, I didn't. I'm sorry. But I'm asking you to choose me, now.'

A beat passed, fire licking the walls and smoke gathering like a thundercloud.

Then Edward lunged at the same time that James darted back, raced up the stairs between raked balconies two at a time. Halfway up, a hand closed around his ankle. He fell hard, ribs smacking against the stairs. Edward had hold of him, face dark with intent. He stabbed, and James kicked with his free leg, catching Edward across the temple with the heel of his boot almost by chance. Edward yelled, clutching his face. The stitches across his forehead had split, revealing the bone and gristle beneath.

A firecracker flashed and James took the chance to flee ever upwards. An arm snaked out of the smoke, hooking him into one of the rings. It was Al. James took in Olympe, a shivering outline of blue sparks, and Camille, as pale as chalk save for the hectic spots of colour in her cheeks.

'This way.' He led them up, up, into the smoke that grew denser and more caustic, looking for the second exit he knew was somewhere along the highest tier. His head swam, the stitches in his arm a burning line. Then, just as his eyes were watering too badly to see, his hand closed on the doorknob, and they were tumbling into a small corridor in the upper reaches of the hospital.

Olympe and Al supported Camille between them as they ran. At every corner James expected Wickham to appear, mallet in hand – but somehow, after an eternity, they broke out through a servants' door into a courtyard at the back of the complex.

In seconds, they vanished into the warren of streets in the old part of the city, cutting first down Butcher Hall Lane, past Christ's Hospital, then along Ivy Lane and Paternoster Row, heading for St Paul's. James had the vague idea of looking for a hackney cab along Ludgate Street, though only the hardiest of drivers would be out this late.

As they reached the soot-blackened, looming mass of the cathedral, Al called for him to stop. There was too much open ground, so James led them to the only hiding spot he could think of: the portico of the cathedral. At the top of the steps, they secreted themselves in a dark corner and Al lowered Camille to the ground. James kneeled before her to take her pulse and her temperature.

A fever, her heart thumping like a moth battering itself against a lit window. She looked as pale as the blood-drained corpses on the dissection table, her face gaunt and skull-like. Only her eyes blazed, a manic, glossy glint that skipped here and there, lacking focus.

An understanding had dawned on him just before she'd left for the pleasure gardens but he hadn't had time to think on it since. Now it was all too clear. It was the doctor's bread and butter, a sickness you could see on any street in the country. The quiet horror of it was almost more than he could bear.

'Loosen her collar,' he instructed. 'Is there any water?'

Al shook his head, but helped undo the cravat around her neck.

'What's wrong with her?' asked Olympe, still glowing with charge.

'I don't know,' James lied. 'We need to find a cab – keep an eye on the street.'

Olympe crouched by a column, watching the road intently. James pushed the hair back from Camille's forehead.

'You're going to be okay.'

Camille didn't reply, only meeting his gaze, then closed a hot hand around his.

'There! A carriage!' The cry went up from Olympe, and they manoeuvered Camille down the steps towards the horse and carriage pulling along the churchyard. It stopped at the gate in the wrought iron fence, but at the last second James hauled them back into the shadows.

And there they were – Wickham jumping from the driver's seat, Edward climbing after him. He made a gesture and they split up, Wickham turning towards Ludgate Street, while Edward entered the churchyard.

'Come on,' hissed James, following the perimeter fence towards the opposite gate.

They barely made it a few paces. Camille sagged in Al's arms, stumbling over her own feet. James lunged to catch her, but she was a dead weight. Her eyes rolled back in her head and she was gone in a faint.

The clouds cleared from the moon, and the tableaux was cast in silvery light: Camille collapsed, Al and James trying to lift her, Olympe smothering panicked sparks that kept erupting from her skin.

And Edward, lurching over the paving stones towards them.

James froze, kneeling at Camille's head, knees pressed against cold stone. Edward stopped, took in their desperate state.

James held his gaze, a silent plea passing between them.

From the street beyond, Wickham was calling.

'Nothing here! Report?'

Edward watched them, his face cast in sharp angles in the moonlight, only the wound on his forehead to distinguish him from the statues surrounding them. His gaze flicked from Camille, to James, and then to Olympe where she glared in defiance, the shadows shifting uneasily across her skin.

James held his breath.

'Nothing here either!' Edward called. 'Move on?'

'Move on,' Wickham confirmed.

Edward lingered, holding James's gaze. It seemed in that moment that their entire history together, shared triumphs of drunkenly celebrated exam results, lows of sleepless nights spent studying, the quiet moments of ordinary friendship, all of it was laid out between them. And James had betrayed it. He didn't deserve forgiveness, but Edward had always been the better man.

He knew it was not over between them.

But for now, Edward had granted them mercy.

13

The Salon, the Duc's Headquarters

Tea was a formal affair. Taken in the plush upholstered salon, the duc had invited several aristocratic sympathisers and brought Clémentine up from the catacombs to celebrate the death of Robespierre.

Ada sat among them, feeling like a weed amid hothouse flowers; she didn't belong, and it must be painfully obvious to everyone there. The rush of the experiment had left her shaken, the thrill and horror mingling as she played it over and over in her mind. The duc had found a way to kill countless people at once, and she had helped him. The Revolution was on its knees, and it was a matter of time before he had all the pieces in place for a coup. She had given him the largest one.

How did Camille make these impossible decisions? In that moment Ada desperately wanted to know what Camille would have done in her position, a whole-body longing that still had the power to surprise her. She wanted someone to stroke her hair and tell her she was right and the doubt and anxiety and dread would be worth the outcome. She longed for Camille like she had longed for her mother at ten years old, curled up crying in her bed.

When a round of toasts was called and measures of brandy were poured, Ada mechanically lifted her glass and drank to the execution of Robespierre, the fall of the Committee for Public Safety and the end of the Revolution. The alcohol burned in her throat. She was glad, at least, that no one expected her to speak. She could still smell the dead rats on her skin.

Just when Ada thought she couldn't stand it any more, the duc left with his allies flanking him to conspire in his office. It seemed impossible that time could have unravelled so quickly.

The Revolution had never defeated the monster; it had only slumbered.

Clémentine and Ada were left alone. Ada stood abruptly. 'Thank you for your hospitality, but I must go...'

'Of course.' Clémentine smiled, though made no move to show her out, as if she knew Ada wasn't done yet.

Ada fought herself, fingers twisting in the fabric of her skirt, then gave up and sat back down. There was nothing left to lose. She couldn't baulk now.

'I'm sorry, but I must raise this again,' she said. 'You know I know Olympe. She told us about her upbringing. She thinks very fondly of you, but the duc – she does not know he is her uncle. From her own reports he did ... terrible things to her.'

Clémentine's face was stormy. She might not have Olympe's swirling, cloudy-grey complexion, but Ada could see her daughter perfectly in her.

'Yes, I thought it best to protect her from that truth.'

'But the experiments…'

'I regret the way things went. I will not deny it.'

'She's your daughter.'

'And I have subjected myself to far worse in the name of discovery. I only wish I could speak to Olympe and explain it all to her, that I only ever saw brilliance in her. To achieve the brilliance one is capable of, one must sometimes do unsavoury things – I thought you understood that.'

She sat, tall and steely, and Ada knew she meant every word she said. It was so hard to reconcile the fierce mother in front of her with the awful past she'd read about in the duc's notes. Ada thought about the experiment she had just done with the duc. The blood she had on her hands. Did she really have the right to judge?

'When your brother pressured us to hand Olympe over, it didn't seem like he wanted her back for family reasons. It seemed he was more interested in how her abilities could be used in pursuit of his political ambitions.'

Clémentine snorted. 'Philippe is my brother and I owe him a lot, but he is something of an idiot. He can't *use* Olympe; she's her own person. She'll either work with him or not, that's her choice. He's never understood that. He uses the people around him to prop him up because on his own he isn't half the person he thinks he is. Why else do you think he wants you here?' Ada flushed. Clémentine shrugged. 'But what's so bad about that? We use him too.'

She turned this thought over. Clémentine couldn't know the truth of how Ada had come to be working with the duc, but she was right. Ada was using him. Getting close to learn his plans, to work out how to stop him.

And, if she was completely honest, using him to do what she really wanted with her life. She'd always thought getting to study and to participate in practical experiments was a dream for the future. She had danced with Camille on a rooftop and talked of university, of planning their life to come. The duc had given her that life *now*.

'There's nothing wrong with taking what you need,' said Clémentine. 'Don't you get tired? Don't you see there's no way you'll ever be good enough for them? You don't have to play by their rules. Use the skills and resources you have to hand, do the things they never could do – whatever it takes. Because no one is going to hand you anything.'

Ada rubbed her temples, suddenly exhausted. Why did everything have to be such a struggle? Months and months with the battalion, railing against forces stronger than them, people who thought they knew better, trying to do *right*. Maybe Clémentine was right. Maybe she was the one making it difficult for herself. Camille didn't doubt herself, Camille did whatever was needed to get what she wanted. Why was Ada so insistent on being a *good girl*?

A good girl – that's what her father called her, wanted her to be. But it hadn't got her anywhere with him. Good and quiet and obedient only made it easier for him to disregard her. With the battalion, she had already proved she wasn't the last one. Maybe there was no reason to be the first two either.

Clémentine took her hand. 'I'm sorry. I don't mean to push you. Only, I see myself in you and it makes me angry that little has changed. And you make me think of my girl. I've spent many months powerless to help her... Maybe I can at least help you. Tell me, what does your mother think of your scientific interest?'

Oh, that felt like a blow. 'My mother ... passed away a long time ago.'

Clémentine's face crumpled. 'My dear, how terrible. So hard for a girl to grow up without a mother. A loss you never stop feeling.'

Ada was crying before she realised it, fat tears running down her cheeks. She reached for the handkerchief in her pocket, then remembered it was tied round her mother's earrings and cried even harder.

Clémentine took a square from her reticule. 'Here, use this.'

Ada sniffled. 'She asked for you. When we rescued Olympe, the first thing she said she wanted was to go back to you.'

Ada felt more than heard the sharp intake of breath. Clémentine turned away from her, a quiet anger clear in her posture. The tears would not stop coming. Ada cursed herself for feeling so helpless.

Clémentine put an arm around her, mopped the

tears from her face. It was a small gesture, but it brought Ada's mother back to life for just a second, in the gentle and protective sweep of the handkerchief against her cheek. Clémentine might have a warped idea of being a mother, but she still was one. Who could they trust more to help them protect Olympe than her own mother?

Ada lifted her face, eyelashes stuck together and cheeks wet. 'I need to tell you something – but you must keep it secret.'

Clémentine's brows drew together. 'You can tell me anything.'

'Promise me.'

'Very well, I promise.'

Ada paused, on the very edge of the cliff. Another step and there would be no going back.

Sometimes it was impossible to tell the difference between bravery and recklessness.

She could only find out by taking a leap of faith.

'I know where Olympe is. I know how you can get her back.'

PART FIVE

L'Enfer

1

6 Bedford Square

James put away his stethoscope and closed his medical bag. His hands were trembling imperceptibly. Camille watched his movements, feeling detached, unreal. It was like the time Ada took her to see the great telescope at the Observatory and showed her the stars and planets drifting through their ancient orbits impossibly far away. She knew they were connected to her life, that they meant something about the truth of their world. But it was too distant to connect.

Standing a few paces away, James was like a distant moon. Alien and unknowable.

Or perhaps he was the Earth, and she was the cold dead thing, floating alone in the dark.

'I'm sorry I couldn't give you better news,' he said, turning his head away as he blinked back something in his eye.

'Don't—'

'I can get you a second opinion. I'm sure you'll want one.'

'Do you think you're wrong?'

He turned to face her and his eyes were ringed with red. 'No. It is quite clear.'

'Then I don't need a second opinion.'

'Cam—'

She stirred herself, enough to train her gaze on him. Let her tone become stern. 'Nobody can know. Promise me you'll tell no one.'

A look of pain crossed his face. Perhaps in another life, she would have comforted him, but that divide still lay between them, uncrossed. Maybe none of that mattered now. She had suspected for some time but until James had said the words there had been room for doubt, for hope. Her fear had come true: her battalion would fall away. But she wouldn't be the one left alone to mourn.

The thought came like a blow strong enough to floor her: it would be Ada. For Camille, all this would end. For Ada, it was just beginning.

She shut her eyes and concentrated on the weight of her body in the chair, the feel of the wooden arms under her hands. It might be selfish and weak and dangerous but *god* all she wanted was Ada to come through the door, wrap her in her arms and tell her it was going to be okay.

But it was not going to be okay. Nothing would ever be okay again.

She didn't fully remember how they got from St Paul's to Bedford Square, just snatches of a bumpy carriage ride and hands lifting her. At the stable block in the mews, they had paused to hide Olympe, who couldn't safely come into a house as crammed with people and servants as the Harfords'.

Olympe had lingered at Camille's side. 'I am loath to leave you again now I've found you, especially if you're—'

'I'm fine,' Camille had croaked, and she had been surprised at the strangeness of her own voice. 'It's only my chest. It's always been weak.'

She had been taken over by a coughing fit. A fresh handkerchief was pressed into her hands. When the cough had subsided, it was speckled red.

'I have my medical bag upstairs,' James had said. 'I'll give you an examination and see what's— see if I can help.'

'That's not necessary.'

James had fixed her with a glance. 'Camille. I insist.'

Climbing up to the open window they escaped from had been out of the question, so Al had pushed money into the hand of the servant who let them in through the back door, and then the two of them had half-carried her up to her room.

Al had left at her insistence, then James had retrieved his bag, listened to her symptoms, examined her bloodied handkerchief. Looked into her mouth, her eyes. Took her pulse.

Grown sombre as the situation became clear.

Now, he looked at her. 'All I can say is that it will likely be slow. You will have time. We can arrange for you to stay in Italy or perhaps the Alps, for the air—'

'No.'

'It's the recommended treatment.'

'No. Thank you for your advice, but no.'

He watched her silently, frustration replacing

distress on his face. Oh, her kind, useless James. She hated him, and she loved him. He had betrayed her, and she still wanted him to pay, to watch him squirm and beg her forgiveness, but right now all that felt so far away, peeled back like a thin layer of paint over the long, shared pattern of their lives that had been forever entwined.

Three broad sash windows broke up the wall opposite her. Outside, the rain had softened, tracing jagged patterns along the glass. Beyond, the sky was a pale grey with dawn. Featureless. Camille watched the trees shift and sway in the wind, let her mind drift back and forth with their movements. They were calm, deep roots and wide branches that stood firm, as if time and decay were just foolish human notions.

'So you're going to carry on with ... this?' he asked.

'Why? Do you think it's over?'

James hung his head, returned to packing his bag. 'No. Wickham was more than clear he won't be done until no one stands in his way.'

'Then I will carry on with "this", as you put it.'

'You're ridiculous, Camille,' he said, but there was softness in his voice.

'And you're a hypocrite, James.'

He snapped his bag shut.

'I suppose things are not over between us either.'

She pulled her shawl closer around her shoulders. 'No. We will talk, not – not now.'

His lip curled. 'Why do I suspect there will be less talking and more yelling?'

'Because you're not *quite* as stupid as you look.'

'I will keep what I know to myself. And I won't go easy on you when we have that – talk.'

She stared him down. 'Good. Don't.'

He smiled, but his eyes were still sorrowful. She couldn't take it.

'Go, get out. Let me sleep. Tell your family – oh, tell them whatever you want, I don't care. Just let me sleep.'

Without another word, he left.

And she slept. A hectic, fevered sleep full of dreams of blood and monsters and in the middle of it all, Ada, faded and intangible, a wisp that dissolved every time Camille tried to touch her.

She woke, sweaty, covers flung off. A cadre of maids were stoking the fire and shutting the windows tight, a hot brick wrapped up at the foot of her bed to sweat out the fever.

James must have said something about her health, because the attention did not stop. A cup of posset was brought up, replaced an hour later by a restorative beef broth, then Hennie offering to read to her before being herded out by servants. And all of it punctuated by a cough that wouldn't settle, a raw, bloody taste in her mouth, her stomach and sides sore, her chest squeezed tight.

Camille let it happen.

It was a role she knew how to play. In Paris when she was a child, her mother had swaddled her and hung her room with bundles of herbs, suggesting that perhaps it would be easier for her to breathe if the air smelled a little sweeter. The more Camille had complained about being stuck in bed, the more her mother fussed. Even

Ada did it, pestering her about doctors and rest and tonics. She would suffer a hundred indignities if only Ada was here to see her through them.

But she wasn't, and Camille felt more alone than ever.

She'd learned that all people really wanted of her was to let them try and help. It made them feel better, and who was she to take that away?

It seemed she did not have much else to give.

2

The National Convention

Ada travelled to her father's house, still wreathed in the smell of burning flesh. No matter how hard she scrubbed her skin, or the clean clothes she'd put on, it wouldn't go away.

She had kept her mind off the experiment while the duc had toasted Robespierre's death the evening before, and while she had cried on Clémentine's shoulder. But now it was all she could think of. Every time she closed her eyes, she saw the sheet of brass. The rats' claws clicking as they snuffled unsuspecting across its surface. Then the burst of electricity. The smell of death.

The carriage ground to a halt in the traffic where the Pont Notre-Dame met the right bank at the Quai de la Grève. Ada pulled at the neck of her gown. She couldn't breathe. From the riverbanks came the scent of rotting fish, raw sewage, run off from butchers and breweries and tanneries, of the livestock driven through the streets and unwashed masses of people pressing through the gaps between the traffic and lurching buildings.

Ada tumbled out of the carriage door, gasping. She couldn't bear to be enclosed another moment more. The city closed in on her, the crush of people, all strangers, all wrong. There was only one person she wanted, and one person she couldn't have: Camille.

But under the longing was fear: what if she had gone too far? What if Camille couldn't forgive the lines she'd crossed? Ada thought of the rats in their cage, carried helpless to their death. Like the prisoners being transported to the guillotine, only this time she hadn't saved them.

She'd killed them.

Would Camille still want her after that?

If she delivered Clémentine as an ally, maybe.

She started walking, making it to the Pont au Change before she realised what she was doing. The carriage was back down a busy street. If she returned to it, it would take her to the duc and she would have to pretend nothing was wrong. She would have to deny every thought in her head until she disappeared into a shadow. A negative. The shape of a person who didn't exist.

She kept walking, along the Quai de la Mégisserie, past the end of the Île de la Cité, past the Louvre to the Jardin des Tuileries, where finally the cramped city opened into sky and green.

On the other side of the garden was the Salle du Manège, where the National Convention sat. Where Robespierre had given his last speech. Where the idea of a France that governed itself, without a king, had formed. And now, perhaps, died.

If Guil was anywhere, it would be here. Camille was on the other side of the channel. Guil was the only person she had left. The only person who could understand.

Ada joined the people hurrying into the galleries above the debating floor and spotted Guil leaning against the railings, watching the exchange below with intensity. She slid onto the bench beside him, caught his hand in hers.

'Ada. What are you doing here?'

'Looking for you.'

His expression clouded over; she must look worse than she'd thought. 'How did it go?'

She swallowed against the bile rising in her throat. 'I – can't talk about it yet.'

Below, a man she didn't recognise was giving a fiery speech, thumping his hand on the lectern. A sea of white men sat on the benches, differentiated only by their cravats. The fiery speaker left and was replaced by a dull man with a mousy face. Then a tall, ruddy farmer-turned-politician. Then a general. Then an old aristocrat.

An air of anxiety prickled like a storm brewing, a whole room braced and ready to move. A question, unspoken: what happens now? Time slipped by, and she tried to concentrate, to understand the implications of what they were saying.

But her mind was in the cage with the rats.

A man sat next to her and she was sucked back into the room in an instant.

The duc was in the same outfit he'd worn during their

experiment, a rolled-up paper of the day's convention business in his hand. Ada could hear her own heartbeat racing in her ears. Guil lurched to his feet.

'Don't run.' The duc's voice was soft and measured and terrifying. 'Either of you. I have men stationed outside.' Guil shakily took his seat again.

The noise of the room blurred into a blanket of sound. All she could concentrate on was her own harsh breath and the duc beside her. What did he know? Had Clémentine said something? Had he known about her talking to Guil before? Had his spies been following her from the start? A thousand things clamoured in her mind. She couldn't speak until he did for risk of giving something away.

The duc studied her, his expression unreadable. 'I am too kind for my own good, because even now, with so much proof of your untrustworthiness, I find myself tempted to allow you time to explain.'

'Please—'

'I said tempted – I did not say which way my thoughts had fallen. Allow me to lay out the situation as it appears to me. I learned that yesterday, you left my house to meet with a man. *Not* the errand I had assumed you meant when you left. When pressed, the carriage driver was able to give a clear description of the man who had hailed him and rode with you a way. So finding you in such company now is sadly no surprise.'

Ada felt light, dissolved by her fear.

Had the driver overheard their conversation about Olympe and trusting Clémentine?

The duc was no longer the man she'd worked side by side with. He was the man who had tried to kill them all only a month ago. He had given her a few kind words and she had forgotten who she was dealing with.

The duc continued. 'Let's skip the part where you try to convince me Guil has changed allegiances too; we both know that implausible. So, I thought to myself, what sort of rendez-vous could this have been? Surely it was no coincidence that you met shortly after I introduced you to Clémentine. Perhaps at that point you could have still fooled me, thrown me off the scent, but then I learnt you spoke with my sister and had a *very* interesting discussion.'

Ada clamped her hands together on her lap to stop them shaking. Oh god. He knew almost everything. 'Can you blame me for keeping some things to myself?'

'I understand your loyalties are torn. Accepting change is difficult. I take you in, offer you the run of my home, bring you into my most secret work – but still, you cannot trust me.'

'It's not like that...'

The cold press of a blade against her thigh silenced her at once.

'It makes me think,' the duc continued, as though they were nothing more than two acquaintances passing pleasantries, 'what else have you said that I should not have believed? Perhaps a feigned interest in my work? A stubborn loyalty to the girl who abandoned you and ran away to England?'

Ada shook her head, unconsciously edging away.

'Guil has nothing to do with this.'

'Try again.'

'I swear—'

He pressed the knife harder, her skirts splitting in its path. 'I know you know anatomy. If I slit the artery here, you would die before I stood up.'

He was right.

And he would do it. What was one more death in Paris?

She took a steadying breath. Thought of Camille's crooked smile, the way she had held her hands before leaving for England, stroked her thumb over the lifeline etched across Ada's palm, and said, *I trust you, Ada Rousset*.

There was always a way out, a choice that could be made.

Play the player, not the game.

Keeping her hands neatly folded, and her chin raised high, she spoke with authority.

'I swear I have told you no lies. I came to you of my own free will' – true – 'I *wanted* to work with you' – also true. 'You have to understand – after what I have been through it would be foolish of me not to exercise some caution when I speak with you. And I could not cut contact with Guil or he would be suspicious. But he has no plan – none of them do. They are children, and I am sick of playing games.'

The duc looked her in the eye, searching her face. Ada held his gaze. She would not blink, she would not falter. Breath held, neck outstretched, she waited for the blade to fall.

At last, he spoke. 'I have made up my mind. You

will accompany Clémentine and I to England to get Olympe back. Guil will also accompany us. This is not an invitation, it is an order. As you say, it would be *foolish* of me not to exercise some caution, so I take you both with me as insurance against any scheme you might be concocting.'

The knife withdrew and he stood, offering her his hand.

'Very well. I am not sure I believe you, Ada Rousset, but I grant you a last chance to prove yourself to me. Spend it wisely.'

Heart in her throat, she reached and took the duc's hand.

'I will.'

3

The Garden at
6 Bedford Square

10 Thermidor
28 July

Camille watched Hennie and Phil bat a shuttlecock back and forth in the garden of the Harfords' townhouse. The weather had eased overnight; the sky still a pale grey wash but it was warmer now, and dry. The long summer evenings left too much empty time before dinner, and so the girls had been thrown outside to work up an appetite and Camille had been settled into a chair on the patio, covered in blankets and told to call the moment she felt a chill.

'The patient lives.' Al arrived and, hauling a chair over, he lowered himself down, looking the worse for wear.

Camille sniffed and frowned. 'Are you hungover? When did you even find time?'

'Does the sun rise in the east? Do the English have terrible fashion sense? Yes, I'm hungover.'

The shuttlecock went flying wide and Hennie dived for it, just catching it with her net as she skidded on the grass. Al clapped loudly. 'Oh, terribly good show,' he said in English.

Camille arched an eyebrow at him. '*How*?'

'I went out to stretch my legs. A little hair of the dog, see what gossip I could forage, that sort of thing.' He leaned over her and plucked a bunch of hothouse grapes off the little table of supplies that had been set up next to her.

'Gossip – you mean the hospital fire?'

'Not even a blip on the radar. Big news was a large sycamore tree fell into Lady Featherstonhaugh's summer room and destroyed some extremely expensive and I expect extremely hideous Delftware vases.'

'Al—'

'You know the type, for tulips, look like a bagpipe gone wrong.'

'You are utterly exhausting sometimes, you know that?'

'Oh, lighten up, Cam. Have a grape. Have a drink. Have some *fun*.'

'Why would I do that? We came here on a mission, and unless you missed it, we have yet to get Olympe and ourselves to safety. What purpose does fun serve?'

Al's head swivelled round. 'What purpose … my god, you're worse than I thought. There *is* no purpose to fun. That's the point. No, wait – the purpose is that you're not actually dead yet, so why not try having a bit of a life? Weren't you the one just telling me that? Christ.'

Camille flinched.

Al picked at the grapes, muttering to himself about what Ada and James could possibly see in her. On the lawn, Hennie belted the shuttlecock into an ornamental fishpond. The game was paused to send a footman to fish it back out.

The thought had hit her harder than she had expected. Al was right. She wasn't actually dead. *Yet.* In that moment, swaddled and prone and helpless, it seemed so incredibly obvious. She wasn't dead yet. She was alive.

When her parents were executed, it had felt like the grief killed her old self. With the battalion, throwing herself into dangerous and deadly situations with no regard for herself, no thought about the future, she'd been living as though she was already dead. She could do anything, risk anything. She'd thought it was *freeing*.

Now death stared her in the face, she realised she'd been alive this whole time. Loving Ada frightened her because it meant she was really still here, still alive. That there were consequences and risk and joy and despair all possible. If she were dead, she was untouchable. But she wasn't; she was alive and she could be hurt again, just as badly as before.

What happened to her mattered. What she did was the only thing that mattered.

It was *all* that mattered. When she was gone, it would be all that was left of her.

Right now, she didn't like the look of what would be left.

If she defeated the duc, would she come out the winner, Olympe in hand, but to a world in ruins?

Was sitting on the fence all she wanted to be left of her?

If Robespierre fell, would the world become any kinder? Would the idea of a new world even survive?

Al interrupted her thoughts.

'Would you like the rest of the gossip?'

She waved him on.

'Wickham has gone to ground. I mean, entirely. Didn't turn up to teach at the hospital, surgeries delayed, patients ignored. He and Edward are ghosts.'

'I don't like the sound of that.'

'Me neither. Sounds awfully like someone plotting a nasty surprise.' He stood, proffered his arm. 'Well. Are you ready for him?'

Camille chewed her lip. He didn't mean Wickham. There was another confrontation waiting, one she would have to face before they could plan their next move.

James was in the stables, notionally examining new tack for his horse. Olympe was at the back of the stall, perched on a stool and looking a little skittish of the sleek grey mare taking up most of the space.

'How are you feeling?' he asked.

'Well enough.' She passed him to finally, finally, embrace Olympe in the way she had wanted to at the pleasure gardens. 'I'm sorry it took us this long. Are you well? How did he treat you?'

James had the good grace to look ashamed. 'Camille – I'm sorry – I never wanted it to come to this—'

'Sorry doesn't cut it,' she snapped. The rage she had been carrying since that night in the foundations of the Madeleine Church finally erupted. Between the attack in the pleasure gardens and the confrontation with Wickham in the operating theatre, she'd had to push it aside, accept James as a tentative ally, and then she'd felt too weak to cope with her own anger. But she was stronger now, and there was no way in hell she was going to let him get away with everything he'd done. 'You pointed a gun at my head, James. You kidnapped Olympe and locked her up – when you *know* what happened to her.'

'And I've apologised to her. We've made our peace.'

She pulled her shawl around her, drew herself to her full height though it only brought her nose to his chin. 'I suppose that makes it better? How did I never notice how completely self-involved and stupid you can be?'

James snorted. 'Because you're so selfless and rational all the time.'

'*You* asked *me* for help. What about making your peace with me? For *using* me. Tricking me.'

'I didn't think you were particularly interested in peace after that stunt with the knife to my throat when you arrived,' he replied coolly.

How *dare* he? Like any of this was *her* fault? He should be on his knees begging her forgiveness but no, he had to have the last word. She wanted to smack that self-satisfied expression off his face.

'Children, children.' Al raised his hands to silence them. 'We're all a little stab-happy here, but maybe let's try to keep the conversation on the two people out to get us, all right? I'm sure you can manage a little truce until we've escaped hideous death?'

Camille narrowed her eyes. 'Oh, I don't know. I don't see why we shouldn't just take Olympe and be done with this. Leave James to clean up his own mess.'

He flinched, but his jaw was set firm. 'Because my father already thinks you're a spy. Disappear, and he'll have every port looking out for you. You'll never get out of the country.'

She hated that he was right.

'You did all this for what?' she said, folding her arms. 'To make your father proud? To make him *love* you? Bad news. He's never going to love you the way you want him to. You made yourself into the villain for nothing.'

James flushed with anger and hurt. 'At least my parents have the potential to love me. Yours are dead. Hard to be loved by a corpse.'

Camille sucked in a breath, reaching for something to throw at his head before she knew it. 'And whose bloody fault is *that*? My mother is dead because your disloyal piece of scum father seduced her, then didn't lift a damn finger to help when she was falsely accused.'

James recoiled in shock, as though it was the first time he had truly put the facts together in his mind, seen the path from his father's actions to Camille, orphaned and broken before him.

Al caught her sleeve. 'Easy now. I don't think we're at the drunken brawl part of the day yet.' He glanced at James. 'Camille does raise a good point. You were a big fat traitor before. A big fat traitor one thinks you may still be. If we stay and help you, what guarantee do we have that you won't make some self-serving move again?'

James ran a hand through his hair. 'Look. You're right, I lied. I made some extremely poor choices because I was arrogant and sure of my own righteousness, and no one regrets that more than me. All I can say is, I want to fix what I've done. And, trust me or not, we have bigger problems now. You don't know Wickham like I do. If you leave with Olympe, he'll come after you. He's determined not to let any of us get in the way of what he sees as his legacy.' James recounted everything Wickham had told him before the pleasure gardens and at the operating theatre. 'But it's more than that – Wickham *hates* my father. While my father is still at the War Ministry, he doesn't think his research will ever be accepted. He wants to take my father out of the picture.'

Camille rubbed her temples, turning through the messy pieces of their situation. Her anger boiled under her skin, but she knew it was time to let it die. She couldn't let it get in the way of what mattered: getting Olympe to safety and returning to Ada and Guil in Paris. James had said they had bigger problems – he didn't know the half of it.

'I want to help.' Olympe spoke for the first time. 'I don't want to leave. Not until I can speak to Edward again. He's – different now.'

Camille shook her head. 'It's dangerous.'

'So? *All* of my life is dangerous, and I don't want to let anyone else get hurt because of me.'

Camille fell silent.

She could still take Olympe and run. Risk Lord Harford sending people after them as accused spies. But was that what she wanted to leave as her legacy? Cowardice and violence?

Goddamnit.

'Olympe is right,' she said. 'There's no risk-free path here. All we have is our choices; that's all that will be left of us once we're gone.'

James looked at her with such sadness she couldn't bear it.

'Can't you try talking to your father again?' asked Al. 'Have this murderous madman arrested? Your father might not believe in Olympe's abilities – and that's entirely fair because, let's be honest, this could just be a wild fever-dream my brain has concocted to comfort me in the moments before I die at the guillotine. But the man tied up his only son, threatened to kill his whole family. Surely he can't ignore that. Killing a government minister seems like a pretty open and shut case for having him thrown in gaol immediately. You English like to make such a fuss about your democracy and law and order, so why not indulge a little?'

James shook his head. 'He won't believe me. He thinks Wickham is a fraud and I've been duped.'

Al shrugged. 'Even a fraud can be dangerous.'

Camille interrupted. 'We need to *make* him believe you.'

James had to be an ally now, they had no other choice; she had to believe their past still meant enough to him.

'What are you thinking?' asked Al.

'Wickham is planning to attack Lord Harford – so we let him.'

'Excuse me?' spluttered James.

'Will anything less convince your father?'

James sagged, frustration and resignation sweeping across his face. 'No. You're right. If Wickham has a gun to his head, maybe he'll start taking this seriously.'

'Not to spoil things,' cut in Al, 'but there is the small matter of James and Camille's wedding in a few days.'

Olympe dropped the piece of straw she had been shredding. '*Wedding*? James, what is he talking about?'

James flushed deep red. 'Ah. Oh. Yes. That. I should have told you.'

'You think? I'm an idiot. Of course you were keeping things from me.'

'Not intentionally! It just … didn't come up. And then we were quite busy with all the mortal danger.'

'You can't be serious.' She swivelled to stare at Camille. 'What about Ada? I don't understand…'

'It's not a real wedding,' Camille explained quickly. 'It was a plot to get close to James, to find you.'

Al was pretending to keep out of the conversation, fussing with mane of the grey mare, but said, 'The preparations seem quite real to me.'

Olympe still stared at Camille in shock and – oh god – disappointment.

'Does Ada know?'

Camille shifted her weight. 'No.'

'Oh.'

'She'll understand.'

Olympe didn't say anything, and Camille felt a void of shame yawn beneath her.

'We are very good at getting ourselves into messes, I must say.' Al jauntily clapped a hand to the mare's neck. 'I think Guil was right about us changing our name to Battalion of the Bad Plans. Trips off the tongue.'

Camille tried to shake off the shame. 'Fine. We use the wedding as bait. James and his father in the same place? Wickham won't be able to resist trying something – we need to be ready for him when he does.'

'While I agree that this is probably our best plan – Camille, this is my father we're talking about. I can't let anything happen to him.'

'It won't. We outnumber Wickham, and we'll be expecting him.'

James looked as though he wanted to say more, but kept quiet.

Camille only hoped she had finally got something right.

4

Camille's Bedroom, Bedford Square

An insistent tap at the window roused her. Camille slid out of the warm cocoon of bed sheets and opened the curtains. Al was crouched outside, grinning like a demon in the darkness.

A faux balcony ran along the back of the house, little more than a gutter a few paces wide and a stone balustrade that connected the windows that faced the garden. Al had used it to hop from his room to hers.

Camille opened the window, a gust of drizzle sweeping in. Her face turned to the fresh air like a flower to the sun.

'What are you doing?' she asked.

'I was worried you might have been smothered to death by well-meaning Harfords. Or died from stress after all that yelling at James. Can I come in?'

A single oil lamp burned by her bed, the wick at its lowest setting. Above her, the folds of the canopy were lost in shadow.

'No – I'll come out there.'

She fetched a dressing gown and slippers and clambered onto the balcony. They sat side by side, feet on the balustrade. The garden was a wild swathe of landscape beneath a dark sky and between the clouds a sliver of moon peeped out, then vanished.

'Seriously, are you all right, Cam? James never gave us an update after he checked your lungs.'

She pulled the dressing gown closer around her shoulders. 'Yes. I'm all right.'

'Is that an actual yes or an "I'm Camille Laroche therefore I must be all right" yes?'

Al's face was carved in shadow and pale planes of cheek and forehead. Camille tucked her hands under her arms; it was colder out here than she'd expected.

'It's an actual yes. James didn't find anything,' she lied. It was the only way she was going to be able to get through this. If her battalion knew the truth, she knew exactly what would happen. After the upset and the anger, they would look at her differently. Maybe they wouldn't mean to, maybe it would be in subtle ways, but she wouldn't be the same Camille to them. She would be weak. Fragile. To be pitied. She couldn't bear that.

And maybe it was kinder this way, to save them heartache over something they couldn't change.

'Just my bad chest. Smoke inhalation from the theatre fire caused more damage than I'd thought, then it was aggravated by the chemicals in the smoke at the hospital.'

He didn't reply straight away, holding her gaze.

She broke first, looking down at her feet, the lichen blooming on stone.

'Phew. That's a relief. Don't know what I'd do if our fearless leader copped it mid-mission.' Al spoke with a forced cheeriness.

A moment passed between them where she almost asked if he knew. Perhaps it was obvious from looking at her. But she wanted to hide it, and if he knew, he was giving her the gift of letting her pretend, so she would take it.

'You'd be fine.'

'No. I don't think we would.'

They sat for a while, watching the stars come and go behind the clouds. On Great Russell Street they could hear the occasional passing carriage, the toll of a church bell from St Giles's or St George's. On this side of the square, new houses backed onto the ornamental gardens behind the British Museum – and then nothing but the churned brown earth of building sites, green market gardens, and tin-roofed shanty towns stretching north and east.

'Stay here with me, Cam. Don't go back to Paris.'

'I have to, Al. It's home.'

'Is it?'

'I meant what I said before. We have to go back, people need us.'

'Do they? That's not our job, no one appointed us. We can walk away.'

'No. We can't. *I* can't.'

'Why not?'

'Because … because I can't,' she said, frustrated.

'That's not who I *am*. Will you really be happy here, just sitting around drinking for ever?'

'Well...'

'Don't answer that.'

'What about your future, Camille? Can you really keep going on like this for ever?'

Camille stared up at the stars and thought of Ada. Thought of the last time things had felt right: the two of them dancing on the roof of the Au Petit Suisse. Ada's skin warm against hers, the smell of her, the gentleness of her hand in the small of Camille's back.

Maybe that was the last time she'd ever get to be happy.

Maybe she wouldn't get to see Ada again.

James said it would be slow, but what if he was wrong?

Camille blinked, her view blurring with tears.

'I know what my future is, Al. I can't change it any more.'

He gave a dramatic sigh and flung himself back to lean against the wall and kick his feet into empty space. 'That's so incredibly awkward for me, because now I have to go back to Paris too.'

She raised her eyebrows. 'That was a swift change of heart. What happened?'

'*You* happened. Look at you, Cam, you're a mess.'

'Thank you.'

'I would be derelict in my duty to let you go back to Paris alone. I mean, you might keel over in the middle of nowhere and then what would happen?'

She didn't reply. She knew it was a joke, but she could picture the scene only too well. A dusty road between Calais and Paris, her money run out and no passing cart to hitch a ride on, stumbling on a wheel rut and falling. No one there to pick her up. Lungs burning, fever-weak. The end of her.

Al inspected his fingernails, mouth downturned. 'And, well, I keep telling you Ada deserves better, but I realised so does Léon. Only a total arse would stay here and not send a word. And I'm only a partial arse at most. Just the one bum cheek. The left, maybe.'

Camille closed her eyes and sank against him, letting her head rest on his shoulder. She was so tired. He wound their fingers together, stroked his thumb over hers.

'Thank you,' she whispered. 'For not leaving me.'

'Never, old thing. You're stuck with me.'

Al's warm arm was an echo of all the moments Ada had held her close. She knew those moments were finite now, perhaps only a handful left, studded like jewels in the rough cloth of her short future.

The night wind was too cold to stay outside so long in so little clothing, but she would linger a while. In the dark, and the cold.

So long as she was not alone, Camille would stay anywhere.

5

A Ship Off the
English Coast

When the English coast came into view, the ship dropped anchor some way from land. In the starlight, the coast was visible, a roll of hill and shore, pocked with a small port town. It looked so familiar; the spire of the church, the jut of the harbour wall. It could be home.

Ada thought of the long sea voyage with her father from Martinique; the ship had rolled and bobbed across the waves for weeks, and she had never once got over her seasickness. She had thought of it as a premonition then, a warning that she shouldn't have left her island.

Now, she thought she might have been right.

Before leaving Paris, Ada had written a letter to her father conjuring a trip to the country with the 'family she tutored' to excuse her absence, Clémentine adding a note in her hand, reeling off credentials and references to promise his daughter would be safe.

They'd been kept apart on the journey over, Guil bound and under guard, Ada free but always watched. The duc had more allies than they had ever suspected. Allies at the ports and in coaching inns, smoothing their journey at every stage. For the most part, Ada kept quiet, watching the duc and Clémentine to read any clue in their demeanour, but it was no use. She had lost their trust, for now.

With the moon hanging low in the blue-black sky, the duc summoned her from her cabin, and ordered her down a ladder on the side of the ship to a waiting dinghy below. Ada and Clémentine sat side by side, backs to the coast as they slipped silently through the waves. Salt speckled Ada's lips, spray splashing the edge of her cloak and drying in a crust along the hem. After a day at sea, her hair was already suffering, dry and frizzy as her curls lost definition. She'd plaited them in a rough French braid that matched the plainness of the only dress she had with her.

She wondered if Camille had arrived in England in the same way: alone under the cover of night, cold and clinging to threadbare hope. It was strange to feel hope when everything had gone so wrong, but, sure enough, it was there; her plan was falling apart but at least she would get to see Camille again.

Whether Camille would still want her was another matter.

'You promised me you wouldn't tell anyone,' hissed Ada. It was the first time she had been alone with Clémentine. 'You lied.'

It wasn't much of a surprise to learn that Clémentine

had betrayed her to the duc; they'd always known it was a risk. But her own failure stung and she wasn't going to let Clémentine feel comfortable about it.

Clémentine tucked her cloak tightly around her. 'You asked me to make an impossible promise. How could I vow to tell no one when I didn't know what secret I would be keeping?' Another dinghy pulled alongside theirs and their bags were lowered into it. 'Oh, my dear, don't sulk. It was a valiant effort, but I was never going to bank on you, was I?'

'I thought you wanted to help Olympe.' It felt churlish to argue, but she couldn't help herself.

'I do, and I believe my brother is better positioned to do so. Look around, Ada. The Revolution is failing, the tide is turning. Men like my brother will soon be in power again. The only way through life for women like us is to hitch our wagon to power and use it to get what we want. And I'm sorry, my dear, but you are not a force worth allying with.'

'Do you know what they did to her? Sewed her into her own clothes, locked her in an iron mask like a muzzled dog. The duc and the Revolutionaries fought over her like an object. If he gets hold of her now, he'll put the people he wants in power and use them like puppets. Who could cross him with such a deadly weapon by his side?'

The moon hung behind Clémentine's head, shrouding her face. When she spoke, there was danger in her voice, an anger that Ada wasn't sure was directed at her, or at her brother for what he'd done to Olympe. 'Perhaps he will try, but do you think she'll be any safer out there in the wild? People will always come for her. I've known that since she was born, and I have done whatever I had to in order to protect her. One must be smart and make a place for oneself that is unassailable. At my brother's side she may be a weapon but, I ask you, who would cross *her*? Ada, stop worrying about what is good and do what is *necessary*.'

The boat bumped against the gravel beach and the sailor helped Ada and Clémentine ashore. The duc arrived with Guil soon after, and their bags were carried to a waiting coach. Ada stood back, thoughts overflowing. But the more Ada thought about what Clémentine had said, the more she couldn't fault her logic. Ada and the battalion *were* a poor bet compared with the duc's power and resources. And perhaps she was right; better for Olympe to navigate a known position than forever be on the run. Who was Ada to say she knew better?

As they climbed into the carriage and set off along the coast road, Ada felt as alien to herself as the unfamiliar landscape around her.

For the first time in a long time, she wasn't sure what she was fighting for.

6 Bedford Square

11 Thermidor
29 July

There was one more day before the Harfords departed for Henley House, and Camille and James's wedding. James had never seen Bedford Square in such chaos: servants loaded trunks of linen and hampers of food onto a series of carts, which would set off earlier; Camille was consumed by a small army of seamstresses come to fit her trousseau; and even James found himself ushered into another room for his own breeches and coat to be tweaked, his hair clipped. In the centre, his mother conducted her orchestra of staff and family, pulling together a symphony from discordant noise.

Al, excused from most preparations, was keeping an eye on Olympe and through a hastily concocted ruse would escort her to Henley separately, having told Lord and Lady Harford he'd had word of distant family in London and must take a day to hunt them down – but of course he wouldn't dream of missing the wedding itself.

James moved through it all like a man in shock. He *was* in shock, he supposed. Their renewed engagement seemed from another life – it *was* from another lifetime, for Edward. James had been so distracted by Wickham, he had forgotten this awful bloody mess; now he could see no way out.

His mother was so happy. A simple, uncomplicated happiness he hadn't been able to give her for years. And it was all a lie. Directing the arrangements, Lady Harford had been more animated than James had seen her in a long while, decisive and beaming with pleasure, as though the sheer joy of the wedding had seeped into her bones, rolling back the slow march of her illness.

Now, at the end of the day, with Camille returned from the seamstress's grasp and James relinquished from the tailors, his mother was finally flagging, words slurring and movements slow and jerky.

'I'll get Maman to bed,' said Hennie, steering the Bath chair out of the drawing room after dinner.

James caught Camille's eye.

'Escort me upstairs?' she asked. 'I'm feeling a little light-headed and I wouldn't want to faint again...'

'Of course.' He took her arm and they went up to her room, where she paused.

'Well, come in, then. We need to talk about this bloody wedding.'

James entered, with Camille on his heels, closing the door behind them.

The room was already occupied.

Standing by the fireplace, hands clasped behind his

back, was Lord Harford. 'It seems you both enjoyed yourselves this evening.'

'Can I help you?' Camille was perfectly still beside him, tension rolling off her.

'I rather hope you can.' Lord Harford was too calm. James knew this look. The disarmingly pleasant smile, undercut by the ice in his eyes. 'You see, in preparation for several days out of town with my family, I had a great deal of work to attend to and planned to spend today in my study. Imagine my shock when I found important papers missing. I enquired about the footman who delivers my dispatch boxes to my study, suspecting at first an error at that stage in the journey. But I remembered something. My soon-to-be daughter-in-law, outside my study, rifling through them, having conveniently disposed of the footman delivering them.'

James's eyes flicked to Camille. He was almost impressed. Stealing his father's dispatch box was more brazen than he'd thought was her style. But Camille was not so easily cowed. She clasped her hands in front of her and cocked her head in a show of concern.

'Yes, I do remember the incident you mention. I can only apologise for being so clumsy. I left the papers at your request and instead looked at wedding menus with Lady Harford. Do you not recall? Perhaps if papers are missing, they have fallen between things? Or something was damaged by my spill and a servant laid it somewhere to dry? I know I often mislay things when I am busy.'

Lord Harford watched her hawkishly. 'I have had

my rooms thoroughly searched, and no servant reports doing any such thing.'

'Ah. How unfortunate. I hope it wasn't anything important.'

Then, there – his father's expression began to shift. In the downward tilt of his chin, the dark line of his brow, James read danger. But he was not a boy now. He didn't have to be meek and deferential.

'Now look here,' he said, 'I don't like what you're suggesting.'

'This requires no input from you, boy,' snapped his father. 'I don't blame you for not seeing what is in front of your eyes; you would be fooled by a man dressed in a sack calling himself king.'

James's cheeks burned.

'I didn't take anything,' said Camille.

'I think you did.' Lord Harford advanced on her, like thunder rolling in across a plain. 'You are a dutiful girl, but I suspect your loyalty lies with your country, not mine.'

Camille held her chin up. 'I don't know what you're talking about.'

'Oh, I think you know exactly what I'm talking about.' His eyes glittered. 'I put it to you that you were recruited as a spy before your parents' untimely deaths, and you have been looking to prove your loyalty since they were called traitors. I further put it to you that when my foolish son appeared in Paris, you saw your opportunity. Your *mark*. In following him home you knew you would be coming to the house of a war minister and it was the perfect opportunity to steal state secrets and feed them back to the baying dogs of the Jacobin Club.'

Camille laughed, cold and harsh. 'If you are seeing spies everywhere, I suggest it is because you are the one putting them there,' she said. 'You live in a world of subterfuge, and you assume the rest of us behave the same. I am not a spy, whatever you choose to believe. The Revolution murdered my parents. How could I ever be loyal to it?'

Lord Harford pulled a sheet of paper from inside his coat. 'Then why did I find this in your room?' Brandishing the paper, he crossed the room in two strides. 'A top secret report on the state of the Revolution that contains the identities and whereabouts of English agents in Paris. What possible other reason could you have for stealing and hiding this?'

Camille blanched. For a moment, James thought the gig was up.

Then she shifted, anxious tension changing into something darker and more raw. 'Fine, I'll admit it. You are correct, I was trying to steal your papers. And I'll tell you why.' James reached for her arm in warning, but she shook him off. 'I know about your affair with my mother. Molyneux told me. Do you know what else he told me? That when my father found out about the two of you he felt so humiliated he decided my mother had to pay for it. With her life. Did you know that? He made up some lies that she'd betrayed the Revolution and had her executed.'

In the flickering candlelight, James watched his father recoil. Shock, anger, sadness passing across his face in quick succession. Though James already knew about the affair, it hit him again how awful the truth was. His father had always been his beacon, the figure carving the way ahead, showing him what a man was, how life should be lived. He had worked and failed, struggled and fought to live up to his legacy. To be someone his father could acknowledge as an equal. Now, he could see it plainly: his father wasn't a man to live up to. Because his father wasn't *above* him. They were both human – fallible, messy, confused, lying to themselves that they were good people and they did things for the right reasons.

Nothing James did would ever be enough, because he was chasing the shadow of a man who didn't exist.

With Camille's revelation, the fight went out of Lord Harford. He reached blindly for a chair, sinking into it heavily.

'I did not know that. I would not have thought Philippe capable of such … vindictiveness. I swear to you, I did not know, or I would have made some attempt to intervene.'

'I suppose that makes you blameless?' Camille was still ablaze.

'No. No, nothing could make me blameless in what we did.'

'If you want a reason for my actions, then you have it. I was looking for any sign that you loved her. That what you both did *meant* something. That my mother didn't die because of petty men and their whims and jealousies.' Camille surged forwards, eyes shining with tears. James caught her, wrapping his arms around her as she shouted. 'Tell me. Did you love her? Did she love you?'

'I … of course I did. I'd known her so long.' Lord Harford looked small, like a child being scolded.

'But did you *love* her? Was your affair worth it?'

'Was it worth her life? No.'

'And will my life be worth it if you throw me to the wolves, chalk me up as a traitor because I *dared* to think the people I called family would take me in when I had nowhere left to go?' Camille's voice was hoarse, the hitch in her breath warning of an oncoming coughing fit.

But Lord Harford wasn't so easily distracted. 'That still does not explain why I found these political reports in your room. What do these have to do with your mother? Why would you take and hide them?'

Back-footed, Camille floundered.

And James knew it was time. Time for him to make his choice. To decide who he was, and what he wanted to leave behind him.

'I took them.'

Lord Harford's head jerked up.

'You … you did what?'

'I took them. Read them. Hid them.'

He'd thought it would hurt to see the ease with which his father believed him – but it didn't. He'd been here too many times.

'Why on *earth* would you do that? You have grown up in this household, you know never to touch my documents—'

'I wanted to find out what was going on in Paris. I

wanted to be able to tell Camille something comforting – she has friends still trapped there.'

Camille looked at James in cautious wonder. 'You … would do that for me?'

James knew what she was really asking. What sacrifice he was making.

He met her gaze and smiled, the first real thing he'd done so far. 'Yes. I would. I have a lot to apologise for.'

'Lord help me.' Lord Harford got to his feet, tucking the paper back into his coat. 'I would say I'm disappointed in you, James, but at this point it's barely worth saying.'

'And yet, you always say it.' James hadn't realised he was going to speak until the words were out of his mouth. 'You have no idea the lengths I've gone to, to try and make you proud of me. But I never will, will I? I'm never going to be good enough for you. Did you ever think that maybe *you* disappoint *me*?'

His father spluttered, an ember of rage about to catch – then he caught it, snuffed it out. 'There will be consequences for this. Give me time to decide what.'

He strode out and Camille sat on the bed, breathing hard.

'Bloody hell. That was tense.'

James shut the door, trying to hide the tremor in his hands. 'Do you think he bought it?'

'Just about.'

Now it was over, he felt strangely light. Untethered. The future had gone from something solid and assured to a wide open plain, where the only certainty was that there was none.

James stuffed his hands in his pockets and turned back to her. 'Jesus, Camille. Why did you need his papers?'

She watched him coldly. 'When you betrayed me, it was abundantly clear I would need every card I could get my hands on to stand a chance against the duc. I didn't come to the home of the war minister to spy, but I'm not stupid enough to let a chance like that escape.'

'And did you find your card?'

'Maybe.'

For a beat, she thought he would reply, but instead he made to leave. Camille rose and stopped him with a hand on his. 'What you just did ... that was—' She broke off, scowling. 'God, don't make me say it.'

He grinned. 'Oh, no, I want to hear it.'

'Thank you,' she said, between gritted teeth.

'Anything for my fiancée.'

Her expression changed at once and it felt like a blow. He knew what she would be thinking about. Or *who*. The shadow of Ada hung between them.

But he meant it. He'd do anything for her. He'd realised it as he'd given her the news of her illness. He'd been hurt by her choosing someone else, and maybe even enjoyed hurting her back, but it seemed so petty now, such small squabbling when the truth was simple: he loved her. He had always loved her. Ada didn't change that. Maybe Camille didn't love him in the same way any more, but that didn't mean he wouldn't stand by her. Do whatever he could to keep her safe.

James drew away. 'Get some sleep. It's going to be

a long few days.'

Back in his own room he splashed cold water on his face and took a long look at himself in the mirror above his washstand.

For the first time in a long while, he could meet his own eye.

Then he thought of Ada. The way Camille looked at her, the way her hand lingered on her waist.

How miserable Camille seemed without her.

The future might be unknown, but some things seemed certain. He had found himself, and lost Camille.

7

A Coaching Inn Not Too Far from Henley-upon-Thames

12 Thermidor
30 July

England smelled strange. It smelled like cowpats and rain-damp grass and sour ale. Maybe it was just that Ada was used to the scent of Paris, the rot and sweat and sewage, but she couldn't adjust. The scenery didn't look too different, and the people were the same, more or less, yet as they hurtled along the post roads leading from market town after market town, Ada felt utterly at sea.

They had driven up from the coast as dawn broke, through the day until the light failed, only stopping to change horses, use a chamber pot and buy food for the next leg of the journey. The duc seemed unwilling to take any risk that Ada's information would grow cold.

The roads were a little better than the French ones, but the ride was still so bumpy Ada could feel her brain rattling around inside her skull. Tucked in her shawl, she stewed, thinking of all the ways things had yet to go wrong. They could arrive at the address Camille had given her to find them long gone. Or perhaps Camille hadn't found Olympe, perhaps James had hidden her away – what would the duc do then?

As much as she desperately wanted to see Camille, kiss her, feel the warmth of her body in her arms – she didn't want to put her in the duc's path again.

Whichever way Ada looked at it, there was no good way for this to end.

They stopped at a coaching inn for a few hours' rest. Ada passed Guil on the stairs as he came down to sleep with the hired muscle. He had been untied – what good would running do him now? They stopped, a step apart. This was the first chance they'd had to speak to each other.

'I'm sorry,' she said. 'I thought telling Clémentine was the right thing to do.'

Guil covered her hand with his own where it rested on the bannister. 'We both knew the risk. So much has changed since Cam left – perhaps we need to be together again.'

'Yes,' said Ada, falling back into thought. 'Things *have* changed, haven't they?'

Before Guil could reply, Clémentine called for Ada. He gave her hand a squeeze, then disappeared into the dark of the inn.

A servant woke her at dawn and she dressed again in the same plain gown she had worn for the last three days. On the road, a new carriage waited with a team of fresh horses. Behind it was a cart. The duc was talking to its driver, and in the back were half a dozen men – farm hands or day labourers from the look of them. With a shiver, Ada realised what they were: more hired muscle.

The inn's servants were loading their luggage onto the carriage; one of them fumbled the crate they were lifting and it landed with a clank. A cry went up, someone had been injured, the crate split. Ada rushed forward to help, but the duc swept onto the scene, barking orders and shooing her away. All she had time to glimpse was a strip of dull metal, and then Clémentine was ushering her into the carriage. The box was repacked and they set off.

An hour into their journey, Clémentine had fallen asleep, bonnet pulled down to cover her face. Ada was alone with the duc, and the conversation she had been avoiding could no longer be put off.

'What must I do to prove myself trustworthy?' She'd had several days to think, and appeasement was the only option left that she could see.

'We do not need to speak of it.' The duc watched the dull scenery of fields and trees and hedges outside the window.

'With respect, I think we do. You have brought me along as insurance against this information being false. So I want you to know where I stand.'

Reluctantly, he gave her his attention. 'Very well. Speak.'

Ada ran her tongue over her dry lips. She had been rehearsing this conversation since she woke up. Now, it was time.

'It is as you said: it is difficult to shed old loyalties, however misplaced I may know them to be. I do not know you well, and I have seen both good and ill in that time. Having made one mistake with my trust, I was not eager to make another.'

The duc seemed conflicted. 'You are cautious, and I admire that about you.'

'Then don't punish me for it.'

That broke his brooding expression, amusement flashing across his face before he schooled himself back into seriousness.

'Very well, Adalaide. Then let me give you some frank advice: do not be a fool. I am offering you a future – a real future – and a place. What does Camille offer you? *Love*? You will do well to grow up quickly and learn that love is not something to bank on.'

She chose her next words carefully. 'It's more than that. My father was a proponent of the Revolution, at least to start, and I confess myself sympathetic to his views.' Feed him a little of the truth, and maybe he wouldn't see where they joined up with lies.

He nodded. 'Many were.'

'People were *starving*. It was impossible for things to go on as they had…' Ada trailed off, acutely aware that she was edging her way across cracking ice.

A shadow passed over his face. 'Of course I don't want people starving. I want France to be glorious, as she was once and can be again. And of course there were things wrong with the old regime, but weren't there good things too? Wasn't France a beacon for centuries? Of art, culture, learning, refinement. Just because some people mismanaged a system doesn't mean the system must be thrown out.'

Ada felt as if she was full of something loose and light, like constantly shifting sand. As if she couldn't get purchase on herself. What he was saying wasn't wrong. There were good things about France too, surely, though she didn't often feel like France thought she had any right to claim them as hers.

She could also see that, in the face of the guillotine, anyone would be scared. They would find the good in the things being challenged, long for a past that felt secure and certain.

She wondered what it was like to have a past you longed for. Then again, how many times had she thought of her years with her mother and seen only the good?

'I have never denied there was evil in the Revolution,' she said, 'as much as there was also good.'

He leaned forward, looking at her with the earnest light she had only seen when he spoke of science. 'Then you must agree: whatever was intended at the start, surely it was never meant for us to end up here. But Robespierre is gone, the nightmare is ending. We have a chance to try again. The people call for a stable hand on the tiller, a hand marked by god, one bred for power and able to weather its storms. Not these weak, selfish lawyers or baying, simple peasants.'

'A king, you mean.'

'France has been led by kings since Charlemagne. Why do we think we are so different from all of those who came before us? A king is order. Stability.'

'He may also be a tyrant.'

'And so may a president. What else would Robespierre be called than tyrant?'

Ada said nothing. She had nothing left to refute his words. He was right. Everything he was saying was right.

'Are you with me, Ada? With your help we can take the path of least bloodshed. We can restore order, law, peace. Can I trust in your help?' He spoke softly, kindly.

She folded her hands in her lap and took a deep breath.

'Yes. I am yours to command.'

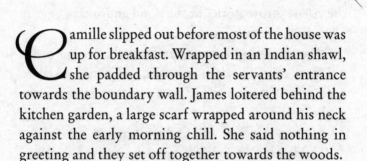

8

Henley House

Camille slipped out before most of the house was up for breakfast. Wrapped in an Indian shawl, she padded through the servants' entrance towards the boundary wall. James loitered behind the kitchen garden, a large scarf wrapped around his neck against the early morning chill. She said nothing in greeting and they set off together towards the woods.

The papers had arrived that morning with the news: Robespierre was dead. James had passed it wordlessly to Camille. She knew things had been precarious, but this still had the power to shock.

Only with the Revolution on the brink of collapse did she begin to understand where her loyalties truly lay, and the mistakes she had made.

Because she might not have time to right them.

The boundary wall ran around the broad expanse of the Harford estate, breaking off an obscene portion of land for the casual pleasure of one small family. Mist wreathed the ground, not yet burned away by the sun. Camille walked faster, relishing the pain in her lungs. She wouldn't hide from her weakness any more – she would make it her greatest strength. There was nothing left to lose, so she would make this fight hurt everyone as much as it hurt her.

On the other side of a copse of beech trees, the wall was broken by a gate, painted green and locked shut. Camille and James knew the gate well. They had stolen the long-forgotten key from the groundskeeper when they were children and used this secret exit to disappear, on adventures to the local village, to bother the cows, throw stones in the pond and smash eggs in a giggling, brattish mess.

Now, James pulled the key from the pocket of his old frock coat. The door was stiff, and it took a kick to get it open. On the other side, a narrow track ran close to the wall.

'Do you think Al will find it all right?'

'He'd better.' Camille leaned against the wall and crossed her arms. 'Come on, you don't really want to marry me, do you? Surely if there's a plausible enough reason to postpone the wedding your father will buy it.'

Lord Harford had interrupted them before when Camille had meant to discuss with James how they were going to get out of the wedding ceremony, and since then they'd hardly had a moment to themselves. The worrying thought was dawning on her that she might actually have to go through with it.

'Don't you think we have enough on our plate without adding in another plan?' said James.

He wasn't wrong. But Camille wasn't in the mood

to be placated. 'Admit it, you were playing this bluffing game as much as me. But I have Olympe now, and you've got us into more of a mess than before. Why bother keeping up the charade?'

James shoved his hands in his pockets, glancing at her from under his lashes with a hollow, smudge-eyed smile.

'To protect you, Cam. I'll always protect you.'

It was like being dropped off a cliff. Anger and longing twined inside her; anger at what he had done, and longing for the easy love that was between them once, longing to hand over control and let someone else take the weight of all the impossible choices ahead.

Liar, she wanted to say.

Please say it again.

Instead, she pursed her lips and looked away down the track, watching for Al. 'You have a strange way of showing it.'

He shrugged. 'It's true. I never meant to hurt you. It wasn't about you; it was about me and my father. I thought it didn't matter who I hurt as long as I got what I wanted. I was wrong.'

She stubbed the grass with the toe of her leather walking boot, grinding the blades into the dirt. 'I forgive you. Mostly.'

Because what was the point in holding grudges? There was a far bigger fight coming: Robespierre was dead, the Revolution would be smothered. The duc would move into the vacuum and use his influence to keep the rich powerful and the poor too traumatised to fight back.

Power operated like abuse. The powerful sold the lie that their rule was inevitable: the logical order of a fixed world. Change was dangerous and would hurt the people more than they were already hurting. They threw sops – pageantry, charity – to show themselves to be not *all* bad. Hungry, exhausted and hopeless, the powerless couldn't risk change. It was safer to stay with the known, even if it was killing them.

The Terror had handed the Royalists perfect proof that change was dangerous. Camille could only imagine what a terrified country might accept in exchange for a return to the known and familiar.

'Marry me,' said James.

Camille blinked. Looked at his mouth, trying to understand what she'd heard. 'What?'

'Marry me. For real. Let me keep you safe.'

He stood close enough she could see his bitten lips and the crepey purple skin under his eyes. She wanted to laugh. A hysterical giggle bubbled against her lips.

'That isn't funny.'

'It's not a joke.'

'It *is* a joke, because you cannot possibly be serious. You know Ada is… James, I *can't.*'

'I won't stop you from being with Ada. Bring her to England. Live with her. Keep loving her. I won't stand in your way.'

She was at once too hot and too cold. Maybe it was just the fever she couldn't shake. That had to be it. She knew where her future lay: with Ada, in Paris. That was the life she'd chosen for as long as she could live it.

But it felt as far away as the stars Ada had shown

her. James was here; the memory of being together on the other side of a thin door she only had to open and she could step into the past. Into a simpler time when her choices were easy and love was enough.

'I don't understand. Why would you do that?'

'I already told you, I would do anything to keep you safe. If you ask it of me, I am willing.' James traced his thumb along the line of her jaw. For a moment so fleeting she thought she must have imagined it, his expression was raw with regret. And want. 'Because I still love you.'

With each breath she felt keenly aware of how close he stood, that only a little air and her flimsy dress separated them. She thought about him closing the gap to cover her mouth with his.

A traitorous thought, bringing guilt sharp on its heels.

Then he was turning away, reaching into the large square pocket in the skirt of his frock coat to pull out a pistol.

Her pistol.

He held it on the flat of his palms. 'Here. This belongs to you.'

Camille took the pistol wordlessly. It was heavier than she remembered, the smooth wood and mother-of-pearl grip nestling into her hand.

She wasn't completely sure she wanted it back. Not now she knew what she did about her father. He wasn't the noble revolutionary she'd thought him. Just a petty man who'd thought his jealousy and humiliation at his wife's affair justified his violence to her in return.

Where the track curved behind the boundary wall, two figures appeared, one heavily veiled. A mud-splashed Al and Olympe arrived.

'What ho!' called Al. 'Two very English and not at all suspicious people arriving at the back door as requested!'

Camille glared, tucking the pistol away. 'I also said quietly.'

'We made it, what more do you want?'

They both looked exhausted. She didn't know where they had hidden themselves after disappearing from Bedford Square, and she didn't have time to find out. They needed to conceal Olympe before too many people were awake. Camille took Olympe's hand as they walked back through the trees, squeezing tighter the more she felt her tremble.

Once inside, they slipped through corridors towards the old ballroom. The last of the old rooms to be renovated by Lady Harford, work had stalled with her advancing illness and now it lay in perpetual disarray, dust sheets and abandoned scaffolding cluttering the once-fine space.

'It shouldn't be too cold, I hope,' said James, pulling a dust sheet off a chaise longue.

Camille surveyed the room. Scaffolding had been erected at one end, where the ornate ceiling cornice was still waiting to be painted with gold leaf. The parquet was unpolished and half-covered in more dust sheets. No one should come into the room, but if they did Olympe could hide herself under the sheets pulled over furniture.

'I know it's a risk,' said Camille, 'but it would be a bigger one to split up. At least this way we're all in the house.'

Olympe sat on the chaise longue. 'I'll be fine. I've slept on worse.'

Camille thought of the straw pallet in the Conciergerie prison cell where she had found Olympe.

Yes, what was at stake was much worse.

Camille plumped a pillow, positioning it at the head of the chaise. 'I still remember my promise. We're going to get you somewhere safe. I don't know where yet but – we'll think of something.'

Olympe had removed her bonnet and veil, letting her unpinned hair spill around her face in gleaming black waves. Despite her captivity with James, Camille thought she was starting to look almost well. The gauntness that had been in her cheeks when they'd rescued her in Paris was gone. Her stormy skin glowed, the colours richer and more complex.

Whatever else happened, they must have helped her in some small way. She had to hold onto that.

Olympe lowered her gaze. 'There's something I want to tell you. Please don't be angry.'

'All right,' said Camille cautiously.

'I don't think I want to keep hiding. I … I can't keep running away. It makes me feel helpless, and I don't want that to be my future.' She looked up, eyes glittering. 'Let's go back to Paris, after Wickham has been arrested. The longer I run, the longer I put other people in harm's way. The duc, Wickham – they've both hurt people in pursuit of me. This is my fight. Let me fight it.'

Camille was silent. Olympe had been through so much more than any of them, and she was braver than all of them put together.

They had offered themselves as bait to Wickham. A human monster walked among them.

Wickham would attack; he wouldn't be able to resist. Their trap would snap shut.

One day more to hold their nerve.

One day more, and it would come to an end.

9

The Dining Room, Henley House

Supper was a lavish affair.

The company had gathered in the drawing room. James was dressed in a freshly cleaned black tailcoat and breeches, after Al had refused to be seen in the same room as someone wearing a frock coat so completely out of date. Lady Harford had, of course, matched James with Camille to lead into the dining room, and they took their place behind lords and baronets and in front of the vicars and lawyers, as etiquette demanded, before the procession crossed the entrance hall to the grand dining room that shone with polished glassware and silver.

The last of the light was dying behind the shuttered windows, and tens of candles illuminated the table in a golden glow. The menu was French as a nod to Camille and Al, despite the current war making it unfashionable and unpatriotic. A stuffed and dressed boar's head was placed centre-stage, surrounded by jellies and deep fried cockscombs, then a whole salmon poached in champagne with truffles, and in between, plates of asparagus, artichokes, hare cake in jelly, petit pastis of veal, all washed down with endless bottles of hock and sherry.

James pushed a piece of salmon around his plate. It was hard to find his appetite. The chatter drifted over him, and he let himself be a pebble in a stream, water rushing past but never moving him.

Camille sat opposite. He allowed himself only glimpses of her, glancing up when she was looking away. She was beautiful in a mint-green silk dress that brought out her eyes, and her hair had been curled and piled on top of her head, a few artful locks left loose to frame her face. She glanced his way, and he hid his face in his wine glass. It hadn't been long since they'd sat at this same table as enemies. How hopeful he had been then. He'd thought his plan only needed a little more time, that he would triumph. What had it been for? Absolutely nothing. Now they could only wait for Wickham to make an attempt on Lord Harford's life, so that they could close their trap.

Having drained his glass, James risked another glance at Camille.

She was staring straight at him.

He flushed, then she smiled and he smiled back. Her eyes were too glossy and her collarbones too gaunt, but he couldn't help feeling some measure of contentment. He was home, with the girl he loved. If he squinted, it almost looked something like the life he'd hoped for. How odd that they had still ended up here, where they had been aiming for long before the world fell apart, before the Revolution had rotted and Camille's parents had been executed. Before Ada.

Perhaps he had drunk too much, but his mood turned like a coin flipping and he felt sour and disappointed. He knew it was fantasy he was indulging in.

Supper carried on, and an array of trifles, sweetmeats, and strawberry soufflé rounded out the meal. The women retired to the drawing room and the men stayed to drink port and smoke. James excused himself from both. In truth, he couldn't stand being around people any longer.

Out on the terrace, he watched the stars spin across the sky, a bank of clouds rolling in from the west. He filled a pipe but didn't light it.

It was almost over now. One way or another.

'James. I was looking for you.'

He turned to find his father had followed him out.

They had hardly spoken since their confrontation in Camille's room, and all his conviction of that evening had fled.

He put the pipe away. 'You found me.'

His father shifted his weight. 'There's – ah – something I wanted to say.'

'Yes?'

It took his father another moment to find the words and James realised with a flash of surprise that his father was *uncomfortable*. It was a first.

'I know things haven't been easy between us.' Lord Harford left a pause that James politely declined to fill. Whatever this was, he wasn't going to make it easy for his father. 'I have been hard on you because you are my son, and I know much will fall on your shoulders when I am gone. I want to know you're able to carry it.'

James almost laughed. If only his father knew just how much he carried already.

Lord Harford cleared his throat. 'Perhaps we don't understand each other too well; we wouldn't be the first father and son to have that problem. But this is your wedding, my boy, and I am willing to take a step towards conciliation if you are.'

'I am.'

'Excellent. I have decided I will escort Camille to the altar; it's the least I owe her parents. We can start your new life off on the right foot.'

His father seemed to think he'd done enough; with an incline of his head he left, and James stood alone.

The Vestry Outside the Chapel

13 Thermidor
31 July

The Henley House chapel was a medieval relic nestled inside the sprawling house. A small space for the family's private use, it had remained while the rest of the building had risen and fallen with its owners' fortunes, finally forming the nexus around which the contemporary house had been built, accessed through an unassuming door off the entrance hall. Only one door opened to the outside, long fallen into disuse.

Camille remembered how terrified she'd been of this place as a child, convinced its Gothic arches and vaulted ceiling were haunted by legions of Harford dead. How she and James would sneak in, in the dead of night, and dare each other to lie on the stone caskets and pretend to be a corpse.

Lady Harford delivered Camille to the vestibule at the front of the chapel, Hennie pushing her Bath chair. Camille was wearing the gown Hennie had suggested, her hair piled on top of her head and woven with purple flowers and silver ribbon. The dress was pale lavender, embroidered in silver thread along the hem and waistband, a shimmering forest of leaves and curling vines and blooming flowers. Camille hated to admit it, but she almost liked how she looked. She wished Ada was here to see her – then remembered why she was dressed up and the very thought of Ada made her feel dizzy with shame.

The double doors to the chapel stood open, and inside the pews were decked with flowers, guests already taking their seats. Lady Harford raised a hand to signal Hennie to stop the chair. With a jerky, fumbling movement, she reached for Camille's hand. Camille helped her take it, coming closer to save her the effort. She didn't know if it would ever stop hurting to see Lady Harford like this. She had been powerless to save her own mother, but for a moment she wondered how much worse it might be for James, to be forced to watch his mother's slow undoing, the helplessness stretched out over weeks and months and years.

Lady Harford was looking at her with tears limning her eyes. 'My dear. How glad I am to see this day, and how sorry I am we didn't do more to make it come sooner.'

Camille only smiled, silenced by guilt. She was repaying Lady Harford's love with deception. She didn't deserve her kindness.

More guests were arriving and Hennie wheeled Lady Harford into the chapel with them. Only Al hung back.

He was dressed smartly in black and cream, an emerald pin in his neckerchief the only show of ostentation. But his face was washed out, his usual insouciance gone.

'Are you sure you want to do this?' he asked. 'There's still time to run.'

A punch of nerves hit her. It was as if her insides had been turned to churning liquid. 'Stop making it worse,' she snapped. 'You know how much I hate this, but we can't let anything endanger the plan now.'

'It's okay to admit you've backed yourself into a corner—'

'Just shut up. *Please*.'

Whatever note of honest pain had been in that word seemed to work. Al said nothing. And then he did something even more shocking: he hugged her, squeezing tightly. 'You're brave, Camille,' he whispered against her hair. 'You got us all this far. You won't stop being brave now, I know it.'

Her face pricked hot with tears and she turned away, blinking furiously.

With a final squeeze of her arm, Al went into the chapel and closed the doors behind him.

She was on her own, a bouquet of meadow flowers clutched in her hands, until her cue came to walk down the aisle.

She thought she might be sick.

The door from the entrance hall opened and Camille brushed away her tears. Lord Harford came in, hesitant. He was too tall for the cramped medieval space, ducking to fit under the frame.

She bobbed a curtsey, lowering her eyes.

'Ah. Camille. I'm glad to find you here. I came to apologise.'

At that, her head snapped up and she looked at him in disbelief. Lord Harford coloured. Clearly this was as awkward for him as it was for her.

'I've – er – made a few unfair assumptions about you. My job, I'm afraid, has a tendency to make one rather paranoid.'

She blinked. Gathered her wits. 'Perfectly understandable, my lord. These are unusual times.'

'Quite. But I can see that you make my son happy, and there are worse matches he could make, so I suppose what I'm here to say is that I would like to give you away. It's the least I can do in memory of your father's friendship. And your mother's...' He broke off. 'Well, will you have me?'

'I...'

She knew she should accept, but she was having trouble getting the words out. She had never spoken much with her father about her planned match with James. Now she knew the truth about her mother's affair, she wondered if he would have allowed it.

Then again, after what her father had done in retaliation, she wasn't sure she cared too much what he would have wanted.

'Yes, of course.'

Lord Harford smiled, an unexpectedly genuine thing, and offered her his arm.

As she went to take it, there was a knock at the door.

Not the door to the chapel itself, or the door to the entrance hall.

A knock on the outside door.

A cold flash of warning passed through her. Lord Harford frowned and went to lift the latch.

'How odd. A late guest of my wife's, perhaps?'

Camille backed away, hand reaching for the pistol strapped to her thigh beneath her dress as the door opened.

Flanked by Edward, Wickham stood on the threshold.

'Wickham!' exclaimed Lord Harford. 'What on earth are you doing here?'

The other man smiled, his mouth a grim, determined line.

'I'm protecting what's mine.'

He made a signal, and Edward stepped inside. In the milky early morning light, he looked at once more monstrous and more human. His flesh had discoloured further, new stitches along his forehead. And yet the handsome lines of his face were undiminished, the gloss of his black curls, the angle of his cheekbone. The smell of death hung in the air, but his eyes were more alert than before, his movements more supple and dexterous.

Lord Harford stared in breathless horror. 'Wickham – my god, man – what have you done to the boy?'

Camille yanked him back by the elbow, placing herself between him and Edward, pistol raised.

'Back. Off. Olympe might not have been willing to hurt you, but I am.'

The muzzle of her gun landed on Wickham, who snarled. 'Don't think I won't kill you if you stand in my way, girl.'

Edward didn't move. His eyes were fixed on Camille and she had the sickening sense she was being studied.

Lord Harford took one look at Camille wielding a weapon and lost his composure. 'Good god,' he yelled. 'Where did you get that pistol? You *are* a spy after all!'

'Will you *shut up*?' snapped Camille, struggling to keep her focus.

'You're working for France! I knew it!'

Her pistol wavered, and Wickham made his move.

He and Edward lunged forward together. Camille leaped back, in too close quarters to fire the gun. Edward overshot and barrelled into Lord Harford, who was slammed against a wall, head making contact against stone with a sickening crack. In the near-collision, Camille dropped her pistol.

But she had no time to retrieve it. Wickham got there first.

She glanced between Wickham and Edward, calculating her chances.

Then she turned on her heel and ran.

The guests were restless.

They had been seated on the uncomfortable pews, with everyone frozen in position for too long. Hennie was pulling petals off her bridesmaid's bouquet, and Lady Harford looked to have nodded off in her Bath chair. Behind James, the vicar shuffled nervously, flipping the pages of the Bible back and forth.

James sneaked a glance at his pocket watch. What on earth was going on?

When his father had told him his plan to walk Camille down the aisle, James had blanched – god knew how Camille would react to *that* – but let him go about his business.

A fight, he'd expected. Camille storming off. Their cover being blown.

Any of it would make more sense than this.

Beside him, Al leaned in. 'Looks rather like you've been stood up, old chap,' he said, smiling blandly at the assembled guests.

James clasped his hands behind his back and nodded at his Great Aunt Tabitha, who gave him an encouraging look from a middle row. 'I don't know what you mean.'

He knew this wedding plan had always been a pretence, but to be left at the altar still stung something fierce. *Camille* had been the one who insisted they go ahead, who said it wasn't worth the risk that his father would act on his suspicion that she was a spy. The least she could have done was warn James she was going to bolt.

'Honestly, though, don't you think we should perhaps check on her?' said Al. 'Camille isn't known for being sensible and staying out of trouble...'

He wasn't wrong. James checked his pocket watch again. Maybe in another five minutes he could send Hennie out to see what was going on.

James had spent enough Sundays of his life in this very room to know every sound it made, and the sounds of everyone who spent their Sundays in there with him. Almost every Sunday, bar sickness or travel, he had been here, wedged into a pew, cold, bored and paying attention to anything other than the sermon.

So when the handle of the chapel door rattled, he knew it was not his father on the other side.

Unthinking, he took a step forward, blindly reaching for Al in warning.

Then the double doors burst open.

And Ada and the duc stormed in.

PART SIX

Begin with Trust

1

Henley House

Camille ran so fast she had no idea where she was going. Pelting out of the chapel and into the entrance hall, she took the first door that was open and ran and ran and ran, the sound of footsteps behind her. At any moment she expected Edward's cold hand to close around her arm, for their fight in the pleasure gardens to repeat with a deadlier end.

Corridors and rooms rushed past, her silk slippers sliding on the polished floors. In a lesser hall, she skidded into a locked door and crumpled, landing hard on her backside. Her chest was spasming, like a fist squeezing her too tight, and for a moment the world was nothing but the struggle to breathe. Her tongue felt thick in her mouth. She hacked up something bloody and raw onto the pale skirts of her dress, a fine red spray peppering her stockings.

And still, no hand reached for her throat. The footsteps had died away.

Camille looked up and found herself alone.

She was on the floor at the bottom of a set of stairs

far less grand than the main entrance hall. The bones of the old Jacobean house could be seen here, in the dark wood panelling, the squat doors and heavy furniture crammed together. It was a part of the house Camille knew less well. The dull, dingy rooms full of dust and ugly old art had bored her as a child, preferring far more to explore the attics and basements and ice houses and stables with James – but it wasn't far from the ballroom.

Her heart rate slowed, the initial panic that had sent her fleeing seeped away and she was left with a stark choice: go back to the chapel to warn James and Al, or find Olympe and protect her.

It was a snap decision, and one she could not regret making.

Knotting her skirts around her waist, Camille padded up the stairs towards the closed-off wing, and Olympe. Honed with new purpose, she stole through the corridors as silent as a breath of wind. The guests were in the chapel, the servants in the kitchens or setting the dining room for the wedding breakfast, leaving her a brief window to act unseen. And oddly, she felt almost calm. They had been waiting in the wings for too long, riddled with nerves. Finally, the storm had broken. Maybe there was something wrong with her, but she had *missed* this. The thrill of the hunt, her life on the line. Everything immediate, vital, urgent.

Alive.

She didn't know how much longer she would be. Better to die in action than live in obscurity.

In the abandoned ballroom, she found Olympe sitting cross-legged by a window, five individual flares of blue current crackling from her fingertips like claws. When she spotted Camille, they died down immediately.

'What's wrong?' she asked, slithering from her perch.

Camille explained as best she could. That Wickham and Edward were here, the time to spring their trap was now.

'We should have known it would come at the worst time,' said Olympe, eyes wide in alarm. 'Where are James and Al?'

'Still in the chapel, they don't know yet. But Lord Harford saw Wickham and Edward, he knows the threat is real – that's something.'

'What good is it if we all end up dead anyway?'

'We're not going to end up dead.'

'You have a plan?'

Camille chewed the side of her tongue. Calling it a plan was generous.

'There are more of us than them. If we find somewhere we can physically trap them – maybe we can hold them long enough for Lord Harford to send for help, and have Wickham arrested.'

'What about Edward?'

Camille shrugged. 'If he sides with Wickham, he faces the same consequences.'

Olympe looked grim. 'They won't arrest him, will they? They won't believe he's human any more. They'll kill him.'

'Maybe so. I won't promise different.'

'I think I can get through to him.'

'Olympe—'

'No, listen. You weren't with us at the operating theatre until the end, you didn't see him. He spared us at St Paul's.' Olympe fixed Camille with her starry gaze, her mouth a thin, determined line. 'Will you at least let me try?'

Camille stood, and pulled Olympe up with her. The blood had dried stiff on her skirt, and her silk slippers had torn. She pulled them off. Barefoot, skirts around her hips and hair falling out of its elaborate series of pins, she felt nothing like herself. And everything like herself.

'I won't stop you. But it's harder to change your loyalties than you think. If you get in trouble, I'll pull you out.'

Olympe's eyes flashed. 'Deal.'

A floorboard creaked outside, and both girls froze. From nowhere, a fly buzzed across the room. The floorboards creaked again.

Silently, Camille raised a finger to her lips, then led Olympe to a door on the other side of the ballroom. They eased it open and slipped out.

They found themselves in the long gallery that stretched the width of the house, lined with windows on one side, and a wall of art on the other.

Footsteps came from the ballroom – and then the doorknob twisted.

Camille and Olympe hunkered down behind a couch, holding their breath. The door opened and

Camille watched a pair of boots cross the floor through the gap under the couch. Wickham walked slowly, almost casually. As he passed them, he began to whistle. He held something in his hand – Camille couldn't see what – but she could hear the sound of leather twisting.

There was only open ground between their hiding place and the door back into the ballroom. In the other direction stretched a long, long expanse of gallery. It was just a matter of time before Wickham found them. Then Camille saw it – their chance.

Halfway along the gallery was a large set of French windows leading to a balcony. From there they could drop to the lawns below. She caught Olympe's eye and gestured to it. Olympe nodded.

'Come out, come out, wherever you are,' Wickham drawled. 'I like a bit of sport as much as the next Englishman, but we've all had quite enough of this, don't you think?'

Camille held her finger to her lips again and motioned for Olympe to follow her.

They shot across the gap as fast as they could.

The French windows were so close she could see the balcony and the wide open space beyond. A breeze ruffled the hair that had spilled around her face, and she realised the door was open.

Wait – why was the door open?

Like a bolt it struck her. It was a trap. Unlocked, enticing. The only way out.

Camille stumbled to a halt, giddy with panic.

Wickham met her coming the other way around the chair.

His handsome face was twisted into a cruel grin. 'Boo!'

In an instant, his arms were around her, pinning her arms to her sides. Olympe flung one hand wreathed in sparks towards him, then hesitated. If she shocked Wickham, Camille would get shocked too.

They had tried to be smart.

Wickham was smarter.

'Run!' said Camille, with the last of her breath.

But it was too late.

Another figure stepped forward. Eyes dark and necrotic flesh beginning to slough from his bones, Edward blocked Olympe's retreat.

Camille felt rather than saw Wickham's grin, the movement of his jaw against the side of her head.

'Get the girl,' he snapped, signalling towards Olympe, 'and end this.'

2

The Chapel

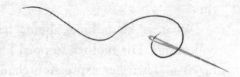

The duc advanced, Ada at his side, striding down the aisle with a gun pointed at James's head.

It took a minute for James's brain to catch up. How was the duc here? This was impossible. It made no sense. Like he had stepped sideways into the wrong universe, into another wedding, one where the duc was leading Ada down the aisle, like the father of the bride.

But this was all *wrong*.

'You have something of mine,' said the duc, stopping a few steps from the altar. His English was pristine, if a little out of fashion. 'I have come to collect it.'

Oh. That.

'Who on earth are you, and what are you doing in my house?' Lady Harford said. Hennie wheeled her forward. She had drawn herself up, every inch fighting against her tremors. Her tone made some instinctive childhood part of James shrivel.

The duc, however, seemed unaffected. 'This doesn't concern you.'

Ada looked at James, standing next to the altar in his smart suit, and frowned. James could almost see her putting the pieces together.

'I very much think it does concern me if you insist on speaking to my son in this way.'

James stepped down from the raised dais and stood in front of his mother. 'Don't worry, I can take care of this.'

'What is he talking about, James? What is he collecting?' His mother stopped him with a hand on his arm. Then her expression changed. 'Did you get yourself in debt?'

'A very grave debt,' said the duc. 'I have waited long enough.'

'Oh, you foolish boy. Is this why you wanted to postpone the wedding?'

James eased himself out of her grip, then turned to the duc, schooling his features into something impassive. 'Not here. Not in front of my family. Come with me and I'll take you to what you want.'

The duc nodded. 'Only you.' He pointed to Al. 'I want no trouble from that one.'

Al was so shaken he made no quip, simply nodded.

'James! You can't leave, what about the wedding?' called Hennie. 'What will we tell Camille?'

He flinched. 'I don't think Camille's coming.'

He hoped she'd managed to run. If he could give her enough time to find Olympe and flee, maybe they stood a chance.

Alone, he knew his own life was forfeit.

Ada thought she should feel angry, but she only felt numb.

James at an altar, at a *wedding*, waiting for Camille – it was her worst nightmare. The thing she had dreaded since saying goodbye to Camille had been that, in England, without Ada around to remind her of what they had, Camille would slip away from her. The past, stability, home – those things would be too alluring to turn down.

Apparently, she had been correct.

God, she prayed it was some sort of clever plan, but she didn't want to delude herself. Sometimes things fell apart.

The duc shut the doors to the chapel. 'Bolt it. I don't want anyone interfering.'

James obeyed, looking as white as a sheet. Ada felt a sour moment of pleasure. Good. She wanted him to be uncomfortable. It was as much as he deserved.

Clémentine had been outside arranging the hired thugs to guard the exits while Ada and the duc had confronted James. Now they were reunited, and Guil had been pushed into the chapel, hands bound, to be locked in with the rest of them.

With the doors shut, a slumped figure was revealed. A tall man, smartly dressed, hatless with a runnel of blood down one temple and cheek. A pistol lay at his side.

James gave a cry and fell to his knees. 'Father! Father, wake up!' He turned to the duc, eyes blazing.

'There was no need to hurt my family. I said I'd help you.'

The duc looked perturbed. 'This was not done by our hand. We found him like this – of course we did not know who he was then.'

All thoughts of the wedding left Ada's mind. If it was possible, James seemed to go even whiter. He was frightened – more frightened than he was of the duc. That couldn't mean anything good.

Ada kneeled with him, putting two fingers to the man's throat. 'His pulse is strong. I think it's simply concussion.'

James didn't look too reassured, but Ada took the opportunity to mouth, 'What's going on?' She didn't know if she could trust him, but they had a mutual enemy in the duc and perhaps that would be enough.

James just shook his head.

'Where is Camille?' asked the duc. 'I would advise against any more of your ill-planned theatrics; you have tried my patience too far already. Pass me the gun.' He directed the last order to Ada, who reluctantly handed it over. She knew the firearm well; it was Camille's.

James stood, dusting off his hands. 'I don't know where Camille is. I thought she was with my father.'

Ada looked at the injury to the man's head with renewed interest. 'You think Camille did this?'

'No,' said James simply. 'I think whoever did this is also responsible for Camille's disappearance.'

Ada swallowed. 'She ran?'

James looked at her, hollow-eyed. 'I hope she ran.'

Ada's blood turned to ice.

She had known this couldn't end well – but perhaps it was going to be worse than she'd dared think.

Ada hadn't realised just what kind of money James came from. As he led their party through the house, she was struck by the sheer size of it. She was familiar enough with the luxury of her father's house, and the grand apartments Camille's family had occupied before their death – but this was wealth on a different scale.

The countless pieces of art lining the walls, the statues and rugs and vases, and room after room of sheer excess. James moved through it casually, as though his wealth was wallpaper. Ada supposed it must feel like that, if you grew up in it.

The duc handed Camille's pistol to Clémentine.

'Protect yourself, my dear.'

The words were so quiet, Ada almost wondered if she hadn't heard them. Clémentine took the pistol with a look of thanks.

Ada prayed James had the sense to take them anywhere but to Olympe.

Whatever it was James was scared of, she had to believe Camille could handle it.

It was easier to worry about that than think about what the wedding meant. Slowly, the numbness was wearing off and she began to sense the size and shape of her anger.

It frightened her.

The four of them followed James into the house, strung out in a line like a hunting party. Clémentine joined James at the front, Ada behind, the duc bringing up the rear to stop anyone thinking of running.

'You're the second man to steal my daughter,' said Clémentine, with worrying casualness. 'Tell me, what did you want with her? You work for the English government, no?'

'No,' said James. Ada could only see his face from an angle, but there was no mistaking the tight line of his jaw. She could well imagine the shock he was feeling, meeting Olympe's mother in such circumstances.

'Then you took her for yourself?'

'Olympe was safe with me, unlike with the duc,' he said.

'You don't expect me to believe it was altruism, surely. Are you a man of science too? Or did you merely want to add another curio to your collection?'

James didn't answer, only gestured them through a door. They had come to a ballroom It was empty.

'Well?' asked the duc. 'Where is she?'

James shrugged. 'She should be here. If she's not...'

The duc cocked his pistol. 'I am asking you again. Where is Olympe?'

Ada's gaze darted between the two men, mouth dry. Her two enemies. Maybe she should intervene. Maybe she could simply step back and let the two of them take each other out. Not that she rated James's chances.

'I don't know. I think you might be too late.'

'Explain.'

James closed his eyes. Then he began to speak.

'It was a man called Wickham who sent me to France. He was my surgical tutor at university; he also studied electricity and the human body. I was meant to bring Olympe to him, but instead I took her for myself. When he realised I had betrayed him, he threatened to kill us to get to her.' He opened his eyes. He seemed resigned to whatever fate waited for him. 'Like I said, you're too late. You have no idea what he's capable of.'

Ada gasped. 'This is the person you think attacked your father?'

James nodded.

It took everything she had not to ask about Camille. She had worked too hard to regain the duc's trust to squander it.

The duc didn't rage as she expected. He drew himself together, sharp as tempered steel.

'Then they have made a grave mistake.' He cocked the pistol, eyes narrowing. 'Olympe is mine.'

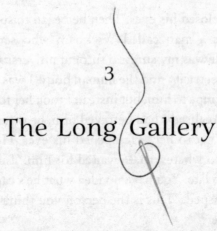

3
The Long Gallery

Olympe stood frozen in fear by the door that could have been their escape, but now Edward was in her way. Wickham's arm was still tight around Camille's neck, holding her in a headlock. The more she struggled, the more she strangled herself.

A cascade of blue sparks washed over Olympe, crackling and flaring like a shield. The air was sharp with the scent of electricity, and Camille's hair began to rise like a halo.

Something had changed in Olympe while she had been in England. Camille had never seen her exert such control over her power – she had always thought of Olympe's power as primal, chaotic, a storm to be contained, not directed.

She'd been wrong.

It stung to think it, because it meant that maybe James had got something right. Whatever work they'd been doing together seemed to have paid off.

'I see you, Edward.' Olympe's voice rang out clear and unwavering. 'I know you don't want to hurt us.'

Edward didn't respond, but he watched Olympe with an intensity that made Camille's skin crawl. The blue sparks of her shield cast a glow over his mottled face. She thought of the way he'd looked at Olympe back in the operating theatre. The curiosity, and the guilt. He'd hesitated before, shown them mercy when Wickham wasn't around. Was it too much to hope he might do so again?

Hesitantly, Olympe took a step forward and held out a hand, letting the electricity pour back up her arm, leaving her palm bare.

'He treats you like a monster to do his dirty work – but you're not one. I think you're like me. Different – but human.'

Edward looked down at himself, the stitches holding him together, the discolouration and rot setting in. 'Perhaps. But I think I'm running on borrowed time.'

Olympe considered him for a moment, then brought her hands together. In her cupped palms the sparks gathered, wound together and bloomed like an eerie flower. 'This isn't like the rest of them either. Does that make us less?'

He said nothing, eyes trained on her hands.

'I think it makes us *more*.'

'For god's sake, get *on* with it,' Wickham snapped, tightening his grip on Camille, who clawed at his arm, trying to draw breath.

'Why?' Edward looked past Olympe, to Wickham.

'Because I am giving you an order. Or do I have another traitor on my hands? We deal with these two first, then James. It's time for a clean house.'

Edward flinched. 'Don't touch James.'

Wickham snorted. 'Your sentiment is touching, but misplaced. Why be loyal to someone who crossed you the first chance he got?'

'Perhaps he saw in you what I was too deluded to realise. You go too far. Why should I take your orders?'

'Because your life is *mine*,' snarled Wickham. 'You would be dead without me, so do as I say and I won't sell you to a freak show.'

Olympe's eyes flashed. 'I think *you're* the monster.'

Still, Edward did nothing, frozen in a war with himself.

'Fine,' said Wickham. 'I will do it myself.'

With his free hand, he drew a knife and stabbed Camille in the back of the knee. She yelled, pain racing up her thigh, and buckled to the ground.

'And stay down.'

She tried to drag herself up, but her leg went out from under her.

Knife raised, Wickham lunged at Olympe.

In a crackle of blue and the smell of singed hair, Olympe threw out a net of sparks that wrapped around him. He gave a grunt of pain. His skin began blistering red where the electricity made contact, but Olympe held steady, keeping the current flowing from her hands. In her black eyes, a thousand stars danced, as cold and blue as ice.

'I am not your prize,' she said, voice low and dangerous. 'I am not an object to be traded and fought for. If you won't leave me and my friends alone by choice, perhaps I will have to make you.'

The net tightened, his hair charring, eyes wide as the sparks bit into his face. Camille held tight to the chair for support; she didn't know whether to try and stop her.

'Please.' Wickham forced words through his clenched jaw. 'Don't kill me.'

'Why not?' Olympe hissed. But the fervour had gone out of her eyes, her control on the net sputtered. As it lifted from his skin, the smell of charred flesh filled the air.

With a cry, the current snapped and Olympe fell back, staring at her own shaking hands. 'I can't.' She met Camille's eye. 'I'm sorry.'

Wickham, now free, fixed his grip on the knife, his face a cross-hatch of raw skin and burns.

But Edward got there first.

In a single motion, he was between Olympe, hand closing around Wickham's throat. There was only a second to see the panic in Wickham's eyes, before Edward lifted his tutor off the floor. Wickham scrabbled at his hand, face red, eyes bulging.

'Stop,' he rasped. 'What are you doing? I order you to put me down.'

With Olympe behind him, Edward's face was cast again into shadow. The light from her sparks had lent him a lifelike glow; now he was painted only in shades of death.

'She might not be able to kill you,' he said. 'But I can.'

Edward looked at Olympe, pain on his once handsome face. She reached for him, but he squeezed Wickham's neck tighter.

It snapped.

Olympe gasped in horror, hands over her mouth.

Edward flung Wickham to the floor like a ragdoll. His head lolled back so that his sightless, glassy eyes looked at Camille. His knife had fallen next to him. Camille saw her chance and closed her hand around it.

'Thank you.' Edward moved towards Olympe, stiff and slow, touching a coil of her hair that had pulled free of its braid. 'Take care of James.'

She looked at him in hope and confusion and fear. 'Take care of him yourself—'

A shot rang out and Edward jerked, toppling into Olympe before collapsing onto the floor. Olympe screamed, a spatter of dark red blood spraying across her face.

A woman Camille didn't recognise strode through the open door. Her hair was wild and loose around her shoulders, her dress elegant but muddied, and she held her head high. Camille narrowed her eyes. There was something familiar about her – something in the tilt of her chin.

She stopped in the centre of the room, pistol still smoking.

'Get your hands off my daughter.'

4

The Long Gallery

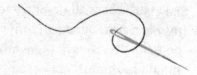

The smell of gunpowder and blood lingered in the air.

Ada stood beside the duc in the doorway to the long gallery, taking in the scene. Two bodies on the floor – three, if you counted Camille, collapsed and bloodied. And at the centre of it all, Olympe.

The battalion was reunited; in a straight game, the numbers were on their side.

But she remembered what Guil had told her: *play the players, not the game.* There were too many moving parts and Ada didn't know where on the board everyone would fall.

Clémentine dropped Camille's pistol and dashed across the gallery to Olympe.

Well, they would soon see where one set of pieces would land.

Olympe drifted forwards, the electric current faded from her, leaving a pale bluish-grey blush to her skin, like a suddenly calmed sea. Dangerously calm.

'Mother?'

'Oh, my poor sweet girl – what did that creature do to you?' She pressed her hands to Olympe's face, smoothing her hair.

'Nothing. You didn't have to—' Olympe's voice broke, and she stepped out of her mother's reach. 'Why did you have to hurt him? He saved me.'

Clémentine laughed lightly. 'I was trying to keep you safe. That's all I ever try to do.' She pulled Olympe into her arms again, and this time Olympe let herself be held. 'It's okay, we're together now. Just like it should be, hmm?'

Despite the complicated woman Ada knew Clémentine to be, she felt a stab of envy seeing Olympe reunited with her mother.

'But … how are you here?' asked Olympe.

The woman's face fell, a mixture of confusion and frustration. 'Aren't you glad to see me? Aren't you glad to know I'm safe?'

'Of course I am. That's not what I mean.'

The duc chose that moment to sweep in imperiously. Ada kept in his shadow. Behind her, Guil, James and Al followed.

'She's here because we have come to take you home, Olympe,' said the duc.

Olympe scrambled back. '*You.*' She glanced between Clémentine and the duc, eyes clouded with confusion. 'I don't understand.'

'Ah – yes. There is something we must talk about, mon ange. It was a mistake, perhaps, not to tell you before. The truth is, the duc is my brother, Olympe. I did my best to keep you apart from the world – all the world. I thought it would be easier for you to think our life simple, to remove any temptation to look for more family, for the dangerous world beyond. But this is what matters: he is a man with money and means and it is clear that he is our best chance to keep you safe.'

'Keep me safe? He's the man who hurt me my whole life!'

'I won't deny that you have been through harder times than most, but we never acted with intent to *hurt* you. If we didn't understand you, how could we know how to protect you?'

Olympe gaped. 'Understand me? You're my *mother*. If that's protection, I don't want it. I want my freedom.'

Clémentine's face fell. 'That is what I am trying to give you.'

'You *let* him hurt me...' Olympe's skin crackled blue with sparks, ripples and twists buckling along her neck, her hands. 'All this time I thought you were on my side.'

'Ridiculous girl, of course I am on your side.' Clémentine grasped her wrist, ignoring the pain of the shock, and the sparks damped down immediately. Olympe wouldn't risk hurting her mother. 'You are the greatest discovery of our times. I told you I was never scared of you, I thought you were a *wonder*. But being a mother doesn't always mean being your friend. When you were three and screamed the house down because I wouldn't let you play with snakes in the garden – you hated me, but I did the right thing and stopped you. When you were nine and wanted to stay up with the adults and drink wine, and I sent you to bed no matter how much you told me I didn't understand you – again, you hated me but again, I did the right thing. That is my job. I must do things you cannot understand and you may hate me, but never, ever believe I don't do this for *you*.'

Olympe had gone limp. Behind her, Camille was on the floor, skirts soaked in blood. She'd ripped off the bottom of her petticoat and was tying it around her knee. It took everything Ada had in her not to rush over and help.

'So I don't have a choice?' Olympe's voice was barely a whisper.

'No,' said Clémentine, gently taking Olympe's arm. 'I am afraid you don't.'

The look on Olympe's face broke Ada's heart. Then it hardened; better Olympe knew the truth than keep believing there was justice in the world. Now the Revolution had fallen, it was dangerous to be so naive.

The duc retrieved the pistol from where Clémentine had dropped it, tucking it into the waistband of his breeches. He surveyed the bodies on the floor.

'So this is the English competition.' He hunkered next to the strange, mottled boy, examining the gunshot wound in his forehead. James joined him, a strange mixture of relief and horror on his face. Silently, he kneeled and closed the boy's eyes, his own limned with unshed tears.

'Yes. But it's over now.'

'I was expecting something a little more intimidating.' The duc gave a harsh laugh. 'Good to know the English lag behind us as ever. All empty threats and bluster. Ada, come and—'

He never got a chance to finish the sentence.

Something exploded at the periphery of her vision. Ada flung herself down, along with Clémentine and the duc. Through the smoke, she saw Al and Guil in the doorway, Al holding a small paper packet. Her heart soared.

'You think we can't pick locks?' he crowed. 'Idiot.'

He lobbed something into the room and took off running. James hauled Camille up by the elbow, and with his other hand grabbed Olympe. Another flash turned the world white, and when Ada looked again, James, Camille and Olympe were gone – a concealed servants' door swinging shut.

For a moment, Ada thought about going after them.

But the pieces were falling into place. The game was still in motion.

And she wasn't finished yet.

5

The Servants' Passages

E ye pressed to the crack around the concealed
servants' door, James held his breath.

In the long gallery, the duc was raging, left
alone with nothing but two bodies and probably a burst
eardrum. Wickham's ambitions had ended in a messy
splatter of rotting flesh, smeared into an Ottoman rug.
James had managed to spirit Camille and Olympe away
in the chaos, but it felt like a hollow victory.

James tried not to look at Edward, sprawled as
lifeless as he had been on the operating table. Death
had only been held at bay for a few days; now his walls
had fallen and death was back to claim its own. There
wasn't time to grieve, and after everything Wickham
had done, he didn't know how to. But Edward – oh
god. He deserved more than this.

The three of them waited in silence until the duc,
Ada and Clémentine had left. They could hear the duc
snapping orders to split up and hunt Olympe down.

Once they were sure the coast was clear, James led
them further into the servants' passage. They were

inside the narrow corridors built behind the walls of the house, a network of unseen walkways to make sure no Lord or Lady Harford need ever see a servant unless expressly summoned. As children, he and Camille had used them as a playground, an echo of the dark game they now played.

Camille let them out of the passage at the other end and into Lord Harford's study, then immediately wedged the door shut with a chair while James looked for the key to lock the main door. The sturdy wood of this old part of the house was as close as they could get to a defensible position.

Just as James found the key, a noise came from the antechamber, where he'd waited for his father to summon him only a short while ago. He moved to lock the door, but Camille shook her head, then held a finger to her lips.

Silently, she lifted a poker from the grate and edged towards the door. One hand on the handle, the other raising the poker like a bat, she yanked the door open and swung.

With a yelp, Ada ducked just in time.

'Good lord!' she said, straightening shakily. 'Well, I suppose that answers the question, are you all okay. You might want to be a bit quieter, I heard you from outside.'

Camille sagged in relief. 'Come in, quick.'

They locked the door behind her and Ada and Camille stood at an awkward distance.

Ada folded her arms. 'I would kiss you, but I'm not sure you want me to,' she said icily.

'Ada – it's not – whatever you're thinking, you've got it wrong.'

'So you *weren't* about to marry James?'

If James could have disappeared, he would. This was not a conversation he should be present for.

Camille looked like she was going to throw up. 'It wasn't real.'

'Looked pretty real to me. You had an altar and guests and everything.'

'Well – what I mean is – it was part of my plan.'

Ada narrowed her eyes. 'Go on, keep digging.' James had never heard that note of cruelty in Ada's voice before.

Hesitantly, Camille explained how she'd used their engagement as a cover to get close to James, and then when his father suspected her of spying for France, going through with the wedding seemed the only way to avoid rousing his suspicions further.

Ada remained at a distance, radiating cold fury. 'I can forgive you a lot, Camille, but this is…' Ada shook off Camille's hand when she tried to touch her, then turned away. 'Do you even think of me when you do these things?'

'I'm sorry – god, Ada, I am so sorry.'

'Were you going to go through with it?' she asked.

'I…'

Camille stood, twisting her fingers in her skirt. James wasn't used to Camille looking so undone. It made the ground feel uneven beneath him.

'You were.'

'I couldn't see another way out.'

It was the wrong answer. 'You never have a choice, do you, Cam?' Ada spun round, eyes flashing. 'You hurt me, and you always say you had no choice. But that's not true, is it? You do exactly what you want and only think about whether it'll hurt someone when I end up crying.'

Camille hung her head. Her cheeks were flushed, her eyes glassy; James could hear the wheeze in her breath. As her friend, he didn't want to see her in pain; as her doctor, he desperately wanted to tell her not to get worked up. But they were too far beyond that now.

'I'm a coward,' she said. 'That's the truth. I know it, Ada. I know I don't deserve you.'

Ada crossed to the window and pressed the heels of her hands against her eyes. 'I'll stay if I want to, I'll leave if I want to. Stop trying to force my hand or you may have too much success.'

There was a knock at the study door.

'It's very rude you started the party before we arrived.' Al's voice was muffled, but James would recognise that smug tone anywhere.

Camille flew to the door, flinging it open and dragging Al and Guil inside.

'You could have told me you had some of the firecrackers left,' she scolded, but there was no heat to her words.

Al gave her a wry grin. 'I got jealous thinking about you having all the fun, so I thought, why not keep a surprise up my sleeve? One more flirt with danger, as a treat.'

'I would like it on record that I thought a surprise explosion was a bad idea,' said Guil wryly.

'What? It worked, didn't it?'

Guil squeezed Camille, while Ada pulled Al into a hug and he patted her on the shoulder. 'Good to see you too, my dear.' Then she turned to Guil, something unspoken passing between them.

Finally, Ada embraced Olympe, who had been silent at the back of the room, tears still streaming down her face to mingle with Edward's blood. 'Don't think I forgot about you. I'm so happy to see you safe.'

'Please don't fight with Camille,' said Olympe quietly. 'I can't bear any more fighting.'

Ada didn't reply, her expression tight. Then she said, 'I'm sorry I told your mother how to find you. I thought she could help us. I was wrong.'

'No … you kept your promise. You said you'd help me find my mother. I suppose I should have realised it might end up that I didn't want to be found.'

Guil glanced at James, one eyebrow arched. 'I assume it is safe to skip the part where you explain that we can trust him now?'

'Ah. Yes.' Camille straightened her skirts. 'Take it as read that I've given him a good kicking over it.'

Ada settled against the windowsill, arms crossed and expression unreadable.

James cleared his throat. 'Er, so, sorry to bring us back to the situation at hand, but … do we have a plan? I'm not sure we can hide here for ever.'

Guil nodded. 'We should make a play while we have the upper hand. I would suggest that Ada and I don't blow our cover yet.' He explained how Ada had infiltrated the duc's operation and gained his trust by revealing Olympe's location. 'The longer he thinks he has allies, the sloppier he will be.'

'Do you think he'll trust you enough to follow you to a location we choose?' Camille asked Ada.

She shrugged. 'I'm not sure. But it's worth a shot.'

'Good, then we finish this. I have a plan.'

Guil smiled. 'Ah. I've missed those words.'

'My pleasure.' Camille grinned back. 'I can't fight like this,' she gestured to the makeshift bandage around her leg, 'but I know what we can do.'

As the battalion drew together for the first time in weeks, Camille explained the bones of her idea. And James began to have hope. Because this was what Camille was good at. Not the Camille he'd known before, the girl still finding herself. But this Camille, the one he didn't know so well. The one with her own life that didn't have space for him. He'd been angry she had moved on without him. Now, he felt pride. He'd always known Camille was brilliant, and now everyone else got to see it too.

'I don't like it,' said Olympe when Camille had finished. 'It's too dangerous.'

'Whatever we do will have some risk,' said Guil. 'This is about minimisation, not elimination.'

Al pulled the paper packet from his pocket. There were no more firecrackers, but something silver glinted inside. 'I might have another surprise we could use.'

Camille pulled her lips into a tight smile and nodded. 'You know what to do.'

Olympe spoke again. 'Please. I don't want anyone to do this for me.'

Camille held her hand up. 'We don't have time. It's my risk to take. If you play your part, there'll be no risk, right?'

Olympe didn't look happy, but she nodded.

'Does everyone understand what they need to do?' Camille looked around the battalion, getting a nod from each of them in turn.

They readied themselves to leave, and Camille caught Ada's hand, fixed her with a burning gaze. 'Can you do this?'

Ada nodded.

'I'll go back to the duc. Let him think he's winning. At the right moment, I'll make my move.'

Then she seemed to make a snap decision. In the space of a breath, Ada had crossed the floor and pushed Camille against a wall, kissing her angrily. A flush burned in Camille's cheeks, eyes glittering, too thin, looking like danger incarnate.

When they came up for air, Ada said, 'I hate how much I love you. It makes life bloody difficult, you know.'

'I know,' said Camille breathlessly. She looked at Ada knowing she held a wonder in her arms, like the whole sun and moon and stars had come to earth to bless her with their light. 'I love you too.'

'I'm still angry.'

Camille looked away, mouth tugging down. 'You have every right to be. I'm sorry. You deserve better.'

'Maybe. But you don't get to choose what I do. I'm

not leaving just because you're a monumental idiot.' She backed off, self-consciously tucking back a loose curl. 'It's been an age since I saw you in a dress that nice. Don't think I haven't noticed you're bleeding all over it.'

Camille pulled up her skirts to show the bandage. 'I'm all right. I've had worse.'

'You know that isn't remotely good enough an excuse,' said Ada. But she crouched anyway to inspect the wound and re-tie the linen strip.

When she stood, Camille pulled her in and kissed her again. 'I've missed you.'

Ada kissed her back, arms winding around her body to hold her close.

Then she stepped away, breathing a little shakily, but resolute.

'Well, you're going to have to miss me a bit more.'

Without another word, she picked up the poker Camille had almost lamped them with, and left, with Guil and Al in tow.

As the door shut, Camille closed in on James, hooking her arm through his. That dangerous light was back in her eyes.

'Now, you have something to show me, don't you?'

James took her into the antechamber and the set of shelves where his father's duelling pistol was displayed. The twin of the one Camille had carried, the one she had kept as a memory of her own father.

Reverentially, Camille lifted it from its stand, ran her hand over the mother-of-pearl handle, checked the store of shot and powder.

Then she lifted it, sighted down the barrel as though tracking her target.

Finally, they were closing in.

6

The Entrance Hall

They found the duc in the grand entrance hall, simmering with frustration. Clémentine had returned and was leaning against a side table, braiding the ends of her hair in a gesture so like Olympe that Ada felt suddenly disorientated. At the top of the stairs where they hid, Guil rested a hand on her shoulder.

'You can do this.' His smile was gentle and familiar and for a moment she could breathe again.

Behind them Al was limbering up, rolling his head and cracking his joints. 'Let's get on with it, before I lose my nerve.'

Ada checked the hallway again, then pushed them forward.

At once Al and Guil broke into a run, crashing into the bannister and stumbling down the stairs. Ada followed half a second behind.

'Stop them!' she yelled, catching herself on the newel post.

The duc and Clémentine responded at once, heading

Guil and Al off at the foot of the stairs. In their haste Guil and Al were uncoordinated, tripping on the last step, tumbling into each other and landing at the duc's feet. Ada leaped the last few steps and threw herself into restraining them. Al gave a few pathetic wiggles before Clémentine got his hands secured. Guil gave a more realistic performance, and Ada prayed he wouldn't push it so far things ended up in real violence. A few swift motions and Guil was tied up as well.

Ada sat back, panting, the tremor in her hands no pretence.

'Did you find Olympe?' she asked.

Clémentine shook her head. 'Well done for finding these two.'

The duc was watching her closely. 'Well done indeed.'

The duc turned Al onto his back with the toe of his boot. 'Do we have an aspiring hero on our hands?'

Al looked faintly disgusted. 'Don't be ridiculous. Heroics are for people too stupid to understand the risks. I'm more in the "let's get the hell away from these mad bastards with guns" camp.'

Clémentine crouched next to him. 'Please, if you know anything about where they've taken my daughter, tell me. I've been parted from her for so long, all I want is to know she's safe and to take her back home.'

'Safe?' scoffed Al. 'My mother was a nightmare, but at least she never let an evil scientist loose on me.'

'My brother and I do not see eye to eye on everything,' said Clémentine brittlely.

'Have you thought about growing a moustache?' Al

asked the duc. 'You could twirl it to really bed into this villain character you've committed to.'

'Be quiet,' the duc snapped. 'If I want to hear the gibbering of an idiot I can pay to visit an asylum like anyone else. I do not need a private performance.'

'Suit yourself.'

The duc pressed the muzzle of the gun to the soft flesh under Al's chin. 'Perhaps this will help you focus. Tell me what they're planning.'

Al's eyes darted around nervously. 'They're planning a charming day trip to Box Hill. What do you think they're planning? They want to get out of here as quickly as possible.'

'And how, pray tell, are they hoping to do that?'

'No idea, but the last time I saw them they were legging it into the grounds.'

The duc lowered the gun with a stream of curse words and turned to the grand front door.

'Come! Bring them both,' he ordered.

Ada and Clémentine got Guil and Al to their feet and followed the duc out the door.

So far, so good.

Now, all Ada could do was pray Camille pulled off her end.

Mist still lingered on the ground, coiling and billowing over the grass of Henley House. The tradition for early weddings followed by a breakfast meant the day had started at dawn, and the weak summer sun had yet to break through the swirling clouds. In the grey morning, Camille thought Olympe looked almost at home, mist and storm come to life.

From Lord Harford's office, Camille had purloined a cane and used it now as she walked across the lawn to the house; the wound to the back of her knee had dulled to an ache that flared each time she put weight on it. They had briefly scouted the edges of the estate and found the duc's men stationed at every escape point.

A few bird calls disrupted the silence, and she was reminded of how far they were from anywhere.

How far they were from help.

The duc stepped out of Henley House, followed by Ada and Clémentine, Al and Guil tied and held between them. Guil had relocked the guests and the Harfords in the chapel after picking the lock to get him and Al out – he'd thought it the safest place and Camille was grateful for that small mercy. Whatever happened here, there wouldn't be any by-standers getting hurt.

'Citoyen Aubespine!' Her voice rang out blessedly clear and loud. Her chest felt tight – but it always did these days. Oh, well. She only needed it to last her a little longer.

'Mademoiselle du Bugue.' His boots crunched through the gravel, coming to a stop a few paces away, the line where the gravel met lawn drawing a boundary between them. 'I hope you are done running?'

Camille's lip curled and she looked down at her leg. 'For now. Let's settle this like gentlemen.' Leaning heavily on her cane, she met his eye, chin raised. 'I demand satisfaction.'

The duc let out a loud peal of laughter. 'For what?'

'You have caused me offence, have you not?'

'You wish for a duel?'

Camille continued, unfazed. 'I believe you have my father's duelling pistol?' Camille pulled the other pistol from her sash. 'Here, I have its pair. Fate, don't you think?'

He took a moment to pull a handkerchief from his pocket and dab the corner of his eyes. 'I said I was sick of your theatrics, and yet somehow you always surprise me with something new. Come, this could be a fair trade. You have someone of mine, I have two of yours.' He raised a hand and Guil led Al down the steps. 'A more than fair exchange.'

Al looked pale, but his chin was set firm. Beside him, Guil was stony.

Camille let a grin spread across her face. 'How about winner takes all?' James and Olympe drew up behind her, sending the mist curling around her bare feet. 'If I win, you give me Al and Guil, and leave. You respect Olympe's choice *not* to be a pawn in your extremely dull chess game and leave her alone.'

The duc raised an eyebrow. 'And if I win?'

'Olympe goes with you, we stop fighting.'

Clémentine joined the duc. 'Olympe! Are you really going to let these two bet you in a wager? I thought you had more self-respect.'

'I thought you had more respect for me than to let your own brother experiment on me,' said Olympe, her voice icy. 'Looks like we were both wrong.'

The duc considered for a moment. Then nodded. 'Very well. It will not be the first duel I have won.'

Camille smiled sweetly. 'Allow me to make it the first you lose.'

The decision made, everyone moved into action. A central point was chosen, James and Ada acting as seconds, and Camille let herself be put into position. Olympe hovered near by, lighting the snuffing sparks of energy at her fingertips.

Not yet. Not yet.

Al and Guil lined up with Clémentine, hands behind their backs. Maybe it was a trick of the light but she thought she saw something silver glint in their hands.

She and the duc exchanged salutes, before preparing the pistols. Balancing her weight on her good leg, she filled her pistol with power and shot and tamped it down. Then she took her cane from James, relishing the security of something to hold on to.

A solitary magpie soared across the sky to land on the cupola of the pavilion she had been carried into when she had first arrived at Henley with Al. Its mate was nowhere to be seen.

Camille and the duc turned back to back. She could feel him clearly through the flimsy material of her dress and felt acutely aware that he was taller and stronger than her.

Good. It meant she would present a smaller target.

With a final shaky breath, they began to walk.

One for sorrow.
Two, three …

Ten slow, heart-wracking paces as they called out the numbers together.

Four, five, six …

The weather was good for it. Overcast meant no sun to get in anyone's eyes.

Seven, eight, nine …

This was it. Her plan would either work or it would kill her. She'd known her time with Ada was running out, perhaps it already had. She thought of their kiss in the study, the softness of her skin, the heat of her mouth.

But then what was death but an inevitability? A coin that could only be spent once.

She would make sure it bought something worthy.

Ten.

Camille whipped round, pistol raised, and squeezed the trigger.

7

The Grounds of Henley House

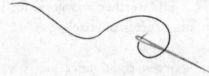

The bullet struck her hip. Her legs buckled, sending Camille crashing to the ground. Someone was screaming and distantly she realised it was her. The pain radiated up her side like lightning, vicious and angry and all consuming. She lay flat on her back, panting, eyes turned to the vast, milky sky.

She never thought it would feel this bad. Her mind felt like it was over-stuffed and every time she grasped one thing, something slid out elsewhere. Dizziness and exhaustion came over her like a tide.

The pistol had dropped from her hand. She wondered where her shot had ended up.

Nearby, the gravel crunched, and the duc loomed into view.

'It was an honourable effort, I'll give you that. But a word of advice, for proving yourself such a worthy opponent.' His face replaced the sky as all she could see. 'Learn when to give up.'

Camille sucked in a shallow breath. Words swam and danced in her mind, getting lost on their way to her tongue. Light flared in a halo around the duc's head as her world telescoped away. She felt as though she was floating away from herself to a great height.

Subtly, she felt for Wickham's knife which she had picked up in the long gallery and tucked into her pocket.

'I'll give you a word of advice in turn.' Her voice was rasping and tired.

'Oh?' he said. 'And what would that be?'

She smiled, teeth slick with something metallic.

'Never trust me.'

Ignoring the screaming pain in her side, she surged, using her momentum and the moment of surprise to topple the duc to the ground. Within seconds she was straddling him. He struggled – then went rigid. Only his eyes moved, darting from side to side.

Lazily, Camille rested the knife against his throat, letting herself enjoy a moment of elation. The blade scratched his skin, drawing a bead of blood.

Then she leaned closer, so the duc could see her as she spoke.

'Looks like I'm the winner. I guess that means I get to take it all.'

Olympe had seen her cue and thrown herself onto the ground beside them, two bare hands on either side of the duc's face to send a burst of electric current through him. But the jolt was larger than Camille had anticipated; she was flung back, off the duc who was trapped under the net of sparks flowing from Olympe's hands. Landing hard, she bit back a howl of pain. A wind had whipped up, static picking up dry leaves and spinning them into a vortex with Olympe at its centre. The sky had grown dark like a candle snuffed out, and a rumble of thunder called somewhere overhead.

Olympe was kneeling, hands like an oil spill, purple and black and grey and shimmering with power, wrapped around the duc's skull. Her eyes had blown into two shimmering stars, all the tiny pinpricks gathered together into a galaxy of light, blue and heavenly and terrible to behold. The duc was like an insect pinned by a god, a frail thing with its wings plucked, soft body easily crushed. A filigree mesh of electricity held him in place, flowing a few centimetres above his body, raw power bursting up at points, arcing to snap nearby trees in half like a lightning strike, burning the grass around them to a crisp. The duc was alive for now, but if Olympe's control slipped even a fraction it wouldn't just be the duc who got hurt; that much power out of control would kill them all.

Camille crawled towards her, mouth full of blood, hair crackling away from her skull. 'Olympe, can you hear me?'

Thunder boomed again and an answering flash of light splintered through Olympe, stray sparks grounding themselves around her like water cascading over a cliff edge.

'You tortured me,' she hissed, leaning over the duc's fear-stricken face. 'You took my childhood and turned it into a nightmare. You want me to be a weapon? Watch me *kill*.'

Camille saw Clémentine move a moment before it was too late.

From somewhere she pulled a second gun and pressed it against Al's temple.

'Enough!' she yelled. 'I have your friend! Let my brother go and I let him go. Olympe? Are you listening to me?'

Hair wild, skin glowing with constellations, Olympe slowly turned her face to her mother.

'This isn't you, my girl! My wonder.' Clémentine held out her other hand. 'Come back to me. You are no killer.'

Slowly, the wind ebbed, the hum of static fading from the air as the clouds paled.

'Maman?'

'Yes, mon ange. It's me.'

Olympe's face cracked, tears streaming over her inky cheeks. 'You left me. I was locked in that prison and you *never came*.'

Her hands fell from the duc's face, and he went slack, his breathing rapid and shaky.

'I'm here now. Come to me, I let this boy go, and it can be over.'

Olympe rose, the starlight fading from her eyes. Camille reached for her hand but she stepped away.

'It's okay,' said Olympe. 'I'll go.'

'No. *No.*'

'Let me do this, Cam. *Trust* me.'

Camille held her gaze, an unspoken exchange passing between them, then she nodded.

Olympe would make her choice, and the rest of them would make theirs.

Dress fluttering around her legs in the breeze, she crossed the gravel to her mother.

Clementine was true to her word, taking the gun from Al's head and pushing him away before helping the duc up and leading him back to their group at the steps. At the same time, James slipped an arm around Camille and she hobbled back to the grass. Al was with them, making short work of the rope around his wrists.

They were lined up on opposite sides of the driveway.

James, Camille and Al.

The duc, Ada, Guil, Olympe and Clémentine.

Ada shifted her grip around the handle of the poker she had taken from Lord Harford's study. On one side was the duc. On her other was Guil, and next to him, Olympe. Something slithered to the ground behind Guil's back, the sliver of blade Al had given him flashing in the light.

'Ada, now!' bellowed Camille.

Ada turned, raising the poker.

And cracked Guil across the head.

He went down like a sack of bricks. For a moment, they were all frozen.

'What the...?' Al lurched forward, shaking with shock, but Camille threw an arm around his waist, anchoring him.

'Al – don't.'

'Ada, what the *hell are you doing*?'

Ada turned to the duc, avoiding their gaze. 'He had a knife. They wanted you to capture him. He cut his ropes and was going to snatch Olympe.'

Camille was numb. She watched it all through Al's eyes, how he crumpled from horror into fury then despair.

The duc smiled, slow and languorous. 'Good girl.' He looked over at Camille, smile widening. 'I knew I could trust you.'

8

The Grounds of
Henley House

Clémentine smothered Olympe in the silk of her dress as Olympe screamed and screamed and screamed. Sparks rushed over her like a second skin, but they died on contact with the silk.

Ada watched through a fog.

She watched as the duc's hired muscle arrived on the scene, summoned by the sound of gunshots. She watched them tie Olympe's hands behind her back with silk ropes, she watched sparks build and burst across her face in vain.

And she watched her friends, a few paces distant and a whole world away, look at her in disgust and fear.

It was worth it.

It had to be worth it.

They wouldn't fight – she knew Camille was too smart for that. They were injured. Outnumbered.

It was over.

Still, she watched James fumble with the duelling pistol, trying to reload it before Camille took it out of his hand and drew him and Al away. Her dress bloomed red at the hip and knee. Ada could smell the blood from here.

Oh god, please let it be worth it.

The duc ignored them, stepping over Guil's prone body as if he was a piece of broken furniture, ordering his men like a general in battle.

In the end, it was Olympe who broke through the fog. Twisting in her mother's arms, she turned on Ada.

'I *trusted* you.'

'You shouldn't have.' Ada couldn't meet her eye. 'I have only known your mother for a short while, but she taught me something important. The world doesn't treat people kindly. So we have to do whatever is necessary to carve out a life we can live with.'

The electric sparks had died away, and the clouds that rolled across Olympe's face had gone perfectly still.

Ada had never seen anything more terrifying.

'And can you? Live with this?'

Finally, she forced herself to meet Olympe's eye. 'I will have to.'

From the carriage, the duc took down one of the boxes they had carried with them from France and opened it.

Clémentine kept her arms around Olympe still, swaying gently, like a mother rocking a baby.

'Hush, now. Remember that I told you sometimes being a mother means I must do things for your own good, even if it makes you hate me.'

'Don't you dare talk to me,' hissed Olympe.

'We can't risk you doing anything out of a misguided

sense of loyalty to these people. It's just until you get back to France. If you show us you can be grown up, then maybe we can rethink it, hmm?'

'You'll have to tie me up for ever because I will *never* stop fighting you,' Olympe spat.

Clémentine sighed. 'I thought you might say that.'

From the box, the duc lifted a large metal object, around the size and shape of a pumpkin. Hinged on one side, it opened like a box, with a slot for a padlock on the other side. Three holes were punched out of one half, and there was a circle of space left open at the bottom.

Olympe caught sight of it and went silent. Her eyes were circles of fear, all the stars snuffed out.

'Monster! Traitor!' Camille still had Al pinned as best she could, while James staunched the flow of blood from her wound, but she couldn't keep him quiet. 'Shame on you. I will *never* forgive you!'

Ada felt sick.

The duc carried the mask over, opening it, ready to be placed around Olympe's head.

Ada waited for her to beg, to plead, to scream again.

But Olympe did nothing. Only drew herself up tall, holding herself steely and proud. She would not let them see her afraid.

So Ada would not look away either. She would not hide from what she'd done.

As the mask lowered, Olympe's gaze flicked to Ada, and the last she saw of her face was that cold, blank stare fixed unnervingly on her.

Then the mask snapped shut, and it was over.

9

A Bedroom,
Henley House

The wedding guests declared it one of the most shocking turn of events that had ever befallen any good, upright citizen.

Lord Harford, attacked in his own home by an envious rival who suspected he had been passed over for funding from the War Ministry for his research. The bride forced to run. The groom kidnapped at gun point. A heroic struggle and the rival driven off.

Camille knew they would be dining out on it for years.

It was enough of the truth that no one looked too closely at where the edges didn't meet. The guests didn't need to know about the two dead bodies in the long gallery, or that the bride had been grazed by a bullet.

It had hurt so badly Camille had been sure she'd been hit – but when James examined her, they found only a bloody score mark along her hip marking the path of the bullet. It hurt, but it was easier to bear than the raw pain of Ada leaving with the duc, her cold expression transforming her from the gentle, clever woman she knew. That memory would linger in her mind for a long time.

James had cleaned and dressed the wound and declared she would make a full recovery if only she learned how to rest for five minutes.

For company, they laid Camille up in the same room as Guil, who had come round after not too long with a nasty lump on his head, but nothing a dose of laudanum and a lie down wouldn't cure.

The thing Camille couldn't stand about rest was all the time it left her to think. Visitors drifted in and out; Hennie bounced in, wanting to hear Camille's version of events, before Lady Harford shooed her out to take a turn dabbing her forehead with a cool flannel; and all the while, Camille's mind kept replaying the last moments of the fight.

The mask closing over Olympe's face.

The men bundling her into the carriage.

The duc, Clémentine and Ada climbing in after, and driving away as if they'd done nothing more than pay a visit for tea.

Ada, never looking back.

Ada, always Ada in her mind. Eyes closed or open, Ada was all she could see.

She had barely got Ada back, and now she had lost her.

Camille closed her eyes against the pain. Love was pain and it was fear and it was half her heart torn out and leaving with her enemy. She had thought she knew hurt, and yet there was always more; always some new thing to pull the breath from her lungs.

In the golden twilight, James and Al arrived with a delivery of toast and jam and tea for the invalids.

'It's the good blackberry jam,' said James, setting down the tray. 'Mother must really be worried about you.'

'Yes, you are both very pitiful.' Al plonked down on a pouffe and started slathering a slice of toast in butter.

And love was her friends sharing toast and tea, the constellation of her family shifting around the hole torn into it.

Lord Harford was recuperating in his own rooms and Camille could only be thankful Lady Harford hadn't thought three was better company than two. James had sold Lord Harford a version of the truth, explaining that he had taken Camille into his confidence about Wickham, given her the pistol to defend herself. She was no spy.

Lady Harford and her husband were the only other people who knew close to the truth of what had happened. They'd needed help dealing with the bodies. They had no intention of hiding a murder, but how could they explain to the police what had really happened? Lord Harford was more than willing to believe James now he had seen Wickham's handiwork with his own eyes. The result of a few muttered conversations and some hastily sent letters was that this was a military matter involving the War Ministry and as such could be dealt with outside the usual criminal proceedings.

Or 'a great big government-conspiracy cover-up' as Al had called it with glee.

Whatever it was, Camille was grateful to have a few allies for once. They had been fighting on their own for too long.

There was something much bigger at stake. Without Robespierre, what would the Revolution be now? She wasn't such a fool as to think the killings would stop. The balance of power was swinging back the other way. It turned her cold to think of what would happen to the ordinary people who had dared stand up to the rich and powerful and demand to be treated with respect.

Retribution was an ugly thing.

She realised this must have been how her parents had felt. Seeing the dream of something better that they had believed in, that they had passionately fought for, slip through their fingers.

There wasn't much she could do, but there was *one* thing.

No one else knew the true threat the duc posed, the destruction he could wreak with Olympe under his control.

So Camille would stop him. She might not be able to save the Revolution, but she would stop the duc moulding the new order to his own liking. If she was going to die, then she needed to leave behind something worth dying for.

James set down a saucer of tea beside her, then pulled up a chair, face drawn tight in thought. 'I'm sorry, Cam.'

'You've already apologised for about ten things. I think you're done.'

'I want to say it again.' He rubbed his eyes. 'I still can't believe Ada did that.'

Camille hid her face in her tea. Her hair hung around her shoulders, glinting gold in the sunlight. 'She did what she thought she had to.'

'You don't really believe that?'

Camille didn't answer.

James shifted in his chair, as though deeply uncomfortable. 'And seeing it made me really understand what I did to you in Paris. So I'm sorry.'

She patted his hand. 'Apology accepted.'

James delivered tea to Guil as well, and for a moment it was like being back above the Au Petit Suisse, exhausted after another job put to bed.

With one big missing piece.

Camille looked at her battalion, ranged around her on chairs and day beds, slurping tea and spooning jam onto toast. Her family.

She couldn't put this off any longer. They deserved to know.

So Camille spoke.

'I need to tell you the truth.'

Postscript

Paris, a Month Before

'Betray me.'

Camille stood beside the window slit in the convent wall, braiding her hair in deft, sharp movements. Her eyes glinted like wet slate in the candlelight.

Ada didn't know how she could stay so calm. Not after what she'd just said.

'Absolutely not. I won't do it.'

'Ada—'

'Cam, it's madness. He'll never buy it.'

'Won't he?'

'No! He won't!'

Ada threw her hands up and thumped down into a wicker chair by the empty grate in the Cordeliers safe house. Weeds were already growing through the cracks in the flagstones, weaving through the ancient monastery to take it apart brick by brick. More effective than any revolutionary effort.

She had thought Camille had already left for England when she'd received the cryptic note summoning her to the Cordeliers. It wasn't easy to slip away from her father without arousing suspicion so soon after she'd talked her way back into his house, though for the chance to see Camille again she would have done anything.

But, of course, Camille had been looking for more than a prolonged goodbye.

Camille kneeled on the floor in front of her and took her hands.

'He will. If you make him. Win his trust; then when the time comes, betray me. Do what you have to to make him believe you're on his side.'

'You're asking me to get in bed with a monster.'

Camille held her gaze. 'Yes. I am. I promise you, I will fight with everything I can to stop him, to keep Olympe – to keep *France* – safe. But right now, I don't think we're going to win. I can get Olympe out of James's hands, but that's only half the fight. The duc won't stop. He's clever and powerful and the only way we're going to defeat him is by working in his blind spot: his arrogance. He needs to think he's broken us, that we're nothing to worry about any more. It shouldn't be too hard; he doesn't think we're worth much in the first place. So do it – don't warn me. Make it real. Then he'll be yours.'

Ada's chest felt tight. Fear, yes, and panic at the overwhelming size of the task in front of her. But something else too – a little flare of excitement. Because this was her chance. To step out of the shadows and show Camille, her father, *everyone*, that she was so much more than they bargained for. Camille was propping open a door and Ada had only to walk through.

Camille squeezed her hands. 'He thinks he knows us so well, that he'll always be smarter and faster. So let him think he's won. Let us move in the places he isn't looking. Do things he won't expect us to. Cross lines he'd never think we would.'

'Camille. What you're asking is a lot.'

'I know.'

'You say we'll cross lines, but you mean me. I'll be the one who has to cross them.'

'Yes.'

'Did you think about what it might cost me?'

Camille flinched almost imperceptibly. 'Yes. I did. And what it will cost *me*. But this is bigger than us.'

'I know.'

Ada took a shaky breath, feeling the future weigh down upon her. She couldn't run away from it now.

'Okay. Okay, I can do this.'

They stayed together for a long moment, Camille's rough fingers wrapped round her own, the twin beat of their pulses humming through their skin. The kiss came together out of nothing, their lips were apart and then somehow not, like they were meant to be pressed together, the taste of Camille in her mouth and the soft press of her breasts against her own chest. Ada could get lost here, in the smell of her hair and the brush of her fingertips and the intoxicating power of knowing Camille was just as lost in her.

Ada drew back, took Camille in. The curve of her jaw, the hectic flush against her pale skin, her glittering eyes. This girl she loved. This girl who dragged her from one disaster to the next. This girl who was her future. She opened her mouth to tell Camille she loved her, but Camille spoke first.

'Betray me, Ada. Hurt me. And save us all.'

Acknowledgements

I think all my books will be for my mum, for a while.

I wrote this book in the last months she was alive. I revised it in the months after she died. Losing her, when I had to live in lockdown isolation, is the hardest thing I have ever been through. That I continue to go through at the time of writing this.

I'll start with the people who meant I made it, exhausted and forever changed, but alive:

Tim, Dad, Kiran G, Chelsey, Saskia, Kirstin, Kay, Coco. My therapist.

I don't know what else to say but thank you.

To all the friends who stood in place of family gone: Jane, Tasha, Ciannon, Allison, Maddy, Jenny, Catherine, Harry, Tori, Tash, Daphne, Kate, Carly, Leena, Karin, Marianna, Constance.

To the company of writers who make it less lonely: Bex, Kylie, Emma, Yasmin, Aishia, Sophie, Mel, Faridah, Ava, Sarah, Helen C, Ciara, Chloe, Helen L, Narayani, Kes, Laura, Hux, Jess Rule, Jess Rigby, Danielle, Charlie. And especially Non and Peta, who dug me out of several holes.

To my agent, Hellie, for having my back. To my editor, Fiona, for her patience, and Jenny, for leaping into the fray. To Laura Brett for my always-gorgeous cover art. To all at Zephyr and Head of Zeus who brought this book into existence and into the hands of readers.

To the booksellers and bloggers, librarians and teachers, readers and reviewers, BookTubers and BookTok creators – thank you from the depths of my stony heart for all the love and support you gave *Dangerous Remedy*. Debuting during a pandemic was not the start I'd hoped for, but you all made it so, so worth it.

Kat Dunn
London,
March 2021